THE GREAT
PINT-PULLING
OLYMPIAD

THE GREAT PINT-PULLING OLYMPIAD

A Mostly Irish Farce

BY ROGER BOYLAN

GROVE PRESS
New York

Copyright © 2003 by Roger Boylan

Published simultaneously in Canada
Printed in the United States of America

FIRST EDITION

Library of Congress Cataloging-in-Publication Data

Boylan, Roger, 1951-
The great Pint-Pulling Olympiad: a mostly Irish farce / by Roger Boylan.
p. cm.
ISBN 0-8021-4032-7
1. Ireland—Fiction.   2. Terrorism—Fiction.
3. Drinking customs—Fiction.   I. Title.
PS3552.O915G74 2003
813'.54—dc21   2003049074

Grove Press
841 Broadway
New York, NY 10003

03   04   05   06   07   10   9   8   7   6   5   4   3   2   1

For my womenfolk: Esther, Elizabeth, and Margaret

Ever tried. Ever failed. No matter. Try again.
Fail again. Fail better.

—Samuel Beckett, one night in the
PLM bar at the Porte d'Italie,
around closing time

Prologue

Last night, I dreamt I went to Spudorgan again. It seemed to me I stood by the roundabout leading to the MacLiammoir Bypass, and I wanted desperately to get across; for a while I could not pass, for the way was barred to me by the press of traffic, mostly spanking-new Jocelyn GTs, with the odd Jag here and there. Then, like all dreamers, I was possessed of a sudden by supernatural powers and passed like a spirit through the cars before me. Uphill Street wound away in front of me, twisting and turning as it had always done. But as I advanced, I was aware that a change—nay, changes!—had come upon the fair city by the sea, my Killoyle of dreams. Mammon had come into his own again, and little by little had encroached upon the city with long tenacious fingers, entarting this tavern, expanding that car park, englamouring that once-barren coffeehouse. And finally, there was Spudorgan Hall, once desolate, once known and unloved as the Rat Palace, now a festive and plush member of Vacation Inns Worldwide. And nor time nor Mammon could mar the perfect symmetry of those walls. . . .

—from *A Poet Does His Nut, Vol. I: Years of Struggle,* an unpublished bildungsmemoir by Milo Rogers, poet laureate of Munster

THE GREAT
PINT-PULLING
OLYMPIAD

1

Miming the petulant moue of, say, a Roman
sensualist of the post-Antonine era, or a Regency brat under the
Younger Pitt, Michael T. "Mick" McCreek's face, that interesting preface to the rather ordinary rest of him, buried itself pillow-
deep in a vain attempt to avoid the probing rays of the rising Irish
sun, a weak sun at best but a game one, bedad, and not a sun to
be shut out of the bedroom window of Flat 16A, Padre Pio
Houses, by a mere flimsy curtain or so. Indeed, by shining persistently and directly onto your man's Romano-Regency face,
it illumined in an unwelcome, glaring red glow the intricate
Mississippi Delta network of his inner-eyelid veins.[1] He
grumbled. Slowly, sleep ebbed as sufficient time dragged itself
along, with the lame determination of a hunchback[2] in heat, to
accommodate the twin phenomena, one tactile, the other aural, of: (1) warmer sunshine splashing onto Mick's gob and (2) a
car outside starting up with hiccupping roars exacerbated by

---

[1] I'm with you here, entirely. The interior cross-hatching of my own eyelids is a holy terror, so it is, especially when it's a hair of the frigging dog I
need and not more bloody tea, thanks very much. Why, there was one time
when for a second or more I'd have sworn I was a chicken enmeshed in the
coop and ready for the guillotine, the pattern was that intense.

[2] "DC (Differently-abled Citizen)" to you—*qv., infra.*

much boot-to-the-floor pedal-pumping followed by the gear-grinding diminuendo of exceedingly slow departure.

There goes that Indian dickhead (shouted the uninvited thought-announcer in Mick's brain) *at the wheel of his effing old Escort that he should have sent to the junkyard long since, the stingy wee bastard, turning his lights off in the middle of the night and spewing clouds of burnt oil left right and centre and no bloody notion in the world of how to shift into first . . . !*

With all this external din and internal mind palaver Mick was distracted, uneasy, a failed sleeper; in fact dangerously near wakefulness and getting closer all the time, what with one thing and another—his Indian neighbour's departure, the sun scorching his face, the new day's being Monday. It was a full sixty-second minute or more before the perfect (indeed only) solution wormed its way into his awakening brain: *Turn over, son!*

He obeyed, and was at once conscious of a coolness of visage counterbalanced by a rapidly warming spot on the nape of his neck where Old Sol, still staring through the halfhearted window curtain, now focused his gaze. Of course, it *was* the morning, and Mick *did* have a job, however ludicrous (very: assistant test driver for Jocelyn Motors);[3] give him credit, though, he was a realist, by and large, and that morning he was, consequently, soon out of bed and well downstairs, in fact in the immaculately white kitchen itself, blearily scrutinizing the controls of his birthday coffeemaker, last year's (and no doubt last, as in lifelong) gift from Eileen, his ex, on the occasion of his fortieth.

------

[3]A small but exclusive, i.e., skint, southeastern manufacturer of exclusive sporting motorcars, one of which—a Blackthorn GTS in, well, British racing green I'm afraid—took the wrong corner twice before running over me poor old gran, and that three times or more, as if to make sure the old dear was dead. She's gone, so she is, but the car's still running, in fact it's in me drive—aye, you guessed it, well, you would, wouldn't you? But a nimbler motor you'll not find in the seven times seven hundred parishes of Christendom.

"Nice of her," he mumbled. "But how typical, for God's sake, to give me something I don't know how to use."

The words *Oh Eileen by the holy Christ I miss ya my sweet machree ah God so I do me own darlin' girl* trembled unwailed in the air. He did miss the woman, too, especially her thigh and hip area and its oft-kneaded amplitudes, but not enough to call her up, or make (re-)overtures, not with her tendency to plunge into the warm bath of Monologue, or was it Soliloquy . . . God, was she a gabber, anyway, and getting worse with age.

So—

He preferred to let things follow the zigzag route of their own unpredictability. The coffeemaker could wait its turn, or disappear entirely. And anyway My Three Buns, the place down the road, brewed up a matchless Arabica, or Colombian, or was it Brazilian—something hot, moist, and dark, anyway, like the inside thigh of an Andalusian whore, plus caffeine . . . Mick, mentally stirred (if also slightly shaken) at this thought,[4] whistled shrilly the second theme of Mimi and Rodolfo's love duet from *La Bohème* by G. Puccini as he sought and successfully deployed navy tie, sky-blue shirt, and crimson underhose (with white piping). There ensued a quick tussle with the belt and trews, a smooth scrape of the stubble and the cursory tremor of a comb in the hair—and presto! *Mick McCreek reporting for duty, sir!* Not that he ever so reported, or called anyone "sir"; and of course the effing job was on the other side of town, and naturally *his* frigging car was in the shop, but what could you expect from a five-year-old Jocelyn GT with twelve valves to the competition's twenty-four?

No, it's the old Number Twelve bus or shank's mare, mister me man.

Well, anyway, first off was My Three Buns, the newly chic trucker's caff down on Blessed Martin de Porres Street limned

---

[4]Nary a trace of caffeine did I find in them precincts, be janey, and I a night watchman on the Jerez-Gibraltar border full half a decade, these two score years gone by.

sketchily in Mick's mind's eye, the eye that never lied but was frequently blurred, more like a bad TV broadcast than the likes of a West of Ireland shanachee's meanderings, My Three Buns in reality being far less congenial than fondly depicted on the bloodshot eyeball of Mick's mind. There it basked in such clichés as "grotty but solid working-class ambience" and "down-to-earth unpretentious food." Truthfully, the place was a bit of a tip, and Devereux, the owner, was quite the rogue, a greedy sod anyway, boasting a ratlike and bewhiskered face above bulbous abdomen and thorax. His missus was no better, only cleaner-shaven, and with deeper cleavage in the chest area. They had kids, too, but that didn't bear thinking of . . . still, the fried bread was top-hole, and the eponymous buns, gooey as a bag of melted Mars Bars on the backseat of the family saloon in the summer sun: YUM!

And none, however well motivated, could come close to the bacon rinds, never mind your classic sunny side up with chips on the side . . . !

Especially those chips: salty, oily, limp: plain delicious!!!
After all, it doesn't have to be good for you to be good, does it?[5]
"Yum! Oh yum!"

Mick was ready, oh he was agog, old tum agurgle, satchel at hand, keys ajingle. He checked the gas above and below, adjusted his tie, and scampered delightedly into the dangerously random Great Outdoors, where it was blustery, rendering his tie a windsock, pointing due East. That way lay Wales, as usual, with England loitering beyond; here in Ireland's north-southeast it was a cracking fine day, what with a brisk wind that danced with the trees and lifted the leaves above the eaves. Not so bad for September the twentieth, when for all you knew it could plunge to five on the Celsius scale, the record for Killoyle City and envi-

---

[5]Of course not. Nothing good I've ever had has ever done me any good at all, and don't you forget it, boyo.

rons, set a twelvemonth ago last September in the year of three governments.[6]

Thanks be to God, a mere twenty-four solid Christian degrees it was, this breezy September morn.

"Sure you'd be hard pressed to do better in the south of France, or the Aegean itself," blurted Mick, fatuously.

A quick step or so took him across Padre Pio Circus down Blessed Martin de Porres Street to the scaley shopfront behind which teemed My Three Buns—or rather, teemed not, for on that day of all blessed sunny days in the calendar there was a sign on the door. Mick, incredulous, peered, then peered closer.

"Closed," said the sign, and repeated itself identically throughout subsequent double- and triple-takes. Through the window

---

[6]Gar Looney, then a bloke named O'Hair they found stretched out down by the North Wall, then Gar again, plus O'Hair in the wings. When they found Gar to call him back to Leinster House, he was at his customary post in Flood's Bar, back turned to the hoi polloi and standing with a pronounced list to the left so as to get a better view of the telly above the bar, more specifically the hurling special on TV3 followed by An Nuacht on Channel 2A (Gacilge). In his left hand was his third pint of the day, in his right his thirtieth fag of the twenty per diem he then allowed himself (he quit soon after, only to start up again under the menace of peace arrangements north of the border and the concomitant necessity to hobnob with Unionists). Well, when the parliamentary committee approached him he pretended at first to be someone else entirely—a Japanese businessman, I think, complete with eyes and accent—then took off at a sprint through the side door but ran headlong into the arms of the law (Sgt. Liam Paterson, shaking off). "It's a fair cop," said Gar. "No, it's me," said Sergeant Paterson, unfairly. "All right, all right," babbled Gar, "I'll be taoiseach again, but I won't go into coalition with that bastard O'Hair, and that's final." (Breaking news has it that Looney's Fine Whiskies party has formed yet another coalition with O'Hair's Féar No Beàn group. "I can scarcely imagine being in government at all without being in coalition with my dear friend and colleague Proinsias O'Hair," remarked Gar last night while sweeping majestically with his entourage from the Long Hall on Aungier Street to the Norseman in Temple Bar.)

an ugly mug hovered, glowered, glared, and vanished behind a hastily lowered blind.

"Go away," came a muffled shout.

Mick obeyed, dragging his feet, one more cosy plan up the spout. He dawdled not, for "work" (such as it was) was imminent, rendering breakfast urgent. He mentally perused the possibilities:

There was the Bay Window, with its pseuds from Killoyle Upper College and prats from elsewhere.

There was McSpackle's Cantina, on the Promenade, with its annoying Spanish decor.[7]

There was the Koh-I-Noor, curry shop of the gods, run (actually) by that Indian berk from downstairs with the dicey Escort, but the Koh was better reserved for late-night homeward-bound stopoffs for Vindaloo and a six of lager.

There was the snooty Balsa Room of the freshly renovated Spudorgan Vacation Inn, where a fiver might just get you a pot of coffee and a table away from the jakes (if you managed to find the good side of the freshly reappointed managing director,[8] Milo Rogers, no easy task—and wasn't Milo a hard man when he was at home, oh Christ, he was that—or so they said, for Mick had never met the poet laureate of the Killoyle hotel business, but the man's reputation preceded (and followed) him like a gang of impecunious inebriates.[9])

---

[7] Finger foods, "Little Hands of Silver" on the jukebox, King Juan Carlos atop an Andalusian (horse); a poster from some Plaza de Toros announcing a forthcoming nonevent between one Sean "El Gran Macho" McSpackle and *el toro*.

[8] Insufficiently acclaimed author of two non-award-winning collections of verse, *Gobbing into the Gutter* and *Stockings in the Dust*—as some of you will know (or not). See *Killoyle, An Oyrish Face*, pp. 1–248.

[9] Arrah. Arrh. Them would be Tam, Paulie, Roddy, Sean, Morry (known to his friends and enemies alike as The Tullamore Jew), Ted, and Shaymus,

Finally, and more realistically, there was McShiny's. The American chain had opened a branch on King Idris Avenue (West), which, given time-and-motion considerations (Mick was first test driver of the day of the new Asphodel LSI, and that in thirty-five minutes) would be the likeliest candidate for brekkers.

And McShiny's it was. Blandly Americanesque in their good humour, the teens behind the counter somewhat oversold their product and the customer's pleasure in consuming it, their pseudo-conversation bookended with anodyne "how are you todays" and "have a good days" designed to provoke the matutinal temper of your average mick; and Mick was nothing if not that.

"I'll take the Shiny Sausage," he muttered. "And chips," he added, irritably.

"Will that be the Super Shiny Sausage with Super Shiny Fries?" inquired the adolescent, plunging Mick into an agony of indecision and despair.

"Oh, I don't know. How big is it? Oh, all right."

As he ate the Super Shiny Sausage—nearly a foot long and encased in a warm sticky bun apparently made of some kind of molten yet edible (just) plastic—across the linoleum his furtive gaze steadied its focus onto a pair of neat feminine legs, neatly crossed, attached to a felicitous lady whose glance was at once winsome and willing. Red-haired was she, and buxom, and greeny-blue of eye; and she purported to be perusing a copy of *Glam*.[10]

God bless and keep yez and yoa wouldn't have a bob or two to spare for a poor man wouldya squire?

[10]It's herself, right enough. This is known as foreshadowing, don't you know. Trust me, she'll pop up again, later on—although not in my house, worse luck. Sob. (Pipes mournfully peeping in something minor—say, C—with harps standing by stage right.)

Now none of that, boyo, grumbled the once-uxorious censor in Mick's brain, where the spirit of Eileen still flitted free (as free as she was now in the bloody wynds and backways of Edinburgh . . . ?); *sod it,* countered the opposition, voice of gruff maleness open to a pint and a quick fondle any time, mate, day or night. *Nice piece,* pursued that voice, offensively. To ward off panic, Mick turned his eyes to a copy of the *Killoyle Clarion* that lay abandoned on the next table.

"City Picked as Site of Olympics," confided the headlines.

"Cripes," exclaimed Mick.

Not *the* Olympics, as further perusal revealed, but the World Pint-Pulling Olympiad, no small event when you stopped to consider the attendance at your average boozer in any Irish town any day of the week, never mind during an event when the stout flowed like the waters of the East Killoyle River for five days running and free pints were handed out like trophies on Derby Day, with the grand prize a wee pub of one's own, location to be designated by the judges; ah a pub, thought Mick dreamily, like the Lusitania in Listowel, or Harvey's Bar in Bundoran, or McCracken's on the Diamond in Omagh . . .[11]

---

[11]Not to mention my personal favourite, McTowel's of Dundrum, run by the late Tadgh McTowel—that's right, the 1958 Kilkenny hurling champion. He had a brief run on the gogglebox, as well, if memory serves. Something to do with a cookery program perilously poised opposite La Finnucane on the other channel that collapsed after one episode when he'd used up his two recipes (cold cuts on a bed of oatmeal and colcannon potage). Anyhow, he fell ill all of a sudden like, overnight, in the pink one day and death's doorman the next. Sudden depression combined with an acute inflammation of the long urinary basin, most likely, according to his doctor, Seoirse "Peachy" O'Buitlear, according to whom also Tadgh was heard to announce from his hospital bed, in an unexpectedly loud and clear baritone, "Stout isn't poured at McTowel's, it's milked from the great tits of Mother Ireland herself," upon which he sat up and stared straight ahead in horror, then fell back—dead.

The lady with the legs went out, using those very legs to precise locomotive effect.

Mick sighed, riven by waves of nostalgia, lust, and acid reflux.

"Well, I drink Coke because my mum drinks Coke," explained a teenaged girl to another teenaged girl behind him. "She says it has less carbonation than Pepsi."

"Cool," said her friend.

"Ah, Christ," said Mick.

He rose, dabbing his lips. His system reacted to the hasty ingestion of sausage grease plus chips with a gaseous detonation. The girls giggled.

"Beg pardon."

Making haste, ten minutes later he was at the Jocelyn works and behind the wheel of the world's first production-model Asphodel TTX. Pats Bewley, the testing supervisor, red-faced with impatience, was clutching his clipboard and emitting a faint hissing sound through his lower mandibles. As usual, Mick noted irritably, he was wearing a shirt with cross-hatching and a shite-brown tie misknotted entirely and only coming down to the middle of his chest. Mick hated Pats Bewley on general principles, because Bewley was a prat, but more specifically because he was a known nondrinker and Hearty Harry type of sanctimonious churchgoing hill-climbing Pioneer arsehole with a full complement of manly condescension and salutary anecdotes for the less-advantaged, i.e., drinkers, smokers, freethinkers, and all the plain people of Ireland.

"Ah, there you are, McCreek," said Bewley. "Another five minutes and I'd have given the drive to Driscoll. Always almost late, aren't you?"

"Kiss my arse."

"That's what I mean. That attitude. No manners to speak of, and what's that on your tie? Now, there's the car. Take her up to speed, but watch the brakes. New antilocks are always chancey lads, I don't have to tell you that. And watch the lean on corners."

Pats stood aside and placed a complacent checkmark on the checklist of his clipboard: 8:46; Tester McCreek at the wheel; all three liters and sixteen valves of the Asphodel LSI ready to throb; nine miles on the clock. The Asphodel was the first of a projected new generation of Jocelyns, uniting elements of the jeep, the claw-footed bathtub, and the family saloon, and powered as it was by a unique seven-cylinder engine developed exclusively at Jocelyn Motors. The inverted-bathtub-like bonnet displayed a scooped-out air intake like the entrance to a cave, and the roof wore a gnarled-steel crown of gleaming aluminium tubes. Thick manly or womanly tyres and shining alloy wheels squatting beneath bold wing flares hinted at the no-nonsense stance of a barge designed for high speeds and deep road-rutting.[12] Also, chrome abounded, not least inside, where Mick already had a headache from the glare.

"Too much fuckin' chrome in here, Pats," he said. "I can't see."

"Get on wichya, McCreek," snapped Pats. "Put on yer shades, then. And mind the brakes."

------

[12]Yawn bloody yawn. Get on with it, can't you? If I wanted to read this automotive rubbish I'd have gone out and bought a copy of *Motorself* or *Speedstick Revue* or *GT Slushbox* or another of them auto mags written by, and for, teenage boys with a wanking problem and bad skin. Enough's sufficient, mister me man. Bloody cars anyhow, eh? Good for going from A to B but that's where the problems usually start, isn't it, just outside B on a cold and rainy night with yours truly squatting on his hunkers wrestling with the bloody tyre jack not to mention two grimy wheels, a tyre iron, and a tyre flat as me owld Auntie Clarissa's chest. Cars, is it? I had one once . . . but hang on a sec. If you're a Kantian, as I suspect you are, you'll be muttering about me not separating cars, as "things in themselves," from my experience with cars, that is, "things as they are for us," or, in other words, failing to distinguish the noumenal from the phenomenal, as it were. I should be seeing (you'll no doubt go on to say) space and time as the forms of our sensibility, imposed on the noumenal world as a condition of our experience of it. Fair enough. But I still had a hell of a time with the spare tyre on the outskirts of B, that rainy New Year's night long ago. That was noumenous enough for me, I can tell you. And thus do I clear my mind of Kant.

Displaying a profile of haughty indifference to Bewley's nagging, Mick drove off and motored about stylishly for a while, imagining an audience of girls. Oh, the machine would make a less demanding man quite happy, he reckoned. Just the thing for the philistines who littered the world's computer shops and university science departments, the T-shirted, unkempt, TV- and video-obsessed imbeciles with their baseball caps and dirt bikes and bungee jumps, the miserable half-witted wee nerds. . . . Truth to tell, Mick, a lover of cars, nevertheless dreamed not of Asphodels, nor of any Jocelyn. A Merc was his motor, black, preferably, with silver paneling, and chrome-tipped dual exhausts, and one of those smooth German clutchless shifters.

"Ah, that'd be the man, all right."

Mick whistled in atonal counterpoint to the overture to G. Rossini's *L'Italiana in Algeri* rollicking away on Breakfast Classics 105.5 FM.[13] The traffic was light at that time of day in most parts of town and almost nonexistent on the MacLiammoir Ring Road, from which vantage point there was a grand view of the sea. As a red light lingered, Mick stared at the view, one of the best things about living in this godforsaken shithole of a town (no Milan, you can bet yer bags). Whatever his preoccupations of the moment, he always gave the view from the MacLiammoir Road a glance of admiration, especially when there was a chance, as there was on extra-clear days, of spotting Wales on the far horizon of fact and fantasy, like Avalon, or Hybrassil—in fact, as he watched, a layer of mist peeled away and *presto!* Thar she blew, a thin layer of crust on the distant line of the sea. It was an inspiring sight:

---

[13]A nephew of mine (wee Colm, Bertie's boy) worked at that place. Seems they walk around starkers most of the time, and shagging isn't the half of it, why they spend day and night on top of each other, so they do. That explains the lengthy musical compositions offered for public consumption, operas and oratorios and what have you: changing the record manually cuts into shagging time, like.

Cymru! The imagination, if so instructed, might even supply the
distant sound of massed baritones lustily rendering "Men of
Harlech" in the melancholy valleys of South Rhondda and
Gwynedd . . . my oh my, ruminated Mick, not for the first time.
So it was across this sea that Tristan sailed to his Isolde's Cornwall
and did battle with stout King Mark; that bloody Cromwell came,
in the wake of the even bloodier Vikings; that the Normans came,
too, and conquered; that, some day long since, the original Celts
had arrived from God knows where to rout the small dusky na-
tives from the cosy comfort of their bogs; and it was over this
selfsame sea that the former Mrs. Eileen McCreek, fed up with her
quondam hubby's obstinacy of habit and innate lack of ambition,
had, in the tradition of the modern Irish exile, sailed away on the
midnight ferry from Dun Laoighaire, away from her green land,
toward a greener love, to Edinburgh, city of Boswell and Burns and
the whiskey distiller or beer salesman or whatever the blazes he
was who had tempted her to sacrifice so much so soon. . . .

"Ah, ya sod."

(It *was* a relief to be shut of her blathering, but. Talk about
carping.)

The sun, as previously noted, was shining full force. The liquid silver sea and the chrome fittings inside the car formed a
confluence of brilliance that had Mick, sunglasses or not, quite
blinded by the time the horns started honking behind him like
hungry geese. In his rearview an oddly distorted face behind the
wheel of what appeared to be a 1970s-era Fiat convertible snarled
silently.

"All right, all right. Jaysus."

Seeing little in front of his eyes but a flock of reddish-blue flying mice, Mick yielded to driver's instinct and coordinated clutch
pedal, gearshift, and accelerator in your standard departure mode,
following which forward progress was normal if slightly jerky (he
made a mental note: too-long throws on the gearbox) for all of
one and a half seconds—the interlude between normality and di-

saster, like the final pre-iceberg half-hour of the Titanic's voyage, or John Kennedy's last wave of the hand on Dealey Plaza, or the still moments just previous to the explosion of TWA Flight 800—when into Mick's life lumbered fate in the guise of: (1) sluggish brakes, per the warning issued by Pats Bewley; (2) Francis Feeley, apprentice bartender at Mad Molloy's Bar, embarking upon a last-minute, hare-brained dash across the street against the pedestrian light; (3) the sunlight ricocheting off the sea, the dashboard, divers chrome fittings, and straight into Mick's eyes.

There came a crump and a yell, coincident with reflexive mashing of the brakes. At the front there was a soft jolt, behind a bang. A man was down, and Mick had been rear-ended.

"Ignorant snail-eating foreign bastards," shrieked the driver of the aged rag-top behind, an epicene young man with large hands and nervous eyes and, it seemed blurrily to Mick, rouge, heavy lipstick, and eye shadow. "I'd take a crowbar to you French fuckers if I had one, so I would. Go back to Cannes, you garlic-eater. *Allez vous-en*, Monsieur Le Poof Français."

"Shite," said Mick.

Preliminary investigation revealed signs of life behind the closed lids of the supine form on the street. A garda arrived, soon followed by an ambulance.

"You'll be charged, you," said the policeman, who appeared to be acquainted with the injured man. "Mother of God, it's Frank. Frankie, lad, speak to me. Aye. Charged, so you'll be. So no wanderin' off. You stay right here, eh, Mr. .... eh?"

"McCreek."

"Greek. It's a bad case, so it is. I'd not be surprised if poor wee Frankie was dead, God bless and save us."

"But he's not dead. Look, he's sitting up already."

"Are you the one who ploughed into me, then? You bastard, you damn near did for me, did you know that?"

"Not ailing in the slightest, to judge by the vigour of his vocabulary."

"Vigour me arse. You're a right bastard. I can't move me legs. Listen here you. If I'm paralyzed, I'll sue you for every penny you're worth. Ah, hello there. Is it yourself, Petey?"

"Just you lie back now, Frank. We'll see to it this fella's charged to the fullest extent of the law."

"Look, officer, this pal of yours jumped out in front of me after the light changed. And I couldn't see anything anyway, with the sun shining in my eyes."

"That's quite enough out of you. And he's no pal of mine, I'll have you know, so never mind them accusations. He's me brother-in-law, Mr. Greek."

"Mc*Creek*. Jesus, Mary, and Joseph."

Briefly, Mick found himself in a world of Kafkaesque disjointedness in which for no apparent reason he had become the scapegoat of public ire.

"Go back to Paris, you," screamed the rear-ender, who by this time had stepped out of his car into full sunlight which clearly illuminated the makeup that overlay his features: lavish blood-red lipstick; black eyeliner; more than a hint of blush on the cheekbones . . . in another microscene stage-managed by the ghost of Franz K.,[14] no one but Mick seemed to notice.

"Listen to that music he's got on," clamored the made-up man. "I'm telling you, I can spot 'em every time."

"Now calm down there," said the guard. "We'd like you to come along and give a statement as well. And don't worry, this man's on me list."

----

[14]The blooming hypocrite. Did you know he went out for five years with a gal named Felice Bauer and only at the end screwed up the nerve to tell her that she had bad teeth? All the time she'd taken his narrow gaze and long brooding silences as signs of something profound, like the lucubrations of love, whereas in reality old Franz was just saying to himself over and over again "Christ what fuckin' 'orrible teeth."

"What list?" bawled Mick. "I've been tried and convicted before I've even had a chance to defend myself. As for this, this . . ."

"What was that. I'm not above administering a bit of physical restraint, I'll have you know, especially to recalcitrant wee spalpeens like yerself."

"Lay a finger on me and I'll have your fucking badge."

"Make way, now." An ambulanceman checked Mick's blood pressure and, alarmed, ordered him to the hospital. He also suggested an X ray.

"You never know, sir. The owld whiplash can muck you up."[15]

In the event, Mick was charged with "reckless endangerment of the public welfare with a weapon the exact size and shape of a motor vehicle." A Breathalyser test revealed total sobriety, and after an hour or so he was released on his own recognizance, with a warning not to leave the limits of Co. Killoyle. He promptly declared his intention to seek legal counsel and have the onus of misdemeanour shifted to the persons of Francis Feeley, perambulating barman, and Cornelius Regan, rear-ending (as it turned out) church sexton.

Mick repeated this plan to Pats Bewley when Pats came to tow away the injured Asphodel, and Pats was quite candid in turn.

"Well, Mick, you're sacked."

"Aw, give us a break, Pats."

"Given you enough breaks, lad. And look at you. Always late, or almost. Nearly cheeky every time you open your mouth. And if you drank on the job you'd be the world's biggest absenteeist,

---

[15]*I* don't know. Thanks to those high-speed motoring nightmares of mine, I've had whiplash every night of my life and damn the harm it's ever done me. The only real problem was a twisted knee after one particularly harrowing night going through the Arnage bend at Le Mans during a rainstorm in what I'd thought was a '67 Lotus Brabham but turned out to be a '76 Reliant three-wheeler. Boys, did I ever lose control of that one.

I can feel it in my bones. There's always something you'd just be about to do. I can't put my finger on it, but it's there somewhere. You're like one of them Yanks that go over the edge and turn up at their old place of employment with guns blazing. And the dear knows the number of times you've almost wrecked your test vehicles."

"Bastard."

"Aye, well, it's a hard world, lad."

Mick's blood pressure was still "a bit to mostly sky-high," they told him at the Mater Misericordiae Hospital, and although preliminary examination revealed nothing, he should, they said, take a day off and rest at home.

"Well, absolutely no problem there. My employer has seen to that."

Moreover, home was where Mick yearned to be, with the world suddenly turning on him the way it had. Home, and the locked front door, were the best guards against the infinite bothersomeness of things. Blinds down, too, and a freshly rinsed glass, and soothing murmur from Fran Leeson on the telly at that time of day: talk time on *Talk Me Talk You* (RTE Channel 4A). The subject was Societal Inebriative Dysfunction, or SID.

"Inebriated what? Oo's Sid?"

Mick only twigged to what they were on about when one of the lady guests held up an empty bottle of Jameson's and announced that she had once gone through two of them a day.

"And did your husband suspect?"

"Suspect?" A tobacco-hoarsened wheeze of laughter like the air brakes of a coal lorry. "Didn't he start me on the bloody stuff? The bastard."

Reassured, Mick chuckled and turned to pour an additional glass of liquid comfort from his own bottle, not Jameson's as it happened but a fine smooth Paddy's, and with a few water crackers to hold things together down there by janey it was going down as smooth as buttermilk from the great dun cow of Connacht.

"Ah God," blubbered Mick. He then found himself dissolving into stuttering hysterics. Somehow the reflection in the TV screen, glimpsed during an all-black commercial for eau de cologne, of his own shirtless form, pale face, and general air of decrepitude, yet seated in (he recognized the association and its absurdity at the same time) the precise pose of Gertrude Stein in Picasso's Cubist portrait of that manly gal, brought home in a vivid and pictorial way the multifarious actual and potential nastinesses of his own situation, and life's abusive absurdities in general.

"Shite. Bastards. Fuck you, Pats Bewley."[16]

He tipped another short one down his throat and gave himself up to random thoughts of despair.

Sacked!

Un-fucking-employed!!

On the Sosh!!!

He'd end up like his father, a jobless chancer with one foot on the barrail and the other in the grave, creator of his own legend and two martyrs: his wife, his son ... and here Mick's lot in life was turning into the bit of a disgrace, as well, what with Eileen dumping him for a job in Scotland (and that job's gruff, manly Scots overseer, Sean bloody Connery in a suit and tie, och aye the noo) and himself being nearly broke anyway, the consequences of divorce leeching away the larger part of his puny savings and the rest siphoned off by his own natural disinclination to put anything aside, *carpe diem, fay ce que voudras,* hasn't the owld motor gone long enough without a fine set of alloys, and I always fancied one of those multi-CD changers, and Hanna's just got in

---

[16]That's telling 'em, boy. I used identical language when management, in the form of a slope-shouldered article named Stiles, threw me out of Pucker's Steel Pens and Quill Manufactory after employing me for three days on on the assumption that I was Ernie Eames, whereas I was, and am, not, and whereas Ernie, as it transpired, had moved to the greater Inisbofin area to try his hand at the repair and maintenance of nets.

a Kavanagh first edition . . . of course, even at the end of the line there were the soft nannying hands of Ireland's welfare state, of whose generosity toward her citizens Mick McCreek had taken advantage often enough in the past, starting without hesitation soon after graduating from TCD with a degree in classical architecture (from Vitruvius to Palladio, inclusive) that—like all college degrees bar those in the applied sciences—turned out to be quite useless except for purposes of adding a dash of spurious learning to barroom blather. Anyway, he'd used his money from the Sosh, plus a packet borrowed from home, to go to Italy to visit Elide, a girl he'd met on the windy heights of Howth Head, the both of them en route to the Abbey Tavern for good crack of a Saturday night (Christy Moore, De Danaan); and when Mick visited and, intending marriage, wooed his Elide in her noble hometown of Milan, he went out to Monza and saw Ferraris and Alfa Romeos being put through their paces and even drove a Dino (hers) at high speed along the cypress-lined highways of Lombardy and Emilia-Romagna from Milan's Piazza del Duomo straight down to rich, wine-redolent Parma and Bologna; and that was that. From then on he was hooked. Something of the same aesthetic-scientific appeal that had drawn him to buildings attracted him to cars, a union of the fabulous and the everyday, with a heavy dose of vanity, as in sartorial taste, also an Italian specialty. More importantly, he'd absorbed the neopagan half-adoring, half-cynical attitude Italians have not only to cars but to life in general. A young Irishman like Mick McCreek was a blank slate indeed, back in the early '70s when Ireland herself was only just ungumming her weary age-old eyes and taking in the new dawn of things . . . then *il capo,* Elide's father, also known behind his back as *il duce,* sussing out Mick's earnestness vis-à-vis his little girl, had one night over *tortellini in brodo* (washed down with a crisp Lambrusco[17]) proudly announced the

---

[17]When was that, 1973 or so? Why, that's just yesterday, isn't it, chum? Sure don't I remember clear as crystal that outstanding haddock-and-chips I had

existence of Commendatore Spadolini, an appointed future son-in-law then in the high command of the Squadra Volante, and with that, or shortly thereafter, in an atmosphere of peerless awkwardness and sweaty palms (his), Mick left, via Geneva; but in his dreams he visited the glorious peninsula yet, wandering across the geometrical shadows of De Chirico piazzas and driving that red Dino south along the cypress-lined highways of an Italianate heaven.

But most importantly, he'd also lost his virginity on that little jaunt (late night; the family *casa* in San Donato Milanese; her room, adorned with posters of the same rock stars who adorned the bedroom walls of Killoyle bungalows; dead silence bar the act itself and the distant ebb and flow of a televisual laughtrack in *il Duce*'s parlour) which had forever, for one thing, ended Mick's blinkered Irish suspicion of the world and all its foreigners.[18]

Otherwise, he'd made a bags of the whole business, as he had the rest of his life, or so it seemed through the prism of the whiskey glass.

"Elide," he elided elliptically, quite langered—and it scarcely three p.m., for goodness' sake.

---

round about ten P.M. on June fifteenth of that year, and didn't I wash it down with a fine vintage Lucozade straight from the bottle?

[18]Not entirely unjustified, let me tell you. Foreigners will be foreigners and there's precious little you or I can do about it. Once I met one who said "oo-oo" and kept on staring at me, like I was some kind of sodding exhibit. I told him to piss off, but no, it was "oo-oo" again and the unblinking stare, like a sheep on a hillside, then "oo-oo" and eyes the size of bloody soup plates. Finally I had to leave the bathhouse entirely and dry off outside.

2

"Now that's enough."

Penny Burke was astounded at the coarseness and fecundity of language suddenly gushing forth from behind the old newspaper shelves.

"Feck off ya feckin' owld shagspot, Oy says. And do ya know what he says. Wait till I tell ya. He says, ya can kiss me arse a hondred and twenty seven toymes, ya feckin' owld hand jobber. He does, so he does, ah well now ye're the nice bugger entoyrely, arencha, Oy says . . ."

"I say, that's enough. This is a library, you know."

Nabbed, the culprit sneered: a red-nosed, double-chinned man in an Aberdeen mac, lecturing a buxom woman twice his height who with weary patience lent an ear while flipping idly through the latest P. D. James;[1] then, when Penny appeared, she walked away, not without a disapproving sidelong glance.

---

[1] P. D. James, is it? The dear knows there's hardly a moment in the livelong day that I don't slew around, convinced I've just heard someone pronounce that name, those initials, that diphthong. . . . Last Monday morning, for instance, I was waiting for the old bus (the 12A, corner of Pembroke Road, brrrr, it doesn't get half blustery there, I had my woolies around my neck for warmth) when I distinctly heard a pair of lips part moistly just abaft of my left ear, a quaveringly wheezy breath inhale, and a sandpaper-rough voice

"I'm sorry, sir, but you'll have to leave if you keep on like that," said Penny to the man. The wretch had a coughing fit, then turned on her with resort to the Irish tongue, not knowing he was deal-ing with a Silver Medalist in the Gaelic from the county Mayo.

"_Imeacht gan teacht ort_," he hissed.

"_Titim gan éirí ort_," retorted Penny. "Now please be quiet, sir. I don't want to hear any more of that kind of language in any language."

The man cowered, cowed.

"Oy won't. Oy'll shut up now, miss. Sorry, miss."

"All right then."

He grovelled, fishing for benisons to gain her esteem.

"_Bail ó Dhia ort._"

"_Bail ó Dhia is Mhuire duit_," replied Penny.[2]

---

declare, or inquire, "P. D. James," with an upward inflection, as if it were less a statement, more of a question, as per: _"P. D. James?"_ but in response to no ques-tion uttered by me (as, for example, "Good morning, are you an aficionado or aficionada of the famous detective authoress P. D. James?" or, "Yoo-hoo, who's yer favourite detective writer, then?"). Gave me a turn, I can tell ya. I didn't stop running till I reached Harold's Cross. And as if that weren't enough, and it weren't, there I was doing my twice-weekly shopping at Strangeways on the Mall a day later and a wizened old bloke with the red nose of a true bottle man accosted me with the bold-as-brass question, "Oy! Are you P. D. James?" Now, these things come in threes, so I'm waiting for the next one, walking on egg-shells as it were, earplugs firmly in place, one left, one right . . .

[2] A fine instance of West Coast blarney of the type as would occur with great regularity in Cousin Monk's life out in Connemara, especially when old Monk fell off his bike and an Irish speaker, ideally Father Harney, S.J., hap-pened by; such conversations, edgy at first—dictating where and how the other party should depart the premises instantly; evoking in vivid terms the pro-found and wide-ranging quality of the other's personal shortcomings—would then ease into mutual blessings via various reassuring degrees of blandness before resuming antagonistic counterpoint a mile or so apart with the foulest imprecations and gratuitous comparisons to elements of excreta, abnormal coitus, the lower primates, et cetera.

She returned to her post at the information desk. The P. D. James-reading lady awaited, her mouth a thin downward crescent of disapproval.

"I want your supervisor."

"Beg pardon?"

"Your supervisor, gell. I want to file a complaint about your behaviour, speaking to my husband that way."

"Your husband? I had no idea. Anyhow, he started it." Bloody hell, what a day so far, self-complained Penny.

"Nonsense. I distinctly heard you say shut up."

"Well . . ."

Well, she *had* said it. The man himself suddenly popped up, like a leprechaun in one of James Stephens's spurious elfin tales.

"That's her," he said, happy as a schoolyard tattletale, barely able to contain his glee. "She said shut up."

"Yes, I know this is she, Victor dear," said his wife. "Now we're waiting for the supervisor."

"That would be Mr. Finn."

Finn was at his desk in his office, rocking slowly from side to side.

"Mr. Finn," said Penny. "This lady's got a complaint."

Finn frowned. He, too, had complaints, mostly centered in and around the intestinal area, which tended to worsen when exposed to the imperfections of others.

"Oh, for goodness' sake," he expostulated, after hearing the issue through. "Somebody apologize to somebody else and leave me alone."

"Now that's no attitude to take," said the lady. "I'm afraid I must insist on contacting your supervisor, Mr. Finn."

"Well, you're out of luck, Mrs. eh . . ."

"Hasdrubal-Scott. Mrs. Victor Hasdrubal-Scott."

"Right. You see, I'm my *own* supervisor, actually. And I'll soon be on my annual hols, you know. Won't be back for a fortnight. Isn't that right, Miss Burke."

"Right," said Penny. "Bilbao, I believe. Weren't you there last year?"

"Ah . . . well . . ."

"Never mind, Mr. Finn, your secret's safe with us, I'm sure."

"No secret, Miss Burke. I had a splendid time. Have you been to the Basque country, madam? Oh, delightful. The Guggenheim, you know, in Bilbao, one of the world's great . . . not that I'm a great museum-goer, don't think I've ever been in one, actually, except perhaps the West of Ireland Jaunting Car Museum out in Clifden . . . oh yes, beautiful, just beautiful. Nothing like a bit of motoring through the hills, eh? Of course I'm not much of a driver, and hills give me vertigo, but I've heard they're fine . . . splendid fishing, as well, if you care for that sort of thing, which I don't, much, never been a fish-eater myself. But the wines . . . my goodness gracious me. Not that I drink wine at all. " He rubbed his stomach, wincing as in pain.

"Spain, you say?"

This seismic bit of info antagonized the Hasdrubal-Scotts into threats of imminent civil action for libel, slander, and/or what have you, with the ground, however, somewhat cut out from under their feet by the colourful metaphors employed by Mr. Hasdrubal-Scott (or plain Mr. Scott, as it turned out, the Hasdrubal being his wife's moniker by right of birth and possible Hiberno-Maghrebi descent), who reembarked on a journey of profanity and insult.

"Feck this for the lousiest little shitehouse of a municipal liberry Oy ever saw. And yerself, Whinn is it? For a royght owld ballocks."

"Careful, them's fightin' words," said Penny, half-enjoying herself; after all, what else awaited her, except the remainder of the day? And wasn't that a guaranteed seven-hour *ennui deluxe*?

"Now I've had quite enough," said Mr. Finn. "Unlike the rest of youse I actually have work to do."

Testily, he arose and, adopting the slightly bowed posture of the chronic hemorrhoid sufferer, he escorted his unwelcome visitors to the door of his office from which, in a straight line, he could shuffle at any time to the bathroom, there to make— on a matchbox-sized cell phone of which he was inordinately proud—clandestine calls to the turf accountant, the talking clock, the twenty-four-hour weather line, and other, less quotidian—and perhaps hotter[3]—hotlines, and also to alleviate his sufferings for a brief moment or twain; and, at the end of said same sad day, with the dreamy gloaming softly glooming over the car parks of Killoyle and another nine-hour block of time under his belt (spent mostly cataloguing and making acquisitions when he wasn't arranging free seminars for the likes of the town's small, mostly Indo-Pak immigrant populace, or presiding over "training sessions" in the hills for the unemployed, complete if you please with hot buttered scones, courtesy of Mrs. Finn), it was his wont to progress unobserved via a trajectory of forty-five degrees west-northwest toward the parking place under the sycamores reserved for the placid metallic-grey three-year-old Rover 175LS with manumatic five-speed that was his sole means of returning in a timely fashion to the trim, well-clipped gardens of Number 115A Anchorite Avenue, just down from the deconsecrated church once known as St. Oinsias and now called Laddi's Disco.

"Good afternoon, Mrs. Hannibal Smith," said Finn firmly. "And you, sir. The main exit is that way. Please don't hesitate to use it."

"Hasdrubal-Scott. Winn, is it? I'll be drafting letters this very afternoon, Winn, you mark my words."

Penny was also en route out the door when:

"Not you, Miss Burke. Stay."

"No."

"I beg your pardon?"

---

[3] Aha! More of the old foreshadowing. Just keep reading, if you can stand it.

"I'm not a friggin' dog."

"Beg pardon?"

"Sorry."

Her position, she feared (being a pessimist by nature and up-bringing) was in jeopardy, in view of her general attitude, recent events, and things . . . ?

"Not at all," said Mr. Finn. "I value your contributions, Miss Burke. Bleeding Jesus, what a pair, eh? Straight from Nightmareland. Brrrrr." He mimed a shiver. "Oh. Right. Actually, I was just going to ask you to take that flemmin' unemployment seminar for me tomorrow afternoon. It's enough I've had of them lads, believe you me. And I'll be away at, ah, a seminar."

"'Twill be a pleasure, my liege."

Finn's eyebrows rose and quivered; he was, as always, slightly irritated by Miss Burke's ironic perkiness, beneath which he suspected there lay aching innocence pleading for attention, respect, nay, love . . . but that was her business, not his. And thanks be to God for that.

As for Penny Burke, she returned to the information desk with a sensation of mild pleasure at the prospect of any kind of blip in the flat line of her routine, and also mildly irritated at herself for being pleased to any degree at anything less than a grand departure, an appearance on *The Late Late Show,* or the announcement of her nuptials . . . but sure anything was better than sitting about all day answering questions like (for instance) "Have you a Dick, Dick, Dickens?" or "Do you happen to know whether seaweed plus iron is a suitable nutrient for the white pinwheel zinnia?" or "I want to know everything about tyres for a '94 Bedford remover truck."[4] And anyway, sometimes there were actually decent folks

---

[4]Or, "How are you today?", or "Do you have Cliff Richard's memoirs?", or "D'yez have books about owld Troyumph motorboikes, loike?", or "It hurts here, no, right here, when I cough," or "When does the next bus for Enniskerry leave?", or "Do you have *The Dominatrix of Langerhans Hall* by Megan Truex?",

at these unemployment seminars, not just down-and-outers and permanent Sosh addicts and compulsive urinators but decent hardworking fellas (she was thinking of the men, mostly, not all of them physically repulsive) who'd stumbled a bit along the winding highway of life, like, concerning which misfortune she'd not be the one to cast aspersions, not hardly, not after the ups and downs of her first five years out of college, and herself a girlish Galway grad thrown into the eddies and whirlpools of Ireland's three capitals (Dublin, London, New York), before following love, back in Ireland, southeastward with the coastal railway on which he was employed as a ticket-taker (following an odd misunderstanding concerning his profession, she, quite the music lover— mostly folk, but occasionally classical—hearing "conductor" and envisaging Rattle, Toscanini, Karajan, and co., whereas he'd intended nothing grander than "fares, please"—besides, how could

---

or "Do the Southeast Ireland Wolseley Spotters meet today?", or "I think Hermann Goering was the bit of a lad, don't you?". . . I did that job once, in England, or was it Wales (actually, a bit of both: Wrexham). Oh, I could go on, and I will. Once a young tough lunged at me on my way out for a smoke and threatened to hold me hostage if I didn't escort him to the bathroom, where other young toughs awaited, he said, full of ill intent vis-à-vis him; well, I promptly did as he requested, of course, and received a sound thrashing for my pains. Another time a lady in a mac came and stood in front of me and hissed, then without further ado she opened her mac wide and exposed . . . nothing, or rather, a perfectly ordinary blouse-and-dress assembly. "Ye forgot to disrobe, Shirley," I snarled, not best pleased, and the silly cow loped off, muttering. Then there was the time I saw the eyes peering at me from across the top of the gardening bookcase, oh evil shiny wee orbs they were, and for a while they followed my every move, lustful wee button-eyes darting wickedly about and sliding greasily back and forth, oh I was that narked so I was but, emboldened by the presence of a policeman (Garda Duffy, in the corner, engrossed in *Musclesleuth Monthly*), I approached the nasty wee peepers with a bold challenge, something along the lines of, "Now, look here, you," only to discover that they weren't eyes at all, but well-polished specimens of igneous rock in the Children's Science display.

he have known she liked that kind of music?) and now, with that particular love gone a-roaming (Iarnrod Eireann a-beckoning), she'd ended up behind the info desk at the Killoyle Public Library, and a nice job it was, really, steady and decently paid, despite which she was desperately desirous of putting pen to paper and pedal to metal simultaneously with, respectively, a manuscript at a publisher's and America or the flakier fringes of Europe (e.g., Barcelona, Berlin, Corfu) as her twin goals . . . not that *that* particular ambition felt terribly fresh or inspiring this morning, which had begun at seven A.M. with the Special Delivery return postage parcel containing the seven stories she'd shipped out to Handyman House (Publishers) Ltd., The Vines, Turbot Lane, Upper Mandrake, Surrey SU4 1BJ.

"There is little here to interest this or any reader," sniffed the rejector, an anonymous editorial dogsbody. "My advice is the bin, or the interstices of your knickers."

"Ohhhh," moaned Penny, uncomfortably suspecting, deep down, that the seven stories were utter shite and that the best you could say of them was that they were correctly spelled and that the author had read Elizabeth Bowen.[5] Still, they were better than

---

[5]Bowen Schmowen. Pen's tales are fine examples of the writing craft, especially the one about the art collector who mistakenly steps onto a country road in one of his prize possessions, Van der Lubbers's landscape painting "Laandskajp Ootsijd Joopdenuyldorp" (circa 1667) and proceeds to rearrange the entire painting from the inside, driving its value up by a million or so every time, all of which nicker goes straight into his savings account—but he can't touch it because he doesn't know how to get out of the bloody painting, so somehow he has to suss out the formula for transmogrification, which involves going inside the tavern and bringing enough of the characters to life to help him out . . . ah, you should read it. Oh, that's right, you can't. Because of the opinions of high-minded berks like the foregoing it hasn't been published. Well, drop by the house sometime and we'll scare it up for you and you can read it over the *glöwein* (Pen's a past master, or should that be mistress?) and finger foods (*olé*).

nothing, a start on the endless rocky road upward into the weeping grey clouds of literary martyrdom, and anything written down on paper was a break with the Burke family heritage of illiterate drunkenness, that fine old tradition extending back through time to the very first gibbering bards and whiskey-bibbing wastrels of the glorious West . . . "Burke," of course, was a Norman, that is, French, name (de Bourgh) way back, so way back in fact it hardly mattered anymore, so unbearably Irish through and through had the whole lot become, over the course of the centuries 'twixt the Middle Ages and now. Penny's Burkes came from Ballycoughley, on the road to the Twelve Pins, near the Burren, a prime site for bird-watching (kestrel, curlew, bittern), drinking (seven pubs, all along the main street, called Main Street) and plain old loneliness (population [1990] 987 and dropping). Penny's da, Big Matty, a land speculator by training, had, in the course of a long, uneventful, and almost entirely useless life (except for the spawning of Penny and her brothers Phil and Finnbarr—although the usefulness of bringing those two galoots into the world was a matter for dispute), spent many a dull hour progressing from third on the left at the bar rail in O'Hare's Bar to flat-out facedown inspection of that establishment's fine tiled floor, and that sometimes on a daily basis; truly, Penny's da would be the most thoroughgoing and well-worn of all Irish clichés, God save us, right down to the Donegal cloth cap, shiny trouser seats and flourishing grog blossoms, were it not for the man's kind and Christian disposition and deepseated love of animals, especially the humble donkey, or burro, of which species the Burkes possessed at any given time at least three (currently Astro, Bentley, and Gandalf). Penny loved the little buggers, too, for their soft indomitable patience and gentle stubbornness, and there was scarcely a time in her life that she could remember without a warm donkey presence.

Thus prompted by the donkeys of Mnemosyne, she mused behind her desk, remembering home and all, and she dared to hope, memories of the past crossing the line into ambitions for the future before you could say "Jack (or Mary) Robinson." Taking advantage of the total absence, for the moment, of any questioners or information seekers, Penny uprolled her eyes to heaven, via the aluminium crossbeams and fluorescent lights of the library's ceiling (a bat peered back, confused) in votive dumb show, pleading with whoever or whatever for whatever, or whoever . . . well, no, more specifically: publication and a fella, and not one of your sensitive New Age fellas, either, but more of your old-fashioned Irish manly kind of article, not too much that way, of course, no drunken drubbings by night thank you ever so much, but maybe more than a hint of actual literacy but certainly none of the ultramodern bisexualized wimp specimens, with their endless apologies and downcast eyes and programmed responses to the Third World, abortion, pop culture, and the environment, Jaysus they might as well get on with it and have breast implants all 'round. . . .

"Excuse me, do you have any books on the dangers of radiation in yogurt?"

Speak of the devil. Penny scowled.

"Check 'Environment,' third bookcase from the left."

"Thanks very much. Ah."

"Yes?"

"Have we met?'

They had, actually, Penny realized, remembering the limp handshake, the ponytailed hair. The venue a folk festival. She only hoped they hadn't . . . ?

"No. Sorry."

Why apologize? Anyway, he wouldn't leave. He stood there staring at her as if she were the bleeding Mona Lisa.[6]

---

[6]Well, she's fresh-faced and clear-skinned, but not overly gorgeous by any means, indeed she possesses a friendly face that might lend itself too easily to caricature: blue eyes prominent, indeed just this side of bulging; nose ever so

She shifted uncomfortably.

"Now I remember. The Listowel Festival a couple of years back. Peggy, isn't it? No," he glanced at her nameplate. "Penny. Sorry. I'm Derek, remember?"

"Sorry, Derek. Afraid you're mistaken."

"Derek Paterson. You don't remember?"

"Absolutely not. Sorry."

"Oh, come on. The Dogues were on. And Pernambuco Ashley-Laura, the Brazilian samba guitarist?"

"Oh dear oh dear."

"Oh, well. Listen," he said, feigning a sudden pause, as of inspiration, his voice rising as if he'd just had the most original and fabulous idea and was about to make a declaration along the lines of "Give me a place to stand and I will move the earth," instead of which he burbled:

"Well, why don't we have a drink when you get off and let me refresh your memory? I mean, if that's all right?"

"I'm afraid not. You see," she lied, with a fluency that disturbed her only slightly, "I have a meeting with a martial artist around that time."

"I see. Well, then."

Derek strode off (it would have been tempting to say *in a huff,* had she been writing the scene), revealing a diminished, and petulantly flouncing ponytail. Touchy, wasn't he. Derek, was it.[7] Folk

----

slightly longer than average; a strong, but far from lantern, jaw; fine skin, however, and ash-blond hair that fans out across her slender shoulders, these atop a figure not quite *zaftig* but more than slender.

[7]Indeed. Derek, eh? I knew a Derek once. (Not this charlie, but. Never fear. More on this later.) Actually, I tell a lie. The fact of the matter is that I lived for a while in a bungalow haunted by the *ghost* of a fellow named Derek, Colonel Derek Godmanchester-Smith of the Londonderry Light Infantry, one-time regimental cook and old India wallah (he still smoked those cheroots, I'd find spectral fag-ends lying in the grate of a morning). Wait till I tell you.

festivals, indeed. Synods of adolescence, all under the not-so-benign sway of having a good time (and pass the doings, darling)! No, the RTE Symphony was more her line these days, or the odd

---

It all started about a month after I moved in, this was back when I was a freelance whatsit, or slightly before . . . well, anyhow. So there I was, and it didn't take long for me to suspect I had a bit of the old ectoplasm floating about the place, what with the standard-issue moaning and wailing and chain-rattling and whatnot. When, needing my eight hours, I told him to feckin' shut up, my ghostly roommate resorted to trying to shock me by barking orders ("Quick march!" "Tenshun!" "Company halt!" "Open fire!" and so on) from the top of the stairs in the middle of the night; then, when that had me so thoroughly cheesed off that I was threatening to bring in his old regimental sergeant-major to straighten him out, he took up more devious means of getting himself recognized, such as handcuffing visitors to the banister and delivering smart flicks to their rumps with a ghostly riding crop. This would excite him no end, you could hear the old mountebank breathing heavily—until I turned up, that is, he never quite got over his fear of me once I'd threatened him with his s-m. "Sir," he'd say, quailing, or "Madam?" Then he sought to gain favour by sitting at the foot of my bed and whiling away the wee hours by droning on about this and that: his amorous dalliances with sex-deprived memsahibs in the hill stations of a summertime; his daring idea for a musical about Indian stockbrokers; his favourite books (*Kim; Monty: A Soldier's Field-Marshal; Memoirs of W. G. Grace; Mrs. Ponywhite's Remove Stains Now and Forever,* and P. J. Rasnakrisnavoram's *Mumbai Days, Mambo Nights*), how he got on in the army despite a grammar-school background; some of his best-known recipes (including his two personal favourites: Burma Squid in Its Own Ink and Bengal Croutes, consisting of crushed toasted almonds mixed with Sharwood's Green Label Chutney, spread on homemade cheese biscuits and baked for about ten minutes), etc. It was all right up to a point but I needed my sleep, so when he wouldn't go away I finally got in Father Doyle from St. Oinsias Church, as it then was, to do the exorcism rites. The good padre was shite-scared and needed a few jars before getting on with it, but once he reached the *In nomine Patre* part heavy footsteps thundered down the stairs and out the front door, which slammed decisively and put an end to the colonel's posthumous shenanigans. I quite missed him after a while, actually, and I still use some of his recipes (but why muck around the Bengal Croutes's exquisitely subtle flavour by adding a balsamic vinegar gravy? Similarly, his

musical (Elvis Joseph, Anthony George Webster and that lot), or
so she thought, like a vice (or virtue) practised in secret, such had
been the pressure of boyfriends, pals, and other peers. She felt,
with the apostle Paul (and, judging by the people she knew,
damned few others), that she had finally come to Man's estate, or
rather Woman's, and had put away childish things like dolls and
colouring books and folk festivals and bumper slogans reading,
Nuclear Power? No Thanks! . . . Still, she'd had her good times,
right enough, and that Derek fellow was cute, in his way, and she
fancied a bit of . . .

From across the room she saw him peering her way, yogurt
book in hand. Guilt prodded her with the tentative yet insistent
fingers of a mendicant.

Well, all right, she *had* been a bit abrupt, but it would hardly
do for her to call out plaintively after him *now,* would it? But then
the phrase "beggars can't be choosers" pronounced itself quietly
in her mind, and she recoiled from the notion. She, a beggar?
Bugger that. For now, for then, for all bloody eternity.

"Sod him," she muttered, and proceeded to put her imprecations on a footing of sound empirical logic. "The friggin' wee folk
guitarist."

(Well, she could always call him later. Now that she had his
name, like.)

"Excuse me, could you help me?" Rheumy eyes, a trembling
liver-spotted hand. "I was given to understand that a new biography of the climber George Mallory has just come out . . . ?"

Now, this one she was quite willing to help; indeed, she went
so far as to accompany the old chap, solicitous hand on elbow to

oversweet jus does no favours to that exquisitely tender, well-hung roast veni-
son with mashed swede and spinach), and every so often I imagine I hear his
gruff tones on the telephone, from a great distance; but gone is gone, as mum
used to say, and wishing don't make it any different.

forestall imbalance, all the way to the biography shelves at the far end of the library and to indicate to him the possibility of his ensconcing himself in a cosy old armchair next to the window through which there was a grand wee view of, if not the high Himalaya, at least Killoyle's silvery strand. As for the Everest book: yes, there it was, and she wasn't about to let it go without a word of strongest recommendation, particularly vehement with reference to the scene in which Odell sees Mallory and Irvine for the last time, mythically, two upward-crawling specks against the gigantic hulk of Everest seconds before the mists descend like a play's final curtain from the dazzling empyrean and usher the two climbers into the land of eternal mystery, viz., heaven itself. . . .

Oh, he recalled it well, said the old gent, having been there himself, having helped them on with their oxygen tanks that very morning, having taken the last picture, having mourned with the world.

Later, Penny handed over the info desk to Naomi, her nocturnal counterpart.

"I had a member of the 1924 Everest expedition in here this afternoon," she said.

"Cripes, he must have been an old fart, yeah?"

"Eighty-six. Or was it eighty-seven?"

Old bones, young heart, as her mum used to say, as well as the opposite.

On the way home, Penny stopped in at Traynor's the grocer's, across from the busaras. A tired face, a wrinkle-wreathed smile, a hundred thousand welcomes.

"Miss Burke. How are you at all?"

"Oh, all right, Mrs. Traynor. Chutney, please. And a can of Foster's."

And that pretty much summed it up: Chutney and a can of Foster's. Not that Penny lived in squalor, picturesque or otherwise, despite the student ambience evoked by the mention of these

comestibles; *au contraire*, her flat on the top floor of the Hoardings, the ambitious yet cheaply built new Maher Properties
development north of the city centre, was exceedingly well-
appointed for a mere flat, with a fancy stereo and lots of books
and on the walls the art of the unartistic: posters of museum ex-
hibitions gone by (Monet at Giverny, Manet at Maubeuge) and
travel pix of exotic places (Sardinia, Manhattan, Mykonos).
Twice-weekly hooverings kept the flat in the hypothetical running for a Fine Apartments and Handsome Houses of Ireland
award.[8] Across the street from the pseudo-ritzy underlighting of
the Hoardings glowed the great diamond Koh-I-Noor atop a
mythical Taj Mahalesque edifice that crowned the tawdrily blinking neon sign of the eponymous restaurant, where Penny frequently purchased sinus-cleansing curries for those long, tired
nights in front of the telly . . . most nights, now, sad to say . . . she
wept, briefly, then took herself in hand, wiping away the tear or
two that glistened, swelled, hesitated, skittered down.

"Ballocks, girl," self-scolded she.

"Grrr. Alph alph alph!" declared Alf, her Jack Russell terrier, a
manly wee tyke but tenderly affectionate when it suited him, or
his appetite.

She fed Alf, then pondered: A nice chicken Madras might do
the trick after all, obviating as it would the need for infinitesi-
mally slow-boiling water, frozen vegetables, a slumgullion of stale
spices, sliced whatsits on the heavily striated cutting board (it had
to go) and God only knew what else (washing up, that was what).

Halfway through the evening news (something in Israel, of
course, and wasn't old Gar at it again, only this time up North;

---

[8]Oh, I submitted my apartment's candidacy for that award once. Came close
to getting it, too, only at the last minute I discovered the flat I was putting
forward wasn't mine at all but Lord Iveagh's. I had to apologize, of course,
and buy drinks all around. On the other hand, that was how I almost met Kathy.

they had pictures, too) Penny rose and shrugged on a raincoat and went across the rain-slicked cobbles of Uphill Street to the ghee-redolent precincts of the Koh-I-Noor, "Killoyle's most venarable [*sic*] IndoPak resturant [*sic*], F. A. Goone, prop.," as the hand-lettered sign in the window stated semicoherently. The grub was grand, but, and they hadn't raised their prices in years, not like that upstart Star of Bihar down on the Esplanade (hadn't she eaten there with train-conducting Owen, painful memory twisting in her heart like a red-hot skewer, no thanks—odd, now that she thought of it, the misunderstanding that had led her to him . . .!), never mind the one out on the Crumstown Road, Hamshri's? Rami's? Hashmi . . . ?

Haresh's Hideaway, that was it.

Maybe Derek would take her there, if she asked him. It wasn't as if she had a surfeit of suitors, or a rich social whirl. And he seemed a nice guy. And it wasn't every day a nice guy came up to her and as much as fell to his knees before her.

She entered the Koh-I-Noor. The submarine gloom faded into a flickering glow that grew slowly less dim and, as an oyster yields its pearl, eventually propelled forth a querulous Indian, frowning:

"Yes? Yes?"

"Hello, Mr. Swain."

"Oh, it's you, Miss Burke. How terrific. Please come in."

"Well I . . . All right. Just a carryout, mind. The usual, you know?"

"Absolutely. Chicken Madras? And a pair of nice cold Tuskers?"

"Well."

"Quite."

The Foster's would have to take its place in the queue. These fellas had Tusker, from East Africa, a legacy of the Koh-I-Noor's founder and former owner, Mr. Patel, who had fled Kenya during the early anti-Indian rule of President Daniel arap ("*L'état c'est"*) Moi and who had, more recently, fled Ireland for (some said) the Maldives, or (according to others) Suriname. Anyway, Tusker lager was his legacy to the Koh-I-Noor, and it was the best brew Penny'd had since Shepherd Neame back in her London days . . . sure now those were the days, or had been, living from hand to mouth and back again, never knowing if your next mode of transport was going to be the tube or your tired old feet or a stretch limo, not to mention the odd jaunt to Dubrovnik or the Costa Smeralda with the odd fella, usually Italian or German, who fancied girls with her, Penny's, laid-back intellectual attitude and stout West of Ireland thighs . . . *well,* now.

The door crashed rudely open and a man stood there, swaying. From behind an assortment of softly clicking beaded curtains and screens of imitation bamboo Mr. Swain stepped out, on the alert and a trifle concerned, recognizing as an old restaurant hand must the unmistakable signs of long hours in the pub or at home among bottles, in any case the vivid emblems of one hard-punished by drink. In this case his downstairs neighbor, that fellow McCreek.

"Oh, it's you, McCreek."

"Give us a Vindaloo, Swain, be a good fella, woncha. I've eaten fuck-all since this morning, God what a day, went down to My Three Buns—by the way he's a nasty sod, that Devereux article, isn't he? Not that I've ever been rude to him, but even then they were closed, Christ what a day, everybody's been at me. Have a go yourself, haha. Got sacked, too, didn't tell you that, did I, no of course not, never saw you did I. Well, hel*lo* there."

His watery gaze fell on Penny. She looked away.

"And so it goes, eh Swain? This young lady here. She won't even give me the time of day. Just like all the others, eh? Well bugger off then, you! No, sorry, no I don't mean that. Sorry. Well now let's see, how are you, Anil? Oh right. What I came for, eh? Vindaloo. Beef, you know. The roast beef of old England, haha? Not, let us hope, in spongiform form, if you catch my meaning, ah haha no, not quite . . ."

"I say, Mick."

"Make it chicken."

"Well my goodness I don't know, you know."

"And a full complement of that excellent Tusker. Say, four cans?"

"Now Mick. By golly."

"Right then. I'll be back for it in five, ten minutes. Just go and get some fags, yeah. Be seeing you. Miss."

He leaned, lurched, swayed, caught a sidelong glance from Penny, tipped an imaginary hat, and slouched away through the door, comically swerving to avoid a collision, the incoming customers-to-be being, as Penny remarked instantly, of a far more respectable, that is, sober, brand. But how much more boring, she thought, recognizing that her relief at the departure of the man named Mick (suitably so named, in her opinion) was combined with spontaneous amusement at the dangerously heterogeneous opinions of the truly erudite drunk and her profound, innate fellow-feeling for the response to the world's venom that made drinkers of men (and women) . . . he had seemed to be Irish, of course, offensively so, if not heavily Paddy-accented; but probably not a local. An educated Dubliner, then, down on his luck?

A jackeen on the skids. In old Killoyle.

"Your Madras, Miss Burke. And two Tuskers."

"Oh thanks, Mr. Swain. I won't be needing those. Let that gentleman have them."

"Gentleman? McCreek, you mean. Well, all right. Three-fifty please. Thank you very much, Miss Burke. Oh, how kind."

Penny departed, content. The single Fosters would do. He could have the extra pair and round out his libations to a six-pack. Satisfied, feeling penitential and—more importantly—less likely to gain weight, she locked the door behind her, sat in her lounge chair and dined on Mr. Swain's chicken Madras, which left the lips a-tingle, the sinuses aflow. At her feet, Alf, expectant; on the telly, an American police drama in which, in each week's episode, slaughter, torture, and mayhem occurred on the level of, say, the Russian Civil War of the early 1920s. Very highly rated by the critics it was, and widely admired by intellectuals of a, she couldn't help noticing (sorry, but there it is), certain left-leaning bias (exposing the dirty secrets of rich America? of complacent Whitemaleworld? of the polluters of Mother Earth?), and of course police, firearm, and S & M fans. The show had been the recipient of critical praise likening it to the Book of Genesis and the works of Fyodor Dostoyevsky, as well as telly awards beyond the counting of them. Penny only watched it for the bloke who played the Lootenant. He looked like a nice fella.

Actually, he looked like that fella tonight.

3

"Well, blow me," exclaimed Anil, quaintly.

"I'll try, Uncle," said Mrs. Swain. "But it's a bit awkward in this position, you know."

"No, no, Auntie, on the telly, look," said Anil, squirming. "It's that bloke again. The silly chap with the ears."

The television's borrowed voices and secondhand images entertained, while soothing to the point of rapture, the Swains, Anil and Rubina. It was late, say half-eleven or thereabouts, with the dreamy night settled in over damp Killoyle, and the Swains were squatting naked on the floor of their top-floor flat, watching the TV screen arms akimbo, legs intertwined, immersed in a Kama Sutra-based calisthenic exercise known as Tandem Monkeys.[1] The lights were off, but the glow of the telly screen was refracted a sparkling hundredfold in the myriad glass animals collected by Rubina over the years—elephants, dromedaries, tigers, giraffes—that adorned the living room.

---

[1]Squatting with arms akimbo, is it? Well, there are those who'd disapprove, although I'm not one of them. (Uncle Jem, now, he'd have turned the firehose on 'em.) No, no, I remember the dear old Kama Sutra, or "KS" as we used to call it out in KL. This is position number one hundred seventy-five, if memory serves (ouch!).

"Bloody good show, this."

"Isn't it?"

"A bit daft, you know. But they're always the best ones."

"So true."

"That bloke with the ears, by golly, he makes me laugh, you know?"

"I know, Anil. I can hear you laughing like nobody's business whenever he's on. And often when he's not."

In tranquillity broken only by sighs and grunts of determination, plus a few rubbery bum-squealing noises on the newly waxed parquet floor, the Swains clinched and clutched at elusive ecstasy.[2]

Suddenly Anil disengaged moistly and slewed around, shocked.

"Oh, no, it can't be over already. Oh, bloody hell."

"Bye-bye, show."

"Oh, damn and blast."

"Anil, it's only the telly, you know."

"Only the telly? What do you mean, Auntie? *Only* the telly? My

---

[2]Not quite making it, I'll wager, but getting a damn sight nearer than any of their Irish neighbours (or you and I) ever did, or do. Sod me, so to speak. When I was growing up the only outlet for that kind of thing was the odd Dutch or Swedish nature mag brought down from Belfast (the only good thing that's ever come out of fucking Ulster, let me tell you, bar Ben Kiely and his chums Neeson and Heaney—oh, and we can't forget the sly wee man of the little horses, can we) containing photographs of purportedly female specimens in ballet tights at right angles to trees and boulders and what have you; well, only by working up a right old lather of pubescent lust could one derive the remotest pleasure from those snaps. Still, they were all we had. Of course, sometimes the bolder of us lads took a turn down by the Royal Canal of a Saturday night, shoulders squared, whistling a jaunty air, Donegal caps at an angle, window shopping only, needless to say, as we were skint to a man, and I could hardly touch my old fella for the financing to underwrite a visit to the whores, now could I? Temperamental, was the da. Why, he once took a belt to the young brother for making eyes at the game show hostess on the television (of which, I hasten to add, the pater, like your man Swain, was inordinately proud).

goodness, do you remember how long it was before we even had a *neighbour* with a television? I don't take it for granted, you know. No, no. I'm not your kind of blasé oh-tally-ho wine-and-crumpet kind of chap, you know."

Silly Anil, thought Rubina with fair-to-middling irritation. He was always considerably more put out by his favourite TV show being over than by, say, flash floods, or unemployment, or epidemics in Tamil Nadu, or the time the police came barging in and took him to gaol for sending signed letters denouncing Bharjee Pal, the local real estate moghul back in Sandrapore ... a brave thing for him to do at the time, considering. And he so low on the totem pole, and in such a muddle, lifewise (as well as, to be quite honest, a bit desperate) that he'd had to advertise for a bride. She still recalled the advert, especially in essence-of-Anil moments like this one:

"Wanted: a Tellugru Brahmin Vellanadu non-Kausiga Gotram bride below 25 years with fine teeth, a bit of money, and no cheeky attitude. Contact A. S. Swain P. O. Box 917 Sandrapore."

Well, she'd been twenty-seven. And not quite the Brahmin he'd originally insisted on. And her teeth were less than optimal. And, oh! Was she ever cheeky! But somehow love had unexpectedly intervened, disguised at first as lust, and made a nonsense of all that nonsense. All that Indian caste nonsense, so far away now. (Thank God, in a way. In another, not.)

Anil and Rubina remained side by side for a few minutes more while boring news of Israel and Gar Looney was boringly pronounced by a news presenter with a mouth like an inverted arsehole (thought Rubina, reluctantly).

"Oh, Anil, turn him off. He turns me off, if you know what I mean."

"Certainly, my dear. Bloody ugly bugger. That must be why they only have him on at this time of night, eh?"

With the casual expertise of long practice, Anil launched an invisible signal from the remote control to the television, plung-

ing arsehole face into oblivion; then, with much sighing and
groaning, husband and wife went off to wash, separately. Half
an hour or so later a boldly nude, sandalwood-scented, slick-
haired Anil Swain made himself a cup of tea (orange pekoe) and
stepped onto the balcony for a smoke, reiterating to himself for
the thousandth time his pleasure at having a balcony to go and
smoke on at all, even if it was a poor kind of balcony, really,
just a kind of extended floor-level windowsill with a railing, not
unlike what they'd call a verandah or *pyol* in certain parts of
India, only smaller, too bloody small but at least there was room
enough for a chap to stand and smoke a bit and peer out at the
city and the sea and down at the car park and the flagstoned
lamplit path (flagstones! what a luxury) that snaked through the
bushes; and all that was a decided improvement over any of the
other places they'd lived in.

Anil lit his B & H and inhaled expertly, thereafter alternating
deep smoke inhalations with rapid sips of tea. The weather was,
of course, on the cool side, but not actually cold, and the breeze
was quite pleasant, really, flirting as it was with his pubic hairs. It
was drizzling faintly, a bit like autumn in the northern foothills,
except for the smells, of course, no cow dung or *bhang* here and
certainly no peat smoke there (and not so much car exhaust, no
bad thing that). Downstairs a telly or radio brayed hollowly at an
unvarying pitch that implied an empty flat, or one in which everybody was asleep, or—this being Ireland, for goodness' sake[3]—

------

[3]Well, I don't know. It's not such a bad old place. Go back to bloomin' India
if you're unhappy here, bukes, is my first reaction, although that's a bit fascist, I know. But still. I mean, it's not as if we didn't have enough to thank the
good Lord for in this country: the poetry, the roads, the sky in winter, the bus
service, the stout, Michael Flatley, Temple Bar, Danny O'Donnell, the people
at the Galway Races, Mick McCarthy, social diarists, The Cranberries, Eddie
Irvine, The Corrs, Irish Country and Western, the old fella behind the bar at
the Stag's head, Willie O'Herlihy, mobile phones, Jackie Healy-Rae, Bono's

drunk, the latter hypothesis gaining the most ground after Anil leaned over the railing and located the source of the noise as almost certainly being Mick McCreek's place, windows wide open and abnormally brightly lit for past midnight.

There you had it. The bloody fellow. How Irish. Just enough sobriety in him to turn on all his lights and gobble up the Vindaloo, then down with those six Tuskers at one go (more than Anil had ever drunk in his entire life; he knew he oughtn't have given him that extra pair) and bingo, there he was out cold with all his lights blazing, running up one corker of an electric bill and probably lying facedown on the floor breathing like a water buffalo into the bargain.

"Bloody hell," said Anil. "What a country."

Well, it was, you know.

No, he took that back. It wasn't so bad, really. After all, it hadn't been that long since Sandrapore, a sweet little town but not much to do, certainly no future at all at the local paper, the *Sandrapore Times* (and the brutal attentions of Bharjee Pal, especially in Rubina's direction—bloody hell!), then, suddenly, England, Wolverhampton to be precise, and a downstairs flat across from the stinking gasworks and five A.M. daily rising for a smelly coughing rocking-back-and-forth bus ride to the tyre factory and the utter bloody hopelessness of a ten-hour stint amid smells of rubber and human sweat, punctuated by occasional shouts of "Oy, Gandhi" and "Wotcha, Abdul," and "Where's your turban, Mohammed?" and whispered threats of *jihad* from the Pakistanis on the crew and every day an English lunch of milky tea and potted meat on flaccid bread taken on a

---

sunglasses, Ronan Keating, *The Quiet Man,* Bloomsday, Brian Cowen, Foster and Allen, Glenroe . . . the list is endless. But it would only be fair to mention, on the other hand, Gar Looney's escapades and that dreadful woman on RTE Channel three.

bench in the fluorescent-lit company caff and home in time for two things: late-night telly and bed, the sleeping kind. And Rubina doing her best in that bloody awful tonic-water bottling plant on the brackish canal alongside all those fat doughy heavily made-up prostitutes who called her, invariably, "Ruby" or "Indira." That wasn't so bad, of course, both of them having been called worse, worst of all back home, by Muslims, or communists, or both. . . .

"Oh I don't know at all."

Anil inhaled smoke from his cigarette as if deep-breathing the freshest mountain air, and drained the last of his tea. In the dark humidity of the middle distance harbour lights twinkled, and to the south the strobe lights on the new RTE-TV5 tower flashed abruptly on and off as a warning to low-flying planes, one of which suddenly droned overhead, a triangle of red lights whizzing in and out of the clouds and grumbling away into the distance.

Shouts, drunken, spiraled upward from the street. A motorbike snarled, creating a Doppler effect like distant thunder against the echo of the narrow street walls (now *that* sounded like home, for a moment . . .) before ebbing slowly into the sea of larger, more diffuse noises of the town.

So Ireland had come as a bit of a stroke of luck, you know (reflected Anil), and even with the bother of getting relocated and finding a job and these days all the political machinations and shenanigans involved in trying to put up enough cash to wrest control of the local Koh-I-Noor franchise from that horrid bleeder Goone (and having to deal with the Irish in general, who as a general rule knew even less about the rest of the world than the English, almost as little in fact as the inhabitants of, say, the state of Tamil Nadu, but who, also as a general rule—there were exceptions—didn't call him Abdul or Gandhi, possibly out of simply never having heard those names), Killoyle was still turning out to be a bit of a haven (if not heaven, ha ha) for Anil and his Rubina. They'd been here a year and a half so far and were likely, bar the unexpected, to stay on a bit, unless they just went home, you know.

And have kids: he was thirty-seven, she thirty-three. It was time, or people'd begin talking.

(Sod them, then.)

It wasn't as if he wanted to be a rupee millionaire *crorepati* or maharajah or even a millionaire in Irish punts; all he asked for, dear Vishnu, was a decent chance to make a bit of money, buy a nice house, and show a bit of flash before the next cycle of life began.

Suddenly, his reverie was barged in upon, rudely. Shadows scudded like spring storm clouds across the lighted blinds of Mick McCreek's flat and an unsteady silhouette, that of the man himself, manifested itself suddenly, tottering, at the window.

"Ahhhhhhhhhhhhhhhhhhhhhh!" roared McCreek, gathering strength. Then:

"Ah, the sweet flowers of the forest."

"Oh, by golly, why don't you be quiet, Mick," said Anil, irritably, his peace of mind in tatters.

Mick looked up, rubbing sleep and drunkenness out of his eyes. With knuckles poised in the air, he exclaimed, hoarsely (eliciting from adjacent apartments grumbles of "Shut it," and "Go to friggin' bed"):

"Swain! Fuck me, you're starkers!"

Upon which, obeying the solemn dictates of inner necessity, Mick folded himself neatly forward over the balcony handrail and disgorged a reddish firehose of vomitus into the night air, with subsequent splattering, as of a sudden downpour, upon the elegant flagstones below.

"Ah-ha-ha-*haaaaaaaa-hooo*-hahh," he declared, approximately, then boringly proceeded to repeat himself three times, aiming in slightly different directions each time, with varying modulations of the strangled-bellowing part but no lessening of intensity at splashdown.

"I'll call the guards on ya, ya shite," hollered the indignant voice of one downstairs resident who nevertheless made sure to stay well concealed in the darkness of his own flat.[4]

"I'm not having any more of this nonsense," muttered Anil. He tapped his cigarette out and flicked it overboard. "Bloody hell. It's too much." After closing the double-glazed French window behind him, he retired to the excessively dry warmth (central heat, a rare comfort in the damp chill of Ireland, but not much good for the sinuses) and snug exactitude of his flat, which was silent but for the ticking of the grandfather clock and Rubina's gentle fluting snores; but outside, as from a great distance over land and sea, came the muted counterpoint of Mick McCreek's retching and more fruitless shouts of protest.

"Silly drunk old *gangaram*."

Anil, shaking his head in the opposite of admiration, retired to his bed, there to sit upright, pondering the immediate concerns of his life. They were, admittedly, few, but they loomed large in his mind, for his mind was that of a man adept at the old back-and-forth mental tennis match of worry and solution (*pock*), worry and alternative solution (*pock*), worry and counterworry (*pock*); indeed, the alternative, theoretical courses of action presented to him by each day's dawning kept him awake a good part of most nights, although he usually managed to exhaust himself, and life's options, by midnight, and again by dawn.[5]

---

[4]I know the type. It's more of an American response than an Irish, but not uncommon for all that: Sure, let the cops take the chances if yer man's packing heat!

[5]Very much in the spirit of yours truly, when I had all the time in the world on me hands and not much to occupy my time with, bar the old navel-gazing. I don't know. Some people never grow up. I mean, on the one hand, say, the trenches of World War I, or the camps of World War II, or life in the Liberties a century or so ago; on the other, sushi or Thai? Or, Should I buy an extra set of roller blinds for the front parlour? Or, Should I use the money for a set of PVC nose flares? And will I be too late to get a reservation at Benito's?

Currently, however, a crisis was at hand in the affairs of the Koh-I-Noor, and his preoccupations were entirely centered thereupon. Anil's ambition to own the restaurant, a seed planted by an offhand remark of Rubina's a few months ago ("Get hold of that damned restaurant, what are you, a waiter for life?") had swollen into a domineering obsession. In his mind's eye Anil saw himself bespoke-tailored, a smoker of gold-tipped Sobranies, a fluent speaker of many languages, a brisk *frotteur* of his own be-ringed hands, a greeter of endless trains of delighted customers.

Namaste, o respected restaurant *wallah!*

But there were obstacles galore to the realization of this trite fantasy: The money was simply lacking, by golly, unless he could cut a deal with the bank, and that blighter Goone was putting up some stiff resistance to the notion of selling out, or rather to transferring the franchise, for there were other Koh-I-Noors on the island of Ireland, one of which, smack on Donegall Place in the heart of Belfast, had been blown up three times since 1982.[6] Ironically, Goone's main

---

[6]In '82, to be precise. I remember it well, my niece's second cousin Lenny "Stove-In Face" MacGoelecanth pulled off that job. Unaware of the precise Indian associations of the name Koh-I-Noor, but associating it vaguely with the word "hoor"—and of course having devoured his Biggles and Rider Haggard as a lad—the crapper took the place to be an outpost or embassy of British imperialism and corruption and lobbed a few seventy-five millimetre shells through the front window before sending in the lads with the flame throwers and body bags. Fortunately, there were no customers (it being an Indian restaurant in Belfast on Sunday night), but "Stove-In Face" took the entire staff—Hosang the cook, Rashid the headwaiter, and Pryanda the manager-ess—prisoner. Blindfolded, they were released on Magilligan Strand. Rashid greeted the alteration in his circumstances with delight, exclaiming, "How beautiful! Who the hell wants to work in a bloody Indian restaurant in Belfast anyway?" as the dusk drew in over fair Rathlin and the air was filled with the sweet unmusic of the organ pipes of the Giant's Causeway. Rashid, self-restyled "Roger," settled in the busy market town of Coleraine, where he met and married a corn-fed lass named Noreen and worked his way up to

objection seemed to be that Anil Swain was an Indian. Was the bugger a racist along with everything else? It was certainly possible. After
all, he lived with a chap who dressed in women's clothes. And he
also owned some kind of doormat factory near Killoyle Airport where
immigrant workers, including Rashmi Vashnapuram, a cousin of
Anil's, toiled in harsh conditions—although Rashmi, a rich girl from
Calcutta, was there voluntarily, semiundercover, as it were, doing
research for her degree in labour relations or something (Anil had
never really worked out what Cousin Rashmi was, or did, but he sure
as billy-o fancied the dickens out of her, God or gods help him oh
yes he did and that was that, you know). Still, here in the sentimental West poor working conditions could do an employer in good and
proper, and with all the cards played right, in the right hands . . . *Blackmail* whispered its ugly name. And all's fair in love and war, as they
said over here somewhere.

　　In any case, Goone had told him point-blank that he, Goone,
wasn't a racist, but how many times had he, Anil, heard that clap-

---

become manager of a farming-implement emporium and publicity director
of the Coleraine Symphony Orchestra. Noreen and Roger now have three
sons—Jamil, Jamal, and Jim—and Rodge's opted for: (1) the Protestant way
of speaking (no "h"), in order not to ruffle his neighbours, who initially suspected him of being "a fockin' Papist"; and (2) casual attire, so as not to seem
a toff. (Rodge also joined the Church of Ireland as an ex-Hindu, and now feigns
devotion with the best of 'em.) As for the others, well, Hosang went into hiding and still resides underground, warily, and, he insists, temporarily, surfing
Internet sites. The third abductee, Pryanda, well she came home with me,
didn't she, and boys o boys was that ever a night and a half: she turned out to
be a grammar expert, and halped me no end with my conjugation! "Stove-In
Face," by the way, got nabbed as he was leaving Portrush: a local member of
the Orange Order pegged him for a taig by the way he picked his nose while
driving and alerted the local chapter of the UVF, but the RUC boys got to
him first, thanks be to God. He's in Canada now, as I understand it, working
on Halifax docks and living for the day he can take ship for dear old Ireland
and breathe her sweet air and walk her trackless strands and see her dear old
smilin' eyes again (sob). . . .

trap before? Plenty, you could believe that, and not just in the West, either, why back home in some ways it was even worse, just you try getting a job in Calcutta if you were a Parsee, or in Mumbai if you came from West Bengal, and never mind the old caste system. . . . It was hard to tell. Something in the eyes gave them away, and he hadn't seen it in Goone's (as they wandered to crotch-level and below) . . . well, maybe he was just a bastard, not a racist.

Anil lay back on clove-scented pillows and revisited in the ringing halls of Memory that afternoon's telephonic dialogue with the fellow:

"Not that I have any objection based on nationality, nor any aversion to you on a personal level as a result of your race or ethnicity, for fuck's sake. That kind of caper's for the likes of Owen Parsley, if you know who I'm talking about. No, it's your experience or should I say lack of same that concerns me. You're not really well-versed in the business practices and customs of our society, are you at all, Mr. Singh?"

"Swain."

"Aye. Swing."

"As well-versed as you, Mr. Goone. Bloody hell, what do you think, that we live in trees in India, for goodness' sake? We Indians are the best damned businessmen in the world, bar none, and businessmen from Mumbai are the best of the lot."

"Are ye now."

"Oh yes. A Mumbai businessman, ha, well let me just say that a Mumbai businessman on top form would eat you for breakfast, spit you out, and find ways to have you again for dinner, Mr. Goone."

"I'd not fancy that, bedad. I'd rather have beef Madras. And that's a fact."

"Well, then."

"Well, I'll consider meself warned, like. Still, I can't help wondering why India's so poor, if you're all such hot-shot businessmen, like."

"Other factors. Socialism. The caste system. Hinduism and Islam, with a touch of Sikhism, too. You know about the dead hand of religion, Goone. You're Irish, for God's sake."

"For God's sake, indeed. Aye. We'll talk later, Swing."

"Swain."

"Who?"

Talk when?

Soon.

About what?

Probably nothing.

A distant bell struck the hour, once, timidly. Anil closed his eyes and slid into a half dream composed in equal parts of longing and remembering: Hurriedly, lingering not, he went home again, for there was a deep-rooted homesickness beneath his chipper, can-do, English-speaking exterior. Down the misty Ghat Road in a long-ago morning he saw Sandrapore. He noted on his way that the Mission School was still in business (hadn't been, in reality, since '89); that the Singh bicycle shop was still there; that the Regina cinema was showing an old movie of Amitabh Bachchan's. The dream-Anil then drifted past Pawal's haircutting saloon and the Maharashtra India Bank, heard the squishy vowels of Urdu and the spit of Hindi speech and his own honeyed Gujarati and the put-put of rusting Hindustan taxis and the mooing of street-bound cows; he smelled the *bhang* and the *beedee* smoke, enjoyed the caress of the humid late-summer breezes off the river, feeling all the while, in every cell of his being, the overarching vastness of the infinite Indian sky built high with fortresses of thunderclouds that trembled on the verge of rain seemingly forever before, finally, the first great drop smacked the dry leaves of the tamarind trees, then another, then another, then the skies would swing open for the torrent that lasted for weeks when the sounds were of rainwater running off tin roofs and tree branches and of cars and *jutkas* splashing through puddles and of the leaking tap-tap-tap-tapping in the kitchen and the sudden flapping of a bird's wet wings and the chortling of the swollen rain in the gutters. . . .

A phone rang in the empty lot behind the Sundaresans' old house on the Narayanasanda Highway. Well aware that he was dreaming, yet impelled by the nagging sense of urgency that drove him so relentlessly in waking life, Anil stumbled through waist-high weeds toward the sound, accompanied for obscure dream reasons by the current prime minister of India, Dr. Rajput.

"Why don't you get that bloody phone?" snapped Dr. Rajput, notorious within and without his Zarathusan Party for his impatience and quick temper. Anil, overwhelmed by a desire to please his PM, nodded and smiled, and ran with a will, but suddenly found himself sinking into the stock quicksand of dreamland and incurring Dr. Rajput's wrath.

"You're a proper jackanapes, aren't you, Swain," bellowed the PM. "And a damned silly little *raanti-sahib*. Never fear, my lad, your superiors will be hearing from me."

Anil awoke. It was, of course, his bedside phone.

"Hello? Cousin Anil?"

"Rashmi? Bloody hell, girl, do you know what time it is?"

"Time to get up, Cuz. It's half six."

And indeed it was, as Anil blinked wearily in the sudden morning light around him, Rubina, applying a *bindi* to her forehead, bustled past in the manic mode of early-morning. She frowned at the sight of her husband puffy-eyed and unwashed with his hedgehog-spiked hair standing up in a disorderly row.

"Oh, do get up," she said.

Aromas of *idli sambar* and *kulcha* floated out of the kitchen. Another Indo-Irish breakfast was in the making.[7] Anil's stomach

---

[7]Indo-Irish? Would that be bangers *korma*? Or streaky bacon and *dal*? Or kidneys in mango pickle sauce? Or . . . hang on, I just caught myself slavering, or was it gagging . . . ?

rumbled. To paraphrase the advertising slogan once plastered alongside every road in Sandra Pradesh ("Feeling Lazy? Drink a Lassi!"): He was listless without his morning *lassi*.

"What do you want, Rash? I haven't had my breakfast yet."

"Never mind your breakfast. This is serious. I want you to come out to the factory today and bring a camera."

"What? What camera?"

"Oh wake up, Cuz. The big boss is coming here today on one of his surprise visits everybody always knows about a day ahead. Goone, you know? The fellow you want to buy your restaurant from? Well, you know he'll never sell unless you put the screws on him, and here's the way."

Rashmi Vashnapuram was a student at Killoyle Upper when the fancy took her and worked at local factories the rest of the time, earning "pocket" money on the side (to supplement her hefty trust income) while doing her research, so-called, and as previously noted only the man or men upstairs knew precisely what that was. She had it in for employers, anyway. As the daughter of militant, if well-off, Calcutta communists—Pico "Pik" Dutt, notorious strike-leading president of the West Bengal Transport Union, and Indra Butt-Dutt, book club director and "La Pasionaria" of the Calcutta and Howrah dispossessed— Rashmi ("Rash" to her near and dear), a purported "student" and "freelancer" of no fixed abode, was a zealous young woman, as well as a militant of the old school, and not half bad as an actress (she'd posed as a prostitute in a police sting operation in Brixton, S.E.), well-versed in union lore and employment regulations throughout Asia and the European Union, and the way they were treating the workers at Emerald Mats, she said, would shame a Hyderabad sweatshop. The latest outrage was typical: The personnel manager, at the tyrant Goone's behest, was reneging on his promise to grant foreign employees an hour for lunch, arguing that, as temporary "seasonal" workers, they were entitled to nothing but the price of a ticket home after six months! Well, Rashmi had already been there for nine, and they'd just asked her to take over (with fifteen minutes for a quick sandwich out of the machine) the supervisory duties of the late Bulent Tülüy, senior manager of doormats, who'd plunged headfirst into his mutton ragout a week ago last Thursday, dead of more than cigarettes (fifty-five to seventy daily, unfiltered, flown in airtight tins from Kurdistan via Türk Hava Yollari Cargo Express). *Murdered,* whispered Rashmi, in thrall to the subcontinental taste for conspiracy and horror,[8] *murdered most foully!*

"He was only forty-five, Anil! And you should have seen the condition of the body when they flew it back to Istanbul!"

"Oh?"

"Yes! Putrefying and gaseous, and the colour, I kid you not, of *aloo saag,* or one of those statues in the Palace of the Winds in Jaipur—or do I mean Jaiselmer?"

"Never mind the bloody hell. The fellow was somewhat greenish, then?"

"Positively pistache, Cuz. Why, several of his coworkers fainted dead away as the catafalque was carried out of the premises. It's monstrous, inhuman, uncivilized, downright, well, Indian, you know, completely contrary anyway to the spirit of the EU!"

"Well, what do you want me to do? I'm not Sherlock bleeding Holmes, you know. And I've a job as well, in case you're forgetting."

"Oh, Cuz, it's easy. No trouble at all."

These were ominous words, but the goal was a noble one; Anil steeled himself to obey.

---

[8]HindoTV Channel nine, Sundays at eight-fifteen (repeated every Monday night at eleven forty-five): *The Casebooks of Inspector Bagwati,* Episode One: *Suttee in SW7.*

4

"You're right, Mick, you were screwed good and proper," said Tom O'Mallet. "Fucked to the hilt, I'd say."

"Too right, Tom. Twice over."

"Twice . . . ? Oh, the gardai. That was no picnic, either, I'd doubt."

"It was desperate, Tom. Wait till I tell you."

"And aren't you the lad for the desperate times, Mick. Remember back in college when we were arrested on suspicion of intent to loiter?"

"Do I ever. Mother of God, that was a caper and a half."

"Not to mention the time they found what they thought was Semtex and it turned out to be your lunch . . . *quenelles,* was it?"

"It was, Tom. *Quenelles de brochet sauce Nantua.*[1] I never believed in being forced to eat student grub just because I was a student, like."

"Whereas I was, and am, indifferent to all that shite." (At this, Mick, although willing in principle to give auld acquaintance the benefit of the doubt, shivered in disdain.) "Satisfied with fried cod and chips, so I was, and am. But that was you all over, right enough.

---

[1] *Quenelles,* is it? The things that just lie there like long pallid jobbies? Wanker.

Always overreaching yourself, eh? But God, the times we had, eh, Mick?"

"Ah sure with the massed saints of heaven themselves swearing on a stack of Bibles you'd not believe the half of it."

"There was the time you were done for drunk and disorderly in front of the president's house."

"Exposing the old gonads to His Excellency, had he chosen to examine them, but he was upstairs exposing his own to the presidential mistress, Mrs. Plunkett. Nabbed be the rozzers I was then, and the buggers promptly gave yours truly a knee or two to the groin on general principles."

"Yet who emerges otherwise unscathed from the brutal hell of police detention in the dungeons of Aras an Uachtarain half an hour later but yourself in the flesh, totally unbruised on the surface, I might add?"

"Spare my blushes, Tom."

"Mick feckin' McCreek says I to meself as I live and breathe. And there you were, danderin' about like you were on a health walk in the Wicklow Hills."

"It's true, Tom, it's true. And didn't I feel like the Lord's own darlin' boy on that day and on many others."

"The blarney, Michael. 'Twas the blarney. If it works once it'll work a hundred times."

"True on ya, Tom."

"Ah well, Mick. *Is fear rith maith ná drochsheasamh*, as the old poets and shanachies have it."

"Or words to that effect."

"More tea there, Mick?" Suddenly the spout of the teapot hovered aggressively in his face.

"I'd not refuse. Ta."

"Say when."

Tom poured. Mick nodded "when" and sipped the overflow and there they were, the pair of them, having a grand old cup together in Killoyle's premier coffee shop, the Bay Window on the Promenade, maintaining with elaborate screens of Irishry the prerequisite distance of old acquaintance freshly renewed: Mick McCreek and Tom O'Mallet, once in the distant long-ago fellow students (of things artistic/architectural and legalistic, respectively) at University College, Belfield, Dublin 4, and roommates in Mrs. Minion's boarding house in the respectable seaside suburb of Sandymount (also Dublin 4)—and unacquainted since then but for an October bank holiday weekend jaunt to London during which time neither came home with a penny to his name, nor drew a breath that could reasonably be described as sober—sat and sipped their tea and stared out of The Bay Window's bay window onto the lilting white-capped sea. Smoke curlicued upward from Mick's morning fag, causing a disapproving frown to transform Tom's bland features into a slab of aged Brie plus eyes, nose, and mouth. He'd been an ex-smoker for a year and a half and as such was about as unbiased on the subject as an Iranian ayatollah might be on the topic of, say, a quick double whiskey before a night's whoring.[2]

---

[2]Ayatollah, me arse. They're nothing, boy. You should have known the Rev. Peter Porter of Portadown, man alive there was a specimen you'd want to shoot at a moment's notice. He was down on some kind of scholarship when I was at college, and boys o boys there was never a moment when the creature wasn't hovering about like a bowler-hatted bluebottle fly, trying to steer me away from the path of vice—in other words, Popery—and toward Protestantism, or rather the particular brand thereof he espoused, something called Sin-Spotters of the Lord, a bunch of troglodytes who went about lowering the boom on suntans; alcohol; any form of sex, human or animal, even interfering with TV nature programs if glimpsed through the lace curtains of a quiet house, in passing (they'd barge in and confiscate the box on the spot, flashing phony badges); tobacco; caffeine; cars; skiing, snow- and water-; smiling and/or laughter, especially when accompanied by a glowing gaze from the eyes; symphonic music, the Rev. possessing an ear of solid tin; etc., all these and more being the work of he whom the Rev. Porter called Stan, omitting for some reason the first "a": "Aha, it's Stan's round,"

"Ah Christ when are you going to quit that filthy habit, Mick?"

"'*Tis* a filthy habit, Tom. '*Tis* that, and don't I know it better than most."

Obliging the prosecution, a cough erupted from his lips, trawling behind it micro-coughs and moist throat clearings.

"You see, Mick. There you go. Gagging up your innards like that and just like me poor owld mum you still go ahead and light up another. Jaysus, you should hear her when she started on one of her fag jags, the pitch of it rose to the level you'd hear at the hurling final with Kilkenny playing, or the Concorde taking off, and didn't she always end it by saying to me (just about when I was sayin' to meself that she'd really bought it this time), 'Och gi'e us a fag, there, son.'"

"Indeed." A slow-burning irritation with this class of sanctimonious blather smouldered like an unextinguished fag end in Mick's soul.

"And she's dead, Mick."

"God rest her soul, Tom."

"I don't know, Mick, I can't understand it."

---

he'd jeer, spying me through a pub window lifting a pint to my lips; or, from behind a bush, "Peek-a-boo! Stan's at the wheel and downshifting fast!" as I, ambling en route from my bachelor digs down Aungier Street to Botany Bay, casually turned to admire, say, a Delage or Jowett Jupiter briskly driven; and if women were involved, well, you won't be surprised to learn that the Rev. and his chum Stan took a very dim view. Anyhow, fortuitously, while tentatively navigating the treacherous shoals of sexuality himself the Rev. ran aground, as it were, on the shallows of sodomy: Terenure, council flats, aging boy-prostitute, slapping sounds, loud hectoring in a bizarre metallic voice (Stan, no doubt, being channeled by your man), neighbours promptly on the horn to the guards, encouraged by yours truly enjoying a cappuccino in the flat above. They let the fool go, of course, and last I heard he was ladling out the soupe du jour at an AIDS soup kitchen in Denver, Colorado. *Mutatis mutandis,* eh?

"Human nature, Tom. A perverse lot of chancers we are, so we are."

Impulsively, Mick blew a thundercloud of blue smoke directly into his lawyer's face—for Tom O'Mallet was, or would be, his lawyer, or solicitor to be precise; he in any event who would bring Mick's grievances to court and lead the charge to victory . . . maybe.

"Put that fucker out."

"Sorry."

"Now."

"Right."

They discussed strategy. Tom was unconvinced by Mick's argument against the gardai.

"Not a good idea to go up against the guards, Mick."

"But the pricks tried to railroad me, Tom."

"And don't I know it, Mick. And haven't we all suffered at their hands at one time or another. Still, I reckon we're on firmer ground when it comes to your wrongful dismissal claim against Jocelyn Motors."

"But, Tom . . . The way that wee peckerhead treated me, and in public, too."

"It's not on, Mick."

"The bastards."

"OK, let's lay out the odds here, Mick. Say you take on the gardai, the all-powerful national police force. Here you are, an absolute nonentity, a zero. A nullity in human form. A piece of dogshite on the underside of society's shoe, with all due respect. Sorry, Mick, but there it is. You're a recently dismissed ex-test driver of Jocelyn cars, now there's a precious way to make a living for a start. And you were once involved in a barney with the guards at the president's house in Phoenix Park in your student days, and you were once and are again a thoroughgoing unmarried bachelor to boot."

"Divorced, for Christ's sake. And that business in Phoenix Park was ages ago. And by the way mine was only the third divorce in county bloody Killoyle since the referendum, I'll have you know."[3]

"You don't say? Quite a place in the sun for you. Only it would make you look like the standard-bearer of an anti–marriage trend, because the good folk of Killoyle aren't quite on the Elizabeth Taylor wavelength yet when it comes to divorce, referendum or not. As you know. Anyhow. Divorced, then, and known among his friends as being an aficionado of motors and the ponies and the idle comforts of the public house. . . ."

"You're saying I'll come across as a waster."

"With the wrong judge even with the wrongful-dismissal claim, and with *any* judge if you go after the guards. On the other hand, Mick," and here Tom O'Mallet gave his old friend the full benefit of what had become known in his legal chambers as the Halogen Stare, "with the wrongful dismissal case, chances are the judge'll be a gas man entirely. He'll be on your side from the word go, you can take that to the bank."

"Tom. And how would you know this much about the judge so far in advance, like."

"He's my da, and he drives a Jocelyn."

Indeed, although the truth was that Tom's *pater*, Judge Gerald O'Mallet, was only one of three judges of Killoyle District Court, and any one of these eminent personalities could theoretically preside over a minor case like Mick's, given Judge O'Mallet's amicable closeness to Ben Ovary, the lord mayor, and his former golf-playing friendship with Police Superintendent P. Talbott, Esq., the judge could pretty much pick and choose his court sessions, even (or especially) if his own son was involved. More

---

[3]A dubious distinction. I should know, I was fourth. Friggin' lawyers. One of them, the belowstairs spawn of a county Armagh publican by the name of Erin Gallowglass, had his left hand in my ex's left pocket before I could wrestle his right hand out of my portmanteau (and he was a heavy breather, let me tell you)—or was it the other way around?

often than not, Judge O'Mallet chose the petty court of the re-
cidivist drunk and unrecalcitrant kleptomaniac, the better, as he
told his son, "put the screws on the bottom-feeders of society,"
which his son had always interpreted to mean "to get out before
opening time." Still, the judge had a fine tenor voice[4] and refined
taste in whiskeys, and he admitted to a soft spot for a rogue of
traditional Irish stamp—one a bit like Mick McCreek, in fact.

And he *hated* his car, so he did.

"A right owld heap of scrap. He's had it in the shop five times
since he bought it, and once it just turned around on him while
he was driving up to Dublin for the Horse Show, that's right just
bleedin' did a one-eighty in the middle of the N1. Then the last
thing to go was the brakes, apparently. He's given up. He just
leaves it parked outside his house. By the way, do you sing at all,
Mick?"

"Not on a regular basis. Only if the craic's outstandingly good."

"Fair enough. But I'd give him a wee rendition, so I would.
Assuming he presides over your case, of course."

"Of what? 'Danny Boy'? 'The Flowers of the Forest'? 'My Way'?"

"'My Way' might be the thing. The old man likes Sinatra. Or
'Strangers in the Night,' you know, or 'Come Fly with Me,' one
of those. I'll leave that bit up to you in its entirety, Mick."

Mick suddenly wondered if his quondam chum might not be
taking the piss, but he dismissed the thought, reminding himself
that a good, or at least effective, lawyer was almost as hard to find
as a decent wife, and that anyway judges were a notoriously fickle
and eccentric lot—and in any event what choice had he, bar the

---

[4]Ah, the judge. Ahem. From the *Clarion,* before all hell broke loose (*qv.
infra*): "During the 1950s he studied singing with Noreen Dempsey; he was a
gold medal winner in both the *Feis Maitiu* and the *Feis Ceoil,* and he went on to
sing with the Dublin Grand Opera Society. This laid the foundation for his
success in the world of musical theatre."

public defender, or an unwelcome (and impossible, given his financial straits) outlay of funds? It was a simple case of wrongful dismissal, as he saw it, one in which his ex-employer, in the person of Pats Bewley, had acted "capriciously and arbitrarily," in Tom O'Mallet's eloquent words; had acted in fact "without and beyond true cause, or knowledge of same"; in order to save the life of (bleeding hearts and sobbing violins for the judge here, now) the misfortunate clod Francis Feeley, Mick had activated the antilock brakes, which had precipitated the understandable yet ultimately destructive dorsal clobbering from one Cornelius Regan, Esq. . . . and so on.

Tom took notes while Mick savoured to the lees the bitterness of his lot.

"Then there was the chrome. Let's not forget that."

"Aye. Chrome, is it? Could this be a digression, Mick? I can guarantee you the judge'll be drumming his fingers at this point, a very bad sign."

"Rubbish. The chrome's the proximate cause. The Asphodel's full of it. Near-blinded thereby, I lurched forward and ploughed into your man."

"Now that's interesting, but that's all the stuff for the gardai, of course, all that rear-ending and Feeley walking out and that. Reckless driving and that, and we'll not be going any deeper into it, as I already mentioned. If they say it's your fault, Mick, why, it's your fault, and that's the end of it."

"For fuck's sake, O'Mallet. Stop slagging me, would you. Are you my lawyer or not? The chrome blinded me, causing the accident, which led to my being sacked, unjustly."

"Now Mick, we've discussed all that. Shift your focus here, boy. Concentrate on telling Jocelyn Motors where they can get off, either by paying a good hefty sum in compensation or by taking you back at an equivalent or higher level of responsibility and remuneration—and by the way, which option are we going after, Mick, as long as I've got your attention?"

Mick opted for the cash.

"Well, that was an easy one. Good choice, but. And man, I can feel their goolies in my hands as we speak. All we have to do is squeeze." He squeezed the air, repeating so precisely the gesture made by Bobby Lee Irwin in that blockbuster American legal drama the other night on RTE5—*Snake Oil*, was it, or *Snails*— no, *The Scales of Justice*, that was it—that Mick knew he had him, his dynamo lawyer Tom had seen the same film and harboured ambitions of lawyerly wealth in lavish office suites overlooking the East (or Liffey) River, symbolically extinguishing the power of arrogant tycoons with that simple gesture: "You just take their balls," as the Bobby Lee Irwin character had said, raspily, the pock-marks in his face accentuated by the side lighting, "and squeeze," squeezing.

(Tom even looked a wee bit like Bobby Lee Irwin, except for the pockmarks; of course, maybe he cultivated the resemblance, and hadn't Mick tumbled onto something here?)

"I still don't like it."

"But it's the way, so." Tom stood up and brushed off his trousers. "We'll see about a court date."

The bill was Mick's to pay, Tom having swept through the door before any accounting could take place. Mick watched him saun-tering away down the Promenade, past the Michael Collins statue, his trenchcoat (a bloody affectation, as if any normal person wore a trenchcoat, for the love of God[5]) billowing like a tarpaulin around his heels, his hedgehog-brush haircut unstirred by the brisk zephyrs off St. George's Channel. Not for the first time—

-----

[5] I don't know. I had a trenchcoat once. But the people down the street laughed so hard (they even clustered outside the sitting-room window, nudg-ing each other and shaking with laughter as I put in on and took it off) I fi-nally donated it to the Seal Fund. I'm not proud of it, but I'm not ashamed, either, if you follow my meaning.

for about the third time that hour, in fact—Mick had his doubts about the whole business, and Tom O'Mallet in particular.

"Well, bugger it," he muttered, enigmatically, and, exiting The Bay Window, lit an O'Mallet- and death-defying cigarette.

On the Promenade a saline sea breeze lurked, timidly whispered, and fled. In the distance purplish stratus clouds sprawled laguidly across the pearly russet sky, denoting calm seas and, to those who journeyed that day, a prosperous voyage.[6] The Strand was empty, seaweed-strewn, a long white crescent arching into the greyish-white distance of married sea and sky. Overhead a massive silver-and-white cloud banner slowly unfurled itself, emitting droplets, against patches of Aegean blue. The scene was calm, peaceful, verging on perfect; fresh and pleasant, too, but for the competing rural and urban scents of cowshit and car exhaust; imminent with rain, as always in Ireland: September, a grey September morn, sweet autumn in Killoyle. . . .[7]

---

[6]Stratus as opposed to cirrus or stratocumulus . . . ? Well, sweet f.a. is what I know about clouds, but I do know that it's only above the vast bronze seas of the Windwards and Leewards that you'd see a towering cumulus out of season, aye, I know that much, having spent a fair old time out in New Angola as a Berlitz teacher, for my sins. God, the constipation, and, worse, its opposite. But the drinks were grand, if a bit on the teeth-chatteringly cold side, Yanks and their minions being the coldest-inclined people on earth, just so they can warm up right after. Be that as it may, you can't beat the odd sun going down into a purple heaving sea in a blaze of crimson glory, the sailboats and yachts and what have you rocking gently on their moorings, in the distance the lulling tunkatunk tunkatunk of calypso, and in the hand a fine strong drink. And then comes the night, the night-o.

[7]Easy with your Hoolihan there. Actually, I always liked the old rogue (except as a poet), and I always maintained it was a national disgrace the government didn't pick up the tab to fly his bones home. I mean, the man could have been poet laureate, of England at least, if he hadn't turned into a violent homeless drifter in the lower forty-eight. Anyway, any one of the following, from his *Prison Postcards,* Cantos I–XIV, would do, or not (composed on the

Head bowed, Mick marched mindlessly on toward his next appointment, a prophylactic visit to the unemployment "clinic" (or was it "workshop"?) at the public library. It was probably a cod, but he'd sworn to himself in the hungover reaches of the past two nights that he was buggered if he had any intention of going without a job for the duration of whatever asinine legalistic maunderings and shenanigans he and Tom O'Mallet and Tom O'Mallet's da—and God knew who else—were in for. These things could take months, he knew that. And Tom was doing it for a nominal fee, as he said, not yet firmed up, like (and Mick liked not the sound of that "nominal"), but a lot less, O'Mallet had said, than a full-fledged brace of barristers would cost, if a wee bit more than your common or garden public defenders and their ilk, all state-appointed sad sacks on the downward slope, according to Tom—although it had occurred to Mick that the state appointees might be a bit less reluctant to charge the cops with wrongdoing, known lefties and supporters of the little man's rights that they were to a man (and woman) . . . the question was, who was the littler man, Mick or Frankie Feeley?

Or another wan entirely?

Mick would nominate Frankie, hands down, but his viewpoint was biased, naturally, in his own favour.

"That arsehole's an arsehole if ever I saw one and not only that but a friggin' gombeen man and horse's arse deluxe," he muttered anent his presumptive defender, impatient at the eternalizing red pedestrian lights, which he spontaneously decided to ignore, then nearly getting run down by a berk in a fast BMW.

---

long walk from Solitary to Old Sparky in the Parton State Pen, Parton, Pennsylvania): "O Old Grey Strand (of Hair)"; "O Bonnie Bonnie Bungalow 'neath the Bonnie Bonnie Elm"; "Dearest Darlin' Haven Mine"; "My Wee Killoylee-lee-lay." The last two aren't half bad, sung to bouzouki accompaniment, half blotto. Otherwise, to be frank, I'd give the stuff the widest possible berth.

"Up yours."

"Eff off, mister."

Still caustic after this encounter, Mick sent his used-up fag-end spinning into the gutter at the entrance to the trendy purple-accented Gothic-revival pile of SS. Laurence and Peter O'Toole's R.C. pro-cathedral:

"Jobbers!" he bawled.

There was no reply, only the merest hint of a chill in the air.

He strode onward, across Behan Avenue, past Killoyle West railway station, and around Haughey Circle, site of so much. Posters garlanded the stately edifice of Gardai Siochana (the bastards—yaaah!) and adjoining buildings, including O'May Chemists, Ltd., and the secluded and ivied front wall of Ben Ovary's Lord Mayoral Manor.[8] These posters, recently rushed into production—as Mick realized upon closer, bleary-eyed inspection, dabbing the still-moist ink onto a sneeze-stifling Kleenex—touted in no uncertain terms the great event, the pint-pulling Olympiad. It was still a few weeks off but already it was the talk of the town, and beyond. Winsome and rubicund, female faces (indubitably Aryan-pigtailed, blond, blue-eyed, etc.) were shown wreathed in smiles above foaming beakers of amber ale, with incongruous Bavarian-type or Alpine mountains looming in the middle distance from the viewer, who found himself inadvertently positioned behind quaint mullioned panes (*or were those peaks meant to be the Knockmealdowns?* self-queried Mick, not waiting for a reply); well, in any event, the Olympiad of beer engines already boasted its very own logo, a cheese-and-pretzelesque triad of pint mugs linked by vines of shamrocks in the shape of interlocking Olympic rings, of all the overworked clichés (thought

---

[8]Behind which, I have it on good authority, mayoral fingers fiddled and interlaced in impatient alternation, all in the service of constant, unremitting ambition and yearnings that dared not speak their names. . . .

Mick, suddenly bitter to the point of near-nausea) (of course, that could have been in part the aftereffects of last night, but we can't discount the general nastiness of recent events in his personal life) ... at any rate, it wasn't an all-amateur event, not a true Olympiad; how could it be in the multibillion-dollar world of ale?

As the posters made clear, there was serious dough behind the whole extravaganza: Big Jimmie's, a Glasgow firm of brewers with a clear interest in flogging their own wares. Rival firms from England, Wales, Ireland, and even Australia and North America would set up competing teams, of course, each with its own champions, and the race would be on, pints being pulled from one end to the other of the vast reaches of the Balsa Room in the Spudorgan Vacation Inn, where the event was scheduled to take place; and there'd be jobs galore then, by God so there would, only the damned thing wasn't until November.

Still, it was worth thinking about, as long as nothing more substantial came along, and you never knew in this life, in this town, in this country, although Mick's true ambitions were set a lot higher than bartending—in itself not an iniquitous profession, not at all, but it was a bit of a dead-end, and a true certainty to lead downhill one of less-than-ironclad self-descipline ... for Mick wanted to be a bard of the road, a Homer of the highway, a chronicler of the passion of speed and the vehicles that provided it, a recorder of the glories of design and comfort married to four wheels (with great cornering and zero to sixty times under six seconds), racing from, say, Milan to Parma down the Via Emilia: yes, that was our hero's longed-for dream, his Ithaca, his reincarnation of himself in his own version of history's innumerable utopias. For him the eternal struggle led simply to a nice earthly type heaven where we all had the jobs we wanted and nobody went about stabbing or blowing anybody else up and we weren't hungry or poor and everybody had easy, regular bowel movements (two daily)—if indeed excretion had not been entirely superseded, and if so, about time—and, therefore, no tummy trouble; and our sex lives exactly matched each individual disposition, from Nil to Nonstop, with no pretense allowed . . . speaking of sex, Mick, once inside the main entrance of the public library, found himself gazing fixedly in a profoundly horny, hungover, and decidedly ungentlemanly fashion—extending the image of unemployed lout a little too far, as he readily acknowledged to himself (still, it *was* a splendid sight) at a prominent female bust clad in imagination-defying T-shirt blaring "COKE!," both of which (bust, T-shirt) belonged to Miss Penny Burke.

Hearing a bold throat-clearing, she looked up from her reshelving duties.

"Good morning to you," said Mick, essaying a smile. "Ah— I've come for the unemployment, the unemployment," *Christ that's the gal I saw in the,* "whatsit." Annoyed with himself, he straightened up a bit . . .

"Workshop?"

It's him, she self-exclaimed. The poncey drunk from the Koh-I-Noor. Unemployed, well she might have guessed.

"Seminar? Yes, it's over there, sir," she said, laying a trifle too heavy an emphasis on the monosyllabic "sir" for her seeming courtesy to be believable; *Au contraire,* thought Mick, she's taking the mickey, oh sure. Now look here, he lectured in his heated imagination, stridently, inwardly; I am a university graduate and a professional of some standing and distinction, don't you know, and I can throw a Pantera GT through the twisties better than— well, better than you, for a start. . . .

"Over there, please, sir," interjected an irascible Mr. Finn on his way from his office to the jakes, clearly ticked off at encountering an all-too-obvious member of the army of the jobless hanging about in the middle of the parquet, right in front of the main entrance where anyone might see him, for goodness' sake. . . .

"You're on, Miss Burke," said Finn. "I'll tell Gladys she's wanted at the shelves."

As he entered the tinkling pseudo-marbled precincts of the bathroom for the third time that morning, Finn, slightly regretting that earlier upsurge of annoyance at the sight of one of life's unfairly-dealt-with, murmured to himself, "Finn, heal thyself," and uttered a prayer for unseen outside forces of unexpected and unlikely benevolence to improve his, Finn's, life, starting with his poor old bod (all he really needed was a bit of relaxation, i.e., ten days at the seaside, watching the tide) and moving on to the discreet phasing-out of his weekend or extracurricular activities, of which, if they were made known (heroic though they were, from one point of view), disapproval would be widespread, starting with Mrs. Finn herself[9] (now, *that* thought scared him, and Finn wasn't easily scared, as we will discover in due course).

Penny, too, once she'd blown off steam, reproached herself. In fact, she was worried that irritation and a short fuse were becoming her standard way of dealing with the world from inside her little invisible bubble of self-preoccupation—especially with men, irritating personalities that so many of them were and the rest not worth a second glance or thought,[10] mostly.

Ah, well, 'tis life, 'tis that altogether, as her old da was wont to say.

She braced herself and followed the coughing, spitting, hollow-chested, stooped, slope-shouldered legion of the unemployed—eighteen men and two women (this being Ireland)—into the meeting room, called "Learning Centre," adjoining. Computers

---

[9] Well, I'm way ahead of you here, Jack Reader, or Jill Lectrice, or whoever you are. I can't say much, but I can tell you this: Bang Bang! Get it? Boom! Boom! Know what I mean? Pow! Pow! Pow! And I don't mean cowboys and Indians. This is Ireland, after all. Follow my drift?

[10] Sod me if she isn't right. Half the fellas I've known had absurdly puffed-up views of themselves and the others were near-total has-beens, with pony-tails to boot. Mind you, the gals weren't much better. Let's face it, people in general are a bit of a *mauvais quart d'heure,* or should that be *esprit d'escalier* (or *escargot*)? (Of course, there was Kathy.)

had been set up, and chairs faced each other across schoolroom desks. Lists on the wall were of jobs available, most of them of the petrol station-assistant and booth-cleaner variety, promptly disdained by the proud among them, of whom there were many.

Penny despaired momentarily, then rallied to start in on the wretches.

"Good morning, good morning. And how are you?"

She was, she hoped, firm but uncondescending, with a cheery smile for those who worked hard for it. In this she was assisted by one Moira from the Unemployment Exchange, an ex-social worker and seasoned expert in the vagaries and pretenses of the lower-down (and outs) of our society and whether true injustice or personal failings had brought them there. Briskly, Moira divided up the room into two sectors, as if sensing by instinct the difference between the permanent derelicts and the rest, who were just out of a job, like.

"Just out of a job, like," she whispered to Penny. "You wait and see. Now, sir," began Moira. She was addressing a red lightbulb of a nose that preceded not much of a man with trembling brown-nailed fingers and a nervous cough.

"How long have you been unemployed?"

"Just out of a job, like, missus."

"And are you taking training courses?"

"Not at all. Can I smoke?"

"No."

"Well, go get buggered, then." His eyes were wet behind the fury of coughing that followed.

"Thank you. Good luck to you, me lissome lad. Next?"

Penny interviewed an even ten out of the twenty-odd who'd turned up, some of them hoping, it seemed, for a bonus over and above what they got from the Sosh.

"No, we don't have any money for you. We're not the exchange. We provide counseling and the odd job listing. We . . . ," and so on.

"Funny you don't offer computer training," said a red-haired galoot with one eye (the right) larger and more fixedly staring than its mate.

"Why's that?"

"Well, you've got all these fuckin' computers, dontcha? And sod-all punters who can use the fuckin' things, yeah?"

"I take your point. What was your line of work?"

"Demolition and disposal up North. And the eye's glass, by the way, as long as you're starin', like."

"Do you have your Leaving Cert?"

"Ya ballocks."

By the time Penny came to Mick her enthusiasm was on the wane and she found herself almost missing the relative tranquillity of the info desk.

"We've met before," he said, by way of introduction. "Well, not actually."

"Yes. You were flewtered. I'm surprised you remember."

"Oh I never get that bad."

"You looked it to me."

Yes, she was cheesed off good and proper, what with this fellow swanning his way in here along with these other miserable slackers, true low-end specimens,[11] and your man here some kind

---

[11]And that's an understatement. During my home improvement days I lived across from the South Killoyle Exchange, and let me tell you, the air in that place was alive with the odours of *tikka masala* and chips and rich with profanity and tobacco smoke day and night. What was worse, next door some bright spark had the bright idea of opening a Turf Accountants Parlour, which meant of course that the fellas never made it to their job interviews at all but promptly lost on the nags anything they'd managed to con out of the Sosh, forcing them back to the exchange to beg and wheedle for more brass, and so back to the betting shop, and so on ad infinitum. I should know: I was one of them, the year Angela's Wheezer won at Fairyhouse.

of university graduate and dilettante who fancied a bit of slumming, did he . . . ?

"Slumming, are we? Or in genuine need of a job?"

"God, you're on your uppers today, arencha?"

"Just answer the question, please, sir."

"And knock off the 'sir,' OK? It's Mick."

"Mick. No one would ever guess."

"And you are . . . ?"

Well, she was wearing her bloody name, wasn't she, on the beastly nameplate on her left tit . . . !?

"OK, OK. Penny. Hey, Penny. From where I sit you could use a drink. What do you say?"

"I say nothing. This is an interview, of you by me, for the purpose of lining you up with gainful employment. Got it?"

"Fire away."

She wasted some time with the initial standard questions that established little and usually succeeded only in raising hackles, but not Mick's; he sat, unmoved.

"Degree in architecture. Well, it's the next thing to design, you see. With a spot of writing. Always wanted to do both, actually."

"Houses, eh?"

"Cars. Automotive journalism."

"*Cars?*"

Her astonishment was nearly palpable: a brief shake of the head, eyes a touch more a-bulge than usual, half-mocking smile: *Cars!?*

Now Mick did feel a bit ticked.

"That's right, Penny. Them things. Transport, you know. Dad's estate wagon. Your '89 Toyota. Bloody motors. That kind of thing. I want to write about them. Believe it or not."

It all seemed a bit boring to Penny; or rather, a straightlaced, goofy, golf-playing, laddish, beer-swilling, suburban-guy-hanging-out-with-the-guys kind of thing, not really artistic at all, just the machismo of motorheads under the new (to her) guise of automotive journalism, or car design.[12] She'd never heard of either—or at least had never thought about either any more than she thought about her car, which was never, bar changing the oil and checking the tyres; oh it was well-maintained and clean, right enough, but that was solely in order to get her to B (or A) and help her retain her self-respect, living among slobs. . . . Briefly, like the wing of a bat, an image of Continental-type smugness—say, Germanic, i.e., earnest and well-dressed; or French, viz., condescending and sloppily dressed in a tasteful way; and as for the Eyeties, well, enough said (Ferraris, Fiats, *vino rosso* and all)—flitted past her mind's eye.

She recommended an office job, say technical writing, and it so happened she had an opening right here in Killoyle, a stone's throw or whisker's breadth from where they were sitting, in fact: NaughtyBoy Computer Services were in search of an immediate candidate with some computer experience.

"There you go. The fella to see's name's Denny. Denny Tool."

"All right, but hang on a sec, NaughtyBoy? Are they some kind of . . . ah . . . ? Well, I mean. You know. Eh?"

"I really don't know, Mick. You see, it says right here: NaughtyBoy. The words are run together like that. And they've this wee logo of some kind of leprechaun or goblin or . . . or is it a mouse?" She peered, frowning.

"I'm not sure I'd be much use as a tech writer. It's incredibly boring shite, tech writing."

"Most jobs are boring. Well, you know that. Or maybe not. You were lucky before, not having a boring job."

"Man, you're on a roll, aren't you."

"But you were a test driver, it says here. Sounds a sight more exciting than working in a library, let me tell you. Isn't that some sort of racing driver?"

---

[12]Good on ya, Pen. Right on, girl. Onto the tip with this automotive blatherskite. Although I quite fancy that late-model Bimmer coupe old Hemmings next door's selling, now that you mention it. . . .

Mick explained gently, with the twinkly patronising tone of a medical professional explaining a fatal disease to the hapless layman (or woman), and throwing in coronary warnings to boot—in this case, corollary warnings, actually, against the purchase of a Jocelyn vehicle.

"Oh I'm not shopping for a car, believe me. Not with the payments I've got. My wee Peugeot has to last me ten years."

Mick frowned, impatient at talk of payments and wee Peugeots lasting ten years. You made payments for worse things than cars—kitchen appliances, mortgages, divorce—and wasn't it worth forking out a few quid a month for a decent set of wheels that would get you over the hills and far away in the twinkling of an eye? (Came a vision of his idolized Merc. Shiny and black with gleaming alloy wheels. Thirty-four grand at invoice. Jesus Christ.)

"Anyway. Worst bloody cars on the road. Well, made in Ireland, eh? Need I say more?"

Penny bristled.

"And what's wrong with made in Ireland? Isn't Waterford crystal good enough for the likes of you? Or do you turn up your sassenach nose at Bushmills whiskey? Or Belleek porcelain?"

"Note the lack of engineering products. Note, also, that two out of those three you mentioned are made in the black Protestant North. Easy does it, Miss Burke. And what do you mean, sassenach nose? It's as Irish a hooter as there ever was."

And so it was that by the end of the interview (by far her longest of the morning: half an hour, give or take) Penny and Mick had achieved a somewhat convivial modus vivendi veiled by apparent antagonism, a televisual formula as well suited to real life as to soap opera.

"A drink, then?"

"Ach you and your drinks."

"On me."

Well.

"All right, then. But just the one, mind."

He minded, and his minding curdled like new milk within him; but he was a stout-hearted man, and soon the cleansing draughts of the water of life drove away his ill humour, and his fair face blushed the blush of health, and his manly laugh rang out once again through the squares and alleys of grey Killoyle Town. And Penny came to him in the hostelry of good cheer named Mad Molloy's, and there amidst the press of strangers their beakers met in the clink of goodwill. And it was good, at least to him; and to her, too, it wasn't so bad.[13]

---

[13] And it was all yer granny from start to finish. Still, I'd hang about a while myself for a chance to see that T-shirt again, if you take my meaning. (What's more, I did, so there.)

5

Fergus Goone slobbered vigourously into his handkerchief. It was September, sinus weather in the Southeast, and Goone was a bold northern man, by crikey, a crude rude Derryman from Coleraine, Co. Derry, oh 'twas a manly place, so 'twas, a place known for its crisp, manly autumns and manly, rugged farmfolk, especially the lads. . . . Goone turned to express one or all of these oft-expressed manly sentiments to Cornelius, but Cornelius, in anticipation, had already left, leaving Goone mute and agape.

"Sacks of sodding horse shite," he hissed.

It was a right pisser, turning around and not seeing the audience you'd counted on being there—especially when you were used to being ignored, sniff sniff. Just like old days, eh? When Fergus was a lad, he used to speak his piece quickly just to get it over with, because everybody found everybody else so boring back in Coleraine—actually just *outside* Coleraine, in Dundreary, on the road to Portrush, athwart the old Derry-Antrim boundary, just past the Dhu Varren halt, say No. 123A (or was it B?): "The Larches," with mum Linda and sister Veronica—that nobody listened for more than a few seconds, unless you were a "taig" insulting "Prods" (and thereby expressing, in that heartland of Protestant Ulster, a desire to die).

Now Goone was a grown man, and a man of means, and the coming man, *yet still nobody listened,* unless money was quite visibly in the offing one way or another in the form of immediate cash payments or bribes. It was a cod, so it was, but when you came right down to it, wasn't life itself the old cod, eh . . . ?

Well, never mind all that. He could slag 'em back with the best of 'em.

Goone, beady of eye and long of shank, with a handful of feeble hairs afloat atop his otherwise bald pate like sea anemones on a coral reef; Goone, dynamic führer of Emerald Mats, PLC, manufactory of exquisite doormats and placemats, with a promising sideline in curtains for shower stalls and floormats for cars and, possibly (see below), an upcoming sponsorship at the Killoyle International Pint-Pulling Olympiad (or possibly not); Goone, proud owner of three Indian restaurant franchises in Ireland's Southeast (The Koh-I-Noor, Killoyle; The Taj, Waxford; Vajpayee's Hindustan Express, Youghal) with every confident expectation of one day owning ten, or twelve, and not just in the Southeast, or even Ireland, but Britain, Europe, North America, the world!

(Except India, of course. They'd pretty much cornered the market there. As that Singh or Swing fella had explained. Best businessmen in the world—ha! Well, he'd not done business with a sharpnosed sharper from Coleraine, had he . . . ?)

"So how's our mat factory doing, Cornelius?" boomed Goone, with a hint of self-mimicry in his plangent Ulster accents, before remembering once again that Cornelius had left, gone, scarpered, departed to wherever it was Cornelius spent Thursday mornings—the church? Not likely. The Strand? Loitering near the beach cabanas? Offering to swab some poor dear's windscreen for five bob? Lowering his trousers in the lee of the Michael Collins statue? Or he might be on his way to the courts to debate that ridiculous traffic accident he'd involved himself in, denting his old Fiat on the tailpipe of one of them four-wheel drive jobs . . .

Fergus worried about wee Cornelius. Oh, aye. The lad had his ways, didn't he, and they were dodgy ways indeed, so they were.

Truly, Fergus fretted, in his fashion, and his fretting was that of a concerned friend and mentor, but there was a catch, for his concern was heavily laced with the desires of the avuncular queer he was; aye, he lived for—let us be frank—Cornelius's glans, an image of which winked alluringly before his mind's eye even now, stirring up randy thoughts of the peculiar ecstasies of their dyspareuniac intercourse. Because of this, Goone lived side by side with guilt, lust of any kind—especially of, of for, *his* kind—being a no-no in the stern Prod precincts of Ulster where he'd grown up, and not exactly the flavour of the month elsewhere, either. But Goone cared not. His feelings weren't entirely physical. It wasn't as if Cornelius's allure could be randomly replaced by just any lad's. No, the powerful locomotive of Fergus's emotions *had* managed to dislodge a shard or two of genuine affection from the granite rockface of his Ulster heart. He loved the boy, in his errant way.

He did, so.

"I love ya, Cornelius," he mumbled, tearily.

Well, there it was, and the world could think what it wanted. His and Cornelius's arrangement was an unusual one, even (or especially) for Killoyle, although Cornelius had a streak of Bohemianism in him that made their ménage somewhat more palatable, being not only Fergus's snuggly-nuggly-nookie-poo but also full-time sexton of St. Derek's C. of I. Church, Behan Avenue[1] who occasionally—very occasionally, if Fergus had any say in the matter—put on women's clothes and paraded up and down the terrace outside, delivering speeches in a fruity David Frost-like voice. (He'd taken to doing that a wee bit too often of late, Fergus had noticed, reminding himself to have a word when

---

[1] "Quite the cleanest church in the southeastern diocese": *Irish Churchman*, Volume six, number thirteen, July 1998.

the time was right.) Neither this nor the overall San Franciscan quality of the Fergus-Cornelius partnership had escaped the notice of their neighbours, of course, but as it happened the happy couple lived in a semidetached house on Dr. Thomas Maher Esplanade, a row of semidetached houses once occupied by low-income families and now renovated and aggressively rented out to students at Upper Killoyle College; and it was natural for the students, most of whom were utterly without morals except for the "If it feels good, do it" and "If Mum and Dad like it, sod it" variety (except for one or two gangling, virginal churchgoing galoots appointed by God to the dual office of master masturbator and avenging angel of the heterosexual majority) to cast a benign, even approving eye on such living arrangements in their midst; indeed, a forced cheeriness—American tropes such as "hi" and "you guys," which on Irish lips denoted TV-based topicality, desperate trendiness, and a liberal point of view (viz., "We know you're queers but hey! that's cool, why don't you come by sometime for a nut-and-couscous casserole and listen to some Peruvian flute music and join in an exposé of the hegemonic Western military-industrial complex?")—was invariably the mark of their demeanour when they encountered Fergus or Cornelius, an entirely unnatural response to Fergus's dour, distinctly not "gay" weltanschauung.

"Ach," growled Goone, dismissing Cornelius and all thoughts of the young fool with a valiant trumpeting, into a plantain- (or snot-) green handkerchief, of the nose.

Pooooooooo-wooooot. Ooot.

He rose and crossed the room diagonally to the turret window, there to seek on his computer the anodyne reassurance of profit-and-loss tables, preserved for all eternity on software, solid symbol of his success in one of life's arenas, if not in others.

"Right."

(*Too many eyes fixed on his every move, for one thing, now that was the occupational hazard of being a millionaire.*)

"Eight million bloody pounds. What do youse think of that then, eh?"

Of course it was nowhere near eight million pounds. Not a fraction of that. Eighty thousand was more like it, but Fergus Goone liked to dream big. Still, eighty thousand was "nae bad," as that chappie from Big Jimmie's in Glasgow had put it over the phone the other day....

"In ane quarter, eh? Nae bad at all, Jimmie."

"Ah. That's in a year, actually, mate. And the name's Fergus, actually, not Jimmie."

"How're ye doin,' Jimmie."

"Fine. Only I just told you, it's Fergus. I don't know where you got the idea my name's Jimmie."

"Och aye the noo. Och. See *you,* Jimmie . . ."

At this point Goone had understood, accurately, that his interlocutor was slightly deaf—or as the Scot himself put it, "a wee bit corned beef, could ye speak up there Jimmie?"—and that the repeated "Jimmie" was a tic of the Glaswegian way of speech, somewhat like "Sheese" or "pal" up North, or "yer man" or "Seamus" in Liffeyside talk. No matter the moniker, or the degree of aural difficulty: Big Jimmie's man wanted to talk business. His firm was impressed by the quality and durability of Emerald mats. They'd tried out four of the standard model dinner placements in a Govan free house one recent Saturday night and all four had survived ten hours of arm wrestling, Newcastle Brown spills, cigarette ends beyond the counting of them, the trial sharpening of a blade, "more than a thimbleful" of blood, the pinpricks of darts gone off course, great lathering sprays of puke ("last call, gents"), a head rammed tableward, and the ultimate test: detergent.

"Aw of 'em's lookin' great, Jimmie. And they're exquisite tae the touch, like a silk necktie. Ye'd never ken they'd been puked upon."

Big Jimmie's were happy to report that the competition, including much-vaunted AlpTech, a Swiss firm of aerodynamic placemats, had fallen by the wayside. Or rather, to winnow the wheat of originality from the chaff of cliché: Like the mercenary armies of old, Emerald Mats had held high the battle standards when conventional forces had long since departed the field. AlpTech's Waterloo, it transpired, had come round closing time, with the first tidal wave of upchuckies, fatal to maintenance of that healthy sheen. . . .

So: What was next? Circumstances as described—the real-life testing situation; the utter rout of the competition; bona fide punters willing to give endorsements in exchange for a free pint or two; cameras set up and ready to roll; easy, no-charge locations (the corner pub)—seemed to make TV commercials an inevitability, with guaranteed distribution of the resultant video gem throughout Britain (or whatever remained thereof) and Ireland (Greater). In fact, the marketing possibilities seemed *unlimited,* throwing Fergus into a quivering fever of greed. Big Jimmie's, in short, was buying him out. At hand finally seemed to be that long-heralded, oft-dreamed-of moment after which life would no longer be the same forever, as in some cancerous airport-lounge best-seller. The Costa del Sol beckoned, and a snug life with Cornelius, and maybe another lad or two, purely in an intern capacity of course, he had so much to teach the young . . . but this was business, and by janey if there was anything a Coleraine man knew better than how to spot a taig, it was how to make a quick quid.

"Aye," quavered Goone. "We'll do it."

"Awright, Jim. We'll do it."

"Aye. Whatever."

"Lazy bloody Irish bastards. Aw right, Jimmie, *we'll* set it up. Cheers now."

"Hang on, don't you need my web address?"

"What woman's dress."

"Not woman's dress. Web address. *Web address.*" This was repeated uppercase so as to dinn into Jimmie's dense Caledonian skull the magic words and thence to the holiest of holies: the Internet.[2]

"Aye. With ya now. Hang on a sec."

A female voice, Irish (southern), took over.

"Double ya double ya double ya dot."

"Yes, I can guess know that part."

"Dot FerguslovesCornelius dot com."

"Dot what? Fergus what?"

Fergus explained.

"Ah, no, Mr. Goone. Change that address for a start."

Fergus expostulated.

"Well, all right."

"Right, then."

Better this way, mused Fergus, regretting the evaporation of his electronic love letter to Cornelius, his attempt to show the world that it was more than just . . . *och weel,* as they'd say in Derry. Best leave the complexities of the web page to the canny Scots. Neither he nor Cornelius—the poor wee boy was a sexton, for goodness' sake—had ever had much training in computers, bar the basics of finding a plug and outlet and turning the switch from "off" to "on" and, when needed, vice versa; so they'd had to hire a couple of likely lads from down the pub who'd come back to the house a couple of times for a drink or two. Well, there they'd been, names of Des and Tex, nice boys, dab hands at the darts (and didn't they look a treat in leather), fine tenor voices,

---

[2]Internet, schminternet. I wouldn't give it the time of day, or touch it with an eight-foot pole. You know what it reminds me of? That space behind Connolly Station across from Phelan's Chemists, where the taxi stand used to be, next to the kerb where the old grey fellow sells fake wristwatches and pictures of Belgian bathing beauties; only it's on the friggin' computer, isn't it, so all those wee shaven-headed half-bearded liver-lipped jewelry-bedecked neo-Neanderthals take it for gospel.

too, and when the recital and the taxi ride were over they did a quite decent web page with a skull and crossbones and the Emerald Mats logo and that, "a perfectly fine accomplishment and superb visual experience," as Fergus found himself blathering thickly and somewhat overenthusiastically while writing out a cheque for two thousand quid; then, of course,[3] he and Cornelius had looked closer, and they discovered that, with a mouse click or so, the viewer found himself magically transported, via electronic flying carpet, from the friendly home page of Goone's Emerald Mats to the neighbouring home pages of Leather World and Gypsy Rod Stripper Express and Great Big Thingie Dreamland with "Hot" links worldwide, especially to Bangkok, Key West, and Tangier: not, agreed Fergus and Cornelius, the ideal marketing tool, save to the prurient, and other admirers of the homoecdysiast's art.

"We've been diddled," shrieked Cornelius. "God how I hate that. I hate them. I hate them."

"Aye. Wee sods."

The offending web page was promptly scrapped and a new one hastily assembled, following the instructions on building a web page from the best-selling *Do Your Own Internet* by Rusty Bolger. "A sexton sells mats" was Cornelius's first contribution, urgently shot down by Fergus, who spotted the inherent absurdity that customers would find off-putting.

---

[3]Isn't there always a "then"? Too true, too true: "Then, he coughed, ominously," "Then, on a whim, they pelted each other with gooseberries," "Then, Odysseus had himself lashed to the mast," "Then, they discovered the left rear tyre had gone flat," "Then, he rummaged through the dead man's pockets and found—nothing," "Then, she emerged in a cocktail suit and surprisingly foxy Gina shoes," and so on. I don't know. Personally I always preferred "but." "You're sacked. But not yet." "I never sleep with men I don't know. But I'll make an exception in your case." "Normally this would be closing time. But it's bank holiday, so we're open for another hour." Etc.

"Well, it's the word 'sex', isn't it. I doubt they'll never catch on to the real meaning. And it sounds like you're sitting in the square flogging the friggin' things, like one of them black African fellas, whachacallem St. Gall, Sandy Gall . . ."

"Senegalese."

"Aye. That lot. Anyhow, it's the word itself. Most punters don't know shite about sextons or what one does. They'll think it's something to do with sex."

"Oh, sod off, you bloody great old feckin' wanker." This loud imprecation was truncated by the sound of a slamming door: Cornelius, petulant as ever—far too much so, if you asked Fergus, for a lad of twenty-six.[4] Such behaviour was, in any case, inimical to productivity, as Fergus pointed out, gently at first, then in loud haranguing tones, over the telephone to the sexton's office at St. Derek's.

"So shut yer fuckin' gob, all right?"

Anyway, despite the passing imbroglio, going great guns they were, with Big Jimmie's on board and a contract well on the way for exclusive rights to mat-supplying the Olympiad. Apart from this, advances had been discreetly made by a "consortium of businessmen" with heavy Belfast accents who wanted to go into silent partnership behind Big Jimmie's overt investment. Fergus had strong suspicions about the extracurricular pastimes of these Belfast gentlemen—in fact, one of them sounded exactly like the fella who'd escaped from the Maze disguised as a woman and had then given an interview to the television, still in drag, in which he'd tried to rally the Prods against the Brits in the name of "Ireland's dead generations" (but he was appealing to the wrong country, mate, as Fergus could've told him)—still, business was

---

[4]And the author of such promising, if earnest, odes as "The Man with Luminous Hams" and "My True Love Is Bald," both clearly modeled on Hoolihan's earlier work, with a nod to yours truly (*qv. infra*).

business, and if anything took care of Ulster's problems it would be just that: business.

It was all quite promising, perhaps *too* promising, for one invested from the start with deepest Ulster pessimism.

"Still, better this way than upside down with a meathook up yer arse, as me owld mam used to say."

Fergus produced a sandpapery sound from the rapid friction of the palms of both hands. He smoked a fag, then, coughing loosely in the Irish manner, he prowled the office in a show of looking for his key ring, finding it (as he knew he would: he checked twice daily) dangling like a spent erection from a hook behind the microwave, cunningly labeled "Not Car Keys" to confuse any passing car thieves.

"Aha! I've got ye now, ye bastards."

Clutching the keys, Fergus hunched his shoulders and emitted a series of oily titters, a display that might have aroused suspicions of imbalance or outright insanity in anyone within earshot or eyeshot; but there was no such eavesdropper or eyewitness— and sure wasn't it all your man's way, just.

"Time to drive, mister me man," he crooned, switching off lights, television, and overhead heater (coin-fed, one bar). He was agog with pleasure at the dual prospect of both the drive in his new car, a Taiwan-built Melanoma Distend XLS—and the chance of confronting the welshers on his payroll at Emerald Mats—for September was nearly over, it was the end of the fiscal year and time for the supremo to visit the plant and make bloody sure no one was spending too much money on "worker's benefits" and that kind of cod. The moment he turned his back, Fergus had discovered, accountants and managers and their ilk had a way of inveigling monies out of the company kitty, usually in the interest of some soppy cause like "immigrants' rights" or "health care" or "maternity leave"; hence the importance of the personal visits. Since the inauguration of the firm in the late eighties—after Fergus had had enough of chauffeuring yobs (the first and last time he'd been employed at someone else's behest, thank you very much) from the docks to the railway station via Madame Walewska's Eurasian Massage Palace (since defunct[5])—this trip to the plant had become a twice-yearly ritual of about the same dreary predictability as a Royal Progress, or rock 'n' roll tour. On the day before the chosen day, the plant manager, Mr. Wallfish, was usually put on alert around ten A.M. by a telephone call in code (*"Valkyrie!"*). Fergus would then hang up, giggling. The next day, if he was in especially high spirits, he might call again and ring off just as Wallfish answered in that sycophantic way he had ("Emerald Mats. This is Wallfish. May I help you?"). Then, Fergus—fallen somber for the occasion— would slowly and thoughtfully change from his usual Ulster-country-lad patched corduroys and stew-stained pullover into flashier threads, say a Vasari suit and Countess Nardi tie, the ensemble enfolded in the embrace of a fine DuChesnil overcoat with faux-fur collar. A rollicking Ulster folk tune[6] might be on his lips. Having carefully locked, unlocked, and relocked his office to test the security alarms, he would then proceed to the garage, there to board the company's (i.e., his) swish silver Melanoma, a model well-suited to the image of the corporate mogul of his dreams. Once settling-behind-the-wheel and warming-up rituals were over, the Melanoma and he would sweep majestically down the drive, garage door gliding soundlessly shut behind them, and merge effortlessly into the late-morning traffic on King Idris Road (West).

Such, indeed, was the sequence of events on the day in question, with this slight but significant departure from routine: As

---

[5]Closed by order of Ben Ovary, lest His Worship might himself be nabbed there on one of his thrice-monthly visits.

[6]"O Bonnie Lads of Omagh," "Trill, Trill, Ye Boys in Suede," "'Neath His Nates He's Mine," and much, much more. . . .

Fergus steered the silver motor leftward at the lights onto Parnell Parade and thence smoothly and silkenly towards the interchange, there came from Borax Drive, a side street off Pollexfen Walk, a mechanical cough interspersed with puffs of blue smoke and the high yammering sound of decrepit tappets, with weakening pistons flailing in despair, this ensemble of aural effects yielding a Ford Escort, eighties edition (its vintage authenticated by the peeling bumper sticker advertising The Racing Heads "Food to the World" Concert '88), in colour varying from rust to pus-yellow, driven (if we may so style its eccentric mode of progression) by Anil Swain.

"Gotcha," he muttered, spotting the silvery Melanoma. After Rashmi's phone call, and a brisk talking-to from Rubina—"I don't know about you but by golly, uncle, *by golly* do you hear me I'm not going to stay in this income bracket for much longer and that's all I have to say on the matter, and you will do what you have to do"—he'd looked up: (1) the mat factory (unlisted, and Rash's telephonic directions had been cut short by the approach of "one of Goone's goons"), and (2) Fergus Goone himself, who at least, as it turned out, had the consideration to be listed in the phone book (GOONE, F. E.—567A Dr. Thomas Maher Esplanade, Killoyle E.—(123) 765–4321).

"Oh, I've had enough; oh, I've had quite enough," softly chanted Anil, who'd had enough of many things, not least his job, viz., lowly social status, endless striving to no avail, and Rubina's poignant sense of inferiority; but also of fruitless daily attempts at scrupulous honesty and taxpaying backbreaking labour that NEVER BLOODY WELL GOT YOU ANYWHERE ANYWAY SO YOU MIGHT AS WELL GO AHEAD AND ROB A BANK OR AT THE VERY LEAST BLACKMAIL THE BASTARD (farewell, desperate night-long hopes and fears)!

"Shit, do you hear me? Shit."

So intent was he on keeping the swift silver car in sight that he set about thrashing the long-abused gears—especially first, unsynchronized—even more than was his wont, with grinding sounds that set teeth on edge as far away as The Shops, and points south. Uncharacteristically, however, this congeries of automotive sound and smell effects, combined with the hesitant, spasmodic kangaroo-rat-like forward motion and an entirely new engine noise that sounded like chattering dentures (Armageddon for the timing belt) provoked Anil, as he wiped away beads of cold-weather sweat, to exclaim, "Bloody hell, I hate this car. Maybe I should be having a decent motor, too, for a change. Eh?"

Nevertheless, by some miracle of mechanical striving and precise traffic-light timing, he managed to keep the tail lights of Goone's luxomobile in view well beyond the intersection of Uphill Street and the MacLiammoir Overpass en route to the T45 ring road and thence past Killoyle's intermittent outskirts into the lush suburbs so unreminiscent of India (except the green belt round Bangalore, and a few miles near Simla).

"I'll get you now, you black," muttered Anil enigmatically. "Completely, you know."

Yes, Goone was the enemy, the evil many-headed Ravana who'd taken Rashmi-Sita hostage. And Anil? He was no Nakula, nor Bhima, no, not he. Dribbling chaps, those. No, we'd have none of their wimpiness, thank you very much. Bugger off, you lot! Then I'll flex the bow and let fly the arrow!

Yes, Anil was Rama, great lord of the Ramayana!

No! Anil was Arjuna, warrior of the Mahabharata, archer, lover, avenger, decreed by the gods to be eternally victorious!

Onward!

In his imagination he turned also to the great imperial tradition of India's and Ireland's former rulers.

"Into the valley of death/Rode the six hundred," he roared, seeing himself as a latter-day player in his own Great Game, for war was war, and this *was* war with, Anil crazily hoped, precise benefits to his cause. In the passenger seat next to him, per Rashmi's instructions, was the wherewithal of his vengeance:

video minicam, notepad, and tape recorder. (Also on the passenger seat, albeit irrelevantly to the mission of the moment, were two back issues of *Bollywood Beauties;* an oil-stained anorak; a half-empty packet of Lakmé Hindustan semifilter beedees; a copy of *E-mail from Eden* by Tom Gore-Grimes, dog-eared as far as page seven, pristine beyond; several menus from the Koh-I-Noor, glued together by the mysterious spirit-adhesive of time, with a *soupçon* of spittle; a linen handkerchief bearing the initials AS, unused; several serviettes, used; a nail file, unused; and an audio-cassette, dribbling tape, of Shari Jaffrey's *Sitars at Sunset.*)

He'd have the bugger dead to rights. He'd corner him and get statements from Rash and her teammates. He'd threaten to go to the law unless . . .

Well, unless Goone agreed to terms!

"Oh, completely, you know," repeated Anil, working second and third gears for maximum propulsive velocity onto the T45A dual carriageway, direction Killoyle Airport Free Trade Zone and Anil Swain's dharma, about two hundred meters aft of the silver Melanoma and losing ground all the time; but within him burned the passion of the righteous, in Lord Krishna's cause as well as in that of the Swain household and Indian food fans throughout Killoyle City and environs.

6

"Well, tell him I called, will you?" A pause, filtered through stentorian breath, stabbed with a piercing wheeze. "Sheila Hasdrubal-Scott. That's right, Hasdrubal. Aitch ay ess . . ."

"Boy Chroyst, Oy'll kell the gobshoyte, so Oy will."

Thus Sheila's Victor (whose ludicrous stage-Irish speech will henceforth be rendered on these pages as if enunciated in purest Oxbridgian on the understanding that shamrockry's moist labials, twisted diphthongs, and mutilated vowels roil beneath the smooth greensward of his apparent queen's English).[1]

"The bastard ballocks," he went on, with a depth of feeling entirely feigned (but it was less boring than wandering about the house with his hands in his pockets). "The smarmy, smooth, condescending intellectual ballocky bastard ballocks. Winn, isn't it? Ahem?"

"*Thank* you, young lady. And your name is . . . ?" Sheila rang off, impatiently, causing the telephone to trill suddenly, as if in protest. "Drat the slag. And he's not in, she says. Good lord, how

---

[1]Jolly good. Bloody Paddies. Time for a pronunciation key, I'd say. I=oy; ou=ay; u, e, o, etc.=ah, ay, or eh; t=ts; th=d; e.g., "Dat's royghts, moyne's ah poynts ehf stayts, uf yay dahn'ts moynd." Jesus. And they call it the mother tongue?

can he not be in at three in the afternoon? What is he, a mad bomber or something?"

"Maybe he's dead," muttered Victor. "He looked like death warmed over, if you ask me. A right goner, I'd say, with or without our help. You know the type. Greyish-green, you know? With yellow-red lines round the eyes, mostly?"

"Now, Victor. Don't be narky."

"Narky farky yourself," spat Victor. In a storming huff he retired to the solarium, repeating "ballocks" rather tiresomely. There he deflated his rage and extracted and lit a cigarillo, puffing hastily, turning his head away from an imaginary companion to bring up phlegm with a loud rattling like the hawsers of an aging trawler. On a side table lay the classified page of the *Killoyle Clarion,* on which a single entry had been encircled in red. Next to the newspaper, in cause-and-effect proximity, squatted the telephone, expectantly.

"Ah, Christ."

Indeed. It was hopeless. Why did nothing ever work out? Why was everyone always nagging him? Why did he wake up in the morning with the feeling that he was being watched from above? (He'd checked: no one there.) Most of all: Why did he, Victor Scott, live in such a place, with such a woman?

Answer to the last one: Because she had money and he didn't. Never had. He'd been skint all his life, then one day he met Sheila at a Lough Derg church picnic-cum-retreat where he'd gone to pray for cash. Answered prayers: A lissom lad, he'd seduced her, a tremulous and voluminous, not especially fetching, lass, in a flash. (Even today she lived with the memory of the Apollonian Victor of yore, not the double-chinned ever-coughing screwball with outsize corduroys and the voice of an asthmatic parrot.)

Answer to the others: Because he was stone mad altogether, or near enough to have been recently cashiered from the following three jobs consecutively:

1. Sales clerk at Brown Thomas, sacked for folding his arms and scowling in silence whenever his assistance was requested (and once for puckering his lips and emitting rude raspberries at a particularly insistent customer, who then complained);

2. Assistant under-auctioneer at Crumbles, Ltd., heaved out shortly after it became obvious that—apart from having read (or rather, skimmed lightly from pages twelve to fifteen to pages 103–105, where the pictures were) Rusty Bolger's best-selling *Auctioneering in Three Easy Steps, Step One*—he hadn't the foggiest idea how to start the bidding, or appraise *objets*. Indeed, his only attempt at art appraisal had resulted in the lady rushing from the room in tears, clutching to her bosom the Limoges vase, later deemed a £5,000 value, for which Victor had offered her fifty pee, laboriously counting out the change from his own pocket;

3. Catering submanager of Dudley's Do-Nut Boutique on the Strand, in which establishment, halfway through an employee morale-building seminar, he'd expressed his dissatisfaction with the whole business—as well as his outrage at having to wear a white smock and chef's toque emblazoned with a smiling face and the slogan "Dudley's Does 'Em Right"—by throwing a glazed cream-and-jelly doughnut at Frederic Thomson, the visiting regional training facilitator, scoring a spectacular silent-film bull's-eye on Mr. Thomson's nose. This incident, and Mr. Thomson's threatened lawsuit, raised serious questions about Victor's ability to live a normal life at all. Sheila, when questioned to this effect by the Gardai, bristled, and took her dear hubby's side against the great venom of the world. Later, however, following a candlelit dinner with Sheila during which, between bites, she moistened her lips with the tip of her tongue and sat in such a way that her bust

was easily the most prominent part of her, Mr. Thomson was persuaded to back away from actual litigation, on the understanding that he and Sheila could "take a drive to Balbriggan"[2] together. This done, he posted himself across the street from the Hasdrubal-Scotts and waved soppily whenever she appeared, but at the end of the day Victor's snarling features at the solarium window were instrumental in convincing Mr. Thomson to retire into the middle distance and take up an expectant position, awaiting he knew not what.

So much for Victor's prospects. He had no connections and his c.v. was a liability that got worse with each job it chronicled. Not that he cared. All jobs were identical, to him: infinite boredom in the service of fools. Consequently, and not surprisingly, he was currently unemployed, and would theoretically be content to remain so; after all, Sheila had enough nicker for the both of them, and without a job to consume his time he could devote himself to his collection of old newspapers, his prime interest and true light o' love. His collection was conservative—the *Grauniad,* the *Ergonomist, Janus Speaks, Truth Times Two, Time's Wingèd Chariot*—but eclectic, with a classic twist.[3] In fact, Victor hoped one day to oversee his own archive as curator or docent, acknowledged worldwide as the authority—actually,

---

[2]Oh, aye. I've been on a few of those in my day. Last one was with Kathy, sometime in the spring of '96, the year Up Trumps won at Leopardstown. Took us all day, and we got caught in a real bottleneck at the Skerries junction, but once we got there . . . need I say more?

[3]Indeed. The headlines of one or two oldish issues stand out as classics of the genre, for example, from *The Jupiter,* June 1934: "Rohm Shot, Buried Dead," and from *The Munster Gong,* 1968, "Students Shun Cafés, Sack Fruit Stand on Place Marceau."

here was where a job might come in handy, if he could get hold of a computer.

Archiving old papers would be a breeze with one of them things.

This consideration, along with Sheila's gentle reminders of respectability, pension plans, etc., had persuaded Victor to scan the classifieds, reluctantly but resignedly, with a deepseated feeling, like pesky ulcers, that it was a terrible waste of effort but somehow all for the best. He had done so grumblingly, muttering a phrase or two from his syllabary of tongues.

"*Hunns*-hinggadabadawah. Ballocks. Ahack. Ah, here we are."

Among all the listings for temps and entry-level secretaries and word processors and editorial assistants and other wretched stations of the workaday cross a single likelihood had deserved the honorific circling in red pencil: NaughtyBoy Graphics Ltd. (*bloody silly name,* thought Victor) was in search of "an immediate candidate with some computer experience." Well, Victor could be an immediate candidate at a moment's notice, and he even had some computer experience. Not at home: Sheila wouldn't have one in the house. She claimed they caused short circuits and attracted burglars and were the reason for so many "unexplained fires" ("but they're not unexplained if you know the computer caused them, are they?" nagged Victor, at which jibe she only smiled, in her wan way). Still, Victor had used a few, here and there, at the library, for instance, and in Galway once, and another time at his cousin Shoots's, in Crumstown, where the two of them had played the ultra-hot video game Wittgenstein II: The Oubliette for two days and nights running. By Jesus what a grand gas time they'd had! Now that was the life, all cigarillos and a dollop of Super-Whip in the coffee and a side of boxty and good solid gin in the proper glasses, not paper cups, and the computer screen flickering nicely, and not a bloody woman in sight, except on the screen (Wittgenstein's mistress, Dora the Dominatrix, ah, well now) . . . So. If this NaughtyBoy rubbish gave him a computer and actually left him alone to get on with what he wanted to get on with—

and didn't force him to type out memos and company reports and ledgers and all that crap—he could get properly started on his old-newspaper archive, and if he had one on the computer, *actually on the Internet, like,* he could charge admission and really rake in the moolah!

Oh, it was a grand idea all right, oh it was that so it was. Why, he even had a name or two worked out:

Victor's Caravan of News.

Vic's What Happened When and Where.

Meet Me Back Then and There.

Well. It was worth a try, and it'd get him away from *her* for a few hours a day. Of course, the pub would perform the same function, as would the betting shop, or the cafeteria at the new airport, but there was something in the archive idea that made him open his eyes a little wider, that suppressed his cough for up to ten minutes at a stretch, and that felt like the genuine article after fifty-nine years of havering and wavering.

He finished his cigarillo, spat moistly into a nearby hydrangea, and threw himself like an athlete into telephoning, head lowered, shoulders thrust forward, thereby mimicking nicely the eager tremulousness of the job applicant.

"Yes, yes, I've had lots of experience with a Macintosh."

Passing by the open door of the solarium, Sheila overheard and wondered what he was on about now, the darling boy, perhaps it was a dry cleaners he was applying to. She had a momentary vision of him standing rigidly behind the counter at the Panzer Laundry on Behan Avenue, reciting to a surly public the fees for a suit, a sports jacket, an anorak, and so on—the dear silly man! How she hoped he'd found a place where they'd treat him right, at least. It just wasn't fair, he'd had a rough time of it, he needed protecting from the horrid big outside world, and that awful Mr. Library Finn or Winn—not to mention his obnoxious girl assistant, the one with the foul mouth and shameless tits—well, that was the last straw, why it was the very next thing to total discrimination it was, after all Victor was disabled in a way, she was sure of it (some kind of new mental disability, it wasn't in the encyclopedias yet but it was beginning to show up on the telly[4]), there had to be some reason for the way he behaved, and to tell the truth she wasn't entirely convinced there wasn't a lawsuit in it, as well, considering the broad applications of the Looney-Nomad disabilities bill they'd just passed in the Dail after three weeks of nonstop hissing and paper-plane-throwing and rude gestures back and forth, the silly wee lads, oh boys were such boys, bless their wee hearts . . . actually, if

---

[4]Tourette's is a good one, one of my faves. Sounds like Vic here might be one of those johnnies. Or take Psychic Utterance Syndrome (PUS), in which the patient, while (for example) buying cigarettes, or inquiring about plane fares over the telephone, or sitting down for a haircut, blurts out, in a shrill, appropriately accented voice, frequently that of a long-dead foreigner, something like, "Pssst! Can maï family stay viis you? Zey are on run from Okhrana," or "Qvick! Go to de bank branch on Denuylstraat and vitdraw sufficient funds to pay for de tickets to Zvitserland," and so on, and then starts up normal speech again, quite nonplussed when confronted with the blank and/or uneasy stares (or telephonic throat clearings) of his or her interlocutor(s). It happened to me once when I was negotiating a fare with a taximan in Harold's Cross. His version is that I'd almost convinced him to settle for five quid (not bad for Swords and back at one A.M.) when I suddenly lost all credibility by lowering my voice an octave and brusquely requesting, in Italian, with ample hand gestures, the phone number of a Signora Gina Grissini, resident at number 232, Viale Garibaldi, Apartment 15B, in Rimini, Province of the Marches. Coincidentally, he replied in the same language—after all, wasn't his name Tullio, and didn't he hail from the east end of Catanzaro itself—and explained that he was unable to provide me with any phone numbers in Rimini, upon which I spat, flung my cape over my shoulder, and stalked off into the night. Two hours later I woke up in a dosshouse in Irishtown with a right old horror of a poteen-scented West Coast bottleman going through my wallet (and lingering a little too long over Kathy's photograph for my taste). I resumed, consciously, speaking Italian, to the extent of saying "*Ciao,*" and took the 12A back to Ballsbridge.

she wasn't mistaken, it was a grave misdemeanour, not only to insult a D.C.[5] in public (slightly milder penalties if the act occurred in private), but to imply an insult to same, into which category that man Winn or Finn fell, as surely as she, Sheila, had a head and a pair of eyes in it, facing forward.

Truly, apart from her robust health she wouldn't have much to keep her going (bar the light in Mr. Thomson's eyes) were it not for her dear wee Victor and the battles she fought in his behalf.

Job discrimination? Unfair practices? Missed opportunities? Just you wait! The Irish are a litigious race, and the race was on!

(Sheila was one of those well-meaning women whose utter lack of common sense makes her a danger to one and all, and that means you and me—and Mr. Thomson, poor sod.)

Sighing like a humid breeze through a reedbed, she curled up, cat-like, on the divan, and reentered the fantasy world of Wallis Simpson on page 354: "Sighing like a humid breeze through a reedbed, Wallis curled up, cat-like, on the divan, and reentered the fantasy world of Edward, her consort, whose first daily utterance, usually made between ten and ten-fifteen A.M. irrespective of whether anyone was around to hear it (kingly habits die hard), was, 'I don't know how anyone can do the bloody *Times* crossword, it's too bloody hard for me, let me tell you.' He'd generally clam up for the rest of the day, except for padding into the kitchen

---

[5]"Disabled Citizen" (*qv. supra, p. 1*), the legal nomenclature throughout the thirty-two counties of greater Ireland and possessions, as of last November when the Association of Handicapped Irish Persons really held Gar's feet to the fire, threatening to publish the address and phone number of that bint he'd been shagging in Portadown, and be janey no sooner did they get that legislation passed in two sittings when the bint in question voluntarily inaugurated her own web site complete with links to Gar Looney pages, including Gaelic Football Heroes of the Past and his high school yearbook (Portara, better known for uppercrust Prods), portraying him in a half-dozen poses wearing that famous guilty look and someone else's blazer.

sometime during the long dull hours after lunch, when he would clasp his hands regally and in an undertone, so that none could hear him, timidly offer to do the dishes, a ritualistic act of maintaining the common touch that no one took seriously, least of all the kitchen staff, who maintained the stony silence more characteristic of their betters.

"At night the ex-king tended more towards volubility, with the arrival of cocktail hour and a spin or two around the dance floor; then he'd wax nostalgic, and recall the mists of Balmoral and the rattle of waggon wheels on the cobblestones outside Buckingham Palace and his one great act as king, the time he toured the Rhondda Valley and visited the miners' homes, which were a damned sight smaller than Buckingham Palace, as His Majesty had observed in lieu of small talk. . . ."

"O Buckingham," moaned Sheila. "O Balmoral. O Rhondda."

She briefly indulged herself in nostalgia for what she'd never known; then, pulling herself together, she fanned through her Rolodex and found the private number of that O'Mallet person, the solicitor or advocate or whatever he was. "Litigation Our Speciality," read his advert, portraying a cartoon figure surmounted by the photomontage head of Tom O'Mallet holding in one hand the scales of justice, in the other a sack of swag. He was nothing if not straightforward, was our Tom, and Sheila was definitely in the mood for a spot of *that*.

"Well, Mrs. . . . um . . . I've a few things on at the moment," said Tom, when she called. "Discrimination, eh? Cool. Sounds like a brickbat to me. Winn, you say? At the library? I know a Finn— ah, it *is* Finn. My, my. Finn, is it! And you say he insulted your husband, who is a D.C. . . . ?"

"Mentally. He has a condition. Sometimes he swears out loud, but it's not his fault."

"Whose fault is it, then?"

"Well, the condition's, of course. As I told you. And Finn— well, that girl, actually, Finn's employee . . ."

"Girl?"

"Yes, but it's his fault, isn't it, allowing his subordinates to speak to their customers like that?"

"I don't know. Maybe he has a condition."

"Mr. O'Mallet, this is a serious issue. My goodness. I would thank you not to make light of it."

Serious issue me arse, thought Tom, if you're not both in it for the money I'd like to know the name and fax number of the man in the frigging moon. But if it's old Finn (he wondered fleetingly about conflicts of interest, in view of those business deals he had pending) . . . *oh well, money in the bank's money in the bank, no two ways 'round that.*

Aloud, he adopted the crooning tone of the professional legal highwayman, apologized profusely, and agreed that Finn probably *was* responsible for the irregularities of his employees. (Anyhow, as it happened, Tom's alacrity was sharpened by the fact that his own dear old da, Judge Gerald, had had a bit of a falling out with this very same Finn over allegations of cheating at *chemin de fer*, resulting in Judge T.'s name being quietly expunged, judge or not, from the membership register of the South Killoyle Golfing Club amid assurances of hushing-up too humiliating to recall; Tom, therefore, loyal to his family name if to nothing else, was only too happy to assume the fault *was* Finn's.) (Then, of course, there was that private business he had going.) (In a word or three, Tom was playing a very dangerous game.)

"Now, let me get this straight: That's really your name? It isn't a stage name or nom dee ploom or anything? Because I don't do pseudonyms, lady."

He assured her, smothering a yawn, that he would look deeply into the matter. This assurance preceded, as the soup the roast, the oft-rehearsed last movement, for bowels and orchestra, of O'Mallet's lawyerly pep talk, in which were summarized the breadth and scope of his human and humane qualities and his deep concern for his fellow man and woman, all the foregoing delivered on automatic pilot per the instructions of old Professor McKinney at UCD, viz., "By all means, boys and girls, remember that any hearts worn on your sleeves should not be your own."

"Conditions like your husband's are quiet tragedies, Mrs. Hannibal, ah that is to say Hasdrubal-Scott." Spontaneity barged in, uninvited. "By the way, as to your really most unusual name, might I enquire . . . ?"

"Certainly. Moroccan Spanish, via Gibraltar. He was a shrimp fisherman from Ceuta, where the shrimp population was never great, it being inland. Consequently, he was a perpetual traverser of the straits in a quest for employment. One day on the Rock he met a certain Molly . . ."

"Bloom?"

"Beavis. My mum. They emigrated in '59."

"I see. Well, now, as I was saying," resuming the standard legal peroration, "regarding your husband's unfortunate condition. It's an old story, I'm afraid, as we in the legal profession know perhaps better than most. Day by day these martyrs and unsung heroes struggle to cope with conditions unacknowledged by the soulless bureaucrats who run our public institutions. The more we can shine the spotlight of publicity onto these cases, the more we can bring their plight to the notice of the general public, and the better it will be for Vincent and all those who, like Vincent . . ."

"Victor."

Tom yawned with a roar.

"Awwwwwwwwwb. Is *that* his name? Well, I'll be jiggered. Cheerio."

7

Coldly, O'Mallet rang off, and spun round two or three times in his leather-padded Ironman DeLuxe swivel armchair, whistling a tune (two tunes, actually, intermingled: Sinatra's "The Wind Was Green" and Hummel's *Rondo Capriccioso in D*[1]) and admiring (1) the view from his tinted windows of Killoyle Harbour, and (2) his freshly chewed fingernails. Seen up close (closer, please), Tom O'Mallet, charm and success incarnate, was a hollow hulk, a husk, a human wreck, a living, breathing "Deutschland" with no Gerard Manley Hopkins to chronicle his demise. What from a distance could pass for energy and dynamism became, under closer scrutiny, a serious case of nervous agitation: the fluttery tic in the left eyelid, as if a trapped butterfly were struggling to free itself; the watery eyes, like a veteran dosser's; the heavily gnawed fingernails drumming the desktop; the desktop itself, on which sat sprawled and towered ledgers, computer diskettes, invoices, and letters in unruly sheaves.

Beneath Tom's ribs his heart danced the kazachok (*Hey! Hey!*).

"What a cod, eh?" murmured Tom to himself. "Hasdrubal-Scott, me arse. Poor Victor's condition, eh? Oh, we'll fix youse

---

[1]Doesn't exist. I checked. The nearest would be Karl Ditters von Dittersdorf, whoever the blazes he was (some Jerry, most likely).

up with a nice owld condition, lady, you just wait. Tom O'Mallet's got things in hand. Yez came to the right address this time! Them owld conditions are money in the bank these days, you wait and see!"

Bettina, his secretary, announced her presence in the doorway with a timid cough.

"Tom?"

He waved her away.

"Nah. Later."

Behind Bettina boomed the voice of Mary Rose Ryan, Tom's legal partner and part-time barrister in the courts of southeastern Ireland, with offices and representatives in Dublin, Sligo, and Donegal . . . as a rose, Mary Rose was fading fast, and—perhaps in consequence—fancied herself more and more as she fancied men less and less. Especially Tom O'Mallet, whose torch was held high by poor Bettina, and no one else. ("I know he's the bit dodgy on the side, like," as Bettina had confided to her friend Nellie Norris, over Babychams in the Balsa Room of the Spudorgan Vacation Inn last Saturday night, "but I think he looks like that American actor Bobby Lee Irwin. The one with the face, you know?"

"Oooooo," had been Nellie's reply, sealed with a giggle and a pout in the direction of Esteban Barrientos, the strapping young Andalusian barman.)

"I need an appointment at three o'clock this afternoon," declaimed Mary Rose. "What do you mean he's full up? What is he, a manicurist or a doctor? Tell him I'm sorry he's full up, but if he doesn't squeeze me in I'll have him up on charges. He'll know what I mean. Just ask that slut who works for him."

A phone slammed, then a door. Tom listened intently, hardly daring to breathe; then, resuming his swiveling, he essayed a refrain or two from some of his and his da's favourite Sinatra songs— "The Wind Was Green," of course, and "Strangers," but also "Where Are You?" ("Y-û-û-û?"), "New York, New York," and

"Laura" ("Laur-â-â-â-â")—primarily in order to strengthen his vocal chords, still a bit rough after last night's unruly sleeplessness (on the old blower a little longer than planned) ... but he slowly became aware that Bettina had retreated only as far as the threshold and was still peering at him through the door ajar, like a rodent in the undergrowth warily beholding a cat.

Feeling a right charlie, Tom cleared his throat and inquired, testily, "Well?"

"Mr. McArdle's here to see you. From Belfast."

"Oh, Christ."

"Hallo, Tom. How's the lad?" A hearty greeting, broadcast boomingly from a broad face of roast-beef hue that suddenly loomed up behind plump Bettina like a harvest moon above the green-breasted hills of Meath.

"Martin, how are you? Listen, could you give me half a mo'?"

"Surely, Tom. Surely. You take your tayme."

Tom laughed the hollow laugh of Christopher Lee as the count in *The Brides of Dracula.*

"Grand, Martin, be with you in two ticks, yeah?"

It was literally all he needed: the hard man himself, down from the Falls to check on his investment. Oh, the Falls boys were beginning to count on the law firm of O'Mallet & O'Mallet a bit too much, so they were. If a tombstone at Bodenstown needed moving, or refurbishing, they'd call Tom O'Mallet, or his da. If the Prods in Weterford (or, as the Lads said in their quaint Northern accents, "Waterford") were getting stroppy, the word went out: Get on the horn to O'Mallet. If one of the government watchdog groups, or the Gardai, were sniffing uncomfortably close: *Alert O'Mallet!* The latter case was, actually, the present case, the reason for Tom's sleepless night, the bane of his ever-anxious existence, the juicy bone for an eager journalist: Not only arms smuggling, Killoyle being an international port (Brest, Quimper, Plymouth, Holyhead), but arms concealment, the biggest cache of AK47s, Semtex, Katyusha rocket launchers, Kalashnikovs, Uzis, and Scud missiles in the Western world, all locked up nice and tight in a self-storage unit off the N101 Killoyle–Dinglederry Ring Road, just south of the airport. Word had it the guards were getting close and a local splinter group was even closer. Tom's da had had to use his connections, including, surprisingly to Tom (at first) the afore-named Finn, who it seemed was not what he seemed, seeming rather—after closer analysis—to be a rabid armchair nationalist of the classic, 1916 vintage school, an avid reader of the blatherings of Casement, Pearse, Connolly, & Company; in short, a perfect dupe, if one were needed, and a front man made to order. . . .

As for Tom, he'd never had much choice in the matter. His da was an old IRA man of the fifties generation, when little more was going on, or off, than policemen's mugs on mimeographed posters and firecrackers in milk churns in south Armagh, but the judge's name was (self-)inscribed on the honour rolls of the movement, and the old Plough and the Stars waved proudly in his heart. The recent emasculation of the people's army had hit him hard, what with smug Unionists chortling fatly on the news at ten, as good as declaring victory, and worst of all arm-in-arm with those who, until the recent Derry charter of cursed memory, had been the foot soldiers and legionnaires of the people's army: It was Collins versus DeValera all over again, it was ultimate betrayal, it was us versus them writ large. Time, in the minds of the O'Mallets (Tom was on board, halfheartedly, for the good of The Nation, partly, and for the plenitude of his own Channel Islands bank accounts, mostly), to step forward and offer their services to whomever might be stepping forward from the other direction with the light of patriotism blazing in their eyes, and that included some odd bods indeed.

Time to revive the cause, to serve the *oglagh na hEireann*, and so on.

Particularly depressed one night after a Stormont news conference on the TV news during which a Unionist politician referred to the Lads as "the defunct Roman Catholic army," Judge Jerry rashly placed a few phone calls here and there, one to Martin McArdle, de facto brigade commander of the Falls and Ardoyne, hardest of the hard men.

"Fock," the brigade commander had declared to one of his officers (Lt. Finbarr O'Hagan of Newry, Co. Armagh) after the phone call, "Yer mahn's mahd. But he's a fockin' judge, and, well. We nayd to faynd aht what he's abayt." (Rich, rolling Belfast accent henceforth taken as read.)

So things had proceeded apace. It was easy at that time, children, to start up a wee pocket-sized army, oh, say regiment or even division strength, and even easier if you'd already the infrastructure in place, and knew one or two chaps with pull in, say, the former Soviet lands; with eastern Europe transformed from a prison camp to a bazaar, a shiteload of armaments was ready for the taking, and trade with countries like Belarus and Slovakia, which had very little to sell apart from aging Soviet ordnance, vodka, pickled beetroot, and big spicy sausages—the flavour of which lingered in the tum for days after ingestion—was booming anyway, and containers emblazoned with names like Hrçko and Kajdarovskij and Sprodj and Kurvi-Tasch were a common sight in Killoyle Harbour.

Moreover, Judge O'Mallet had done his apprenticeship in European commercial trade law and knew all the ins and outs, as well as one or two plugged-in blokes in the corridors of power in Strasbourg and Brussels . . . indeed, it had been in wintertime in Strasbourg in 1979, with the snow lying heavy on the deep rooftops of La Petite France and icicles hanging from the sagging eaves of the ancient houses Goethe had once known (ogling that Charlotte of his idle dreams), that eighteen-year-old Tom O'Mallet, already big 'round the biceps for his years, had gained admittance to "le quartier rouge" and, head spinning with (1) Gewürztraminer, (2) lust, and (3) being eighteen, had absolutely and completely abandoned his virginity to the safekeeping of Maria Coelho of Oporto, Portugal, EuroParliament secretary and after-hours gal on the go (or make)[2] . . . meanwhile, Judge Jerry then, briefly, a TDE on borrowed time (Fine Gael B list, Killoyle South, snap by-election soon annulled), would have been across town at the Parliament bar on the Place de l'Europe weaving fine nets of acquaintanceship in his best after-dinner style, punctuated with whiskey and cigars and the occasional backslap and false confidence ("Let me tell ye this one, Jacques, and believe me lad I've not told another living soul, well, would you credit it, I'm a lifelong believer in unleaded petrol, so I am, and that's just between you and me and the potted palm, eh?"). Result, twenty years on: Jacques Neckar, rising French parliamentarian, and Carl Marks of Newcastle, onetime muckraking Trotskyite newspaperman, now chairman of the European Parliament,[3] were

---

[2]Make. Actually, Maria'd be a fine lass to lose your cherry to. Dark good looks, but so dark as you'd get lost finding her eyes kind of thing—you know, Tamil- and Ibo-style, or whatever. Why, it was only last year that she was made minister of docks in the new Catholic-Christian government of Jose Neptuno os Pinheros, the former pop singer and tennis pro. "Anyone for tennis?" he'd say with a ringing laugh, by way of kicking things off at Cabinet meetings (true bill: I had this from the gossip section of *O Pais*), and if any of his ministers was foolish enough to pass comment, Neptuno would spend the next half-hour singing *fado* in a low, husky contralto, with the curtains drawn and a single candle burning. Still, there's good seafood in Lisbon, and the trolleys are a trip and a half, take it from me.

[3]Ah, Carl, Carl. The number of times he and I sat in his treehouse together, sharing a smoke and a chew of the rag and, I don't deny it, a wee nip from the old jar. The vista was vast, and frequently grey, under the twisting cloud-panorama of East Wales, near Wrexham (near-England). The intrusive snarl of passing tractors would, at odd moments, interrupt our perorations, as would the occasional shout of opprobrium from a passing peasant steeped in ignorance and superstition. Too, there was the day Carl provided the biscuits and whiskey and after a few toasts fell straight out of the tree, poor lad, dislocating his pelvis something fierce. He always walked a bit like John Wayne after that, although he was never actually mistaken for the Duke, not with his wispy

on the judge's Christmas list. And it was Judge O'Mallet's plea-sure to deliver the goods whenever an urgent call came from Strasbourg for, say, cut-rate CDs of Irish music, or Donegal tweeds, or Aran wool, or bargain-rate software.

Anyhow, back home, what with the Derry charter and the in-exorable worldwide triumph of capitalism (until the next "ism" came along), the lads were getting bored. Bored with war, bored with peace, bored sitting about with their thumbs up their bums instead of . . . well, *diversifying.* So they diversified. They made investments left and right. They had more front organizations than you could shake an Armalite at. Too many front organiza-tions. You couldn't keep them straight anymore. There were too many acronyms, too much snake oil, too much smooth palaver of the Wall Street-City of London-Paris Bourse variety. With all this moneygrubbing, devout nationalists of the Judge Jerry stripe self-inquired, Whither Erin? Soon the IRA'd be advertising on the Net, or on the sides of buses. It was too much. The old crowd were dazzled by the financial possibilities of the brave new world into which Derry had thrust them. They couldn't be trusted any longer, said the judge. Truly, he'd been having doubts about the lads for a while; and with an Irish twist of irony like a knife in the old sow's farrow it had taken this so-called peace treaty to bring out the worst in the bastards—*cease-fire, is it, well wipe me arse with a sprig of nettles,* self-expostulated the judge inwardly. Hadn't one or two of the "lads" already been nabbed smuggling stuff north-

---

ways and shrill Welsh intonation. It was shortly thereafter that he straight-ened himself out and applied to join the Trostkyite parliamentary party, with a view to acquiring some kind of decent lifestyle, i.e., no more of your scruffy eternal-student rubbish: a decent motor, a nice house, and handmade clothes. Anyhow, Carl later launched himself into Europolitics with his usual aplomb and savoir-faire, dining out on his acquaintance with me—well, I don't hold it against him, I've done the same myself.

ward? The Pure IRA, or the Soldiers of O'Brien, or whatever they called themselves? He'd read something in the papers. Then a boat containing Semtex and detonators had been stopped by the Coast Guard off the Blaskets. Loud had been the protestations from the quondam general staff, of course, oh your claims of peace-loving harmony, etc., had filled the air with their bilious babble. They were like car salesmen to the nth degree. It was all so, so . . .

So *unlike* the fuckers. After all, they'd been trained for one thing and one thing only, that is, murder, mostly of innocents and the occasional British soldier; and here they were, quite undefeated when you tallied up the war record but losers right enough, sure they'd never been vanquished on the battlefield but they'd fallen well short of the united Ireland of their quare owld dreams—and now they were expected to bend over to the Brits and the Unionists, please pass the vaseline m'lud? And, once fucked good and proper, meekly surrender their guns? Divil the chance (and here Judge J. found himself in sudden deep sympathy with the insurgents)!

Ballocks in shallot sauce to that one!

The very notion was ludicrous, absurd, the worst kind of wishy-washy wishful thinking and media-spawned drivel! *And look who'd half-fallen for it!*

"Sad to say, but the old crowd have turned into wasters and shilly-shallying spineless, whinging pockmarked jellyfish," he declaimed to the empty air, alone in his chambers. "A bunch of travel agents and fucking restaurant managers, if yez take my meaning."

So he hit upon a plan, hard, as if swatting a fly.

"Simple," said the judge to Tom, by way of explanation. "We get the Rah to sell us their decommissioned weapons, that lot out at the airport. Then we sell the whole kit and caboodle back to them through front men from Europe and pocket the difference."

"It's nuts."

"First thing you learn in life, boy, is that things change. Sometimes you even have a hand in making them change. If you're lucky."

It was a dangerous game, right enough, but the thrills, ah the thrills ...

And the spills ...

"*And the Spoils!*" thundered the judge, by now pissed as a newt. "If we play our cards right."

"Like taking on a poker pro when your game's gin rummy," muttered Tom, dubious but determined nonetheless (father knew best). . . .

Actually, *diversifying* was the actual word McArdle used when Tom, having hastily washed down three aspirin with a draught of harsh but effective Larkin's Blended Private Reserve, invited the ex-commander in, and ushered him to the leather armchair strategically placed to catch the light.

The bottle towered reproachfully between them, proclaiming dissolution and decadence.

"Drink?" offered Tom, with bland insouciance.

"Ah you know I'm strict tee tee, Tom. Anyhow, isn't it a wee bit early? Not worried about anything, are you? Relax. It's a lovely time of year. I'm down here on a house-hunting mission, basically, the missus wanted to get shut of Belfast weather and visit the Shrine of the Invisible Virgin and I fancied a break from business up North. I'm looking at a house later on but I thought I'd drop by first. Now. First off I have a wee favour to ask."

"A favour, Martin?" Tom flexed his knuckles under the desk: *crick-crack-crrrrrck*. A favour as defined by the hard men could run the gamut from suicidal to much worse.

"Well, yes. First things first. Once I find a house I'll be needing a housekeeper. Word has it your da's char—Mrs. Delaney, is it?—that she's fairly competent with the old mop and duster, and I reckon if your da's satisfied I'll be, as the dear knows he's a hard one to please. So can we split up Mrs. Delaney between us? Do a time-share deal, like?"

"Oh, absolutely." Tom breathed audible relief. "She only cleans me da's place three times a week anyway. Sure you're welcome to her. Here's her number." Overly eagerly, he delved into his Rolodex.

"Ta very much, lad. Aye. Like they say, reality bites." McArdle pocketed the number and sat back, readying himself for the real business. "Or is that *sound,* heh heh? Blessed be the peacemakers, anyway, eh? You know the way it is up North these days. Swords into ploughshares, and so on. So we're diversifying, so we are. Oh, aye, we'll keep our hand in. We're not about to hand over our entire inventory. We're not fucking daft. But we can spare a bit. And we'll be needing a cash-flow generator, like."

Jaysus, thought Tom, it sounds like the old bastard's been reading our minds.

"So . . . we unload the stuff, but . . . ?"

"The inventory? Right. Well, almost." McArdle sat forward. As he shifted his weight, the friction of his beefy haunches against the leather of the armchair produced a querulous farting noise that Tom enjoyed. He betrayed his pleasure with a booming laugh. McArdle paused for a second, then resumed coldly.

"I'd start by selling off a few of the big-ticket items. You know what I mean."

He was being uncharacteristically coy.

"The . . . um . . . aye . . . things."

McArdle's reluctance to speak plainly was the clearest indication that a sea change had overcome the tough old ex-brigade commander; his clumsy embrace of euphemism was a sure sign of incipient respectability. His newly acquired jargon limped along with the bland ennui of sports talk.

Tom tried to elicit a little frankness. (He was a bit cheesed off, anyhow.)

"Things? Those would be the Katyusha rocket launchers, Martin?"

"Aye." Martin stared at his hands, then looked up suddenly. "Them's the men, Tom. Get rid of 'em. Dump 'em. Dispose of 'em entirely, if you would, and I don't much care where, as long as it's not to the so-called Soldiers of Nolan, or the Pure IRA. Or the SAS, heh heh."

"True for you. The Pure IRA are the right bastards."

"More Catholic than the pope. There's always some. And face it, some of the lads can't imagine life without a gun in their hands. Not that I don't sympathize. But the rules have changed."

"Well, Martin, we'd best dispose of the materiel then, eh?"

A foolish exultation welled up in Tom's heart: *It was all going his way!*[4]

"Aye. Try your contacts. The Basques should pay top dollar. Unless they're having one of their cease-fires just now. Or the Corsicans, I can't keep track. Otherwise sell 'em at a discount. They'll be clamouring for 'em. Think of all those national liberation movements. The Occitanians, the Jutlanders, the Manx, the Orcadians. It's a seller's market out there, Tom. And if we ever need ordnance of that power again we know where to get it, eh?"

In both their minds, the name of a certain desert oildom unrolled itself like a magic carpet.

"Oh we do that. Oh yes."

The point was, McArdle said—sitting forward in his chair with such eagerness he looked like an enormous beef-bird about to take ponderous flight—that the movement needed to continue to exist, but out of sight, in disguise, behind a front of respectability, until it was needed again.

---

[4]Here's a tip, based on life: Whenever things seem to be going your way, they aren't, unless you're blooming Hitler, and even then there's the bunker at the end of the long hard road.

"And we want to make a profit," said McArdle. "We want to go into business and make money, and what better way in Ireland these days than the Internet and the hospitality business, eh?"

"Hospitality? You mean open a hotel? The Provo Palace? The Sinn Fein Sheraton? Bobby Sands Towers?"

"Not at all, boy. Aha, you're a card, so you are. No. Hospitality. Catering. Drinks and that. Supplies to hostelries. You'd hardly look for the old Rah in a serviette factory, would you? All on our new Internet shopping site. With links. And with this beer-pulling Olympiad coming up, Killoyle will be the venue of choice. Oh aye."

"My God, Martin."

"It is a shocker, isn't it, Tom. More so than if I'd told you we were planning to set off a bomb in the jakes at Number Ten."

"The hard men, selling placemats and serviettes. I don't know whether to laugh or cry."

"Aye. I know, I know. But it's better than disappearing altogether. And it's a lucrative business, don't worry. I've had it checked out. We want you to draw up a sleeping partner arrangement with a local firm called Emerald Mats, PLC. Tidy wee business, and it's run by a fella from Coleraine. I've been in touch with him through intermediaries in Belfast. A man named Goone. I think he's a Prod but I'm not sure. With that name you'd think so, but we're not supposed to ask anymore. And these days it isn't supposed to matter, is it? All of us cogoverning and happy as hogs in shite up at Stormont. Still, you'd best check out that angle."

McArdle stood up suddenly, catching Tom off-guard.

"So I'll be at the Spudorgan until I find a house."

Bettina, still peering, quietly closed the door, then opened it suddenly, as if just entering.

"Show you out, Mr. McArdle?"

"Thanks, girl. I'll show myself out. This way, Martin. Thank you, Martin."

McArdle's departure was accompanied by diminishing gusts of laughter that Tom interpreted[5] as being downright sinister. He felt an obscure sense of having been railroaded, somehow. So they wanted to get rid of the weapons after all, did they? Yes, well, he knew the damn things had been a millstone for months, ever since the lads had decided to clean up their act—but they wanted to keep a guarantee handy. There had to be recourse, McArdle himself had said as much. The weapons had to be hidden, yes, but a source had to remain available in case of emergency to the nation. And now here was McArdle, hardest of the hard men from down the Falls, perpetrator and mastermind of a dozen heroic outrages against the Brits, escapee of legend (from Crumlin Road, dressed as a Shankill housewife in blue housefrock and hair rollers), hero to some, villain to others—here was McArdle, so squeamish about those weapons he couldn't even bring himself to call them by their true names; no, he'd rather sit there and blather on about floormats and doormats and God knew what else—here was McArdle saying, "Dump 'em."

Well, what had to be done had to be done, and there was less and less point in procrastinating.

Suspecting, accurately, that poor smitten Bettina was still watching him through the door ajar, Tom sang out, "Got your van handy, ducks?"

Soon thereafter they were both were speeding in Bettina's van along Pollexfen Walk. With a legal practice feigning illness ("Closed for the Day") behind them, and under Tom's hands the throaty power of the Ford Elastolite eight-cylinder engine, it felt good to be on the road, if only for five minutes. Tom was tired of the song and dance. In a way this was the best thing, it demanded action. Aye: They'd go on a recon.

---

[5]Accurately. Poor Tom, the stupid bastard.

"We'll go on a recon, eh, girl."

"Oooh," ooohed Bettina, feigning a frisson.

It had been a wee while since Tom had had the nerve to actually go and eyeball the arsenal, and he'd forgotten exactly how much space it all took up, relative, say, to his two-room flat on Behan Avenue, or the carrying capacity of Bettina's van, or Bettina's ample bedroom. Now they'd need to make at least three trips, he reckoned, preferably at dead of night, with a fast run down to the coast and over to Brest, Quimper, the Channel Islands, and the windblown Ile de Ré—unless America came calling, as it had in the past, with Irish accents frozen in time and mentalities of another age still in their prime.

Tom was quite jolly as he piloted the mighty van down the T45, even allowing himself the short-lived luxury of a snatch of "It Was a Very Good Year," which Bettina joined in.

> I think of my life as vintage wine from fine old kegs
> From the brim to the dregs it poured sweet and clear
> *It was a very good year.*
> (*And o! The longing behind it all.*)

The warehouse in question was part of Nolan's Self-Storage, on the perimeter of Killoyle Airport. Various manifests and dockets listed the contents as "Camping Equipment," and indeed the AK-47s, when bundled right, did resemble the tent poles of a weekender's gear. Less so the RPG-7 rocket launchers, wrapped in (as Tom recalled) mattresses, now those would be the real buggers to shift. Then there were the "tent-pegs" or Drçka pipe bombs from Prague; the "guy ropes" or Nrçka 75 mm automatic rifles from Pres'ov; the "propane stoves" or Petrushka clay mines (causing many a Saracen to give up the ghost on the lanes of south Armagh) from the region of the Prpet marshes in the west of Belarus. . . .

A security guard appeared at the gate, a grim-looking lad with a close-cropped beard. His humorless eyes were sponges of malice.[6] Tom abandoned his customary unctuous bonhomie, knowing without a doubt (thanks to a penetrating ability to assess the nature of your everyday gurrier) that it would never work with this specimen. He launched a surprise attack from a different direction.

"Ex-commando, yeah?"

The bloke, nonplussed, gave them the once-over.

---

[6]Sponges of malice, eh? Reminds me of Wee Willie Major, or Billhelm the Minor, as we called him, a small chap with eyes that were more like X rays than sponges, if you want my opinion, and who, although he was from Sligo, had a powerful Swiss-German accent, acquired at a considerable distance from Switzerland, which to the best of my knowledge he never visited. (This concurs with experience of the late great Onion McBryde, Nobel Prize winner and idolized lefthander, a Liffeysider born and bred who nevertheless spoke all his life with a thick French accent, except at moments of stress when his inflexion was pure *italiano.*) Well, Billhelm had them glittering eyeballs that shone with unalloyed malevolence whenever you tried to take his electric train away from him, as we did, with monotonous regularity, even long after he was married and had three kids of his own: "Oh, Dad," they'd say, but he never replied, just glared. Even his horn-rimmed spectacles did nothing to diminish the hard glitter behind them; *au contraire, mes amis,* they quite simply enhanced the laserlike potency of his unblinking orbs. "Sponges of malice," someone (Benny from the Liberties, who later moved up the way to Mountjoy via the Falls) called them once, and the phrase stuck in my head. Odd to come across it here, at several removes from reality, so to speak. And Billhelm? Why, don't you read the papers? He's now Gar's Assistant Minister Under-Par. Recently remarried, Bill lives with his new wife and their seven dwarfs in a woodman's hut in the dense reaches of North Phoenix Park. Occasionally he slips out to feed the gibbons in the zoo, but otherwise, Billhelm's a hermit, folks, and not even Gar can cross his threshold without an invitation. The electric train, I understand, still chugs merrily away, but under lock and key, with heavy insurance coverage from the eminent south Armagh firm of Herschel, Pooter, and Bland.

"Ye're not a guard, are ya?"

"I don't think so," said Tom, waggishly. He winked at Bettina. "Are we guards, darlin'?"

"Perish the thought," Bettina tittered.

"Well, there ya go," said Tom. He turned his attention to the watchman, with the casual manliness of camaraderie. "What's yer name, then? I'm Tom."

The man shifted his feet uneasily.

"Seamus."

"So where were you, then, Seamus? Burundi? New Caledonia?"

"Sinai. And yourself?"

Well, it turned out that, as far as Seamus was concerned, Tom had done a spell in the Irish contingent of the United Nations peacekeeping forces as well, not only in the murderous back-country of Somalia, under the notorious Col. Paddy O'Whisker, but in Bosnia, too, under Brig. "Big" Cormac McFall, at the risk of both their necks, and under constant bombardment by Serb artillery just outside Sarajevo.

"Them Serbs, eh. I've heard they were the right bastards."

"Too right, lad. One day a letter arrived for Big, postmarked Ath Cliath, with a woman's handwriting on the envelope. Well, great, home mail, eh? So Big opens it with trembling fingers—'I don't know any bleedin' women in Dublin, Tom,' he says to me—and boom, I dive for cover under the box of Armalites. Next day we find his left eye and three fingers from his left hand on the bonnet of his Land Cruiser."

"Mother of God."

"Exactly. It was grand crack, oh it was that. And since then, Seamus? I mean, like, domestic action?" With heavy significance, Tom laid a forefinger against his nose. "Up North?"

Seamus looked nervously left and right, then confronted Tom with an angry scowl.

"Listen here, what's yer game. I mean if yer not guards what the blazes are ya playing at?"

Tom's time at Judge Jerry's side hadn't been a total waste. He'd learned the power of the halogen stare, and then some. He'd also had a password or two whispered in his ear over the years, some of them inserted, casual-like, into pillow talk, and one of them from fair Rosheen Brown, sweet Rosaleen of the Lower Falls and Andersontown, Mother Ireland to all and white-limbed lover of many a winsome lad—"Cruiskeen Lawn," she'd murmured, murmuring too that those words, as well as the name "Faustus Kelly," if spoken at the right time in the right place, would open many a back-alley door in the Falls and Andersonstown and, it was rumoured, Divis Flats and environs as well;[7] as for the Bogside, she said, don't even think of it, you'd need an entirely different set of open sesames for Derry, but Belfast was the hard core, that was where you really needed to be on the *qui vive,* and in Belfast it went far, as did Rosheen, all the way out of it and down under to Melbourne, Victoria (now married, a kid, a boring job at SuperTemps); anyhow, thanks to the magic words "Faustus Kelly," Tom not only managed to drink in exclusive backstreet clubs but also escaped serious mutilation at the hand of one of McArdle's lads who'd got it into his thick skull that Tom was a Paisleyite operative and/or UVF commando: "I'll get thaht bahstard. Don't try on stop me."

But at the last minute, gun readied, target in crosshairs, Tom turns and comes out with "Cruiskeen Lawn." Well, it worked then, and it worked now. Seamus blinked, looked nervously about, and sidled closer.

"Who did you serve with, then?" inquired Seamus, one elbow inside the driver's door, chummy all of a sudden, even extending a cigarette to nonsmoking Tom.

---

[7]As well as the frosted-glass portals of certain newspaper offices known to a certain ex-Triestine Belvedere College and Clongowes grad as "The Cave of the Winds" (a.k.a. "Gas from a Burner") on D'Olier Street.

"No thanks. Gave 'em up, Seamus. Isn't life short enough as it is? Anyway. Your business, I suppose. Who I served under, well, hold onto your hat, boyo. Does the name Martin McArdle mean anything to you?"

Seamus gaped obligingly, and embarked on a tedious rendition of his three years as a runner for the Rah, the long and short of which discourse was a hymn of praise to the Lads, an invective contra Unionism, a dithyramb to the sight of Belfast from the Antrim Road and Black Mountain, and a lament for the demise of the cause. It was all good old-fashioned Irishry, and as boring as an accountant's supper. But then Seamus issued an open-ended invitation to Tom and Bettina to come and go as they pleased and even suggested they meet for dinner at the Koh-I-Noor.

"That way yez could meet my fiancée Claire. Ye'd get along like a pair of owld boots, Bettina. I can guarantee it."

"Done, Seamus. Ah—I wonder if you'd open up for us, as long as we're here, like?"

"Be glad to, Tom."

He did so. They peered inside. Seamus examined the manifest.

"Camping gear, is it?"

They stood in the doorway, blinking in the gloom, as faint shapes resolved themselves into more distinct, although still mysterious, shapes. In the stale air lingered . . . the explosions of yesteryear? It was a faintly gamey, acrid scent, redolent of wild animals in flight and overcooked breakfasts in seedy roadside caffs.

"What the hell *is* all that, Tom?"

"Classified, I'm afraid, Seamus," said Tom. Again, the forefinger athwart nasal flange. "And by the by some lads may be dropping in to have a look at it, too. Actually, they'll most likely be taking it away with them."

"Ah, you'll need permits for that, Tom."

"Permits me arse. What would I be wantin' with permits, and me in daily contact with owld Marty McArdle, who still knows a thing, not to mention a name or two? Anyway, Seamus, I can tell you this—and I'm tellin' ya this because I like your face, and I want to make every effort to keep it looking the way it does right now—if that's camping gear in there, I'm a fuckin' two-humped Bactrian dromedary."

Seamus beamed.

"And humped you aren't," he said, with the faintest hint of insouciance. "At least, not at the present moment."

8

The days were long, *too long, o lord;* but there was the Internet on every computer screen, and when no one was looking, Italy came calling. Ferrari, for instance, had a fine web site, as did Alfa Romeo, and Madolini, and the Scala Theater, and the cities of Milan, Parma, Bologna, Gransportivo, and Florence, and various restaurants, and the Grand Hotel Jolly-Roger in La Spezia. The great tenor Espiano Frescobaldi was featured in numerous pages maintained by monomaniacal devotees in various of the home counties (with a bias toward Herts) and the United States (notably Oregon, California, Massachusetts, and Maine). Mick imagined these disciples as plump, panting, feline spinsters masturbating earnestly to images of the florid-faced, broad-hipped maestro and pleading with their sterile household gods—their mournful, forgotten, cat-loving *lares* and *penates*—to one day stop the earth on its axis and simply deposit the great rumpled Frescobaldi at the little squeaky gate at the end of that meticulously tended garden path in Essex or Portland, Oregon, the gate whose squeak had for so long heralded arrivals of no importance, and have him *push it open,* the all-too-familiar squeak at last heralding the miracle: Il Prestissimo himself, redolent of manly sweat and tomato sauce, come to greet and warmly embrace and carry passionately off upstairs to bed, *Ah mia cara, mia cara, Aï 'ave so long longed for you, ever since Aï saw your Wab a-site!*

Anyhow, most of those Ite sites were super. Mick spent many an easy moment drifting from one auto manufacturer to another (Ferrari was offering a discount on its new Marcello Speedster S, dragging the price down to a bargain-basement hundred grand), and on to the superbly amateurish, therefore most evocative, hotel pages like that of the Gran Federico Palace in Rimini (three stars, fax machine and "personal frigidaire" in every room), Splendid-Astoria in Cattolica (satellite TV, Internet access, private parking, trattoria in the cellar), and of course the Corona in Domodossola (Province of Novara), "soundproofed the rooms and so all very quite also." Road tests galore abounded on the web, and fine glossy photos of cars, and naked female limbs, and long misspelled rants about this and that. Mick was in clover. He hadn't a home computer, and had only used the Internet once or twice before. This time he took advantage, and explored the tunnels of the cyber labyrinth. Fortunately, supervisors seldom patrolled, being themselves too preoccupied with clicking on one web page after another—technical and pop-culture sites Mick disdained—but when they did put in an appearance, radiating false geniality and the most obvious condescension to "old guys" like Mick (said with a laugh with no humour in it), it was relatively easy to skip out of the web and back to a civilian page grey with dreary office prose of the type Mick was supposed to be turning out for NaughtyBoy's "promotional literature," which had about as much to do with literature as he himself did with the royal descent of the fucking High Kings of Tara . . . still, he'd had worse jobs (and better), and the least of it was the work.[1] In truth, minimal mental effort was needed. Appearance and attitude played the starring roles. Mick

---

[1]And that's not always the case, let me tell you. I once did an apprenticeship at Callow's the taxidermist's in Tobymug Street. Apart from the daily unloading and disposing of the guts, the worst part was old Callow himself. He was a hard taskmaster, chewing biltong, a legacy of his youth on the South

had sloughed off the shriveled skin of his caustic self and was trying for a somewhat more contemporary image (he *was* only forty-
one, for Christ's sake), with silk ties knotted loosely around the
button-down collars of Oxford shirts. Trousers, too, he sought to
match, choosing only the finest grey flannel. In opposition to
Mick's sartorial flair was everybody else at NaughtyBoy, starting with Denny, the young American in charge, a T-shirted and
blue-jeaned denizen of the software age, forever sipping from a
soda can and recounting, during his rare spells of "downtime,"
his travels to the Great Barrier Reef and Ayers Rock—Australia
was enormously popular with him and his kind, offering no culture at all to tax their brains and plenty of sunshiney beaches with
poontang à go-go—as well as other, excessively remote places like
southeastern New Guinea ("great surfing, oh man, hey Mike you
should go," "Ah that's Mick, Den," "Whatever") and the back-
country of Thailand and Baja California, as well as his exploits
as a hang glider, bungee jumper, and mountain biker in all those
locales and many more, none of them in Europe except Barcelona.
He drove a black VolksBilliard GTI, Mick noted, noting also the

---

African veldt, as he tormented his team—me and an old toper named Ned—
with his endless checklists, as follows:

1. Whiskers loosened?
2. Starch applied?
3. Eyeballs plucked, stored in appropriate receptacle?
4. Claws extracted with handy pocket wrench?
5. Synthetic claws, eyeballs, whiskers, installed?

etc. And if you missed a single item there he was humping your back like
one of the wild cats he especially favoured as display pieces and *"pièces de
conversation,"* as he unwittily put it, appealing for no reason known to me to
the housewives and Conservative voters of Tunbridge Wells and environs.
Well, I can tell you I couldn't get shut of that caper soon enough. It was the
rush job on the narwhal for the Newgate Indigent Sailors' Home that finally
did for me.

fine blond young lady who shared the driving. Indeed, the view from the window adjacent to Mick's desk in the corner of the first floor, Building 2 (Ops HQ IA), took in not only the cinematically sculpted legs of Denny's girlfriend emerging from the constraint of VolksBilliard quarters, but also:

A scud of clouds;

A stand of sycamores;

The spire of S.S. Laurence and Peter O'Toole's R.C. church;

The humbled tower of what was once St. Oinsias but which now, as Laddi's Disco, vibrated nightly to the godless rhythms of Space Musik or Tip-Top Rhythm;

The anachronistically Mediterranean-red rooftops of Maher Village, the new upscale housing development to the northeast;

And on the horizon, oddly seeming to loom above the land: *The restless silver sea.*

Yes—there was Wales, too. (Or was't a cloud?)[2]

---

[2]Aha. Gotcha. That's from Hoolihan's *Atlantic City Cantos,* IV–VI:

Was't England or
Was't Wales?
Was't you or
Was't me?
Was't Da or
Was't Mum?
Was't high or
Was't low?

Was't a pint of Old Workingman's Nut-Seasoned XXX Easter Monday Double Chocolate Amber Lager in Hagan's Bar—the one on Thimble Road, just down from Roaches Chemists, next to St. Michael's on the High Street across from old Mrs. Dwyer's and a stone's throw from Bernadette's Hair Salon (you know the place, it used to be called Sheila's back when Sheila herself ran things, Sheila Kelly from Navan, that is, Bertie Kelly's eldest, she was the one as you may recall who ditched her hubby of six months, "Tubby" Leeson, future president of the Ard Fheis, and ran off with "Pop" Henry, the blues guitarist, well I could have

Mick spent a good part of the first day surveying this horizon while yuppily consuming a chicory-and-cinnamon latte coffee purchased at Sparkles' Coffee Cantina on the Strand. He felt like a million, for about an hour, and momentarily forgot his own crushing insignificance in the NaughtyBoy scheme of things. These were indeed the small pleasures of the job. The actual remunerative part, the technical writing and the memos, in which only the most clichéd and anodyne of phrasing and vocabulary would do ("Per your memo of the eighteenth, key to our strategizing is a hands-on approach to right-sizing the company mix in a proactive fashion, pending further issues"), were, of course, mind-bendingly boring, especially to one who hoped to one day make a living from his pen, or word processor ("The first thing that struck me as I settled myself into the crushed Connolly leather of the driver's seat, behind the walnut-trimmed wheel of the Berlinetta 275GTS, was the elegant, dare I say Brunelleschian, simplicity of its ergonomic design . . ."), but this was as he'd predicted, and it was a job after all, it would do until he found his feet again—or until Tom O'Mallet managed to get satisfaction from Jocelyn Motors, a chancier and chancier proposition to Mick's way of thinking. Indeed, in the days that had intervened since the accident and his meeting with O'Mallet, Mick had had no word from the man, and all incoming calls had been false alarms. Twice, in fact, he'd answered the phone to a total stranger bawling insults in schoolboy French (well, not *total:* he suspected it was the wee shirt-lifter who'd rear-ended him, there was something telltale in the high pitch of his voice and his unaccountable conviction that Mick was a Frenchman): *"Allo, monsieur le français?*

---

told her he'd never have much of a career, but did they ask me, well the answer, surprise surprise, is No They Bloody Well Didn't, and anyway the latest I hear is that they got a Nevada divorce and she's working as a frumpy temp in, or should that be on, Long Island) or

Was't plain old stout?

C'est moi," "Vous! Vous êtes un grand salaud," "Vous! Je vous déteste! Vous êtes une crapule," "Je vous dis merde, merde, merde," "Avez-vous mon numéro de téléphone, chéri?", etc.

Penny Burke, too, was incommunicado (or should that be, wondered the on-and-off romance languages scholar buried deep within Mick's soul, *incommunicada?*), uninterested he supposed since their drink at Mad Molloy's that had turned into the bit of a booze-up, actually, surprise surprise of course, himself accounting for a good five pints plus small shots (Kirk Watson's Indian single malt, neat, straight up) but with her joining in pretty lustily, actually, after the inevitable ladylike demurrals. . . . Nice girl, by and large—yes, quite large (Mick spiralled away into mondo erotico, oblivious to the Castello Visconti Hotel in San Pellegrino on one screen and the technical readout of NaughtyBoy's new NaughtyMan ScriptBrowser office software on the other.) Man, did she ever have a nice . . . ! And nice . . . !![3]

Oh, dear.

---

[3]This kind of vulgarity is right out of line, boy. What do we care for the man's sordid fantasies? Best not delve into such matters, as me owld da said one night after a long rambling confession by our aged one-eyed neighbour, Mr. Toomey (British mortar shell, GPO 1916), to the effect that he'd been applying his single eye to the small end of a telescope for years, the large end being trained on my aunt Clementine's bedroom window—that's Mum's younger sister, the one that was a wee bit touched in the head, a regular Gypsy Rose Lee of the Liberties, she was; anyway, needless to say, the amount of abuse occasioned by Toomey's addiction was almost limitless, especially to himself. Mrs. Toomey wasn't best pleased, either, but the owld git never paid any attention to her, really, except on alternate Saturday nights when he (not she) customarily tried for conception of a sixteenth or seventeenth child. The upshot to this whole affair was that one night old Toomey set up his telescope as per usual, only to find an even bigger telescope peering back at him from the direction of Aunt Clem's room!!! Their lenses locked, it was true love, they eloped to Gretna Green and were wed a week later . . . no, hang on a sec, I've the wrong storyline here. That's right: it was the da's affair. "Apology

Mick swooned briefly in remembered lust.

Still, a bit prickly was Penny, but so were they all, nowadays, armed with their sisters' feminism. Reaching reluctantly into the dusty repository of memory he recalled his ex-wife Eileen, for a start. Yes, the ex-missus could be better described as downright stroppy, at least until she'd sussed you out as a halfway decent fella and not a howling pint-swilling sex-obsessed misogynistic caveman (that was the word, wasn't it, they all had to say it at least once an hour, along with some fake compound construction like "gender-specific": "caveman," along with "misogynist," too, or even better, compund-adjectivizing it as "caveman-misogynistic," which only succeeded, in Mick's opinion, in making whoever said it sound like an American postgraduate student in, say, political science). Well, Penny was a bit like that. Oh, Mick foresaw potential pains in the general arse arca there, right enough. The girl was frustrated, of course, that no one noticed her, or her writing, and quite royally cheesed off at things in general, well there was no harm in that, he was cheesed off, too, for the love of God: Cheesed off he was, right and proper, just let Pats Bewley (or, increasingly, Tom O'Mallet) show his ugly mug within spitting distance!

Of course, there'd been the sadly predictable and somehow desultory play on his part for enhanced access to the hidden parts

---

accepted," he boomed, on the heel of this uninspiring tale. "Now don't do it again." "Apology be damned," screamed Toomey. "I've come for the woman I love." Well, now, was that a fine old how d'ye do. Ultimately the da had to escort the wretch from the premises with a pair of blackthorn sticks. Heavy curtains and a twenty-four-hour watch were the regimen from then on, but we found out later that Aunt C. still managed to slip out every other night and (I know, I know, who was the one who was ranting about probing into filth) snuggle up to Toomey as they both peered through their telescopes at the room she'd just left, and goodness knows what was going on behind them drapes!

of her peaches-and-cream bod, this en route to his place or hers—both, as it turned out, separately, sealed on the unromantic corner of Uphill Street and Maher Esplanade with the most chaste of sisterly kisses, followed by a furtive dive into the darkness and waving (or drowning—or just adjusting her hair, he couldn't tell through the shadows and the incipient tears of self-pity welling up in his eyes).

Since then: silence. He'd tried calling, and had damned nearly launched into manly invective at the placid unresponding recorded voice every time, but, remembering one occasion when he'd gone off his nut to an answering machine, not thinking that the lady he was trying to talk to would be sitting beside her phone listening in horror as his inflamed roaring "you stupid cow, why don't you pick up your fucking phone" modulated after the beep into phrases of purring obsequiousness along the lines of "well, hel*lo* there" and "hey there, guess who, why don't you give me a call," while the only call she wanted to make was to the flamin' guards . . . anyway, he'd caught himself just in time, this time. He did, at least, have a sound excuse for calling, apart from being so randy he'd get up on a ewe in a field: The job, of course, which was, after all, just a job; but it was, at least, *a job,* and he'd been out of one for only a week, something of an all-time record for him.

Yes, in the locked casemates of his bourgeois soul stirred gratitude, but this somewhat weasly sentiment warred with the fire-breathing dragon of his autonomous, all-male, hunting-gathering self that utterly despised and rejected jobs, normality, the nine-to-five, suits, ties, Kleenex, and respectability of every description[4] . . . *but the bloody job paid the rent,* and Penny had, in a very precise way, been instrumental in finding it for him. And he'd

---

[4]If you call that respectability. As far as I'm concerned, respectability belonged to the fella who just left. You know, the one in the electric-blue tie and threadbare corduroys? Can't recall his name.

otherwise be supine on his sofa, lachrymose and half pissed, with
the classifieds crumpled across his lap and not enough nerve in
him to pick up the phone . . . on the mental subject of which, Mick
turned from the window (after a double take taking in a rather nice-
looking damsel, say thirtyish, all in sculpted red, trotting trimly
from her colour-matched red Ford Octagon to the mirrored-
glass front doors) and stared at the phone on his desk, wondering
if he should risk the innumerable misinterpretations and false
starts of a call;[5] then, squirming comfortably in the endless cosiness
of procrastination, he decided not to, not just yet. He hadn't tried
since yesterday: Let her make the first move.

(Women never did, but . . .)

Well, he'd have a drink or so and call from home.

In short, things were grey, dull, worrisome, but just bearable, as
opposed to *nearly* unbearable, as they so often had been, except
when he'd had a purring six- or eight- (or once, twelve, that Bimmer
850, oh Lord what a morning) cylinder under his hands with the
curves of a real thoroughbred all the way through the Arnage corner

---

[5]Brings to mind one call I won't forget in a hurry. There I was, ensconced
abed with Kathy, when the bloody phone prrrps and interrupts everything
(not that much really: K. was going over some blueprints for the new treehouse,
and I was paring my toenails, slowly and methodically, as is my wont) and on
the other end of the wire I heard . . . nothing. At first, that is. Then, shallow
breathing and the merest hint of a risible "Ha . . . Ha . . . Ha . . . lo?"
Burlily, I sat up with arms akimbo and boomed "*Yes?*", frightening him or her
into silence, of course, and wasn't I well on my way to hanging up entirely
when the voice ventured again, with a bit more spirit: "Captain?" And would
you believe it, I wondered at first if it wasn't me he (or she) was addressing,
although deep in my heart I knew it was a wrong number (I never made lance
corporal, let alone captain) and, consequently, lost no time in bellowing bru-
tally into the receiver and, quite frankly, ringing off, upon which, my blood
being up, I promptly fell to fondling Kathy with the precise yet languorous
gestures of a florist arranging bouquets for display. The gal dropped the blueprints soon after that, let me tell you.

and the Mulsanne Straight, romping home to victory (i.e., never). . . .
No, the real nuisance, apart from having to have a job at all, was
Victor, with whom Mick shared the grey partitions, twin desks with
computers and phones and corner window of his half office. Victor—he of the impossible name, Hassan Dribble or Drool or something or other, plus Jones (or was it Smith?)—had come on the day
after Mick had started, shuffling into the office, coughing lustily,
reeking of Wintergreen muscle balm like an old-age pensioner
entering his final bedroom in the nursing home, regarding, therefore, all established denizens, viz., Mick, with deep and overt suspicion ("Who're you, then?", "Are you going to stay here?", "When
do you leave for the day?", "Are ye gone yet?") and already
whinging about something or other, possibly Mick himself.

*As if he'd expected to be ushered into a private wood-panelled suite with
a view of the Bay of Naples, silly owld git.*

"Bugger," or "ballocks," and hearty spasms of coughing, punctuated Victor's workday, and possibly because of this, or perhaps
just out of the innate sadism in dealing with their elders that lurks
genetically in the young, Denny and his cohorts paid greater attention to Victor, and what Victor produced, than they ever did
to Mick. This inhibited Victor in his loudly announced intention,
interspersed as usual with coughs, "buggers," and "ballockses,"
to simply spend the day reading old newspapers on the web.

"Useful, those buggers," he said. Mick reluctantly lent an ear.

"Who's useful, Vic?"

"Don't call me Vic."

"Sod off, Vic."

"I said don't call me Vic, you great bawling ballocks. Ahack."

"Sod off, then, *Victor.*"

"All right."

Mick waited for a small typhoon of coughing to subside, then
continued: "Who's useful, Victor?"

"Not who. What. Them old newspapers. I'm trying to get a few
together, you know."

"Old newspapers?"

"That's what I said, isn't it, what's the matter, are you completely deaf? Old newspapers."

"Great, Vic. Ah—Victor."

"Aye."

"So do you just pile 'em up in the entrance hall?"

"Pile what up?"

"The old newspapers."

"In the entrance hall? What entrance hall?"

"The entrance hall in your two-up two-down pebbledash semidetached in the suburbs, for Christ's sake. Where you keep your friggin' old newspapers."

"Now just a second there, you buggering ballocks. Who ever said anything about a two-up two-down ballocks?"

"Whatever. Your house."

"In my house, the old newspapers are in the study." Victor consummated his remark with a shout: "*In the study!*", as if the importance of that fact could not be overestimated.

"Well, that's a relief," said Mick. "Always nice to have a pile or two of old newspapers lying about."

This *dialogue de sourds* was terminated by the approach of Denny Tool. Tool was cool. In fact, in the boss's world everything was "cool" and/or "exciting." On formal and informal occasions alike, he sported, as now, a T-shirt and jeans. A mobile phone accompanied him on his rounds, attached to his ear like a bear cub clinging to its mum. Mick flinched slightly, inwardly, at the sight of Denny's black T-shirt emblazoned with huge pouting scarlet lips enclosing a red-and-white-striped straw protruding from another, more gleamingly rubescent pair of lips, the ensemble surmounted by the slogan, in neo-Gothic lettering, "Thou Suckest."

The mere thought of the existence of such a man was offensive to one of Mick's stamp, but the world was the world of the Dennys now.

"Hey, guys."

"Ah, Denny, good man yourself," said Mick, exuding the nervous flippancy that had always characterized his relations with superiors in the workplace, especially kids young enough to be his own. Victor emitted a complex coughing, snorting, and throat-clearing-cum-mumble in token of opposition to the diminutive form of his name (not, Mick couldn't help noticing, actually *saying* anything, not to this twenty-three-year-old prat whose word could heave two superannuated old fuckers like the pair of them onto the street in double quick time) and slowly and deliberately turned away to engage in a mock surveillance of the slow movement of traffic on the MacLiammoir Bypass. Denny didn't mind; Denny didn't notice (but Mick did). Denny Tool was too young to take account of whomever he was addressing, unless there was something—that is, money, sex, or power—in it for him. No, Denny didn't care. Something cool or exciting was coming along all the time. Today it was coolly exciting for him to announce the inception of a new project and concomitant "team," a word and, worse, an *idea* that Mick hated, reminiscent as it was of Pats Bewley and his goody-goody hill-climbing hearties, not to mention Mussolini, Stalin, Pol Pot, and Nazi Germany (NaughtyBoy *über Alles*!). . . . Anyway, today Denny was driven, to use one of his favorite locutions, by something to do with computer graphics-generating cinematic illusion in the guise of Whitney, a humanoid rat in plus-fours, the latest whelp of American entertainment-computer giant Thirtieth Century Colossus's corporate heavings: a blockbuster film for young and old alike.

"And they've outsourced the rat's outfits to us."

"Great," said Mick, against utter indifference in his soul to all company projects, teams, or rodentine wardrobes.

"Cool," amended Denny. "So I want you guys to lend a hand. This is really exciting news, and the two of you are going to be part of one of the most leading-edge concepts in the industry." He paused for the approbation that might have come from those less intelligent, or twenty years younger.

"Yep," he continued, unfazed. "Bleeding edge. So no more memos for you for a while, Mike, Vic. OK, let's get onto it. Mike, I need you to do a search for me. Check out all other rats, mice, hamsters, whatever, in movie history. We don't want any like problematic issues here. I don't want to find another little guy in like plus-twos with a lawsuit in his back pocket, you know what I'm saying?"

"Like, absolutely." The word was deftly ambiguous yet somehow decisive: Can do, boss! Ya can count on me, boss!

"And Vic."

Again the blurred mumbling half snort.

"Why don't you troll through some old newspaper sites on the web and find something on like golf attire from like the 1940s."

Victor abandoned his study of the traffic on the MacLiammoir Bypass and slewed around, his eyes for once wide open, as in awe. "Ah, old newspapers, did you say, eh, Denny?" There was a tremor of passion in his voice, and his use of the sprat's name was in itself a symptom of profound feeling.

"Yeah. You know, 'it happened on this day' kind of stuff. Old news sites, whatever. Educational sites, you know. Face it, this shit's all kid-driven, anyway. So find out what goes with plus-twos. We'd look like real assholes if we dressed the guy in like plus twos and a tank top."

"Ah," ventured Mick, boldly, "I reckon that should be fours, Denny. Plus *fours* is what your man the rat wears if I'm not mistaken."

"Whatever. That's your department, Mike."

"Um. I'm Mick, actually, Den."

"You're not kidding. Catch you guys later. I'll be expecting a like status report? Sometime in the early P.M? Cool. And guys. We might need to pull an all-nighter on this one, so cancel any like dinner dates, OK?"

As soon as the dread import of the little bastard's words had sunk in, Anguish, like a skywriter, scripted its unambiguous message across Mick's face (actually, down, diagonally, right eye-brow to left lower lip). He cleared his throat and raised a shaky hand like a timid schoolboy.

"Ah, Den. Sorry. Cancel . . . ?"

Irritation was the answering expression on the bulletin board of Denny's mug as he stabbed at his mobile phone. Mentally he was already well away.

"That's right, Mike, you got it, all leave cancelled until we have a mockup to show the guys in Design. It's your ass if we don't have something by six o'clock. This is a rush, so like—rush rush rush, guys!"And he was gone, hallooing heartily into his phone, leaving in the air (of Mick's imagination) a miasmic trail of self-importance.

Oh dear, oh dear, this wasn't right at all at all, mused Mick, in deepest agitation, split sixty-forty between noble outrage ("*How dare that jumped-up little shag-spot talk to me in that way?*") and mea-sly acquiescence ("Well, it was all part of the job, and a job's a job for a' that"), but noble outrage was gaining fast: *Tonight, of all nights?* He was forty-one, he was already knackered, and tonight was when RTE6 was showing reruns of the first series of *Ballykilloran Bells,* his favourite soap opera bar none, three episodes back to back, including the pilot;[6] and there was always the soothing pint,

---

[6] Oh, Jaysus, it's me all-time favourite. That jingle, sung by "Satchmo" Armstrong—or was it "Scooter" O'Noonan, the Castrato of Roscommon? *Bal-LEEE-killoran, Oh dose be-e-e-ells, dose bee-e-ells!!* Sometimes I sit up belting it out in the morning at such a pitch they're all lined up next to me bed, bawl-ing "Shut up," in unison. They said the din was only worse when the old fella used to fire his Lee-Enfield breech-loader over their heads at breakfast to test the acoustics of the kitchen (first-rate). Now, the TV episode in question was the one, if I err not, in which the bishop, already in trouble, trips and falls over Mrs. Spine, recumbent on the main street after her morning jog and subsequent health-giving dose of Powers, thereby precipitating the subplot involving the two of them being perenially at loggerheads until the season

the evening, via radio, at a symphony concert distant in space and time (tonight's dinnertime fare was a visit to Toscanini in New York, circa 1940), a good old read or so (Twain, Higgins,[7] O'Brien, et al., not to mention *Autoself* magazine and the collected works of Solly Mosses, Order of the British Empire (OBE), one-time Monte Carlo Rally champion and role model to drivers every-

---

finale when the bishop, by then defrocked, somewhat over-eggs the pudding by enfolding Mrs. Spine in his shirt-sleeved arms and pledging eternal neighbourliness. His reward: a right hook to the jaw. This was another sub-plot trigger leading to that evening's cliff-hanger and a nail-biting three months for RTE viewers until the next one in September, by which time Mrs. Spine, all cleaned up and wearing a divine leather creation, poses as an aging rock-and-roll legend (female), but the bishop (C. of I., needless to say), now in top form as a cyclist, matches her curve for curve in his maroon Spandex. You said it: there's something for everyone on dear old BB. *Oh dose bells, dose bells, dose wacky old bedtime b-e-e-e-llls!!!* No, it was "Scooter" O'Noonan, all right. I can still hear his fetid screech in the cavities of my noggin, especially during a quiet evening's meditation in the washroom, with the purling of the waters in the background and a clurichaun or two looking on.

[7]Twain, of course, and O'Brien, natch; but Higgins? Ah, Higgins, Higgins, we hardly knew ye ... Bert Higgins, that would be, author of *The Groin* and *Peas, Please.* God, what density of prose, what prolixity of style. Here's a sample, gratis, from *The Groin,* chapter 1: "Born in July, he was the ignoblest, least significant of the July-born, with the basest character of all God's creatures; hare-lipped and hunchbacked was he, with trembling horn-sheathed fingers eager to snatch. Pearly-grey was the ever-pendant snot on his nose, and loud his inhaling thereof. Other babes howled at his approach, and woodland beasts passed him with a snarl. Grown up, he was worse. No woman was safe in his vicinity, and boys gave him a wide berth as he patrolled, cackling, the purlieus of Ballymun, crunching between his black-and-yellow teeth a bulb of garlic, or codliver lozenge. Long and ragged were his clothes, and atop the wisp-crowned dome of his head perched a workman's cap stained with tobacco juice and unguents best unnamed. Flap flap flop went the outsized drover's shoes in which his malodorous feet were shod ..." Well, you get the picture. That's purely autobiographical, by the way. He got married soon after, and retired from writing, or so they say.

where), and of course (alas) the still-flickering hope of an orgiast's dream coming true, that any minute now the phone would ring and she (Penny or whoever) would murmur breathlessly, et cetera, et cetera.

And now this wee gobshite of a Yank speck of sputum had cavalierly tossed a spanner into the works. Boys oh boys. Man. The thing was an outrage, so it was.

Mick brooded. *Oh, how he longed to dump the job.* Well, the pay was decent, but not outstanding. And the hours, on paper, were flexible, and civilized enough. The office was OK, and the Internet was a gas. But Vic was a real liability, and all those twenty-year-olds ordering them about had a smell of decadence about them, like abusive minor Roman emperors (Pertinax, say, or Florius Vicinius), and he'd not counted on this all-nighter, well beyond the norms of the thirty-five-hour week mandated throughout the EU from the Arctic fastnesses of Spitzbergen to the Dodecanese Isles of Greece. It was the shaft, with knobs on.

Being of a generous, even gregarious, disposition, Mick tried to recruit Victor to the cause of proletarian exploitation. He'd heard little from that quarter, not even a cough, save querulous groans and the urgent, plasticky, and somehow moist-sounding click-click-click of the keyboard.

"Bloody outrageous, isn't it. What d'ye think, Vic, ah, Victor?"

"*Do* you mind, you. I've a job to do. I believe you have, too, mister me man. Didn't you hear what Denny said?"

Piqued, Mick glanced round the banks of computers and spaghetti or vermicelli tangle of wires, cords, cables, et cetera, at his office mate. Victor was hunched forward like a parachutist about to launch himself into the void, frowning in concentration at the computer screen, tiny miniatures of which were reflected as limpid blue rectangles in the maniacal sheen of his eyeglasses. His protruding tongue lolled limply in the corner of his mouth, from which mutterings of emotion also emerged. Mick took this display to be a token of concentration on the task at hand, viz., the long-hoped-for search for old newspapers, the silly old berk's own personal Eldorado.

"Gotcher fucking old newspapers now, eh, Vic?"

There was no reply, only the kind of rumbling semicoherent eructation of protest, followed by vehement hissing, that a badger or ferret might make upon being prodded awake, say from hibernation (or a long nap, just). Mick gritted his teeth. Outside for a smoke, he studiously avoided the gaze of the bright young things who trotted past; somehow, he felt, he exuded subversiveness, old age, obsolesence, doubt. He sighed, fanning smoke out across the air. There was a moral dilemma in front of him, with one way out: He supposed he had to keep the job. Enforced freedom from work was, after all, imprisonment of a different sort, and hobnobbing with the lowest of Ireland's low in the piss-scented and detergent-scented purlieus of the Employment Exchange was in itself a nightmare to avoid—and there was Penny, of course, and if he fancied any forward progress in that direction (not that he was betting the bank on it or anything— far from it—he already had his eye on another couple of likely dark horses, but being women they'd also be just like women in all their opinions, wouldn't they, the bloody women that they were) he'd better have a job to hang onto for a while longer, at least until Tom O'Mallet got him his job at Jocelyn Motors back (but contrary clamouring in the realistic side of his brain assured him that this last was a long shot indeed). . . .

Extinguishing his cigarette beneath his heel with the offhand panache of the seasoned smoker, he returned with the burden of true martyrdom on his shoulders to Victor the Newspaper Hound and Whitney the Televisual Rodent.

9

"Don't move, I have a gun."

Anil could scarcely believe he'd said it. For one thing, he didn't. It was only his minicam, concealed under his big blue McShiney's hankie. For another, he was a Hindu, for goodness' sake. Hindus didn't go around sticking people up, not in Ireland, anyway. But having said it, he couldn't take it back, or apologize. What would that sound like?

"Oh no I'm sorry my mistake I don't have a gun carry on."

No, it wouldn't do. *In is in,* as his uncle Arrunjee always used to say, belching into his jar; *and out is out* (belching into the air).

Yearning to be free as a belch in the air, Anil glanced toward the exit (a plate-glass-and-wire-mesh door marked "Exit," through which he caught a tantalizing glimpse of the rust-bedecked left rear wing of his old Escort and, beyond, a stand of oaks spelling Freedom): too far.

He was in.

And there was no time to waste. Goone was coming round, fast, he could sense it; but he could go the other way at any moment.

"Don't do anything foolish, now, lad," Goone said, raising a restraining hand. "We can work this out, man to man."

It was all Rashmi's fault. Damn the girl, thought Anil. She'd hissed enough inflammatory rabble-rousing blather into his ear to incite the whole state of Sandra Pradesh, or Tamil Nadu in all its teeming entirety; and he was the sap who'd fallen for it, and now she was somewhere else, in the west wing, he thought, where the Nissen hut was, raising the consciousness of the canteen serving staff. But she'd read Goone the riot act, and no mistake, my goodness his face was a sight worth waiting a lifetime to see, the pompous arrogance of the man deflated—pop—just like that, like a suddenly emptied bag of chapatis, or samosas! Then all hell broke loose, and the words "security" and "guards" were loudly repeated and doors opened and closed and people rushed in and out. That was when . . . well, Rashmi turned on her way out and mimed the gesture clearly enough, and he suddenly remembered that movie *Elephanta Nights*, with Sohrab Rustam, his (and her) favourite actor, where Sohrab takes a really nasty old Moghul rajah or maharajah hostage (now, all that would have been back in the what, eighteenth century? Nineteenth?) and forces him to take the tabla side of the *sawaal-jawaab* dialogue between tabla and sitar[1] while untying the poor bastards he'd had string up by their toes swaying gently in the hot winds of the Rajput fort like peppers drying in the courtyard . . . all this was madness, yes, but necessarily so, like the great battles of the Mahabharata.

Actually, the tension in the air was somehow, perversely, festive; it was like the spirit of Diwali, only instead of smiles and

---

[1]Ah, a lovely moment, that. Entire Internet pages are devoted to it, I hear. Expertly tuning his thumbs on the hollow body of a nearby fakir, the rajah (not maha-) of Bihar produces a drummed quilt of pure silken sound, in reponse to which the Rustam character (Jamil, stationmaster on the Chennai-Hyderabad line) extends his tongue, widens his eyes, and presto! He does a parody of the morning raga on the sitar, sans sitar: Triiiiiiiiiiiiiliiiiiiiiiliiiiiiii, or damned near, in opposition to the rajah's burburburburburb on the old man's stooped back in lieu of tablas. The dialogue sparkles with an economical wit: "No, Sahib," says the elder, at the end, on being ordered to make the coffee (no tea: too close to Darjeeling, thank you very much). He is, of course, soundly thrashed by unquestioning flunkeys while the chaps formerly hanging by their toes are all over themselves with expressions of gratitude. Just goes to show you, eh?

good cheer and a drink or two and a spot of roulette behind closed doors (and the lights, the lights, drifting peacefully above their own reflections in the mirror waters of the Barji-Ghapta Canal) all the doors opening and closing heralded spite, and shouting, and a horrid parcelpost load of pink English or Irish faces with lots, indeed splashes, of horrid freckles (one bloke in particular, by golly didn't he look like some kind of speckled lemur or why not, baboon while he was at it), staring, Anil thought mockingly, at the lone little Indian, "ye wee Ay-rab Paki-jobby," as MacWhippet the Scottish foreman in Wolverhampton had called him. . . .

"All right. Now."

They were in the office of the Senior Manager of Doormats. Goone was seated behind the desk, that of the late Senior Manager, Bulent Tülüy. A framed photograph of the now-widowed Mrs. Tülüy (a wizened chattel but loyal for all that) still occupied the place of honour, in a direct line of sight from the occupant of the swivel chair . . . that occupant being no longer poor hard-working exiled Bulent Tülüy, dear departed, and father of three (according to Rashmi), but:

The bugger Goone.

"Pop goes the weasel, eh?"

Anil brandished the minicam vigourously—*too* vigourously, because the hankie damned nearly fell off and wouldn't he be up the old rias of Bandipur National Bloody Park without an oar *then*, with Goone's beady eyes on his every move! The man wasn't convinced after all, Anil could see that a mile away. What he'd taken for compliance was prevarication, no more and no less. Best bring down the curtain on this silly Bhasa play, and fast.

"All right. Now."

"That's what you just said, lad. Feeling a wee bit nervous, eh?"

"Not at all. You know I have you dead to rights."

"In what way? Seems to me you're the one waving that thing about, and on private premises, too. And I doubt I'd have no trouble persuading the police that you broke in, oh aye. After all, where's your invitation?"

"Oh, be quiet, Goone. Never mind the police. I'm talking about the way you treat your employees. Disgraceful, and you know it."

"Ah, that's all your granny. Was it young Rashmi who told you that? Everything's quite aboveboard here. Don't they have jobs? And aren't they living in a civilized country, thanks be to God? And the class of insurance they've got is a cut above what they'd get back in Pakistan, I can tell you that, lad. And in a way, by the way, I'm not blaming you at all. Put that thing down and we'll forget it happened. I'll not press charges, nor even alert the guards. No, it's that wee cousin of yours, that Rashmi, now she's a holy terror and don't we both know it. And I wager you'd not care to have her working for you, either. She's a right stroppy number, so she is, and you know it, Mr. Singh."

"No. All that's nonsense and anyway it's none of your bees-wax!" shouted Anil, suddenly bereft of all patience and self-restraint. He felt stressed. He waved, brandished, pointed. The lens of the minicam was, fortunately, long and narrow, much like a gun barrel; if anything was peeking out, why, it could as easily be the snout of a Beretta, or a Mauser, or even a Changuli TT-36 semiautomatic like the ones they'd issued to the Gurkhas in that film *Loves of a Mountain Ghat,* starring Ranjay Vohraswami and Lulu Ampwatt. . . .

AT-AT-AT-AT-AT-AT . . .[2]

---

[2]Ah. Pure poetry. Reminds me of Jackdaw Place, SE1, where every morning was an operetta, and nighttime was woven of condors' wings: tat-tat-tat-tat-tat went the pile drivers, and tra-ala-lalalalala went I, in the shower most of the time, soaping down or rinsing off (and once, both, and not unaided, if you take my meaning, nudge nudge). Aye those were the days, and we won't see their like again.

"Now. Goone. Listen up." (As they said on that American TV show, the one with the swaggering black fellow in the leather mac who always lurked flashing his eyes in the shadows of those underground parking garages Americans loved so much—"Hey man, listen up," as he always said, maneuvering his shoulders in alternating fugues of American-style manliness.) "Here's what I want you to do. I want you to," suddenly Anil realized he was desperately close to making all this shit up, "to negotiate something fair for everybody. Write this down. 'I, Goone, will be fair to you forever.'"

"What the blazes are you on about now?"

"A full nine months Rashmi's been here and you won't give her vacation time. And the others. They're suffering terribly. That Turkish fellow, for instance. You hounded the poor bloke to death."

"Bloody nonsense. The man was involved in arms smuggling or gun running or something in his free time, did you know that? He was no Turk. He was a Kurd, or so they said. Sure wasn't I going to alert the guards anyway. And he smoked a million fags a day, that was what did him in. And vacation time, is it? Och for goodness' sake. Is that what all this is about? Vac time? The old summer hols? Benidorm, Malaga, and co.? They don't have enough? Let them go to Bundoran, then. They've a sight more holiday time here than they'd get back in Bangladesh, I fancy, you mark my words, son. But all right, if it means so much to you I'll give it to 'em, then. They can all have five days paid holidays. Happy, now?"

"Not unless I get the restaurant, too."

"Well now that's a horse of a different colour. That shifts the focus from the shall we say general, even humanitarian, to the personal, dare I say even greedy, you must see that."

"It's for me, yes, but it's for the good of the restaurant, too, and all the diners of Killoyle, and Indian cuisine, and humanity in general. Bloody hell. *You* can't run an Indian restaurant, Goone, not with all the pictures of the Taj Mahal in the world. You can't even make decent nan, for goodness' sake. My God you couldn't even spell Koh-I-Noor at first, do you remember? I had to re-write the sign three times. Now, I have money, Goone. Not much, not as much as you have, but enough for a down payment on the franchise. You know that. But you turned me down because I'm a nigger. Isn't that right?"

"A nigger? Get out of that." Goone, indignant, rose to his feet, but with the barrel of his pseudo-gun Anil gestured for him to sit down. Goone obeyed, but spluttered, "I never said such a thing. Nor are you. I mean, after all. You're a Paki, aren't you, not a Thingie. What flaming codswallop."

"Balls to you, man, big-time balls. Now. By golly. You must write it out. I'll pay for the franchise. I'm not a thief. But you must agree to transfer ownership. Or I am shooting you, starting right now or very soon, you know."

"All right, all right. But we'll need a lawyer here to draw up the terms. Why don't you let me give my solicitor a call and we'll set up an appointment."

"No. Why should I?"

"Well, you have to, don't you, man. If you want this to be legal at all. I mean I could sit here and write down the maiden names of all me seven married aunts and the names of all twenty-six of their pet budgies and it would have about as much legal author-ity as what you want me to write, in the absence of legal confir-mation, like. We need notaries, boy. And a lawyer."

"Quiet down or I'm firing at you very soon, you old Nazi." Shrill was the timbre of Anil's voice; emptier and emptier, he felt, his threats. He thought, despairingly, of Rubina, and how peril-ously close he was to disappointing her utterly. Face it, he self-jeered inwardly. You're an utter failure, you silly bloke. You've really cocked things up, now. But in for an anna, in for a rupee, as Uncle Arrunjee also said, usually (as Anil recalled, a catch in his throat) with his gnarled old hands over his eyes, late at night, when he was on his second hot chocolate Lassi laced discreetly with champagne (Veuve-Cliquot, none better). . . .

"Now, now, lad."

"I mean it. Bloody hell."

Goone heaved the heavy sigh of the much-put-upon, reluctantly reached for his pen, and poised it nonchalantly above an adjoining pad.

"All right. We'll let the lawyers sort it out later. Dictate."

"OK." Anil, feeling his bluff called, started sweating properly. At this crucial moment he had, of course, no idea what to say. Words welled up randomly like air bubbles from a frog in a mudhole. "I, Goone, or whatever your name is, I, Goone, do solemnly swear to abide by the ah . . . ah . . . ah . . ."[3]

---

[3]Good lord, is it ever going to end? I'll tell you what this scene reminds me of, only with a bit more pizzazz: That old lad with the grey crewcut and merry eyes, the one who lived in Paris and always smoked those foul French fags and was a lifelong Gaelic Athletic Association (GAA) supporter in spite of his being a Prod: Sid something, or was it Sean, what was his name now, Bennett? Burnett? Something along those lines. Anyhow, didn't I once sit through an eternity of a composition from his pen, down at the old Peacock of a Saturday night during those terrible days when they were renovating the PVC banquettes at the Abbey Mooney's and I hadn't the strength to go up to the one on Parnell Street . . . ? So there I was, sitting through something that they jokingly called a "play," by this berk Burke or Burdett. Well, anyhow, near as I could figure, it featured, exclusively, cunningly concealed stage lighting, i.e., near-utter darkness, and some unshaven old git dressed in a subfusc frock coat and a clown's striped trews hissing and groaning through his dentures, which were very loose, and wasn't he taking them out and attempting, toothlessly, while facing the audience, a rendition of Patrick Kennedy's "The Merry Month of May" that came out sounding something like this: O! PHIPEELLEEEEEEEEE-EEEEEEEEEEEEEEEEEEEEEEEEP-EEEEEEEEEEEEEEE-PIPIPIPILILIPHEEPEEEWEEEEWEEWEEPIL ILILILEEEEEPEWWWIRRRSS AND SSSSSAAAAA RRAAARRRAPLL LLLLLPPP AND PLLLLLBIBIBIBIBIBIBIBIBIBIBEE AND SSSSSS BIBIBIRRRRRRR IN MAAAAAAAAAAAAAAAAAAAAAAAAAAA AAAA AAAAY, et cetera; then, if memory serves, he put the choppers back in, turned his back, and for the next two hours or so confined himself to deep

"Following conditions?"

"I'll tell you what, you write it and I'll ..."

"Look it over?"

"Oh, do hurry up."

So Goone put pen to paper and wrote, training the corners of his rapidly darting eyes on the dubious silhouette of the putative weapon aimed now at his head, now at his midriff—according to the plainly agitated impulses of young Singh or Swing or whoever he was—and once, directly, at his crotch (ouch); if that's a gun I'm a ladies' man, said Goone, no fool, to himself, suddenly catching (he thought) a glint at the end of the barrel, a glint not as of metal, as might be expected, but as of ... *glass?*

A lens?

A camera!?

Of course! To film the cads in the act of torturing their wretched Third World workforce. It was a pure leftie maneuver. Only the Paki lad was impulsive, he had no idea what he was doing. That wee bitch had led him on, just, the way they do. *Time to act*, me *man*, self-instructed he. Still writing out his pseudo-legalistic nonsense ("and we the undersigned do pledge under these terms to fulfill our duties and responsibilities before God and man ..."), he glanced about the room, assessing points of entry and/or exit, noticing a shadow flitting past the door (A security guard? Wallfish? The girl Rashmi? Arab terrorists?). There was no one else in the room with them, the boy

---

sobbing, as evidenced by the up-and-down play of his broad shoulders, barely visible in the ambient dimness. "Bravo!" screamed the critics. "Encore!" hollered the pseuds. "Where's the jakes?" demanded I. Truth to tell, I'd take a tale from the Banim brothers, or one of Carleton's fireside nightmares, over this tripe any day of the week, Sundays included. Let me tell youse: that Burkett chap may have been a fine automobile mechanic, and the GAA are eternally grateful for his annual membership dues, always paid promptly on January 1, but he was no playwright, God rest his soul.

had seen to that, waving the camera thingie about; and Rashmi (who'd never work in this town again, for a start, never mind the thirty-one other counties of greater Ireland) was doing whatever she was doing over in the canteen, with the rest of the employees, rousing them to action no doubt, and in Urdu or Hindi or Arabic or whatever, by janey this thing could get out of hand if...

He needed the steady hand of his second-in-command. Wallfish, that was it.

Where was Wallfish?

Happily, like a djinn, Wallfish was there, as if conjured up by Goone's thought of him, barging awkwardly in, as was his wont, with his usual look of desperation, mouth hanging open displaying the bad teeth of a previous generation of Irishmen (chipped, orange, askew), perspiration befogging his glasses and, for no apparent reason, holding a half-eaten chicken sandwich in his left hand.

Anil snapped to attention and raised his implement.

"Who the bloody hell are you? Stop or I'll shoot!"

"But *that's* not a gun." Wallfish gangled to a halt. "*That's* a camera." Obligingly, the McShiney's hankie fell off, revealing the pathetic truth of the matter. "I've got one of those," Wallfish said. "It's a Nagano Triple X, isn't it? Great for sunlight scenes, but I've had a wee bit of trouble with the resolution indoors, like." He took a reflective bite of his sandwich. "You must have forgotten your gun somewhere else."

"Thank you, Wallfish," said Goone. He put down his pen and stood up. "Now I reckon we can stop this arsing about and get down to brass tacks. Put down that silly thing, Singh, and come with me."

But Anil, hunted, haunted, increasingly haggard, declined. Instead he legged it for the great outdoors and the venerable Escort, which, miraculously, raised no objections to starting. Driving at high speed (mostly in third gear, with desperate for-

ays into fourth), Anil made it back to Killoyle City just in time
for the early evening rush.

Saying nothing to Rubina, Anil hid the camera under a pile of laundry and hurriedly showered away the sour scent of madness and
humiliation. He then shaved thoroughly, with heavy application
of Geneva Nights cologne. An hour later, punctually at six o'clock,
he was at his post in the restaurant, dressed in his customary
headwaiter's garb: burgundy jacket, black trousers, bowtie, white
shirt with lace frills. Diners were arriving, three grey-haired couples
of peerless respectability, as smooth and suburban as an advert on
the telly, with the English-inflected voices of ardent BBC watch-
ers, or expats (or both). Anil glided as on oiled casters from one
table to another, distributing menus, silently hovering, miming the
smile of servility. In the kitchen the cook, Thackeray Singh, former
head mess officer for the Royal Inniskillings, was having a final
preprandial tussle with the dishwasher, Pedro, from Oporto (*anglice*
Porto), soccer player (centre forward) and part-time male prostitute, hired on sight by Goone one night down by the Western Docks
(Cherbourg/Brest/Quimper).

"Not very good, are you? Eh?" bellowed Thackeray Singh.
"One day I'll really be teaching you how to box, you bloody
shrimp, so be on your guard."

Anil peered around the door. Thackeray, a big chap (eighteen
stone, with forearms to match), had Pedro, a wispy lad, around
the neck in a half nelson. "Eh eh eh eh eh eh eh," gasped Pedro,
whether in anguish or pleasure it was impossible to say.

"Shut up," Anil said, hoarsely. "People are here."

In short, it was just another night at the old Koh-I-Noor—only
tonight Goone was absent, and every minute of his absence drilled
its significance deeper into Anil Swain's skull: Was Goone at the
police station? Was there a warrant out for his, Anil's, arrest? An
APB, as they said on those American police dramas? All ports

watched, posters circulating bearing a smudged but recognizable likeness? Would he spend the rest of his days in prison while Rubina rutted with half a hundred Irishmen? Was deportation the only solution? Suicide?

"I say," bleated one of the silvery diners. "I say. You, my dear fellow. Yes, you. Chapatis, please."

Anil welcomed the opportunity to explain the difference between chapatis, northern (Delhi, Jaipur) congeries of inferior crap suitable only for export, and nan, glorious unleavened bread of the gods, originally from Sandra Pradesh and Pune, that earthly vision of heaven itself along the fabled Marmagao Coast of the Arabian Sea. . . .

"But we always have chapatis."

"Well, tonight you won't. Nan or nothing."

Anil retired to the waiters' alcove, fuming, chewing his lower lip, fumbling for a fag. Briefly, he took refuge in the kitchen, where at least he could smoke and watch Thackeray Singh's mini TV set. He watched the news, smoking, torn between hope and dread: hope that nothing would be mentioned at all, dread that his mug would appear on TV screens nationwide.

"Hurry up with that nan, man," he snarled at Thackeray Singh, who replied—while toiling over the correct mess of condiments in the balti, or curry bucket—with an array of Punjabi insults beneath his clove-redolent breath. Pedro pouted, peevishly, surveying his fingernails. Anil snorted in disgust and turned up the volume on the TV perched on a shelf behind the sink. The news was being read by a reader he'd never seen before, some bony galoot with horn-rimmed glasses and a tweed jacket and a mouth like that of a stonefish.

"Stupid bloody twit," growled Anil. "Fishface. *Qus em'ma*," he added, in Punjabic Urdu, much to Thackeray's delight.

The main themes of the fishy TV man's disquisition concerned a failed, viz., nonfatal, bomb explosion in South Killoyle, courtesy of the Soldiers of Brian O'Nolan, a once-obscure but suddenly prominent splinter group; news from Brussels; free trade with Afghanistan, Kirghizia, and Mongolia; Gar Looney's latest sexual indiscretions;[4] the sudden death of a long-doddering royal;[5] the rising price of petrol; turf battles at a Bord na Mona plant in Co. Laois, at which point Anil felt his temper fraying badly; an Ulster rock band's demise;[6] a strike in a local factory. . . .

---

[4]I'm well up on these items. This peccadillo involved the headmistress of a girls' school in Offaly, soon to be featured on her own web page with links to ladies' fashion outlets offering for sale sartorial and decorative designs of her own creation.

[5]Ah, that would be Prince Anaximander of Wells, God rest his soul. His obituary appeared in last Sunday's *Ulsterbus Telegram*. I have it right here, as it happens:

"Anaximander Arthur Eustace Houghton Stoughton Noughton Isidore Pheidippides Oscar Fingall Flaherty Wills Wells was born in his mother's bathroom at Claridge House, then home to the Duke of Rathgar, on December 2, 1917. He was christened in the Chapel Royal, St. James's, in the presence of George V and three Queens: Mary, Alexandra, and a third who gave her name as Doreen. Two of Queen Victoria's daughters were also at the ceremony, Princess Ted, Duchess of Heath, and Princess Charlton, Countess of Heston, who was a godmother and held the infant Anaximander during the service. According to one report: 'the little fellow repeatedly relieved himself, with joyous spontaneity.' Other sponsors included the Prince of Wales, later Edward VIII, and King Alfonso of Spain. Wells was also closely related to the Swedish, Danish, Iraqi, and Norwegian royal families. His aunt, Princess Zeta of Tyne and Wear, was the first wife of King Faisal of Sweden, and he was thus a cousin of her daughter, the late Queen Cyrus of Cyprus. Anaximander ('Sandy') Wells was a playmate of the present queen when young and in 1937 was a front page at the coronation of King George VI. He went to Eton, and in 1938 was commissioned into the Grenadier Guards; his grandfather, the duke, was colonel of the regiment. 'Sandy' fought with them in North Africa during the Second World War, and in 1943 lost his right leg below the knee as a result of a wound sustained during an erroneous battle near Merguez, Algeria. Thereafter he made use of an artificial limb; his disability never prevented him from wearing the kilt, or participating in contact sports.

And there was cousin Rashmi, lunging like a Moray eel for the reporters' microphones, basking in her element as workers' saviour. It was *aux barricades* for the lass, it was Dresden '48, Petrograd '17, Paris '68 . . .[7]

"From 1944 he was for three years ADC to his cousin Basil Ffolkes-Ffawlty, Duke of Torquay, who was Viceroy of New Zealand. Halfway through his time there, 'Sandy' was lucky to escape with his life when his car became trapped between two baggage carts at Auckland Airport and was sliced in half, along with Sandy's left leg above the knee. This additional injury in no way dampened his ebullient spirits, and on his return he joined the Wicklow Irish Dancers.

"On leaving the army in 1947, Sandy went up to Brasenose College, Oxford, to read Bulletin Boards and the Racing News . . ."

The obituary breaks off here—tragicomically, I used the rest of the paper to wrap last night's fish heads—but I can take up the slack, having a good bit of experience in these matters. Later in life the old chap—Sandy, if you will—barricaded himself inside the ancestral manse of Hound Haven, near Battenberg Marsh, with strict instructions to the staff to shoot to kill, should anyone approach. Rued he that day when, per said orders, the butler and chambermaids opened fire on a merry yellow van that came lurching up the drive piloted by Rick the hapless Satellite Dish man, and they (the butler, an ex-SAS marksman, and two heavily armed chambermaids) riddling him with .38 bullets, thereby proactivating his pension plan and putting paid to the prince's hopes for crystal-clear reception of 275 television channels from across Europe, North America, Asia, the world . . . "What, no telly?" were His Highness's first and last words, on hearing the news. Soon thereafter a shot rang out in the parlour—but alas, he missed, the old fool, succeeding only in bringing down onto his head the massive oil portrait of his ancestor Prince Caspar, Duke of Chemnitz and honorary burgermeister of Karl-Marx-Stadt. Sandy, of course, had to be professionally put down, occasioning the foregoing news report.

[6]As I heard it from Kathy's nephew Dan Dunne, aspiring photojournalist/ jazz guitarist, the group was the Foques, a folk-fusion band from Limavady, long riven by dissension between rival factions: The pro-Israeli Druse vocalist, Sammy Henderson; and the Syrian-backed coalition of Sunni and Shiite Muslims led by lead guitarist Wolfman O'Byrne.

[7]Ah, indeed. "Bliss was it in that spring to be alive/But to be young was very heaven," as Willie the other bard (known far and wide as "The Udder Bard [hic],"), has (or had) it (where?).

"Complete shutdown, yes," she was saying, "until management have agreed to sit down and negotiate fair and equitable terms. We have a total lockout, and no scabs will be permitted. Management is aware of the problem but so far has obstinately refused to even discuss a deal."

Cut to management: Goone and Wallfish, the latter discreetly chewing, the former belligerently, overcoat flapping, taking on interviewer, camera, the world.

"It's an outrage," he thundered, "that a wee minority of spoiled brats from well, let's be honest, a Third World country, or countries, should be able to shut down a vital local industry like this plant and thereby imperil the livelihoods of dozens, even hundreds, of local citizens."

Anil nearly swooned in relief. God bless crazy Rashmi. She'd shut down the plant. A hundred employees were on strike. That was big news, next to which his ludicrous fiasco paled in significance. No one was looking for him; his little episode was forgotten. Goone hadn't mentioned him. Goone had bigger balls on his tray, as they said back in Assam (and portions of West Bengal). After all, what harm had been done, really? He'd waved a camera about and pretended it was a gun. That was it. He hadn't injured anyone, or made (really) life-threatening statements. No, it was well and truly over. His humiliating little crackup would have no repercussions, after all. Nothing would appear in the local press, no jibes would dog him on his peregrinations through life. It was true: No one gave a bloody damn.

"Thank you, Vishnu," murmured he. "Thanks a whole lot, man."

Shoulders slumped in relief, walking with the self-confident masculine ease of a Mastroianni, or a Sohrab Rostum, Anil gathered up a warm, steaming armload of freshly baked nan—rebuking with a sad shake of his head Thackeray Singh and Pedro, locked yet again in a nelson, or half as much—and returned to the restaurant, beaming, insistent in his kindly attentions to his diners, presenting them not only with nan but the finest, freshest nan, at, as he assured them, no cost to them.

"On me," he said, grinning. "All of it. So bloody well eat up, you jills and johnnies."

"I say, jolly good, Mohammed," brayed one of the silver-haired gents, measuring with his eyes the distance between his table and the door—through which, as it happened, at that very moment, burst the visored and helmeted Gardai Special Services Unit, Plexiglas shields in one hand, automatic rifles at the ready. They deployed themselves in approximate battle formation, all facing Anil.

"Anal Swine?" huskily inquired the first intruder. The black, gleaming barrel of his gun nosed toward Anil's chest like the muzzle of a wolf. Anil's only comment was wordless.

"Ah."

"On the floor."

"Good heavens," exclaimed a diner. "It's like the telly."

"Or Belfast," said another.

Anil hesitated, incredulous that such an absurdly cinematic thing was happening to him. It was like that TV miniseries they showed back in India, *Crisis in Calicut,* the scene where the Gurkhas, misled by a Chinese ploy (or boy), break into the gymnasium to arrest Vijay Sundaresan.

(*And what does Vijay do? He buggers off PDQ, that's what.*)

"On the floor."

"No."

Indecision suddenly gripped the human ironclads. One stepped forward.

"You are Swine, Anal of that name?"

"No. No swine here. We're Muslims. Anyway, restaurant's closed. Sorry."

With which, and a clear memory of Vijay Sundaresan's next move in *Crisis,* Anil hurled the remaining nan at the garda's visored face (the tray connected with the Plexiglas with a loud click) and turned smartly on his heel, following these actions with a concerted zigzag sprint in and out of the tables. The diners sat back, some gaping, others fumbling for their outerwear. Anil ran into the kitchen, past Thackeray Singh and Pedro—noticing, parenthetically, that this time Pedro appeared to have the upper hand, anchored as it was in Thackeray's turban—and sped down the rear corridor in which lurked sacks of rice, beans, and onion *bhajee,* and so out through the back door and into a dank courtyard around which the echoes of the thunderous pursuit grew louder and louder, punctuated by curses and, once, the hollow clang of a dustbin lid. Anil tarried not. He dodged nimbly through the darkness, hiding now behind this car, now behind that; most usefully, a minivan transpired, concealing him utterly as the commandos took off in exactly the opposite direction from Padre Pio Houses, whither Anil tended his step.

In short order, he had arrived home, apprised Rubina of that fact, divested himself of his waiter's garb, and stripped down in the bathroom.

"What on earth are you doing?" inquired Rubina above the volcanic hiss of the shower.

"Getting out, that's what."

"But your job."

Anil stuck his damp head out between the shower curtains. The leer of a mad Dravidian pixie played across his features.

"Sod my job, darling," he said. The leer, bad enough in itself, was instantly replaced with a mad-Moghul grimace Rubina couldn't recall ever having seen before. "Sod my job, sod Goone, sod the lot," barked Anil. He disappeared behind the curtain and began soaping himself vigorously, with bold slaps, as he began singing *"Mere sapno ki rani kab* (Queen of my dreams, when will you come to me?)," one of Rajesh Khanna's golden oldies (top of the pops for two years on Radio Sandrapore FM 95).

Rubina stood by in uncertainty.

"Well, will you be wanting dinner?"

Anil paused in his soaping, singing, and self-slapping. Was it a trick question? If he replied yes, would she say, "Then get it yourself"?

"Yes and no," he muttered.

But it was sincerely meant, and in no time, or so it seemed, they were sitting down to it (dinner) like the old married couple they were; only, Rubina kept noticing, his mannerisms were parodies of his usual ones. Instead of quietly tucking his serviette into his collar, as he usually did, he snatched it up with a flourish, snapped it whip-like in the air, and laid it across his lap like a saddle on a mule. With the wrist movements of a card player or conjuror he plucked a *pakura* from the pile on the table and simultaneously turned his attention to the pork *rogan jhosh* on his plate, chewing heartily, theatrically. On the television another face stared into his.

"Know what I mean?" it said, winking.

"I love this programme," said Anil through a mouthful of *jaggery* and coconut. "Know what I mean?"

"I know, I know," said Rubina, irritably.

"No, no, that's what it's called. *Know What I Mean?* It's a . . . what do you call it, a quiz show. You can win money. Look."

It was no good, he was mesmerized, whatever was troubling him—whatever lay at the root of his newly developed tics and leers—whatever was compelling him to snap at her one minute and stare with undivided attention at the idiot box the next—whatever was wrong with her Anil—would have to wait.

Although (she recalled) he'd been like this once before, just before they left India, when Bharjee Pal was really becoming intolerable, and things seemed to be going from bad to worse, and her parents were bickering constantly over everything from the way she dressed to the price of hair dryers and it was nearly impossible to get anyone at Air India to answer the phone, especially when she had to go and pick up their laundry three times a week and run the risk every time of having her bottom pinched by that dreadful Bharjee Pal hanging out of his office window with the *Hindustan*

Times in one hand, no doubt looking to see if they'd finally published one of his silly letters ("Dear Sir, When are you going to do
something about that whistle at the Tata plant? It's driving me quite
bonkers, you know"), while with the other hand readying the index/
thumb combo for action (followed by the most awful snorting and
guffawing, dear Krishna, why hadn't she told more people about
it? *Because she was a frightened small-town Indian girl, that was why*). So
Anil had been exactly like this before, it was the way he was when
something big was about to happen, or had just happened: Round
about the time they got out of Wolverhampton, for instance, and
headed for the Holyhead ferry, he'd acted strange, he'd been leaning out the train window with a leer on his face all the way, but
she'd hardly noticed at the time, that was during her first hysterical pregnancy ("Great! Terrific! What are we going to name him?
Rohit, for my dad? Aniket, for yours? Sohrab, like Sohrab Rostum?
Anil Junior? Oh shit, it's only gas!"), unbelievable the combination
of guilt and longing a person could feel at times like that. . . .

"Know what I mean?"[8]

---

[8]Absolutely. I mean this show's as real as my gran's mahogany sideboard,
I knew because I've been on it. Wait till I tell you. It was on an iron-grey
Tuesday, after work, with the spit of rain in the air from the east and me feeling the wee bit let down, like, after a long day's grovelling and incessant artificial laughter at the office, that I called in to the show and before I knew it
there I was in front of a million viewers, doing my best to maintain my dignity with the host, Pratt Wilkinson, ushering me across the stage and taking
care to (1) shove me hard in the small of the back at regular intervals (2) utter
a loud whinnying sound every time I attempted conversation, and (3) extend
a well-tailored leg and trip me up three times, all of this against a harsh, deafening laughtrack with the telly cameras trained on us en masse, each time, of
course, the applause-o-meter registering a little higher. Well, finally I managed to seat myself and was tending to my injuries when I looked up to see
Pratt rushing at me with a bread knife. Fuck this for an evening's entertainment, I said, and left, tripping over me trouser cuffs on the way. Later they
sent me a scarf and a cheque for nine punts. I ditched the scarf and donated
the cheque to the Seal Fund. I mean, honestly. (But look at their ratings.)

"Oh, shut up."

He paused in his voracious chewing. His lower jaw hung low. In his eyes was the expression of a trapped rabbit, or pheasant.

"That was him," pointing with a half-eaten *pakura* at the silly TV face. "I didn't say anything."

"Oh, God."

Briskly, he resumed mastication, as if on a TV commercial himself, demonstrating fraudulent joy at the taste of this oversalted snack, that bland packaged pasta . . . Rubina despaired, inwardly. Couldn't they talk, at least? Was that too much to ask? Was he that much of a slave to the television? Or himself?

But dinner was over before she could summon up the wit to propose anything of the sort. Anil, upon completion, summoned a cavernous belch from the just-replete corridors of his tum (something else he rarely did, thank God) and, cigarette already bobbing from his lower lip, he made haste to wheel the TV on its trolley from the dining area, or "snug"[9] into the sitting room. This chamber, slumbering quietly in the flickering light of Rubina's glass animals, was immediately jolted awake by the glare and blare

---

[9] I'm with you here. Reminds me of our old neighbour Mr. MacPhelimey, a pooka. His entire house was a snug, vastly larger on the inside than out; a dwelling fashioned of oak it was, or ash, with easy means of ingress and egress, and ample aeration for the volume of richly scented pipe smoke a MacPhelimey of the pooka class might emit, and did . . . and he was one of those, not at all common in south Dublin in those days, who could face several directions simultaneously, "the way," as he always chirped in his sparrow-like voice, "I can keep watch on the north- and southbound bus lines at one and the same time as keeping me eye on the clouds for rain, the meters in the taxicabs, the state of health of Mrs. Boland's old Pomeranian Ivan, and the front door of me own wee house in the event of unsolicited incursions." Later, he moved and his house with him, somewhere down the dell, a stone's throw from Ardee and half a mile from the tidal waters of Ballymaree . . . but I forget myself. Sure, these are *Indians,* boy.

of the television. It was Friday, a good day for televised game shows, *Know What I Mean?* being followed by *How Much Do You Want?* and *SuperNaff.* Anil sought asylum in that mindless realm of deafening sound and blinding light ruled over by ever-smiling overpaid gogglebox monarchs of (like ferrets) astonishing shrewdness but few brains, all arrogantly pandering to the insensate mass of viewers ("You halfwitted losers, how much money d'you think *I* make? Eh? Eh?" "Cor, wonder 'ow much 'e mykes, ven? Eh?") . . . But at least an excursion into this nonworld of entertainment enabled Anil Swain, briefly, to obliterate from his mind the events of the past few hours. Furthermore, he ignored the phone, which rang once or twice. Rubina, dishtowel reluctantly in hand, played back the recorded messages. The first, from Rashmi, was raucous and incoherent and communicated only the girl's excitement and ended with the words, "It's not an empty slogan, Anil." The other call was from an insurance adjuster who wanted to arrange an appointment to examine Anil's papers. Rubina sighed and shook her head. Something was up, that was certain; but he wouldn't tell her, nor would he even let her watch the telly. There was something more demented than usual about his fierce concentration on that nonsense. Maybe she should call someone, but who? They hardly knew anybody. The Indian couple they saw from to time, the Roybals (he a medical intern at Mater Misericordiae Hospital, she a physical therapist) were on their annual hols back home in Mangalore, and there was hardly anybody else. Well, that McCreek fellow downstairs, Anil was friendly with him, but she always thought the fellow was a bit of a wastrel, and she'd never liked the way his eyes started somewhere around her breasts and managed to wander south and north somehow at the same time, and more than once she'd caught him ogling her bum behind her back as it were . . . no, he wouldn't really do, but who else was there, apart from that Moon or Goon chap Anil was always going on about, his boss at the restaurant— and come to that (this had been vaguely flirting with awareness in her mind all the time), *why wasn't Anil at the restaurant?* Good God, it was Friday and they'd be chock-a-block, that was the expression he always used when he came home from a Friday "service," as they called it, flushed and, let's admit it, really quite bloody happy. There were aspects of being a waiter he actually enjoyed even if he wouldn't admit it in a hundred, no, a thousand years. . . .

Goone, then. He was the man who'd know. (Perhaps he'd sacked him, even.) She had to find the phone number, because she knew Anil wouldn't tell her. She glanced in at her husband. He was sitting in his favourite armchair, his knees drawn up to his chest, eyes wide and staring at the television, looking for all the world like one of those hideous king-monkey mummies they'd discovered in the Karakorams or the Hindu Kush or Kashmir or Uttar Pradesh or one of those places up north (and oh how the strings of nostalgia stretched taut for a second as those names tumbled through her mind from the long-ago days when those places were truly north of where she was, physically and mentally, somehow, and herself being south of all that, again both literally and psychologically; anyway, not having just a bunch of boring chilly places called Dublin and Berry and Delfast to the north, and what was north of *them* God only knew; she imagined very pale blond people standing around morosely in fur coats, with thatched cottages and dwarf pines on the horizon); he was smoking, of course, and still transfixed by some stupid programme . . . only it wasn't the ridiculous game show he'd started out watching, thank goodness; it was that arsehole-faced newsreader chap again, and he was reading the news, and in the background was . . . Goone.

Then he was in the foreground, and behind him was Rashmi, raising her fist.

"*Haila!*"

Rubina dropped her dishtowel, in which moist serviettes were wrapped. They landed on the polished parquet with a soft "blatt."[10] She watched in amazement and dismay, sensing a connection to Anil's sudden eccentricities, as Rashmi was interviewed ("the greatest crime an employer can commit is the one Emerald Mats is committing, and I mean exploitation of the underprivileged and turning a blind eye to common human decency and respect for human rights"), by now well used to the intrusive eye of the camera, glaring back with her own angry eye . . .

"Boycott," she bellowed. "Nothing short of a boycott will do."

"By golly she looks good when she's cheesed off, doesn't she," blurted Anil. Rubina, struck breathless by the remark—and *really* cheesed off herself, actually, at the brazenness of the wretch, sitting around slobbering over his little cousin while paying no attention whatsoever to his long-suffering wife.

That was it, actually. She'd had it. She gathered up the ends of her sari and stood directly in front of Anil, blocking his view of the television.

"Hoy," he said. "I can't see."

"Never mind if you can see or not. You're going to tell me what's going on, Anil, or I swear by holy Mahavishnu I'm going to pack my bags and go."

---

[10]Yiddish for "page," as in "a blatt of Torah." Sneaky, that. Worthy of my ex's ex-husband's great-grandad, Rabbi Flowerfield of Cork. Or one of Jumbo Wyde's oritundities in his best-selling *Zemlinsky's Chin:* "Magically, his neckpiece collared his neck as a collar might, per Byron, or Shelley, or another Romantic swordsman, all self and bluster; when lo, he was hanged, self-hoisted he, and his landlady alert only to the brisk drumming of heels upon a distant mantel . . . alas, alack, too late the police (Nazis, anyway)! Troutman was dangling, his jowls blue, his eyes all a-bug; gone was he, all because of an ill-fitting Ascot scarf and an aging coathook as obtrusive as a jokey footnote on an otherwise pristine page." Stay tuned for more of Jumbo, anon. (Or skip ahead to where it says "The End," my favourite part.)

He gaped.

"Oh, really? Go where?"

"Home. India."

"Oh, get out of it. You wouldn't."

"*I would, uncle,*" she said, enunciating loudly and clearly, "*And I will.*" That did it; she almost saw something snap in him. She heard it, too—*or was that something outside on the landing?* (She listened: Nothing.)

Anil sat up and shook his head.

"Now," said Rubina. "Tell me what's going on."

"All right, Auntie. Well, it's been quite a day, let me tell you. I hardly know where to begin, actually."

Rubina was thawing ever so slightly and he was sitting forward in his chair, not looking at the television (thereby missing the brief flit across the screen of a fuzzy facsimile of his own face purloined from the mug shot archives of H. M. Customs, Heathrow) but looking her straight in the eye as he did when he expressed thoughts of tenderness, or wanted the chequebook; ah this was it, she said to herself, he's going to come clean—

When ...

The front door crashed open and the Gardai Special Services Unit thundered into the apartment.

"Anal Swine?" roared the vanguard, as before; but, as before, Anil, much to everyone's astonishment (Rubina and the cops), was too quick for them. A shattered glass eland or gazelle and an overturned ashtray marked the wake of his passage, as did a deep fold in the Mughal-era carpet in the dining room and in that same room the French window ajar, admitting the evening's moist breezes and billowing the drapes thereby. The militia rushed over to the window and squeezed five deep onto the tiny balcony; but, as in an action thriller that takes chances with the audience's credulity, their quarry was nowhere to be seen.

"Swine?" shouted two of the helmeted legionaries, somewhat forlornly, into the indifferent night. Rattling past in the street below was a Panzer Laundries van, to the other side of which Anil would have been clinging, James Bond-like, were this an actual thriller flick; but it isn't, so he wasn't (although one or two of the lads wondered, briefly, frowning at the taillights of the blameless van).

"As if he'd turn and say, 'Yes sir, I'm here, come and get me,'" said Rubina, following her contemptuous comment with a snort of deeper contempt. "Whoever he is. Swine, indeed. Now you. Go get me a locksmith to fix the front door you broke, then get out of my house." (How she loved those words, even at such a time: *my house.*)

"Sorry, madam. We'll give you a chit for the door."

"Chit shit. Give me money, or call a locksmith."

"Actually, we're on duty, madam. That will be taken care of. And you are?"

"Bloody peed off, you know."

The young commando proceeded blandly.

"We're looking for the man named Anal Swine. Are you his wife?"

"I know no one of that name. Now get out."

"We can obtain a warrant, madam."

"Go obtain a warrant, then. But not before you obtain a bloody locksmith, do you hear me, young man?"

Great cakes of mud and a faint but insistent odour of vulcanized rubber were the mementoes of the departed squad (they were five in all, actually, although their bulk and noise made them seem twice, even thrice, as numerous).

"Goddess Parvati, what was that about?"

Rubina shakily cleaned up the shards of the shattered gazelle (or eland), mindlessly scrubbed away the mud, and drifted into the bedroom, there to remove—for the first time in months (eight)—a cigarette from Anil's not-so-secret hiding place: the onyx snuff-box from Chandigarh, where some silly Sikh third cousins of Anil's great-aunt lived (the hot Punjabi sun; the shouting of street-corner urchins; the strong pong of weed; the put-put of decaying mopeds; the confident lowing of kine). She lit up, eager for the therapy of a deep smoke.

Well, what do you know! Uncle *had* been quite the lad today, hadn't he?

(Deep inside, although she hardly dared admit it even to herself, there glowed a kernel of wifely admiration.[11])

------

[11]Well, I don't know about you, but I like a bit of cabaret. Hang on a sec, wait till I tell you, this whole nonsensical business reminds me of Chettie Byrne, back in Mullingar. One night a sot of an American author named Don Libby on a book tour crawled in her window booming out his name (*It's Don Libby it's Don Libby it's Don Libby-o*), having mistaken that particular window for that of the local pub, which was closed tighter than a drum at that hour (two A.M.)—as was Chettie, who awoke to your man's lung-top reiteration of his name ("Don *Libby*! Don *Libby*! O!") and, barely awake, found your man snuggling between her and her hubby of nine years, "Mole" Mullins ("Mole" was impotent as a beached jellyfish, but fancied himself the defining class of grand old rake and light o' love in many a wench's eye nevertheless), a bit nonplussed at "Mole's" presence, to be sure, but soon reassured by the voluptuous warmth of Chettie's substantial form . . . but I digress. Suffice it to say that the long-disused (indeed, dust-festooned) underbed shillelagh, a souvenir of St. Pat's celebrations in faraway Boston and New York, finally came in handy, and that the oaths of vintage New Yorkese that blued the air contrapuntally with the even rhythm of the shillelagh's thumps, were Don's, not "Mole's," although "Mole" had spent a fair wee while Stateside—Providence, Rhode Island, if memory serves—and was soon roused to action by memories thereof (mostly of dingy bars and dingier parlours with mud tracked in from outside and a mangy dog or two and in the background the perennial winking glass eye), but not before several visits to the jakes and a quick scan of what was on the telly ("Columbus" reruns, mostly, at that hour) . . . Chettie later filed for divorce, and last I heard was set to become the third Mrs. Don Libby. "Mole"'s a yacht captain in Monaco. Just goes to show, doesn't it.

10

As he was emitting, somewhat self-consciously, the standard, indeed clichéd exclamations of sexual consummation—*ohs* and *ahs*, certainly, and your token *Oh Gods* and, more Irishly, *Jaysus Christ*, lathered in sweat all the while—Mick was becoming mildly curious as to why his partner in passion, Penny Burke, lay so silently under him, bucking ever so slightly in counterpoint, responding to him not in kind but in short, barely audible gasps, as if straining to open a tin of tuna.

"Wasn't that OK?" he inquired, postcoitus, crowning the occasion with another cliché: a fag, flamboyantly inhaled and exhaled.

"Oh, of course it was OK," she said. "I don't know how long . . . oh, never mind. Yes, it was fine."

Ah, the liars, mused Mick. Eileen was the same (when she wasn't gabbing). They'd had a grand innings for the first couple of years, then what with one thing and another (her social life, his visits to the local, her bloody career, their stupid jobs) they just gave up; not that he hadn't felt pretty much as randy as before, in fact he'd prowled about in the kitchen in the buff, trying to get her interested but having the opposite effect, the more so with the steady growth width- and amplitude-wise of his now-several bellyshelves; no, it was just that some people, like animals, went on and off heat, depending on the season, and Eileen'd been one of them—and what was more, he suspected all women of being that way. Once in a while you'd hit one at the right moment, then *whammo*. Otherwise it was like this, great fun for the fella but you knew she'd just been being nice, so it wasn't much more than a grand old wank in 3-D, really.

But God knew it was better than the one-dimensional variety, with the intoxicating reality of kneaded flesh and . . . well, anyway.

They lay quietly for a time, admiring the blue light of the streetlamps filtered through the draft-driven whorls and wisps of Mick's cigarette smoke above their heads. Mick mused, as did Penny, each unaware that the other was musing, let alone musing about the same meretricious rodent, Whitney the Rat, without whose cartoon self they would not be carnally interlaced, or indeed in any way entwined; for Penny had made it clear (when Mick, unable to stand it any longer, had finally rung her up and learned that the official explanation of her prolonged silence was her absence in Ballycoughley to mourn the passing of Astro, thirty-nine-year-old donkey and the best friend human or animal that Penny had ever had) that she had no intention of socializing with the unemployed, so if he wanted to see her again he'd keep his job, Whitney the Rat or not, and be bloody thankful he had it to go back to, blah blah *blah*!

"In this world of wasters, try to stand out a little," she'd said over the phone, with a hint of the motivational speaker. "Swallow your pride. Jesus knows why you have so much of it in the first place."

"Only child," he muttered, not half narked by her tone, but he had dutifully stuck it out behind his desk at NaughtyBoy Graphics. It was true that he felt no great yearning for the prospect of unemployment, even in the shadow of Whitney the Rat, but life had to move on, and him with it, in tandem heading ever upward, or at least onward, wherever that might be (not the Sosh, at any rate)[1] . . . so, with a judiciously applied dose of arse-kissing at work that morning, even putting in an extra hour through lunch working on Whitney's wardrobe (Denny's comment: "Cool, Mike! Way to go! But lose that hat! And those pants! And that shirt, whoa! Start all over again, and give me a mockup by tomorrow lunchtime! Hey, catch you guys later!"), Mick found himself *in the course of a single day* given responsibility for:

1. Whitney;

2. Clothes for Doc and Drooley, a pair of orange caterpillars who had recently cut a swath of popularity across America's college campuses (but a panel of American educators with a streak of puritanism a mile wide had pointed out that the caterpillars were identifiably orange because they were naked, so it was now Ireland's solemn duty to expand their appeal with a wardrobe);

3. Victor, now expectorating with boring regularity onto the floor, so engrossed was he in his old newspapers on the web. ("Did ye know that Winston Churchill had a poodle? Eh? Can ye imagine it? Ahack? That owld ballocks with a poodle? Hwwwwikkkkk! Splat!")

And then, at the tail end of the day came the phone call, the dinner, *spaghetti alle vonghole* with Frascati and grappa at Signore Rimini's . . . and thence homeward, and wild scuffling of sudden disrobing, et cetera.

---

[1] Hang on there a sec, pal. I'm not at all sure about this onward and upward, oh-so-Victorian-progressive notion of life as a forced march to sunny uplands. Why, if I sat on my arse all day, or stood facing the wall, things would still happen, with no evidence of progression, and nary a sunlit upland in sight. Perhaps, I says to meself, perhaps a better analogy for things as we know them than the tried and true old life's journey (per Bunyan, and Chaucer, and half a hundred wizened divines) would be the doctor's waiting room, with at the end of it the diagnosis, good or bad, and a pile of tattered old mags—*GeoWorld, TimeWeek, Mum's Diary, Glam*—to ease the wait (but whose trite outpourings anent the latest elections on Bosnia-Herzegovina, or the slave kings of Ghana's gold coast, or *How to Raise Your Children in a Multicultural Society,* will bask forever in the half-remembered half-light of bum-puckering apprehension as to the good doctor's, i.e., the high priest's [or even, why not, God's], verdict).

Penny, too, was in the aftereffects of a daze, and could still hardly believe it—but somehow found it all too easy to believe at the same time, the way it was with sex, and banal encounters such as these. Yet in truth she'd hardly expected things to go anywhere with a man she'd sussed as a head-to-toenails waster and shirker extraordinaire whose only apparent interests—cars, writing articles about cars, reading car mags, travelling to predictable places like Florence and Capri, beer, beer, and more beer, interspersed with short whiskeys and maybe "a splash of *vino rosso*"—struck her as dull and mundane in the extreme. Still, she'd concede there was authenticity in it, and a genuine masculinity devoid of any up-to-the-minute affectation or trendiness. But it wasn't for her, it wouldn't last, and she'd lied just now, of course it hadn't been "fine," she'd had half a dozen rolls in the hay that had been twice as good, and she was no sex therapist, nor a Madame de Pompidou, but Mick McCreek was the kind of wham-bam-thank-you-ma'am kind of very Irish fella who'd get on like nobody's business with the da, or her brothers, or Uncle Fergus, which pretty much ruled him out as a long-term prospect for her, demanding as she was, sensitive to the soul and needy in ways Mick could never satisfy . . . and anyway, Alf didn't like him. Which was why they were here, in his flat, not hers.

And Alf usually knew, didn't he?

Good God, Alf had liked Derek, hadn't he, that one time they'd run into him, down by the quays. . . .

Sounds from without probed them in their haven. A dog barked in a light tenor voice; several cars passed at high speed; a moped stuttered; in the car park voices rose and fell, modulated by hoarse laughter; heavy footsteps suddenly tramped down the corridor; a door slammed; more shouts, this time from inside the building. . . .

"What's all that fuckin' din," muttered Mick. He stubbed out his cigarette and swung his still-sweaty body up and out, caparisoning his midsection in modest Y-fronts (blue).

"Just the neighbours," murmured Penny, flopping onto her side. "Mine are a noisy lot, too." (Had she walked Alf?) "And it's the weekend." (Yes.)

"They're never this loud, but . . ."

Louder shouts, followed by the dun-dun-dun of running feet on the ceiling. A faraway television voice was raised in sham emotion. A woman screamed. It was beginning to sound like a war movie, complete with the galloping of the Gestapo in full pursuit.

"Seems to be coming from upstairs," Mick said, approaching the half-open window through which currents of moist cool air insinuated themselves. "The whatsits' place." He lifted the curtain and peered out, feeling for no precisely accountable reason the roiling of concern in his gut (or was that just the letdown after, um . . . ? Hard to tell, at his age, at this stage). No shadows darted suspiciously from lamppost to lamppost, though, nor was anyone visible beneath his window, say in fedora and leather trenchcoat.

"No one there," he said, and was turning away from the window when a sudden human figure landed with a soft thud on the balcony behind him. Penny sat up with a muffled shriek. Mick slewed around, adopting for some reason an absurd martial-arts pose.

"The fuck? I'll call the guards, so I will."

The intruder, unfazed, boldly barged in, then hissed his name.

"It's only me. Anil Swain. From upstairs. Relax, Mick."

"Swain! What the fuckin' hell?"

"No, no, Mick. Please relax."

"Ah, relax, is it? Oh, all right then, if you say so. Please drop in! Have a cigar! Put your feet up! Turn on the telly! And meanwhile the world and his nephew swings in through the bedroom window like fuckin' Tarzan."

"Ah!" Even under the press of events, Anil had not forgotten his manners. He inclined his head slightly and pressed the palms of his hands together. "*Namaste*. Good evening, Miss Burke."

Penny smothered a chuckle, coyly concealing her nakedness

under a bedsheet—or rather, as a child of the postmodern age, *making a show* of so doing, with a knowing half smile on her face.

"Mr. Swain, isn't it?"

"Oh dear oh dear it looks very much as if my arrival was rather ill-timed. I do apologize, but the coppers are chasing me all over town, you know. I'm afraid I'm a bit of a wanted felon. A fugitive from justice, if you can believe it, ah ha ha."

Mick, reasonably, inquired why. Anil promised to reply but first insisted on closing and locking the window behind him; then he drew the curtains and went into the sitting room, there to request a cigarette and a radio. He then explained, boldly leaving out no details.

"Ah, poor Rubina," he said, when he'd finished. "I feel like such a bloody bounder, you know. And she's the goddess Parvati to me."

"Good for you, lad," said Mick with hearty blandness. "Sure she's fine, they've nothing against her, and this is Ireland, man, not bloomin' India . . . sorry, I meant Russia. Eh, Pen, could you pop up and check on Mr. Swain's missus, there, at all?"

"No," said prickly Penny.

"Very well then, I will, so I will."

"No, no. I say, Mick, do be careful, you know. Those horrid buggers might still be about."

"Ach, never you mind." Mick, emboldened by the first legover he'd had in a year or so, manfully dismissed such niggling, pulled on his trousers and sauntered upstairs, there to back away in fear not from heavily armed militia, who were nowhere in sight (although Mick fancied he did hear a hollow clunking, as of colliding rifle stocks, coming from somewhere above) but from a wide-eyed, rolling-pin-wielding (as in a lame fifties television comedy) and evidently deeply agitated Rubina Swain, streaks of teary mascara zigzagging Pagliacci-like down each of her cheeks.

"Where is he?"

"Ah, downstairs, ma'am. In my flat. Won't you, eh?"

When reunited downstairs with her husband, Rubina metamorphosed rather impressively into an avenging angel and clocked poor Anil a good one on the noggin with the rolling pin, per the best of Flintstones/Blondie tradition.

"Stupid," she shouted. "The police, is it, now?"

Well, it all came out, you can bet your bootstraps, over a pot of Mick's mediocre tea (bag-brewed Earl Grey). Penny poured, enjoying despite herself, in the heart of the moment, the sham domesticity—the false wifeliness—of it all, enjoying also Mick's plain enjoyment of same, his sidelong winks, his proprietary air (as long as he didn't go too far) . . .

"I don't know what came over me. I really don't. I just had it so much up to here with that old fairy Goone."

"Fairy Goone? You mean . . . ? Is he, now?"

"Oh, yes. Not that I care. Everybody knows. He lives with a chap who uses lipstick, or something. They're all fairies in the restaurant business. You should see the pair I have in the kitchen!" Anil sobbed, briefly, from nostalgia. "But never mind that." He sniffed and sat up straight, peering at his wife, eyes narrowed. "I was upset at the restaurant, the job, the complete and utter lack of . . . well, you know, Auntie, how often have we discussed this, for goodness' sake?"

"So you went and played Mr. Moghul and threatened to shoot everybody. With my *minicam,* for pity's sake."

"Well. Yes, I did. But my goodness, nobody was harmed, you know. And anyhow Rashmi's demo was the real focus of events, wasn't it? The whole bloody factory shut down, for God's sake, and she got them all to go on strike. My word. You'd think that would be a slightly bigger concern to Goone than my silly antics, wouldn't you? It was just because he knew I was after the restaurant—he knew I had the money but he wouldn't give it up—it was because of that that the blighter gave my name to the police. That's quite clear. The question is . . ."

"What the fuck do you do now," said Mick. Anil nodded, as did Mick, then they both nodded, spontaneously, in unison. Such was the sudden depth of their mutual understanding that they exchanged cigarettes in their newfound spirit of camaraderie and civility and, with due deference, each lit the other's fag, oblivious to the womenfolk and to the circumstances that had brought them together, both men of the world who could understand each other (and isn't *that* a rare thing in this life); smilingly, with many an elaborate inhalation of smoke followed inexorably by the dribbling exodus, via nostrils, of lung-filtered same, Anil offered up a prelude upon which without further ado Mick, like a long-ago long-bearded shanachie of Erin's golden West, started spinning a leisurely litany of long-forgotten (till now) memories and aspirations, all of them of, at best, marginal relevance to the present situation:

- His college days;
- The first deceptive hints of talent;
- That first test drive in Italy;
- The scent of a woman;
- The thousand and one things a fella had to put up with on a daily basis, like.

Which narrative enlarged itself ad infinitum, much to Penny's and Rubina's dismay, but this digression had the virtue of leading the women to exchange confidences of their own, and it soon became plain to Penny—who'd not have known Rubina from Eve before this evening, or cared to—that the gal was in no fit state, that she had a fool of a husband, and that she was no fool herself.[2]

---

[2]But how much of this was genuine observation and how much was woman's intuition, that is men are all bastards and we gals are just perfect, eh? I know: I'll ask her meself. Thinks: Why bother? I know the answer already.

"Did he come all this way just to go crazy?" implored Rubina, tears in her eyes. "I understand he wants to better himself. But he spends all his time looking up his bunghole, you know."

"Oh, I do see that, actually."

"Not that I'm unhappy."

"Quite."

"Because I married him, after all. Oh, it was arranged, of course. Bloody India, you know."

"Exactly." Just like Ireland, Penny wanted to say, feeling the impulsive Western-liberal need to make a cultural counteroffer, even if it was all ballocks: "Just like Connemara."

Then, in exuberant fashion, Penny sketched her life, with all its stops and starts and one-way streets and absurd interludes, in the midst of one of which she currently found herself. Ah, how life seemed even more fictitious than usual when she talked about it, on the one hand charitably intending to distract Rubina from her current problems and on the other motivated by a quite selfish need to, for once, spill the beans to a sympathetic listener who wouldn't pooh-pooh everything from start to finish or get up halfway through to make a phone call. . . .

"Astro, was it?' inquired Rubina, poised on that fine line between politeness and exasperation (but Penny seemed like a nice girl, really, even if she did go on a bit about her silly old donkeys).[3]

"Yes, and he was my favourite, easily. When I was quite young, oh not twelve itself, it must have been . . ."

---

[3]Well, I'd have to join with you on this one; I mean Pen's a sweetheart and that but get her started on her old donkeys and man oh man you might as well use the time to book a flight to Tashkent and have one of your suits sponged and pressed, while admiring the complete works of Jan Vermeer Van Delft on the one hand and making the salad dressing on the other, if you know what I mean.

And at the same moment Anil was trying to pitch a rare comment into the breathing intermissions of Mick's genial monologue ("Ah let me tell ya Anil—need a light? Sure, no problem, use mine—like I was sayin', conditions back then weren't what they're like today, I mean I don't know what it was like for you in India but let me tell you here in Ireland it was a desperate situation altogether, why didn't I actually contemplate emigration, preferably to Italy, if you can credit it?"), when the front door abruptly buckled inward and admitted a sudden crowd, wordless but rushing, with much creaking of oiled belts and the hollow bumping of gun barrels.

A voice thundered:

"Anal Swine?"

And seven fully armed members of the Gardai Special Services Unit clattered into the entranceway and took up positions, pointing guns. While amazed at the turn of events, Mick found himself, with annoying petty-mindedness under the circumstances, dreading the repair procedures, not to mention the expense—unless, he thought with an inward gasp of horror, he got himself turfed out by the landlord for all these ructions. . . .

"This is outrageous!" shouted Penny. "Police brutality if ever I saw it."

"Then you never did," said the cocky youngster in charge (Inspector Donalson). "Because it isn't. And you me lad, we've finally gotcha. Anal Swine, we are present in legal execution of a warrant for your apprehension as a known fugitive from the law. Hands up and over, *if* you please."

"Haila! Chaaylaa!" shrieked Rubina, reverting to Hindi imprecations in her emotion. "Bastards!" She hurled herself, fists flailing impotently, at the Plexiglas shield held up by one of the guards in a manner reminiscent (but not to her) of a Roman legionary. Strong hands bundled her aside; handcuffs snicked crisply onto Anil's wrists. Head bowed in the manner of a thousand years of convicts, he was led away and, true to the age-old form of the

scaffold-bound, he turned for a mournful parting gaze before disappearing through the door. Rubina gasped and sobbed and covered her eyes with her hands.

"We'll send someone 'round to take care of the door," said the commander. Mick betrayed his inner confusion by simply opening and shutting his mouth after the fashion of a guppy, or cod. "Everyone have a good day."

And they were gone, and with them Anil.

"Not to worry," said Mick in the awestruck silence that followed. "He needs a good lawyer to get out of this, and I know just the fella. Could ye get me the phone directory, darlin'?"

"No."

"All right then, I'll get it meself. Now let me see. O'Nan, O'Prique. Ah, here we are, O'Mallet, one two three four five six . . ."

11

In a scene of postbreakfast funk in Square-stairs, Judge O'Mallet's mock-Queen Anne manse, the judge and his boy Tom were sitting in their boxers (pink stripes for Judge Jerry, manlier azure polka dots for Tom) at the breakfast table, staring out the window at a clamorous circus of wee green birds tussling over crumbs in the crook of the 103-year-old elm in the garden, both O'Mallets uncomfortably aware that three cups of Mrs. Delaney's coffee had transformed their bladders into burstable balloons.

"Those lads bear watching, that's all I can say," remarked the judge, after a visit to the comfort station and a deep languorous sigh that coaxed off the dining table onto the floor a pair of doilies hand-stitched by the long-deceased lady of the house (New Year's '89, too much Babycham, ineptitude at the wheel, patch or two of ice).

"Ah, those wee birds?" said Tom, following the paternal gaze. "What are they now, starlings? Or, ah, sparrows? No, what do I mean, swallows? Or . . . ?"

"The Soldiers of Brian O'Nolan, you shagger, not the birds. Anyhow, time for them to be away soon. Morocco, I believe, the lucky bastards."

"The lads are off to Morocco? Well, that changes things. It's good news for the rest of us, if you ask me. Ah, closer to Libya, I reckon. Prime source of weaponry in the old days, eh."

"The birds," boomed the judge. "They're linnets, by the way. As you should know, having grown up in this house and garden and with the number of times you fell out of that tree beyond the counting of them."

"Aw, shut up, so. Birds be fucked."

In the awkward silence that followed, mental maneuverings, as of coracles through fierce tidal eddies off the Blaskets, steered the next installment of dialogue around into the shallows of the prime mutual interest, the topic that weighed on both their minds like a two-ton boulder on MacGillicuddy's Strand, and that without any possibility of confusing birds and bomb throwers: the storage unit at Killoyle Airport and its contents.

Judge Jerry was first into the breach.

"So you saw no evidence of tampering when you went out there?"

"No.

"And what about that boy Seamus?"

"He's on board. He thinks I'm Rah."

"What about the others?"

"No evidence of visiting."

"Visiting?"

"Aye. That lot from France, you know. Or Spain. The Basques and whatnot. What McArdle told me about. But let me tell you this. I reckon it's all cobblers. I reckon"—and here Tom leaned forward, as if eavesdroppers were teeming like linnets behind him—"I reckon it's the Belfast lads who're behind it all. Divil the chance they'll give up their guns and owld gadgets. You and I know that."

"So why do they need us, I hear meself askin', as if I needed to?"

"Aw, yer granny. Bloody obvious, isn't it. They need a smokescreen. A front. In case things go wrong. We're the charlies caught with the goods. Judge O'Mallet, once drummed out of the local golf club. Long suspected of involvement in blah blah blah. And his son Tom, grade A ambulance chaser. Also linked to, blah blah. And now there's this ridiculous toy army of Brian's Soldiers or whatever the frig. So hey, presto, it's off to the Curragh with the both of us and your man washes his hands clean of any involvement."

"Nah, they don't use the Curragh for that anymore."

"Whatever. The point is, we'd better take action soon or we've as much chance of staying unfucked as a pair of whores down the Strand on Saturday night."

"Do you say so, do you now."

During the silence that followed and endured for the length of Tom's absence in the jakes—a silence pinned to the glorious empyrean (for it was another fine day) by the distant thundering of Tom's waters and the merry chirping of the linnets outside[1]— the judge mused hard on the matter. His at-times unbearable brat of a spalpeen bawn was probably right, after all, he said to himself, sternly. They *were* being set up, the two of them, and by the best in the setting-up business, the maestri of framing, the Machiavellis of manipulation: The Belfast Brigade, who, to give the impression to the world that they were divesting themselves of all their weapons (they knew word would get out, they were counting on it, probably via paid informants in the local media and a tame garda or two) while in reality, circuitously, buying all that murderous shite back, probably (hopefully) at a profit.

A small fist of fear politely but firmly closed around the judge's bowels. It didn't look good, it did not. At all. (The situation, that is.) There they were, father and son, a nondescript pair of provincial lawyers with, as Tom had delicately pointed out, records of somewhat tarnished probity with which to seal the public's contempt when the case of O'Mallet *père et fils* closed behind them

---

[1]Merry to *you*. To *them*, screams and shrieks of competition, lust, and outrage, and may the winner take all, and devil take the hindmost, or more likely push him out of the nest to be eaten by a passing dog or so. An all-natural formula, no preservatives!

along with the great iron gates of Kilmainham Jail . . . or Haughey Circle? Or Crumlin Road, or Wormwood Scrubs? There came then mental excerpts from lurid films, some of black-and-white vintage: Papillon, the Birdman of Alcatraz, Colditz, the Krays; battlements silhouetted against turbulent skies; striped-trousered inmates; brutal screws, typically boasting facial scars of acne or drug-taking origin; tiny grated windows through which, distantly, a tree rocked its palm, seen through the teary eyes of the lifer whom hope has quite abandoned . . . No matter. The point was, such images concentrated the mind wonderfully.

"We've got to get out of this," muttered the judge. It was utterly unthinkable that he, Gerald O'Mallet, who had progressed along the usual path—Loreto, the Christian Brothers and boarding school, at twelve to Blackrock College, then triumph in the legal lists at University College Cork before being called to the Bar on the Killoyle Circuit, back in the halcyon days of the late fifties (Christ, he'd known Jack Lunch, they'd come up together, and hadn't he actually dined with the great man when Jack had convened a conference of hurling-playing judges, oh the steaming roast, ah the blushing spuds, eee the Black Bush on ice), then of course marriage and success joining hands as he himself had done with his blushing bride and beckoning him along the gilded road to the pot o' gold at the end of Finian's bleeding rainbow . . . well, life had dealt him a few hard old boots in the arse, right enough, but it was his own fault he, and Tom, were caught in the cold shadow of The Lads. That was the grand illusion for his generation, and their fathers', and their sons'. For all Ireland.

"Shite," he declared, crisply. The linnets paused in their feeding, then surged forward; then as one they paused, motionless as Household Guards on parade, then suddenly exploded upward and were gone. The judge wished he were a linnet. Simultaneously with the thought, Tom returned and there was a loud crash outside the side door, followed by curses mumbled in the coarse voice of Mrs. Delaney the housekeeper.

"Damn the woman," said Tom. He sat down and clasped his hands. "All right," he said. "I've gone through this in me head. We've got two courses of action. One, we can go along with 'em and trust that they don't deliver us up to the guards as bait. I'm not willing to take that chance, not with everything that's going on these days, the boat nabbed be the coast guard, them lads with the detonators. . . . No, we've got to outwit them."

"Very well, son. Easier said. Are you mad, so?"

"Yer a fine one to say that. Whose bloody idea was all this shite to start with? Anyway, if I *am* mad, it'll help, because we've got to think like nutters for a while. One thing those guys don't expect from their stooges is any kind of courage, guts, or originality, I mean they're terrorists, aren't they, they're brainwashed, and they're experts in all the infinite varieties of fear, but for a couple of their patsies to turn around and stiff 'em up the arse—that's not part of the game plan."

Well, the game plan as devised and revised by the O'Mallets was complex on the surface of it, like Mack Gilhoon's forward play in the 1994 Kilkenny–Armagh championship match, yet somehow startling in its simplicity and/or mind-boggling in its stupidity, like the policies of many a recent British prime minister, as follows:

Using Tom and Jerry's Continental contacts, Tom would move the arms about a bit, essentially from Killoyle to Crumstown with a couple of side trips; and he'd recruit a bloke posing as a buyer named Seamus who would purport to purchase the arms, with the O'Mallets casually transferring funds from one to another of various of the offshore accounts (Isle of Man, Jersey, Guernsey, the Maldives) they maintained for their own benefit or that of sundry clients. Then, after a few days, he'd pass on the items to another bloke, wired for sound, who'd sell them on the sly back to the IRA, recording the proceedings all the while.

"Not a prospect for a relaxing time of it," said Tom. "Right enough. But as you pointed out, we stand to make a quid or two once it's over."

"Aye. But bloody hell, I'm having serious second thoughts here, boy," gasped Judge Jerry. "I'm half inclined to say forget it, you wouldn't get me involved in a scheme like that for a million quid."

"A million? Bread crumbs, dad. More like six mil, if you throw in the Katyushas. Half for us, say three? They're bloody pricey on the black market."

"So why not just take McArdle at his word, sell them to the highest bidder, and pocket our percentage? Why this song and dance? Why this exposure, for the love and grace of God and all the saints in heaven?"

"Because they'll get us by the goolies unless we get them first. And don't forget them Pure IRA and Soldiers of Muggins fuckers. They're lurking in the wings somewhere. In any event, divil the chance we'd see a penny. Plus, we'd be branded the warmongers, not the Rah, and they'll parade themselves as the peacemakers. But if we sell the weapons back to the lads, and somehow manage to distance ourselves sufficiently from the transaction so as not to be fucked, actually, by our own dicks, as it were—it'll prove *they* have no intention of disarming. It'll make 'em look like the devious sods they are."

"And then they shoot us, so."

"In the old days, maybe. In Belfast or Derry. But not these days, not down here, and certainly not if we deposit a signed statement in a safety deposit box for immediate distribution to the media in the event anything happens to us."

"Oh aye. I saw that film."

"It's not a bloody fillum," boomed Tom, teed off right and proper, switching on the halogen stare—to no effect, as his da had patented his own version before Tom was a wee nonhalogenic gleam in his poor dear mum's eye—and pounding the table with his fist, gently at first, then, by the fourth blow, hard enough to make the crockery rattle. Another doily slid silently, despairingly, onto the floor. Mrs. Delaney appeared and disappeared silently through the side door.

"Get that out of your addled old Swiss cheese of a brain, Da. This is for real." (Hard transatlantic speech suddenly evocative of Bobby Lee Irwin, that pockmarked thespian genius; ah, the toughness that united them, true men all. . . .)

Net result, assuming they didn't get shredded into ragout in the process: Money in the bank for the O'Mallets; threatened exposure for the Rah; end of parlous two-step between them and us; and, most importantly, long life and prosperity to the descendants of Grainne O'Mallet.

"And."

"Well?"

"We need somebody to drive a van for us. I don't fancy schlepping the stuff out of Killoyle meself. Crumstown's safer. So we need a patsy of our own to drive the shite down."

"Who's good for it?"

"Oh, a moron of my acquaintance by the name of McCreek."

"McCreek, you say?"

"Mm. Ideal, believe you me."

"I'll drink to that."

They had no drink, it being too early for the real thing, so orange squash had to suffice; but high were their hopes (although threaded with wee doubts), and full-blown their hopes of redemption, that bright September day.[2]

---

[2]And shame on the both of youse, and may it be a long day of low clouds and spitting rain before the bright eyes of your sweethearts shine on youse again; and may the wind blow no good thing from the east, and the choughs set up such a clamour in the yew trees beyond the bracken that no sweet sound of flute nor whistle can be heard in the dales and woodlands of your townland; and may there be nowhere for the pair of youse to sit in the boles and crossboughs of oak trees; and may there be nought but stale tobacco for your pipes. And if all this will not suffice, then to the devil with the two of youse. *Go n-ithe an cat thú is go n-ithe an diabhal an cat.*

12

Cornelius was an impulsive young man (or woman), especially for a sexton. Mentally, he lived on the edge. He rarely, if ever, thought things through, buying, for instance (and he the joint resident of a hilltop house), an ancient lady's bicycle with one uphill gear merely because it was the right colour match (vanilla-aquamarine) for his study (eggshell-white, with blue trim), or bidding sight unseen £100 on a bronze bust of Antinous, the distinguished Greek catamite, only to discover it was made of pewter doused in brownish-gold paint, estimated value £2.75.

"Shit!" he screamed, peeved, and with his bare hands soon reduced the deceitful bust to a powdery deposit of lime.

The Rev. Granville Perker, minister of St. Derek's and Cornelius's employer, concerned as much for the public image of the church as for his mad young sexton's welfare, had more than once offered brochures and coffee evenings and outreach sessions in the chapter house, only to be met with freshets of spit and loud insults, some of which, the good vicar was sure, were in French.

"*Grand salaud.*"

"But Cornelius, I'm here to help. You know that."

"Help schmelp," snapped Cornelius, while scrutinizing in a

pocket compact mirror the sexiness of a new mascara. The vicar clasped his hands limply in an involuntarily symbolic gesture of inadequacy.

"But Cornelius, lad."

"Save it for the old dears who want a shag with their favourite vicar. I've promises to keep and tombstones to sweep before I sleep, *if* you don't mind. Tra la la la dee da."

"Could you at least turn down the music?"

In the background of Cornelius's black-and-purple-themed office thudded and groaned a recording of the latest megamechanical hit by Vile Bodies, the cross-dressing techno-metal group from Rotterdam.

"Oh all right." He turned down the din, then rose and spun 'round on one foot. "Vicar," he said, coyly.

"Yes?" The Rev. Perker turned on his way out, apprehension carved into his blancmange-pale features (incipient jowls, no jawline).

"Would you fancy me if I were a girl?"

"Oh, honestly, Cornelius. Get on with whatever you're doing now."

"No, honestly. Just imagine me with tits. Wouldn't you fancy a roll in the old hay then?"

"Cornelius!" shouted the Rev. Perker. "Enough, lad. Enough. You have responsibilities before God and man. Fulfill them."

With those ominous but essentially empty words, the vicar hurried out. *Counseling,* he said to himself, *the lad needs counseling and a firm hand. Society's spoiled him rotten. And that boy, er, man friend of his is no help. Oh, Lord, Lord,* pleaded the Rev. Perker, victim of a confluence of disbelief and nonbelief. *Help me understand the lusts of men. Or at least ignore them.*

But Cornelius responded instantly to his inner impulses, including lusts of a most bizarre stripe (to most folk), and was in intense negotiations with them even while sweeping the accumulated detritus of a couple of nights' rainfall off the tombs of

Killoyle's distinguished Protestant families: the Smyths, the Oxen, the Pratts, the Ovarys.

"Gina Lollobrigida," he breathed, imagining sultriness and curves like a guitar. "Yes, it's me. Darling. *Chérie. Carissima.*"

When he decided to take Fergus Goone hostage a short time later it was, therefore, a spontaneous decision that made no allowance for such commonplace trivia as bathroom breaks or the fact that he'd forgotten to do the grocery shopping or the existence of long stiff prison sentences for such acts. Mindless of these or any other possible consequences, he informed Fergus over tea that day of the new regime, and what with rashers, scones, a pot of black Oolong and the evening *Daily Clarion* as competition, he had to repeat himself twice to make an impact on his lover's consciousness.

"Eh?"

In token of earnest, Cornelius brandished his father's still-serviceable Maxim .45 service revolver (Royal Inniskillings, Malaya and Cyprus, 1949–1956).

"Did you hear me, Fergus?"

Fergus looked up from his newspaper, in which the name "Goone" in reports from the front was variously rendered as "Goom" and "Goote."

"Silly bastards. What's that, lad? What are you saying? And what the blazes are you doing with that gun?"

"I said I'm taking you hostage."

"Ach away. Finish your tea."

"I'n not joking, Fergus. As God's my witness."

Fergus folded first his paper, then his arms, adopting the attitude of the patient sage, or wise granddad. True, he thought, the lad does look strained.

"All right then, dear, it looks like we need a wee talk. I'm listening."

"Nothing to hear. Just that I decided to take a hostage and you were the most logical candidate."

"Och, I can't believe this." Goone briefly pondered the odds of being taken hostage twice in as many days. "Why, for heaven's sake?"

"I hate you."

"What?"

"You never give me any money. You use me as a vessel for your empty pleasures. I'm a mere sodomite. Like a Grecian slave in a Roman villa. But I've had enough. Now I'm taking matters into my own hands. Unless you give me a hundred thousand pounds, that is, which you could, because that stupid bloody tea-doily factory of yours has you rolling in the stuff, but you won't because you're such a tight-fisted old sod. So I've had to contemplate direct and drastic action. If they don't give me a hundred thousand pounds, I'll kill you."

"What do you want a hundred grand for?"

"Well, for a start, I need to change sex."

"Och, for Christ's sake."

Cornelius sprang to his feet.

"You see? I hate you!" he shrilled, brandishing the revolver.

"Get out of it," said Fergus, with hollow bravado. A second-rate vaudeville expression of extreme nervousness (eyebrows raised, eyes shifting uncertainly) played across the shabby stage of his face. "Put that bloody gun down and be reasonable, lad."

"Shut up shut up shut up shut up shut . . ." Cornelius was working up to an access of tragicomic agitation when a detonation rocked their eardrums. The air was suddenly redolent of scorched gunpowder. Shards of plaster drifted down like snowflakes from the bullethole in the ceiling.

"Cripes."

"See what you're doing, you wee eejit? Now put that bloody thing down and let's talk. First off, when did you decided you wanted to be a girl?"

"Not a girl. A woman."

Cornelius sat down and, somewhat melodramatically, turned his face to the wall, emitting long, low sobs. The barrel of his gun, still pointing at Fergus, wagged up and down in sympathy with his heaving shoulders.

"All right, all right, a woman, then. Jesus, boy, girl, or woman, I don't like this shite one bit. For one thing you're pointing a gun at my head. For another, there's the woman angle. Do you think I'd prefer it if you were a gal—sorry, a woman? Is that why you're doing it? Well, as it happens I don't like women, surprise surprise. I'm a *bugger*, boyo, and so are you. And a pair of happy buggers, we are. Or so I thought, and anyway that's how God made us, that's why we're here, and *I* thought we were reasonably well-suited. So let's just have a wee talk, shall we? And put away that bloody gun."

Cornelius slewed around. The gun pointed upward, tentatively, like a reluctant erection.

"You see?" he wailed. "You see? Not a *shred* of comprehension. If there were *anything* in all your talk you'd love me as a woman just as much as you claim to do now. But *no*. All *you* want is your wee *bum*boy. O ye of little faith, eh?" He aimed the revolver again. "Enough's enough. Call the media, Goone, or I'll splatter your brains all over that hideous wallpaper."

"Och, for God's sake. Cornelius."

An avid, expert, and long-time viewer of many a bad film, not all of them blue, Cornelius employed a gesture he'd only ever seen in the flicks: he pointed with the gun to the phone on the wall. He quite enjoyed the gesture—it reminded him of that Dutch actor he'd always fancied, Dyk Van Dijk, in *A Citroën for Vandervalk*[1]—and repeated it with a flourish; but the flourish, and

---

[1]Said Citroën seen only once, as I recall, in the middle distance, in front of the windmills, skidding across one of them Dutch drawbridges, with tulip farmers dozing on the riverbanks—and plop! in she goes. Van Dijk, I believe, went down with the ship, unless I'm thinking of another film altogether. (Unlikely, though, with that acting.)

the general atmosphere of high nervous tension, conspired to discharge the weapon again, this time with the household's daily to-do list on the fridge door as a bulls'-eye.

"Oh *sod* it," sniveled Cornelius. "How many do I have left?"

A brief slapstick scenario ensued in which Goone, bawling "Fuck this," made a dash for the door, knocking over two kitchen chairs in the process, and Cornelius, mindlessly chanting "*Hate! Hate! Hate!*" squeezed off yet another slug, this one zipping ominously near to Fergus's noggin as he ducked, lurched, fell to his knees, clasped a nearby overturned chair, rolled over once or twice and for the first time in many a year mouthed a prayer to the Almighty and/or whichever of His agents happened to be on duty.

"God help us. Bloody hell. You're mad, so you are."

"Shut the door and call the papers," shrieked Cornelius. "I've still got two left, I just checked. That's enough to take us *both* out. Come on, what do you say? A suicide pact? Lovers unto death and beyond? I can just *see* the headlines."

"Look," faltered Goone. "Why don't I give you the money and you can go out to Monaco or Thailand or wherever it is and have it done? Why go through all this mad carry-on?"

"Too late! I want publicity! *Shut up!*"

Goone was numb, as well as recumbent on the floor. But he'd had it, in his Goone-like way. Slowly he pulled himself to his feet, brushed off his knees, and righted the chairs. On his face an expression of stern determination arranged itself.

"I'll be arsefucked sideways with a meat hook," he said, coldly, "if I'm going to let you order me about in me own house, gun or no fuckin' gun. So carry on. Blaze away, boy."

"There you go again! See? See? *Typical.* Never mind *me*, eh? After all, what am *I*? Nothing but a wee *poofter*, eh? You see! *That's* the attitude I'm opposing here. *That's* what got us into this mess, Fergus. Your innate misogyny and hegemonistic chauvinism. When I'm a woman I'll show you, you just wait and see."

Goone tacked onto the truceward bow.

"Aye, well, who knows, lad? Or should I say lass, he he? Maybe when you're a woman you'll force me to go straight, eh? Tell you what, Cornelius—once it's all over, can I propose marriage?"

On his face he sketched an unlikely and unpersuasive attempt at a jocular smile; then, having repositioned the chairs, he sat down, picked up his cup, and blew nonexistent steam off the surface off his tea. It was a fine show of nonchalance, and would have been a model of restraint in itself; but, Ulster gambler that he was, he couldn't resist lengthening the odds against an amiable outcome.

"Well, what are you waiting for? Go ahead, lad, blaze away," he said. To add insult to injury, he even casually reached for his cigarettes; then Cornelius obligingly fired again. His aim was improving: This time the teacup in Fergus's hand shattered and splattered cold tea all over his shirtfront. Nonchalance went out the window, and Fergus did his best to follow, in a flurry of yells and churning thighs and more overturned chairs and much scrambling for purchase on the windowsill and wrestling with the window latch, never mind the twelve-foot drop; but sad to say, Cornelius was enjoying himself, and with his last bullet he took steady and careful aim before sending it on its trajectory directly into Fergus's heart from behind. It tracked straight and true, and the shot would have won Cornelius the gold medal in a shooting contest. Death was instantaneous; by the time he rolled over onto his face, having slid bloodily down the wall, leaving long wobbly crimson tracks behind him, Fergus Goone was well out of it, gone to whatever oblivion or punishment cell or flowery field awaits us all, gay, straight, and in between.

Cornelius stared, expressionless, then approached with the tentativeness of a big-game hunter. He even prodded the body with his toe.

"Oh come *on*," said Cornelius. "He can't be *dead*. Fergus? Get up, won't you?"

But he could be, and was. And lamentations followed, ex post facto plaints on the air of *I shouldn't have done it,* or *I made a mistake, can I take it back?* But no expiation was possible, nor could time be reversed, as so many millions have prayed throughout humanity's slice of it; because there was the weapon, emptied; and there was the corpse, prone between the overturned kitchen chairs.[2]

---

[2]You know, I don't know that I don't find all this blatherskite insulting, deeply offensive, and highly slighting of the great gay race. I mean, just because it happened's no excuse for telling us about it. They're fine men, the gay boys, all of them. I mean, good God, look at the buggers (as it were): Michelangelo, de Sade, White, Black, Grey, old Oscar of course, Simon the groper back in college (or was that Mr. Miller the math teacher?), Angus, André, Giovanni, Gianni, Piotr Ilich Tchai Bloody Kovsky, and God knows who else . . . how about that chap behind the screen at O'Meeley's, for a start, down on the Strand, Merv's the name, or Elton, or Elvis, or something vaguely—well, you know. Something in the way the eyes eschew an eye-level gaze during conversation and linger on the crotch area. Or the deft wrist movement. Oh, he's one of them or I'm a Cuban rumba dancer. Not that I've anything against, of course. Just think of funny old Rog Casement and his wee bathing boys, and didn't he raise himself to the highest level of martyrdom for sweet Ireland the green? God bless the lot of them and the music of their spheres, I say.

13

Next day, the O'Mallets and Mick McCreek conferred on neutral ground, like Israelis and Palestinians in Switzerland, in the cafeteria of the county courts building, against the aural interference of persistently clashing cutlery and the harsh gobbling of the underpaid.

"Well, now, I'd say this works out to everyone's advantage," said Tom, slitting his eyes Orientally against the windward drift of Mick's cigarette smoke. "Goone being dead. His company gets taken over by his lawyers, i.e. us, until a receiver can be appointed."

"Terrible," said Mick. "I mean good for you, but terrible, you know, in the general way of things . . . ah. Did you hear anything about Anil Swain?"

"Oh, he's still cooling his heels. Charges pending, you know."

"And what about, eh . . ."

"Your accident? No doubt it came up at the interview with the cops?"

Mick nodded, grimly.

"Well," Tom went on, "now that the fella that ran into you's been jugged for murder, I reckon you'll not have a great deal to worry about there. And by the way, could you sit, ah, downwind of me there, Mick?"

"Feck that for a lark."

Although semirelieved by the outcome so far, Mick was edgy,
fed up, in no mood. The murder of one man by another was a
perverse act of God, indeed, to intervene in behalf of Mick
McCreek's peace of mind. Stupid, so it was. Bloody stupid and a
thoroughgoing cock-up, in the finest tradition of life itself. So he
smoked in short, sharp bursts, aggressively. Some weekend he was
having, he repeated to himself like a movie tough guy (the inner
voice of Sam Spade or Philip Marlowe). First there'd been the
third degree down at garda headquarters in the morning because
they claimed he'd been harbouring a fugitive or plotting with said
fugitive to overthrow the president or some such silly shite, the
bleeding slow-witted Neanderthal cretins; the worst of it was, they
wouldn't even tell him what it was that the putative so-called
fugitive had done. Murder? Kidnapping? Rape? The doctoring
of reheated chapatis?

And what had that imbecile of a policeman kept on repeating,
like a third-rate actor (say, Vincent Edgbaston) in a B picture (say,
The Troilists [1947][1])?

"Never you mind, sonny. Just answer our questions."

"Sonny my arse. The name's Mick."

"Now, you watch it."

Well, that had dragged on until past eleven, by which time the
news of Goone's murder was in and the plods conceded that Mick
was, if anything, the victim of an unwanted incursion on the part
of said Anal Swine, purported terrorist—apologies all around,
muttered sullenly, faces averted like much-yelled-at dogs—but

---

[1]Ah, there's a lot of grunting in that one. Grunt, grunt, grunt, then a shot
of Wrexham Row or some other dreary cobbled alleyway in London's East
End. Spectacularly, the star descends the staircase two at a time and loses his
balance; then it's "Full Moon and Empty Arms" on the soundtrack and back
to the grunting—or maybe that was *me* doing the grunting, alone as I was in
the back stalls, one dun-coloured winter's day?

then Inspector Sherlock Neame, as bright a spark as any in the four provinces ("Ah, God bless us, it's not Mick *Creek*? And here I was thinkin' it was Mick *Greek!*"), uncovered damning evidence of Mick's heinous involvement in that stupid bloody traffic accident; but (and here fortuity intervened for the first time) Neame's sidekick, Sergeant McFay, promptly came out with the reassuring news that the putative victim, Frankie Feeley, Sergeant McFay's brother-in-law, as it happened—the wee jobber—was being had up over in Wales on charges of public drunkenness/urination and private soliciting of, and interfering with, a lady not previously of his acquaintance, wouldn't you know it, the worthless article, well why didn't Mick do the job and finish the stupid bugger off while he was at it?

"Bad aim."

"Then there's this chancer Regan the transvestite sexton up on a murder charge. Far as I know, he doesn't even deny it. They were, um, you know . . ."

"Drop the charges, Inspector?" inquired Mick, phlegmatically.

"Oh, I don't know. We'll keep 'em around a while longer, I reckon, especially in view of this aiding and abetting and carrying on."

"Feckin' shite. Ya ballocks."

"Now that's enough of that, sonny."

Left alone, Mick had then spent more time than he would have ever dreamed possible staring at a calendar on the wall behind Inspector Neame's desk, a September photograph depicting (presumably) the inspector's family on holiday: himself, herself, the kids (one of each). Bundoran, apparently. Yes, there was the promenade, there Obie's chippie, there the Royal Seasplash . . . Mick, too, had done his time in Bundoran as a youngster, with his mum running off the local girls and himself with an eye only for the latest dream-on-wheels, Escort GTs and tuned Lotus Cortinas the coming thing back then . . . anyway, that had gone on until one, then they'd sullenly let him go, and hey presto, who'd been

orbiting round the bulky planet that was Judge O'Mallet but his
son, Mick's putative attorney Tom, with whom he'd agreed over
the phone on a rendezvous immediately after the garda specials
had hauled Anil off to jail. Now here they were, beaming broadly
after a decidedly submediocre meal of spuds, bangers, and beans,
and Mick was actually being asked to go on a *secret mission*, for
Christ's sake, no cod, true bill, scout's honour, by the father-and-
son comedy duet, not precisely the typical programme du jour
of your man's up-and-down existence—although his existence,
once a saunter, had turned into a roller-coaster ride; and anyway,
this particular mission carried a promised pay-off of a thousand
quid . . . no, *two* thousand.

"Three thousand, actually."

(He must have misheard.)

But the charges would be dropped, said the O'Mallets. They'd
expedite it that very day. All Mick had to do, they said, was take
a couple of hours to drive a van down to Crumstown and back.
For two or three grand. Three. And three grand was three grand,
and driving a van beat designing clothes for cartoon rodents,
didn't it?

"And aren't you the lad for the cars," said his worship, inspect-
ing Mick's features in a disconcertingly dispassionate way, as if
scrutinizing a menu. "Tom tells me you've had quite the old career behind the wheel."

"Aw."

"Aw, indeed. Now. Wasn't there some kind of court case pending, as regards your reinstatement with Jocelyn Motors . . . ?"

Mick conceded, grudgingly, that there might be such, or its like.

"Well," the judge settled himself comfortably, leaning forward
on folded arms in the pose of a confidence-giver, or insurance salesman, "you know how these things go. I'd say there was a strong
chance you'll find yourself back in harness *and* well compensated
for the hours lost, if we can come to some arrangement . . ."

Mick protested, invoking NaughtyBoy Graphics.

"Ach, get out of it, you're not telling me that's any kind of job for a man."

Mick mused. He thought of Denny, and Victor, and the sartorial rodent. He heard, briefly, in his mind's ear, Victor's mumbling and hacking. He bethought himself of the old fucker's old newspapers, and the searing arrogance of the young Yank.

Then he thought of the Sosh.

"Well, it's a job."

"It's shite. Now listen. You see us right, Mick me old love and I can virtually guarantee things will work out with dear old Jocelyns Limited."

"And isn't it a fine Ford van," enthused Tom, "a '96, but well-maintained, with all service records. Oh, you'll love the thrust, Mick me lad. Like getting your leg over. Grand old six cylinder engine . . . or is it eight? Tell you what, you can have it when you're done."

Mick's subsequent gape wiped all traces of intelligence from his features.

"Have what?"

"The van. Keep it. It's yours."

Judge O'Mallet frowned and made utterance laterally, through the corner of his mouth.

"What're you on about? That van's not even yours to give away, you fuckin' young eejit."

"Shut yer gob," hissed Tom. Then, sensitively—and sensibly—father and son shelved their differences long enough to beam blandly at Mick, like the president and vice president of a regional bank posing for a publicity photograph. Tom went so far as to lean across the table and squeeze Mick's shoulder, an unprecedented gesture of amicability that only heightened the falseness of the occasion, all the more so when he overturned Mick's cup of tea while withdrawing the shoulder-squeezing hand.

"Ah sorry there, Mick." Brisk scrubbing with serviettes, then, "So what say you, mister me man?"

Mick mused, bemused; then, responding to the heightened blood that was coursing in his veins, he grasped at courage (or a lifelong sentence to mediocrity).

"Ah, no thanks."

"Ah, now, Mick ..."

"No discussion. I'm not the dimwit you take me for. I don't need a bloody great van, where would I stash it? Anyway, you haven't said a word about what you want me to transport and that's dead dodgy if you ask me. And I don't play if I don't know the rules."

"Ah, God bless you, Mick McCreek. A couple of things going out to our European colleagues ex-tax, as it were. Nothing major. Bathroom fixtures, towels, whiskey, things like that. Pretty run of the mill, only the two of us are that involved in court battles to see that things work out for the likes of you, among other things, that we don't have the time to take care of it ourselves."

"Bathroom fixtures? Towels? Feck that blarney. Semtex, more like. Or cannibalized car parts. Mother of God, you're the right pair of beauties, arencha. What do you take me for? A moron?"[2]

---

[2]Indeed: *qv., supra.* Incidentally, if memory serves, those were Cousin Monk's exact words when he was taken into custody at Galway Circuit Court for "disturbing the peace" during a concert given by the esteemed Romanian maestro "Big Enesco" Enescu, who was reckoned quite a catch for a quiet provincial place like the city of the tribes ... well, let me back up a little here and explain that it was always—at least as long as I knew him—Cousin Monk's habit, being a bachelor and therefore free of any constraints on personal habits or behaviour, to yawn vocally; that is, rather than stage the usual genteel "ho-hum" kind of yawn, or indeed to smother it altogether behind a fist or handkerchief, Monk would loudly transform every yawn into an exercise in vocalizing by affixing meaningless syllables such as "ah-la-la-la-la" to the underlying spasmodic gasp for oxygen. Unfortunately, the night of the Enescu concert Monk was that tired, having stayed up the night before to watch *Balzac II* on ITV9, that he was yawn-afflicted with greater and greater frequency. During the passage in Thaddeus Flatow's "Zeffirelli nella Trattoria" from *Topolino sulla casa mia,* in which gentle winds, whispering breezes, and mur-

The O'Mallets' dilemma was that of football club managers, say of Manchester United, presented with a dull-witted yet recalcitrant player, say Archie Rowe, whose abilities they nonetheless needed in a forthcoming match, say against Arsenal (5–2, in the event); salaries might go by the wayside, extravagant promises would no doubt be made, contracts could well be discarded and redrawn, all to placate the fool, who would only persist in his folly and get himself swapped to another team anyway. So they shrugged it off and let him have his way.

"Whatever you say, Mick. In for a penny," muttered the judge.

"All right, Mick," said Tom. "I only hope things work out for ya on the legal end. Well, we'll handle it, boy. You go along home and we'll be in touch."

Mick was unduly elated by his defiance. Seized by the momentary, volcanic self-confidence of the manic depressive, he rose and left the caff abruptly, not even turning to wave. In the wake of his departure, the O'Mallets commiserated, fleetingly.

---

muring rivulets are captured in the lapping, sublimely lyrical *adagietto*, Monk brayed "AH-LA-LA-LA-LA" at ear-splitting volume, unnerving more than a few of his fellow concertgoers. Finally, Signor Enescu turned around and waved his baton. "*Vai de cel ce merge singur că, când va aluneca, n-are cine-l ridica*" (or words to that effect), he screamed, his delicate Dacian features simian with rage. "No more 'ah-la-la-la,' OK?" Of course, Monk chose that precise moment to yawn again, louder than ever: "AH-LA-LA-LA-LA," he roared. Well, Enescu had a good old-fashioned tantrum at that point, as you can well imagine, breaking his baton and dialing for help on his mobile and all, and soon the guards were on the premises. It was at this juncture that Cuz spoke the words that led me down this stretch of memory lane. "Yes," was the sergeant's prompt reply, "'tis the felonious Monk. I know him well." Of course, it was only Sergeant Neeson, an old friend, and they whiled away Monk's brief time in pokey playing the radio and arm-wrestling. As far as I know the experience never persuaded your man to adopt a more discreet approach to yawning, but of one thing you can be sure: They're not about to rename Eyre Square after the great Enescu anytime soon. "Band of bashi-bazouks!" exclaimed he, flouncing off the stage and out of Galway's collective life.

"Well, kiss that one good-bye. You found a right corker there, boy," said the judge, with heavy irony. "I'll give you credit."

"He's not the first corker in the land of Ireland, nor the last," said Tom. "Although I'm willing to concede that he twigged faster than I'd have expected. Still, it was worth a try. Now tell me, Da. Wouldn't you take the chance to drive a van for, say, five hundred quid, if your only alternative were deportation to India?"

As Mick emerged from the front door of the courthouse, the tails of his overcoat flapped about his ankles, and gave him momentarily the image of a manly buckaroo, or Gestapo agent. Smoke filtered through his nostrils in roughly parallel streams. One hand, his left, was planted firmly in the left-hand pocket of his coat while its starboard mate waved a cigarette, and he cut a fine figure, for a minute or two, atop the courthouse steps like a colossus astride the world; but the wind soon assailed him and uplifted his coat-tails, exposing to that very same world the threadbare corduroys that barely concealed our man's spotted boxers. Concurrently, lank hanks of hair raised themselves in the breeze like a lobster's antennae wandering in the ocean deep. Too, were one to zoom in mercilessly, one might spot pimples adorning his jawline, half concealed beneath the heavy growth of three-day stubble.

"You look a right wanker," Penny had said that morning, re-coiling from Mick's ever-uxorious efforts to plant a farewell kiss on the little woman's cheek. "And you smell like an alkie."

A plain-spoken woman, by God, but an honest one; and wasn't it time after all for one like her, if not actually herself; a bit of stability, anyway, wailed Mick's inward voice. A little *normality*, for once, and never mind the hardships of the job, Whitney and the caterpillars be damned. Nine to five and the cozy common-places of home and yellow-lit window shades and the patter of loved ones and the weekend's devoted labours in fruit patch or rose garden. A pint of mild standing sentinel on the highly polished side table, a folded pair of gardener's gloves, a shaft of early evening sunlight, *The Pimpernel Hour* on RTE3, the autumn leaves yet to be raked, the lawn beneath them scheduled to be mown on the morrow—but not too early; there was always the plush warmth of the eiderdowns, the lure of slumberland a while longer . . . *wrong way,* wailed the voice, and Mick swerved to avoid a lumbering van—a Ford, actually, and a '96, or near enough.

Mick looked after it regretfully.

"Get out of my way," he muttered. "I'm the king of the road."

No doubt about it, he thought (and not for the first time), life went about its machinations in cute ways, entirely.

14

Alone of all his race, Anil Swain, having dismissed his court-appointed barrister, "a wet little monkey's dick" in the defendant's words, ended up awaiting another lawyer in a one-man holding cell on the first circle of limbo, otherwise known as level two of the Charles Haughey Memorial Internment Facility on Haughey Circle. Anil was alone, lonely, and depressed. All around him was brutality, and the unwelcome noises of strangers. At around noon, however, some relief and distraction were provided by cousin Rashmi's arrival. She came to stay in an adjoining wing, having herself been arrested at the gates of Emerald Mats, PLC, when, after deciding that the strike was "too naffing boring," as she put it, she grabbed a bicycle chain from a nearby bike and used the chain to (1) strike a passing security guard (Eamonn Salmon, father of three), and (2) chain herself to the rear bumper of a Gardai van (a '96 Ford), not without some difficulty. Once chained, she'd spat gratuitous insults at the normally placid plods who came to chastise her.

"Piss off, fuzz."

"Fuzz? Now that's not on, miss. You come along with me."

"I can't, I'm chained here."

"Here, allow me."

"Naff off, you fuzz."

"Now, stop that."

"Pathetic. That's the word. Just pathetic."

"What's pathetic, miss?"

"You are, fuzz."

"Fuzz on me arse. It's away on down to HQ for you, young lady."

Driven to gardai headquarters, she was booked on various charges (disturbing the peace, resisting arrest, insulting an officer of the law, squirming suggestively while in custody) and escorted past her cousin to the women's cells, hidden from the mens' by a loudly clanging gate and a flimsy cardboard partition of snot-green hue bearing a faded reproduction of Millet's *The Angelus.*

"Hallo, Cuz," she said, as she passed. Anil sprang to his feet.

"Hallo yourself," he exclaimed. "Bloody hell, Rash. What are you doing here? Oh, damn and blast."

"Shaddup," roared the screw, as matter of form.

"Yum-yum," lip-smacked connoisseurs.

"Your lawyer's coming," shouted Rashmi. "Hang in there, Cuz."

"Wotta piece," clamoured various whiskery hard cases for whom feminine attractions had long since entered the realm of myth. Wolf whistles and heavy breathing followed Rashmi's progress through the male quarters, then the gate closed with a clang and she was gone, plunged deep into the well of loneliness—for now. (Her solicitors and distant employers were already assembling bail, release notices, offers of cooperation, et cetera—but all in due time.)

Part-silence descended, that part that was not silence being the muttering of the ill-at-ease and the shuffling of feet and a distant radio tuned to flailing pop music, and the occasional roaring, gut-wrenching cough from the holding cell, captioned by a moist expectoration and the satisfying splat on the concrete floor of a subsequent mucus wad, or wads. . . .

"Oh Vishnu," Anil was heard to murmur, head in hands.

Later that afternoon, however, came another distraction: Cornelius Regan, heavily made up and wearing a taupe Bruce

Oldfield cocktail dress with matching suede gloves. This, quite expectedly, elicited howls and whistles from the man-ape fraternity on the male side of the wall. Cornelius's appearance also seconded the news of Goone's death, the initial details of which had been purveyed to Anil by a sympathetic young guard who'd once been engaged to a Pakistani girl (Nandeena) and who supplemented his gossip with regular copies of the *Killoyle Clarion:* "Guy [*sic*] Lovers' Spat Turns Fatal," boomed the headline, modulating the volume in the subhead to sneakily announce, "Dress Fabric Stolen from City Warehouse; C. of I. Sexton Charged."

So Goone's dead, said Anil to himself, disinclined to mourn, under the circumstances; rather, his primary concern was the hope that this unexpected, indeed farcical (if tragic) development would signal freedom, because with Goone dead and his bum buddy under arrest, who would bring the charges? But you never knew, and after all, back in India people rotted in prison for decades awaiting trial, Rubina's great-uncle Farwat, for one, now he'd been accused back in 1967, or was it 1968, of taunting old Mr. Nawar's dog Jahangir over the fence, and there he was, still an undertrial prisoner in Hyderabad subjail, waiting for his case to come up—although his lawyer wasn't entirely sure he was still alive, nor was he, come to that, and Jahangir had long since moved on to the next cycle of life, possibly as a lawyer . . . but this was Ireland, Europe, things were done more efficiently here.

Yet here, too, life could be chaos, unchecked by reason.

Anil held his head in his hands and rocked gently back and forth on the orange plastic chair in his cell that clashed so effectively with the dun drab walls and that gangrenously green partition.

"Oh, great Vishnu," he crooned, "give me a hand."

A hand, not Vishnu's, reached through the grate and, as in an emblematic First-Third World friendship poster of the socialist era, extended a packet of Woodbines, full strength, of course, and none of your namby-pamby filters or low-tar nonsense: Just the thing, good as a beedee, by golly.

"Fag?"

"Pardon? Well, yes, you know, I believe I will. I say, thanks very much. It's been a while since I had a smoke. I'm not even sure they allow it in here."

"That's all right, you go on."

"But who are you?"

"O'Mallet. Tom O'Mallet. Solicitor. Here you go. Filthy habit, but we all have our weaknesses, eh?"

Anil extracted, lit, inhaled, and exhaled voluptuously.

"I can tell you, sir, that I'm so grateful for just this one little smoke that I'm quite prepared to discuss anything you want—up to a point, of course."

"That's fine, Mr. Swain, is it? I want to make sure I get it right. Puts things on the wrong footing, doesn't it, if you start off by mispronouncing a fella's name."

The compliant guard unlocked the door, and Tom entered. Anil rose to his feet, impelled by headwaiterly instinct.

"Oh, my goodness, I know what you mean. Please come in, Mr. O' ... ?" Anil felt a momentary surge of warmth for this unexpected and amiable lawyer chappie. Who, once they had shaken hands (his exaggeratedly firm and manly, Anil's somewhat limp, given the circumstances), fastidiously plucked upward the knee creases of his pinstripe trousers, and lowered himself onto the unmade sheet swirls and churned-up blankets of Anil's cot.

"O'Mallet. That's right. Now, Mr. Swain. I've been following your case. I understand you were, eh, less than pleased with the court-appointed barrister."

"Oh, a horrid little wanker. All he wanted to talk about was racism and racial discrimination, like he had it on the brain, but I wanted to ask him, What the hell do you think I am, a nigger?

Anyhow, I canned him. Poof, like that." He snapped his fingers. Tom smiled and flashed the halogen stare through especially obnoxious upribbonings of Woodbine smoke that soon forced him to blink and wipe his eyes, thereby compromising the stare's potential. The wee bastard was a bit of a hard case, he could see that. Tom leaned forward, taking care, despite the smoke, not to blink again, and, like one of those legendary fakirs from Swain's own teeming homeland, he sought to mesmerize, to captivate, to draw into his one-man circle of power.

"Well, I wouldn't dismiss the race argument out of hand, Mr. Swain. It may prove extremely useful. But in any event I'm reasonably sure we can get this silly charge dismissed on the grounds of extenuating circumstances."

"Bloody hell, what does that mean? Oh, I don't like the sound of that, oh no, by golly, you're not going to argue that I'm a loony so I had no idea was I was doing, are you? That's not on, let me tell you right now. The family at home wouldn't approve at all. My God. Disgrace and banishment are bad enough, I can tell you, without adding being a nutter to the list."

"No, no, not at all. And that's the beauty of it, Mr. Swain. Extenuating circumstances can be anything you and I decide they are. A boil on the bum, or a wrongly installed microchip, or a visit to the chiropractor."

"A visit to Cairo? Chips? A boil on the bum? What? Please, Mr. Awmley, what on earth are you talking about?"

"What I'm trying to say is, we can work something out without necessarily resorting to desperate measures, although it's good to know they're at hand should we need them. Like the race angle."

Somewhat placated, Anil lit a second smoke from his first, again clouding Tom's halogen stare.

"You mean they threw me in the clink because they hate Indians."

Tom forced a cough, glaring balefully.

"Must you smoke that shite? Oh, all right. But no more, OK?"

"I say, listen to me, Awmley or whatever your bloody name is, I say, do fuck off, won't you? I mean, honestly, here you are, barging into my prison cell and offering me fags and then telling me not to smoke, then inquiring if I have a boil on my bum. My goodness, what are you, some kind of loony or pervert, I'm thinking, eh?" Anil fumed and smoked simultaneously. "There's no way around it, you know. Every time I set foot outside I'm jiggered, and that's all there is to it." Tears shimmered. "Plus, in here, they won't let me watch television. I can't begin to tell you how many programmes I've missed." Tears welled higher at the thought of his telly and the normality it represented. He imagined it standing silent and despised in its corner at home, gazed upon contemptuously by Rubina's glass animals, bereft and abandoned like the household gods of the Dravidians, or, for that matter, its owner. . . .

Tom raised his hands, palms out, in a priest-like gesture of benevolence and calm.

"Now, now, Mr. Swain."

"Now, now, yourself." Anil, his feet tapdancing in distress, turned his back on the now-annoying lawyer and stared across at the next cell, where a game of draughts was in progress between Ironman Smyth and his cell mate (and second-in command of the Munster Aryans, according to prison chitchat) Pewterhead O'Gorman. Both were in a holding cell awaiting trial on charges of bank robbery. Neither had shown racist, or homosexual, tendencies, thus far; but of course Anil had only been a jailbird for a couple of days, and there was certainly plenty of time for anything to happen. Like this buffoon of a lawyer suddenly popping up and waving his fags about . . .

Ormlet, was it? Anil half glanced over his shoulder.

"I say, Ormlet, have you spoken to my wife?"

"No, I haven't. But I'm here to tell you that I can do a whole lot better than that, Mr. Swain . . . actually, that sounds awfully formal. May I call you Anil?"

"Call me what you please. Just make sure you pronounce it right."

"Ah-*neel*?"

"Close enough."

Tom swallowed and applied himself.

"You know, Anil, in the world of the law, here in Ireland and, well, in India, too, I expect, there are such things as compromises and even, well, agreements, not to say deals, that reasonable people work out among themselves. Now, I'm sure you're aware, just by looking around you, that you're at the end of a fairly long queue as far as coming up for trial is concerned. Why, they hadn't even assigned you a new lawyer until I turned up."

"Just like India."

"Exactly. But we want you to get out as soon as possible, eh?"

"Well, Mr. Ormlet, I do, certainly. But I don't know what you want."

"Whatever's good for you."

"Oh, for goodness' sake. Do bleeding well bugger off, there's a good chap. And get me a television, will you?"

Further dialogue of a sentimental nature only contributed to the retrograde quality of the proceedings, and Tom was beginning to wonder if there was any way to win over this recalcitrant and rather truculent wee Paki bastard, the workings of whose back and shoulderblades he had ample time to contemplate as the sod sat hunched away and smoking a *third* filthy fag . . . there appeared to be no swift means of ingress into the man's heart, at least not on the route traditionally taken by the usual Western liberal guilt tripper, such trip deftly sidestepped and circumvented with moral absolutism by the vain and testy Swain ("What the hell do you know about racism, anyway, Ormlet? Are you black? And what do you care if I'm discriminated against?").

It was then that Tom, at the end of his tether, decided— like Pétain at Verdun, or Maradona in the '78 World Cup— that a direct attack was the best—no, the *only*—way, so without further ado he gathered up his haunches, metaphorically speaking, and launched a leap of faith into the moral darkness beyond.

"All right, never mind all that. Tell me this, Swain. Can you drive a van?"

"Of course I can drive a bloody van."

"Then I can get you out of here."

"Can I have the restaurant, too?"

Tom was nonplused, but Anil soon explained, sandpapering eager hands. The franchise would be up for bids, he said; so why shouldn't he have it?

"Well, for a start, because you have a criminal record," explained Tom, who was only beginning to gauge correctly the depth and breadth of this Indian's eccentric ways—and yet, there was cunning there, and no lack of "intestinal fortitude" (as Bobby Lee Irwin might say, closing his fist in, and on, the air). "Secondly, because you have no money."

"But I don't need money. I want you to get it for me. Or you can shove your bloody van up your arse."

Their negotiations were soon over amid soothing benisons of Tom's legalistic half promises. Miraculously, a couple of brief phone calls soon determined that Judge Jerry O'Mallet had managed to sweep clean a few dockets in District Court that afternoon: nothing more serious awaited his ruling than two cases of drunkenness public and private and one of public lewdness (viz., a heavyweight pub denizen well known to local law enforcement nabbed for loud smacking of lips and suggestive gestures, mostly

arm-folding, up and down, while waiting outside Heron's Minimart
for the 2:44 to Newmanstown[1]).

At four o'clock that afternoon, Tom O'Mallet's legal partner,
the noted barrister and ex-Miss Tipperary Mary Rose Ryan,
followed by a slump-shouldered Anil Swain, swept majestically
into the gray drabness of courtroom number three, Killoyle
District Court, Jerry O'Mallet's favourite courtroom for its view,
through phony leaded windows, of the spire of Laddi's Disco,
and for its proximity to Oliver's House of Giant Oysters across
the street, as well as for its relative proximity (two streets away)
to Mad Molloy's, the poteen tavern with its famous (or infamous,
depending where you come from, or in) games room in the
back, absolutely no applicants, Catholic, Protestant, Jew, or
dissenter, under the age of eighteen, or before the hour of ten
post meridien. . . .

In the background, rendering most conversation inaudible, was
the exuberant purring of Frank Sinatra at Madison Square Garden in the early spring of 1967. Mrs. Ryan pouted, so the judge
reached under his podium and made fiddling motions as of turning down volume controls, and it was softly thereafter that Sinatra
could be heard, declaiming in the purity of his middle period
anent girls with perfumed hair.

"Ah, Mrs. Ryan, this would be the redoutable Mr. Swain, I
take it?" boomed his judgeship jovially, beaming. He turned to
the accused, tentatively flashing hints of the xenon stare he'd

---

[1] I expect the local rag has a piece on that, but I haven't been able to turn
it up. However, as one of the few surviving eyewitnesses, I can attest to the
aggressiveness of said gestures, obnoxiously accompanied as they were by
lips alternately puckered and pouting and explicit hip swaying—some *sayan*
actual rendition of the Hawaiian welcome dance, especially unattractive in a
great hulking slob weighing fourteen stone and standing six-three in his bare
feet.

been working on in the shaving mirror all morning. It was quite a job, as the judge had discovered, for unlike the halogen, which merely required unblinkingness, the xenon demanded opening the eyelids as widely as possible so as to convey the impression, if not the reality,[2] of their (the eyeballs') near-bulging out, with the intention of inspiring doubt as to the mental stability of their owner and concern, even fear, in one's interlocutor . . . but Anil, at least, was unintimidated, uninterested, uninvolved. A deep Hindu resignation had taken root in his soul, consigning pretty

---

[2]See *Being Nothing,* by Jean-Paul Prawn, Vol. 2, p. 123: "Suddenly an organ-grinder in the street below began to crank his instrument, eliciting shrieks from his monkey. Such was the shock of this sudden assault on his sensibilities, and his corollary realization of the horrors of existence, that Julien's eyes froze in their orbits and became thereby permanently fixed in splayed dispositions: the left, pointing symbolically leftward; the right, alas, to the right . . ." Prawn always did his best work while napping facedown, I'm told, and soon came to adopt that posture permanently, causing his girlfriend Sinead (or was it Sylvie?) to move out and take up with, well quite a series of lads, I'm afraid, starting with Monty Pea, that muscular bluejeaned American worker-poet of hers, and moving briskly along to Nicéphore, the languid Verlaine-spouting doorman from the VII arrondissement, Dario the craggy Italian bird-tamer, a weatherbeaten Greek ferryman named F. Kharistopolis, that manly Spanish gentleman farmer Andrés Garcia y Garcia de Vino Tinto y Un Poco Mas, a relatively obscure alcoholic Swiss portraitist named Uli-Peter Tschüdi, a few solipsistic English actors—Nigel, Ken, Tony, Sid, that lot—and even a greyish, dour, ludic Irish man of letters who lived around the corner from the Santé prison, a playwright or poet or some such, a quare old article of Saxon or Runic descent he was, name of . . . Burnett? Burgess? No, *Bassett,* that was it. Stan Bassett. Great grey quiff of hair standing up like a shoebrush. Odd fellow, when you got down to it. I met him, once. "Wotcha, mate," says I. "Ah! It's you," he said, never having met me before, and promptly vanished into the November fog, whistling the main theme from Prokofiev's *Peter and the Wolf* and simultaneously supplying the narration to that charming piece at the top of his lungs, the ensemble fading rapidly into the gauzy lamplit expanses of the Place de la Bastille. "Cheerio," I said, forlorn but not displeased.

much all outcomes of this quasiendless melodrama to the oblivion of cosmic indifference, or divine Ganges of the soul. Not even the sight on the public benches of Rubina's anguished face (well, irritated, really, but with one or two creases of concern down her narrow brow) could quell the despairing resignation within him.

"Do what you will, Krishna," he muttered. "Send me to prison, execute me, make me drive a van, bugger it. Whatever you want."

"Well, now," crooned the judge, "let me see, Mr. Swain. In view of the regrettable and unexpected, if fortuitous—although appalling, of course—demise of your chief accuser in the case, Mr. Fergus Goone, I wonder very much if the charges still stand. . . . Mrs. Ryan?"

A wizened slick-haired man in a maroon waistcoat stepped forward, with an urgent nod of the head, or tic, and whispered something in the judge's left ear, interrupting himself twice with a spluttering openmouthed cough, which caused the judge to wave him impatiently away, flapping a flag-sized handkerchief. Mrs. Ryan then approached the bench and conferred, with a glittering sideways glance at her freshly manicured hands and the tiny gold and silver amulets that tinkled on her wrists. The judge smiled toothily, as if informed of his continuing attractiveness to women, or the winning draw in the Lotto.

"Splendid, then," he said. "Good news, Mr. Swain. Well, good and bad, I should say. It is my considered opinion, having examined the facts of the case, that racism was clearly at work here, oh aye. Now that's bad, and believe me I know racism when I see it, ah believe you me, boyo. Any Tipperary man in Dublin knows what I'm talking about. Slagged off left and right he is. Country culchie, bog squatter, negrohead . . . the list of insults ready-made by those jackeens would turn you white, so they would. Sluggish service in restaurants. Disdainful taxi drivers, oh you can believe it. And loud jeering in certain neighbourhoods. Dubs slagged off by Corkmen and vicey versy. Sheer stupidity, of course. Not to mention prejudice and bigotry, well haven't we all suffered enough, eh? So if you ask me, Mr. Swain, the circumstances of your arrest, having been motivated exclusively by unreasonable dislike formed on the basis of your name, appearance, and ethnic and/or national origin, exclude any further charges in my courtroom." He leaned back with a sigh and drummed his fingers on his straining paunch. "Of course, there is the small matter of some community service in lieu of prison time, as I'm sure your barrister explained to you."

"What barrister?" inquired Anil, puzzled, as Mrs. Ryan shifted her glare from her nails to him.

"Yes, well. And I'm being very lenient here, Mr. Swain, with your poor wife in the courtroom"—Rubina discreetly brandished a fist—"and given the bizarre events that led to this accusation in the first place, not to mention Mr. Goone's death . . . well, anyway. I hereby sentence you to, eh, four hours of community service, precise nature of which to be determined by your legal counsel in consulation with the bench, i.e., me. Case dismissed."

The gavel fell with an authoritative whack.

"They want you to drive a van for them," explained Mrs. Ryan, afterward, as Anil eagerly devoured a liver-and-salad sandwich fresh from the cafeteria vending machines. Mrs. Ryan coolly lit a Joop den Uyl filter-tipped cigarillo[3] and fanned out her scarlet

---

[3]Ah, yes, my God, yes oh yes, I say yes, the good old den Uyls, or "Joops," as we called them, tasty wee things once you'd put out the fires they invariably ignited in the nosehairs and any ambient whiskers, ah I remember them well, picked up the habit in my teens while hitching across Holland with my roommate from Longford College, a Dutch lad named Ruud, who later did quite well, going on to become prime minister of the Netherlands or

fingernails for purposes of further assessment and scrutiny. "My goodness, is that one chipped?" she muttered, peering. "Ten quid I paid for this job. . . ."

---

something and briefly (until she became fully aware of his predisposition to the recitation in bed of dry economic data), Princess Katje van Otterkaat's boyfriend . . . anyhow, there we were in a wee crossroads in the sleepy south of Brabant called Doerpburg, the two of us freshly arisen from bed in the local youth hostel, minding our own business (looking for a jakes, as I re-member) when (and I still have nightmares about this) who should come swinging around the corner like the great gate of Dublin Castle itself but a chap I'd met once back in Cork at some kind of boring writers' pub (cheap ale, two bob a pint) and had sworn never to meet again—but the best-laid plans, eh? It was Jumbo Wyde, the man of letters, author of "Felinoptera" and "Ballyknocknee: A Semtex Romance"; "film-critic slash pop musician slash novelist," as his potted bio has it, neglecting to mention his most memo-rable quality, that of being a bore extraordinaire; and there he was, "doing research," as he had it, in his amiably sadistic way, taking care to trap us in the doorway of Mynheer Underloo's Apothek (closed: it was a Sunday morn-ing), thus blocking any means of egress with his broad frame (and snacking all the while on a powerfully aromatic mixture of mayonnaise and the local chips wrapped fatly in a kind of cone made of the TV listings of the local newspaper, *Den Blaad*) "on my new novel, which is going to be about the fruit-gathering expeditions to the East Indies, of course knowing me you'd expect I'd include a bit about the IRA and sure enough there it is in chapter three"—he paused for a forceful hand gesture that briefly revealed the spire of St. Weselius Cathedral pointing towards the freedom-enhanced Dutch-landscape Dutch sky, just visible beyond his vast and ever-widening bulk—"complete with explanations of the genesis of 'Buster the Terrorist'—OK, look, I'm a pop culture freak and I make no apologies for it, especially to you Eurosnobs, no offense—you know the story about the first episode, don't know, stop me if I've told you this before." "Stop," we wheedled, fruitlessly, unheard. "Well, you know Pete Hedges, the guy who directed Amanda Major in that East-meets-West action romance, *Bao Dai's Schooldays*? Now that was a real surprise, a real seat-of-your-pants romance and martial arts

"Um, Missus," said Anil. But the die was cast, and Anil's fate with it. Mrs. Ryan was growing impatient, and rapped out instructions. "Listen to me, Singh, and don't interrupt."

---

thriller rolled into one, as I said in my review for the *Wellington Boot*—that reminds me, did I ever tell you the story of how I first saw that movie, it was back in Galway when I was working on the fishing boats, and living, let me tell you, on the cheap is hardly the way to describe it, there I was in a cold-water flat on the south side of Salthill—that was when I met Larry 'Lead' Drummer, by the way, you may have seen him in *Bluebeard's Girls*, he was knitting pullovers—pretty good poet and wow, was he ever the clichéd two-fisted drinker, one night I went to a party where he was reading and at first I could hardly understand a word he said, then I noticed two things: one, that he was speaking German; and two, the empty pair of whiskey bottles he was holding in each hand, man was he stocious—wait a minute, I think Maureen Titus was there as well—you know, the lead singer from the Racing Heads? The surfers' rock fusion group from Sligo? Back in the nineties? A real babe? Anyway, she was there, too, or that might have been in Mullingar, when I was assistant curator at the Don Levy Wax Museum and Chamber of Horrors—stop me if I've told you this before." "Stop," I gurgled, unheeded. "I think my old girlfriend Tracy worked for the Italian director, I don't know if you've heard of him, Dario Gran Turismo? What did he make, *O Insalata Verde* I think, and *Te Spacc' Il Grugno* (sorry, I was forgetting myself, your Neapolitan dialect's probably a bit rusty, that was *I'll Split Your Gourd Open* in English, but they renamed it *Amalfi Freak Show* for the States). She worked for him for five years or so, that was before she met Brad, of course, and now they have two kids, man what a handful, I don't think I'll ever have kids myself—well, I lack a certain essential ingredient, ha ha, to wit a wife, or girlfriend, or female partner of some kind, ha ha, and that's pretty much a sine qua non—anyway what are you chancers doing here?" Incredibly, he paused in his gabbing for a life-giving second or so, munching the remainder of his mayonnaise-and-chip concoction before losing interest in us and our openmouthed lack of reply (we were scouting urgently around his vast bulk at what we could see of the world beyond (a DAF automobile driving slowly up one of the few hills in the southern Netherlands; two ladies dressed

Anil was to be at the eastern docks that night at ten P.M. to collect the van and its merchandise from a man named Seamus; then he would drive southwest along the coast (fine views by

----

for churchgoing going, in fact, to church; an old man standing on the street corner opposite and unfolding the *Sontaags Blad*), to no avail, as the wall that was Wyde expanded ever sideways, ever outward, sealing all exits—"Anyway, I'm here because I got a grant from the West of Ireland Arts Council to do a book on pop culture in the seventeenth century, so my book's all about the fella that invented Het Poop, a kind of ginger ale, named Piet Uit Huis, he's an actual historic figure, you can visit his house right here in Doerpburg, they even have a web page linked to the United Presbyterian Church site in Bangor, county Down—hang on a sec, that reminds me of something that happened back in Ballykilloran, county Antrim—that's my hometown, you know, about twenty miles north, no, northwest, or maybe north by northwest—cripes, there's another grade-A movie, loved it, just loved it, all except for that ridiculous crop-spraying scene, you know Hitchcock filmed that because he was hard up for money and he'd just lost his first unit director, Paul Urbanite, to Universal, you probably haven't heard of him, he's the guy who directed that terrific little indie pic *Little Bags, Big Eyes*—yeah, lots of Presbyterians there, real right-wing conservative types, no, it's not much of a place compared to a lot of others, I mean it's no Amsterdam, but man, when I was growing up it was great—not that we lived in luxury, or even syle, nah, our house was a typical two-up two-down ranch-style suburban pebbledash pseudo-Tudy prefab semimansion but it was just down from the river so my friends and I"—at this stage Ruud made a dash for it, but as luck would have it his blazer snagged on the watchband on Jembo's right wrist, distant from his left by what seemed a mile or so, and hapless Ruud was slowly reeled back in, clouds of despair darkening his frank, open, manly features: "Three boys I still keep in touch with after all these years, great fellas, oh believe me we had some grand crack together, it was a real prelapsarian kind of existence, fishing for sea bass— well, I'm in touch with Ken, anyway, he's working in the Ballykilloran fire department, now he's the touchy article, so he is, well he did a lot of dope in the seventies and eighties, like, but you don't want to ask him about it,

full moon; maps provided) to Crumstown, where another man, coincidentally also named Seamus, would meet him at midnight sharp outside the Orinoco Bar on Poole Parade, or somewhere nearby. The van's contents would then be transferred to another

---

he'll stare at you like Jack Nicholson in *The Shining*—the exact same expression, in fact we used to call him 'Jack Nicholson' behind his back—you didn't want to say a thing like that to his face, you know, he'd look at you like Robert DeNiro in *Cape Fear*—now, wait a sec, maybe that's what we called him behind his back, 'Robert DeNiro'"—here another puff of life insinuated itself through the stifling mesh of his blather and it was my turn to break free, under the vast forearm that momentarily lifted, like a Dutch drawbridge, in a gesture of scalp-scratching puzzlement; I'd made it as far as the far end of his trousers when the forearm fell heavily on my head and I staggered backward in defeat—"Sorry about that, man, didn't see you there, you OK? Yeh I honestly think we used to call him 'Robert De Niro,' man, I wouldn't have liked to be there when he heard us call him that, Ken was an easy-going guy except when he did drugs, then he'd have looked at us like Nigel Hawthorne in *Yes, Minister*—in fact, that was . . ." And suddenly my faith, so sorely tested, was restored, for with a clang the shutters of a nasi goreng-and-rijstaffel shop across the street were flung open, the old newspaper-reading man folded his paper and went inside, and Wyde, incredibly, fell silent and wheeled slowly around like an oil tanker in Killoyle Harbour. "Hoy, is that one of those Nazi Goering places?" he inquired, rhetorically, for his no-longer-captive audience had rapidly made its escape through the gap that had suddenly opened up between his left thigh and the wall of Mynheer Otterloo's Apothek. "Hey, I'll be seeing youse, I'm pretty hungry," he said, but we were well on our way. Our last sight of him, as we glanced in retrospective horror over our shoulders, did not bode well for the old newspaper-reader, upon whose frail person the fiend Wyde's gaze had fallen, as they both took their places at the counter. "Myn God," gasped Ruud, when we'd got clear. "I tink I go to church now and pray for protection of all peoples against dis guy." I chose gin, the local variety in earthenware flasks, and smoked my first den Uyl. Tasty, if a bit harsh, at first.

vehicle, in all likelihood, as Mrs. Ryan said, breathing stertor-ously, with eyebrow twitches of enigmatic significance: "*another van*" . . . at which time Anil would proceed to the public phone box at the corner of Modern Dance Street and Peterpewter Place and dial a number previously prearranged . . . conve-niently in numerical sequence for easier commitment to memory, viz. 12–34–56–7.

"One two three four . . . God, this is like a bad dream," said Anil.

"A worse dream," said Mrs. Ryan sententiously, "awaits you *there*," and she pointed with a manicured index finger in the di-rection of the prison whence he had so recently emerged.

"Good, good. Very well. I understand. Didn't I tell you, I'll drive the bloody van," bawled Anil, causing nearby heads to slew about. "Just get me the restaurant franchise."

Bail, for some reason, having been proposed by the now-impotent lawyers for the prosecution, had promptly been waived by the judge, but there were still probationary concerns that de-tained Anil and his counsel (for Tom O'Mallet had reappeared, sharply dressed in a Prince D'Arcy suit and Lady Catherine de Burgh tie, the better to allay suspicions), such as the desirabil-ity, or not, of Anil's criminal record being expunged of all mis-deeds, assuming that night's expedition went satisfactorily for all concerned.

"Now don't worry, son," said Tom. "You just show up at the designated spot. Ah, there's your lady wife." He half rose to his feet, displaying the pseudocourtesy of a legal hack in thrall to his own ego and the pocketbooks of others.

Rubina came over and combined a kiss on her husband's mouth with a crisp openhanded slap across his jowls.

"Ouch," said Anil. "Bloody hell, Auntie."

"I don't know what to do with you, Uncle!" she cried. "I don't know what to do with him," she blurted, turning to Tom (who mimed a worried frown) and Mrs. Ryan (who was on the verge of discovering another unseemly nick in the nail-varnish sheen of the middle finger of her right hand).

"Don't worry yourself, missus," said Tom. "He'll be performing a little community service, just. We'll take care of him."

That's what I'm afraid of, thought she.

15

The old Daimler lurched around the corner, Victor trapped behind the wheel. Valve lifters thrashed, joints clunked, a fraying fanbelt chirped, a gasket hissed leakage. At the side of the road (N45A, Killoyle–Ballywen–Derrydingle–Weterford–Crumstown–Youghal, a bracing thirty-three miles as the crow flies, slightly less behind the wheel depending on weather conditions, intestinal health, wind velocity, etc.), several dustbin lids shifted audibly in the Daimler's wake, imposing on nearby dogs the responsibility of alerting the dozing populace to the monstrous passage.

"Arf arf arf arf," screamed the doggies. "Arf arf arf," et cetera, until they faded into the sonic Doppler distance of long ago and far away. The beam of the car's single functioning headlamp shone on stone walls, shuttered windows, overhanging trees, the narrow mouths of hedgegrown boreens and the wide-open mouth of a late-night jogger—Ted Johnston, twenty-nine, up-and-coming software engineer from Cirencester, over here for a training course, like—who pressed fearfully against the wall in the face of the rattling, whirring one-eyed juggernaut . . .

"Fuck in '*ell*," he gasped.

Then the wild whooshing of asthmatic hoses and the probing beam of light were gone, and the beast shrank to a pair of fast-fading red taillights that wagged wildly from side to side as control of the car's outsize steering wheel slipped slowly from the driver's hands.

"Shite, ya bastard," expostulated Victor, his fingers scrambling for purchase. The balding tyres squealed in a double helix of mad zigzagging, then, happily, on a stretch of dead straight just past Ballywen (population twenty-four), our man finally reasserted control and drove for a short time in an approximately straight line; but upon coming to a hairpin bend above the coastal cliff— Snakey Drive, to the locals—he negated this success by joyfully mashing the accelerator and plunging into oversteer with rear wheels squealing, a maneuver made riskier by his spontaneous decision to lean out the window at that very moment and expel lung gobs into the night. The night flung them back into his face. Again, the Daimler lurched; again, roadside objects and concomitant dogs signaled its passage.

"Wangsadangsadangsadang," gibbered Victor, wiping his face with a handy pocket hankie and wresting the wheel back to true, or near enough, just in time to dodge a roadside marker ("Killoyle 16; Crumstown 19; Youghal 32"; "Vote Fianna Fail"; "Call Aisling for a great shag"). "Jaysus. Sod and bugger this fakin' car. Ahack."

Of course, it was hardly the car's fault. The Daimler was a valiant, once-doughty machine dating from the second miniskirt age;[1] it had been Victor's since '82, having belonged to an ex-colonel in the Falklands War (Royal Irish Fusiliers) now happily retired six feet under the soil of county Down, next to his wife, also reposing thereunder. True, at first Victor had doted dottily on the Daimler, fussing over it for all he was worth, indeed spending the odd night in uneasy brooding about too much wax damaging the window frames, or excessive (or insufficient) air pressure in the tyres, or

---

[1]Aha, with the BeeGees, rather than the Beatles, as background. I'm with you here—but I wasn't there, believe you me, I spent most of my time in the miniskirt age pretending to climb stairs even if I wasn't, if you take my meaning.

the possible existence of an owl's (or rat's) nest in the boot.[2] Too, it was his habit then to run off with a growl and a stream of sharp invective interlopers, or any who proposed borrowing his car keys; but gradually, as the years passed and his life lurched downhill, his heart shifted its compass, calcified birdshit ate away the Daimler's

---

[2]Now that was Uncle Mel to a T. Didn't that man sacrifice his life to keep his car clean. True bill. The car was a '64 Neptune, nothing special, but it was the apple of Uncle Mel's pink-rimmed eye, let me tell you. Days and most nights he was in the garage, shammy in one hand, beeswax polish in the other, "Do Not Disturb" writ large across his honest Ulsterman's features (paradoxically no Ulsterman he; a Leinsterman born and bred, as were we all on that side of the family), ready with a snarl if any of the multitudinous children spawned from his loins (including young Monk, before he grew up to become Cousin Monk of That Ilk) allegedly dared enter, or otherwise disturb his concentration. Frequent were our hushed comments, and obnoxious his rancor ensuite. "You'd be better off in Mexico," as one averred, "or Arizona itself. Divil the rainy day you'd see in that class of a place." "Aaarrrrgh," opined Mel, brandishing a tyre iron, or crowbar. "Bloody silly to wash your car when it rains every day," remarked another, soon quelled by raging Mel, honest sweat dappling his brow, clutching a weighty bottle of Buff'Em Good, or its twin, a fifth of Bushmills Black. "*Urrrrrr*," roared he. Well, sad to tell, over a period of years—say, five to ten—the waxing and polishing grew to gigantic proportions and crowded out everything else from his routine: walking the dog, evenings with the family, the job (an easy one, granted: gamesmaster at the local Loreto convent), shopping (except for car-washing products), even church (R.C., St. Jude's, prayers for his soul and the cleanliness of all cars everywhere). Mel rose early and waxed once a day and more than twice on the Sabbath if rain had in the interim insolently stained the flanks of the noble Neptune, which it duly daily did, this (or that) being Ireland; so there was mad old Mel, garage-ensconced on and off from dawn till dusk, arms working like pistons, sweat flying off his brow like freshets of spume from the whitecaps off Malin Head, working the rags and shammies and engine vacuums and buffing machines like nobody's business. . . . The tyres, of course, needed their daily gloss, the glossier the better. Chrome fittings must dazzle or their very existence was futile. Windows and headlamps, too, must shine to blind, and the front and rear wings had to reiterate Fabergé jewels in their

once-gleaming exterior, the tyres went soft and slowly exhaled, the struts sank to their knees, the fluids stagnated, and all the outward signs of inward surrender were plain to see. Even so, Victor would let no one else drive the beast, any more than (as he'd once put it) he'd "share his knickers." It was, and would ever be, *his* motor. Cantankerous, bulky, outmoded, and barely functioning, it was an

---

shiny glow, and as for the running boards—ah! Epics of limpidity. Well, it didn't take long for Mel to start devoting the little time left over from the cleaning, including sleep and visits to the commode, to crisscrossing the nation—in a hired car to obviate the risk of besmirching the Neptune—in search of ideal waxes, shammies, dust blowers, detergents, et cetera; and it was toward the end of his fifty-ninth year that it became apparent to one and all that he was living his life *for the sole purpose of cleaning his car* (go ahead, laugh, but it put him head and shoulders above most of us clueless punters if you ask me, I mean, at least there was a meaning to the man's life—what's the meaning of *your* life, mate?). Alas, as he passed into his sixties a permanent trembling took hold of his arms from elbows to oxsters, caused partly by fear of what the weather might bring on any given day (rain, of course, but also hail, snow, and, worst of all for the automotive carapace, *sleet*), and partly by palsey, a hereditary Ulster disease (oddly, however . . .or so above). It could not fail to have a deleterious effect on his car-washing, of course, and soon he had to hire a man to assist him; this was Mr. Eamonn Daffy, B.A., a right sharper. Well, it was no surprise when said Daffy made a bid to take over the operation, forcing Uncle Mel out of the garage and into the sitting room, so to speak, where he crouched and twitched, yearning for the cleansing agents. It was no easy transition: Shammies flew, waxing utensils were hurled, and once a windscreen cleaner landed squarely on Aunt Nuala's lap. "That does it," declared that lady, mother of seven, and, bringing her formidable powers of persuasion to bear on the situation, she swept all protests aside. Daffy's duties were enhanced to include kitchen polishing, window washing, and general maintenance, while Mel was packed off to relatives in New Zealand (Auckland, I believe, or was it Christchurch?); as I heard it, he was still making waxing gestures the day of his death, last year round Christmas. Poignantly, his last words were reported to have been, "Hand me that cloth, will ya, then get out of the feckin' garage." 'Tis true—the likes of him will not be reflected in our rearview mirrors again.

automotive version of its owner—who was driving it at the moment, by the by, because he was intent on solace for his ruination of a life, old newspapers notwithstanding. Earlier that day young Liam, one of NaughtyBoy Graphics' local recruits, had jocularly called him "da." "Cheers, da!" he'd piped up in the hallway as Victor was bustling eagerly to his desk. *Da!* Devil the old-newspaper web sites that would make up for that, mused Victor, and what was worse, he'd said nothing memorable to the horrid wee ballockbrain in reply; in fact (he dreaded the memory, photographically etched) he'd actually smiled a soothing, if edentate (i.e., suitably da-like) smile, and had even ventured the feeble rejoinder of the apparatchik currying favour: something like, "Oh, all right, son," or "Should I call you Junior, now?" or "Well, me owld eyes are that blurry, ya know. . . ."

It was the limit. Just like the other jobs, this one was turning into a grand old waste of his own time just to put money in strangers' pockets, in short: a bloody insult to common sense. Well, he'd show 'em. He'd do overtime, all right. But he'd not do any of their shite, no, thank you very much. Old newspapers, that's what he'd do, as many as he could find on the ever-expanding World Wide Web.

Victor's aha! So you needed to ask after all!

As for Sheila, she was away somewhere with some chap (in his indifference he'd forgotten to ask where, or who), and that evening on the telly there'd been nothing but strange faces talking rubbish, and for some reason the old-newspaper web page was unavailable on his computer screen (if *he* ran one it would be available worldwide around the clock, so help him God). So at around half nine Victor had allowed himself a snarling fit ("aaarrgh! snagsadagsadagsadags") and had up and left, destination Crumstown and Cousin Shoots's bachelor bungalow on Layperson Lane. In store, hoped Vic, lay a round or two of the new video game Shoots had just got in, Wittgenstein III: The Tractatus. Raunchy was the word on the street on that one.

Music suddenly intruded via the radio, a '79 Blaupunkt un-serviced since the Argies surrendered at Port Stanley. Like Victor, it was given to outbursts unalterable by reason.

"OK, boys and girls, here's one of those oldies that really stirs up the memories, at least for me, but I'm pretty much over the hill now so I reckon it'll be new to a lot of you out there in listenerland: from the long hot summer of 1977, here are the Yum Yums and their platinum single 'Oh Yammatummmatum.'"

"Oh-ay," brayed the radio, "ah-yeah, oh yammatummmatumma tumm, yam tum tum tum tum yamma yamma tum tum tummy tum tummy tum yam yam yamty yam yamma yamma yamma tum yammayummatummatum . . ."

"Yamma yamma tum detum tum," repeated Victor, dutifully but doubtfully. His musical tastes were more in line with the once-popular compositions of Messrs. Gilbert and Sullivan. Still, he could no more control what his car radio was resolved to play than he could regulate the winds, or the rain, or the sky itself; in any event, Crumstown was nigh. He breathed a sigh of relief at this minor miracle, he and his motor having been spared from destruction en route. Exurban shops swept by, including an ill-lit petrol station and a series of ominous outlets, "everything for a quid or less." A church stalked by, holding high its spire. A purple-stockinged prostitute waved, swinging a handbag. (Victor licked his lips.) Finally, intricate strands of bronze pearls beyond a bend in the road ahead indicated civilization, or at least society, or at the very least a town, Crumstown no less.[3] Utter blackness to the left of the lights of the town positioned the sea, or St. George's Channel, to be precise; upon its waves there floated

---

[3]Intimately linked in its glorious past with the likes of Sir Walter Raleigh and Lord Lumley and other dashing buccaneers of the age of good Queen Bess, Crumstown's now a minor port and a retirement haven for the second-raters who couldn't afford Killoyle, let alone Marbella.

a late-night ferry, gaily asparkle, that September night, like the iceberg-bound *Titanic,* that distant April eve.

Shoots's was on the left, just after the right turn, then left (or was it straight?).

"Whisht, if it isn't himself in person," said Shoots, responding to the doorbell's unwelcome summons to find his cousin on the doorstep smiling through a shoulder-heaving cough.

"Arrah, Shoots. Doin' the best, are ya? Grand, grand. Ahack." Adopting the casual pose of, say, Alberto Sordi in *I Vitelloni,* or Paul Newman in *Hud,* Victor braced himself against the door-jamb and hawked into the bushes.

"Ah, come in yourself then, Victor, for the love and honour of God, and may that same God save us all from the eternal damnation we—or at least you—so richly deserve, ah ah aha."

Shoots O'Bass (of the Carlow O'Basses, distantly related to Turlow O'Bass, founder of the Irish navy) stood six feet in his bare feet, in which tapered to a sorry end the slack remains of the once-strapping scrumhalf for Ireland in the Tournament of Nations, 1958. Hairless was he, bar a wispy fringe and forlorn goatee, and the sad gaze he wore was that of one who had been a watcher, not a doer, all his lifelong. Professionally, from the heights of Senior Steward at Aer Lingus in 1970—in which *annus mirabilis* he had actually bedded a girl (the wrong way, but still)—he had descended in long low steps, as down the terraced side of a Chinese mountain, to his current status: departmental coordinator of lunches and dinners at Ramses International, the software firm. His life was, as he put it on his resume, "the slime trace of a slug on a leaf—if that."

"Just drove down from Killoyle on a lark, like. How's that new Wittgenshteen caper of yours?" Victor swaggered in, coughing boisterously. "Hack ahack. Eh—got any of that gin goin, like?"

It was 10:15 P.M. and Shoots had been at the moral crossroads of every drinker's day, to wit: bedtime, or another quick one? The quick one won, of course, with Victor on the premises—and it should be pointed out, by the way (allow me) that Victor was by no means a boozer, not at all the standard stage-Oyrish article slurring witticisms and cynical weltschmerz over his tenth double whiskey of the day; no, it was strictly on social occasions such as this that he unbent to the extent of sipping a few, leading, it is true, to mild intoxication on more occasions than one, but invariably in the company of Shoots who, as a lifelong bachelor, had a great respect for whatever might illuminate the dark watches of the night.

"Gin's the ticket," said Victor, in the face of Shoots's feeble protests that his stock of gin was low, perilously so (whereas Victor had, like a dog, flared the scent of juniper berries on the man's breath, and there was no disguising the murmur and chuckling in the background of the long-anticipated video game to which a couple of tumblers of Tanqueray's were the natural sidekick).

"Wittgenstein?" asked Victor.

"Tanqueray," replied Shoots, rattling past on another, unparallel, train of thought. Ice cubes clinked; drink splashed. "Oh aye, Wittgenstein."

"Here's to him."

"He's run into Dora the Dominatrix. She's putting the boot in."

"Oh, dear."

They repaired to the sitting room, dark but for the aquamarine glow of the computer screen.

"Here's a nifty feature, look. See how you can drag the cursor across the link on the left side of his nose? Well, have a dekko at this." Shoots settled himself onto his command perch. "Here we go." His bony hand grasped and wielded the mouse with the dexterity of a Gascon swordsman. The cursor raced diagonally across the screen and responded to an urgent double-click by freezing Dora the Dominatrix in her tracks; then, instead of advancing upon the hapless Wittgenstein (engrossed in mid-flagrante in the composition of his Tractatus, volume three), Dora turned to the viewer and stepped inside a picture frame. Tinny bump-and-

grind music started up and the entirely nonexistent, and therefore so utterly satisfying, pixel beauty proceeded to perform a
striptease, following the user's commands.

"Oh, well, now that's a cut above that other shite," said Victor.
"Ahangsadangsadangsadansgadag." His poached old eyes shone
with an unholy luminescence as he aligned himself in tandem with
Shoots. The two aging cousins watched the screen like small boys
at the circus without, let it be said, the innocence of same; rather,
deeply burnt the eternal flame of sexual frustration, and well-
rooted was the denial by old Ireland of nature's simplest joy (bar
the morning stool, some might say) to their generation and all
the dead generations of the nation's glorious past.[4]

"Arrah," remarked Victor, caught between a sip of gin and
glimpses of pixelated titillation afforded by the movement of the
mouse and the user choices on the pulldown menu, to wit:

------

[4]Well, and if you ask me thank God that's over and no mistake. It was a bloody
disgrace, so it was, the amount of misdirected self-tinkering below the waist that
took place on this benighted island, and among respectable husbands and wives,
too, too perishing timid the lot of 'em to inquire of their spouses if they might,
some day, lie together entirely stripped? Of course not, *chauffage central oblige.*
When I was a nipper it was commonplace to say that 90 percent of the Irish
race had never been totally nude in their lives. Imagination ran riot, and one
old article out on Inishmore caused quite a stir by claiming to have photographic
proof that women had three buttocks and at least as many breasts "as Mab, the
great cow queen of Connacht herself." Result: mental mayhem and a booming
black market in Swedish nature reviews. Nowadays things are different, of
course, although I grant you sometimes it does seem like every Johnny and his
chum are pushing the envelope, as it were, of arse banditry. And you just try to
score points with one of them flappers over at Trinity College Dublin (TCD):
she'd brain you, then call the guards, and that lot would side with her these days,
no questions asked. But it's a sight better than old times. At least the crumpet's
where you want it: front and centre, not excessively clothed and huddling
under the malfunctioning electric blanket in a cold-water flat somewhere in the
Liberties, and it raining cats and dogs outside, with himself on the warpath
after missing a round at the Brazen Head. . . .

1. Starkers, full frontal;
2. Starkers, dorsal;
3. Topless, frontal;
4. Bottomless, lateral;
5. Bottomless, dorsal;
6. Et cetera, et cetera *ad nauseam.*

"Pisht," said Shoots, striving for manly indifference but slewing constantly around, dry-mouthed, with pulse aquiver. (He contemplated making a crazy dash for the jakes, there to lock himself in with the screen-images of Dora the Dominatrix fresh in his rotting mind and . . .)

Then came a sudden crash from the street outside.

"Hangsadangsadangsadag.What the fuck's that?"

Victor's crude inquiry introduced an atonal note into the evening's placid *sprachgesang,* but he had, after all, responded to the dissonance from Layperson Lane: that of an ear-splintering, glass-crunching, metal-crumpling collision between two or more sizeable and sturdy objects, as if an entire brigade of Territorial Irregulars had marched through a scullery into a greenhouse—or, suggested Shoots, drawing on long-untapped funds of imaginative rhetoric:

". . . as if a single Turkish air force plane—say, a Dassault Mirage, vintage 1977 . . ."

"Hawker Siddeley," amended Victor. "Or Vickers. Not that froggie rubbish."

"Or, well, Lockheed F-4 . . ."

"Nonsense. Out of business. Make it a Dragon."

"As if a Dragon, then, had mistakenly attempted a loop-the-loop on a course that included both the Topkapi Palace and the Mosque of Hagia Sophia, thereby encountering both, with dire consequences . . ."

"Ah go see what it is, for fuck's sake."

Shoots, too much the gentleman to protest being ordered about in his own house (never mind give the orders himself) meekly obeyed, and returned with garbled reports of a large vehicle, very probably a van, attempting (here he raised a cautionary finger: vroom-vroom, roared a powerful engine, as if on cue) to extricate itself from a tangle of barbed-wire fencing and a row or more of dustbins, all courtesy of the warehouse firm next door, Dereks Ltd.

Victor was now double-clicking on menu five: "Starkers, All fours," and disinclined to be bothered.

"Ah, God, will you look at that now it's nothing short of a frigging miracle what you can do on the old computers these days. . . ."

"Anyway, it looks like there's an Indian driving it."

"An Indian? Well, there are more and more of them lads. A billion or more back home, eh, so no shortage for export . . ." Victor expressed an elaborate, eyeball-loosening coughing seizure, drowning out the first part of Shoots's reply.

". . . coming straight into the house after."

"You wha'?"

"Aye. Invited him in, poor fella. Said those dustbins just rolled into the street while he was driving past. Gave him quite a turn."

Who was the greater idiot, Victor paused to inquire, with some acerbity; the idiot who came up with that one, or the idiot who believed him?

"You silly fucking old bugger. You'll let anyone cod you up to your two eyes, won't you?"

"What? You have some neck, you old you old."

Shoots, quite heated, had flushed the colour of underdone roast beef, or just-ripe strawberries. His feelings were hurt, especially so in the face of Victor's endless grumbling, because no matter what you did for the love of God the old bastard was liable to wheel about and fire off an insult, or a wad of phlegm, or in some way make you feel the size of half a vermicelli noodle and *never* offer to clean up, or buy the drinks, or do the dishes. . . .

Shoots steamed.

And the sheer bloody brass of him turning up at half ten at night.

And the damned dreary depressing sight of him hunched over the computer with his greedy old peepers fixed on the screen.

And the fact of his being Aunt Edna's son suddenly being not quite sufficient to render his presence under Shoots's roof a welcome one.

All this simmered to a boil, and suddenly long-placid Shoots flew at Victor, fists twirling like the propeller on a Stuka dive bomber. Victor, under assault, reacted like France under the assault of such Stukas in June 1940 and capitulated instanter, diving for the floor under Shoots's barrage of feeble but persistent and well-aimed punches—at which moment the front door opened and Anil Swain blew in like a trade wind off the Coromandel Coast (say, from the Andamans, via Chennai).

"Goodness gracious me," he exclaimed, on beholding the combatants. "Quite a barney, isn't it? Am I interrupting? I say, this isn't some homosexual ritual, is it?"

"Sod," gasped Victor, from the prone position, "off."

"No, no," said Shoots, wrenching himself back to a position roughly perpendicular to the floor and hastily attempting a fingers-through of his limp comb over. "Please do come in, Mr. . . . ?"

"Anil Swain, at your service."

"Delighted. Shoots O'Bass. And this is my cousin Victor Hasdrubal-Scott."

"Aha. Cousins, eh? Splendid. My goodness, I was afraid for a minute I'd stumbled into a den of buggers. They seem to be everywhere these days, you know."

Anil sat and took in his surroundings with a beatific smile, then, glimpsing the great staring blue eye of the computer, he started.

"Good heavens," he bellowed, "I thought that was a telly at first, and do you know I was all ready to go over there and sit down and have a look-see, by golly it's been *ages* since I had a quiet evening with the dear old idiot box . . . but I see it's only a computer, and I say," his eyes narrowed, "that's not your standard computer programme, is it?"

"More like the Kama Sutra, eh, Mahatma," wheezed Victor, once again in control of Dora: Lateral, Half and half; All fours, clothed; All fours, topless . . .

Losing interest in the old men's pornography, Anil lit a cigarette (thrust at him in a silver box by unctuous Shoots) and expounded on the doings of a very odd day, indeed.

"Well, chaps, you'd scarcely believe it, but this very morning there I was in the clink, yes sir, I said the clink, the prison, you know. Oh, please don't worry, I'm not a criminal, no no, I wouldn't worry about it, you're quite safe from me, safer from me than you seem to be from each other, ha ha ha. No, I'm not about to carve you into little tiny bits of flesh or anything, no actually it was all a great big silly misunderstanding from the word go. Terrorism, you see."

"Ah, terrorism," said Shoots, nodding in mock sagacity while simultaneously running his fingers through his remaining few strands of hair. "We Irish are old hands at that game."[5]

"Precisely. But it's a game I never played. *Anyway,* there I was, and now here I am. And outside there's a blooming great van with all sorts of things in the back, camping equipment, they said, but if you ask me that's a load of damned codswallop, as they say in Wolverhampton, begging your pardon. And believe me it was about as much fun to drive that thing down those country roads as it would be to, oh, I don't know . . ."

"Ride a warthog across Africa," proposed Shoots.

"I suppose so, having never done it or anything remotely resembling it. . . ."

"Fuck a warthog, then," growled Victor.

"Well, there you are. I hardly think that would be a pleasure, eh? Ha ha ha?"

---

[5]Too true, too true. Ten members of my own family were or are Semtex experts, and the ones who aren't keep a close watch on the others.

"Drink?" interposed Shoots.

"Not usually, no. Hinduism and all that, you see, not that it's actually banned, not like Muslims, but most people just don't . . . well, that's not true, my goodness there are parts of Mumbai where you can't move for the soaks (could they be Parsees, though?) . . . well, anyway, I know it's a bit boring to Westerners, but there you are. But this once, as long as it's all part and parcel of the traditional Irish hospitality you hear about, well . . ."

"Gin? Say yes, it's all I've got."

"Oh, I say. Gin, is it? Good-good. Gordon's, like the adverts on the London buses?"

"Tanqueray's, I'm afraid."[6]

"Oh, well."

Libations were poured, admired, consumed.

"Golly, that's nice. Maybe I should do it more often." Anil interjected a shrill laugh before going on. "So no one was here to meet me when I arrived, you know, no Seamus or indeed anyone of that or any similar name or in fact any name at all, although a lady named Dora in a roadside petrol station asked me the way to Cork and when I confessed ignorance invited me back to the lavatories, if you can believe it—my goodness, do you think she was a prossie?"

"Undoubtedly. They're ten a ha'penny round about here these days."

"Makes me wonder why you can't get a shag, then," roared Victor thickly, smarting from his recent defeat.

"I don't pay for my pleasures," retorted Shoots loftily.

"Ballocks. How much did you hand over for this particular pleasure, you old tosser? And what price the Merc in the garage?

---

[6]Admirably suited to slapstick encounters such as this, although I'd go for a Crystal Beefeater's martini myself, stirred, not shaken, and hold the limes—*hard,* as they used to say for a laugh in Neary's whenever Brits were present (daily; twice on Sundays).

That was free, I suppose? Not to mention the bloody house it-self, oh, you're an old wankspot and no mistake . . ."

"Aaaaahhh," wailed Shoots, and before Anil could intervene he had flitted angrily across the room, arms flailing, to renew his attack on Victor, but this time his cousin, already on his feet and turning to meet the menace, was prepared: "Let's haste to th' encounter," cried Victor, hoarsely, as they clenched and caught and staggered side to side:

> To battle with this man;
> The ford we will come to,
> O'er which Badb will shriek!
> To meet with Shoots
> To wound his slight body,
> To thrust the spear through him
> So that he may die!

But as a one-time assistant presenter at the West Cork Ard Fheis, Shoots was more than equal to the occasion, and in pun-gent Erse:

"*Fai sund nech rat méla/is missi rat géna,*"[7] he declaimed, hero-ically, although in a somewhat strangled voice, with an unfriendly cousinly hand squeezing his Adam's apple; still, he soldiered on,

---

[7]Ah, "And see you, laddie," or words to that effect, "I'm the one's going to settle your hash," et cetera. Big fellas, those, with hips the width of a moun-tain pass, and biceps so broad an army of men could play handball against them, and they the handball champions of the four kingdoms; and shins of such a height that the cloud armies of Ulster met in their shadow, and brows so lofty it was said the thought that was born behind them took half the age of the dun cow to descend to their lips; and their lips as wide as the golden strand of Magilligan beneath the shadow-strewn reeks; and eyes the brightness of two suns and as bright as the Ga Bolga of great Cuchulain himself. (These two being a pair of silly old farts diminishes, but shouldn't entirely eliminate, this analogy.) Hang on a sec—this gives me an idea. (See below, a few dozen pages on, between here and where it says The End.)

at one with an ancient Irish tradition and his own memories of schoolboy fantasies of great Cuchulain on the bridge beneath Ulster's epic skies. The two old fools fell into a mutually entwined heap of pounding fists and clutching jaws, a true spectacle of Irish madness and determination akin in the mind of anyone but, say, an Indian onlooker, to the battle in the *Táin Bó Cúailnge* between Ferdia and Cuchulain themselves.

"Oh for goodness' sake," exclaimed Anil, "do stop that."

The vigour of combat was wearing fast, but still they heaved and punched. Enjoying his gin, Anil was reluctant to intervene, too late rising to his feet to step between the champions. Behind his back a draft trickled, the front door clicked shut, a strange voice spoke.

"Good evening."

And lo, a stranger stood on the threshold of the sitting room, like the Sunday visitor imposing a hush, even a truce, on the proceedings. The bringer of calm was a man. Anil hated him at once. (Victor and Shoots barely noticed him at first, each preferring to concentrate on encircling the other's neck with as many fingers as possible.) He was slim, dark complected, and black clad, indeed French-tailored if somewhat Levantine-vulgar, revealing the glint of a gold watch loose on the left wrist. His hair, close-cropped, was of uniform density and restrained from upwinging by indiscreet applications of a gel the citric tartness of which faintly scented the air. A certain fluidity of movement, and the ease with which he stood, legs planted firmly and evenly apart, implied athleticism, fitness, ease in his own skin, an expertise in martial arts—even, thought Anil, danger: This man, he stated firmly to himself after a rapid mental *tour d'horizon*, was a bully (just like Hosang Jaffrey back in Mr. Mukerjee's English class in college, come to think of it, only this bloke seemed to have some class and that greasy bags Jaffrey was about as classy as a shit-stained *dhoti*)—a barely controlled maniac, a potential murderer, an egotist. All of which added up, these days, to one thing, when you stopped to think about it: *terrorist.*

"Hi," said Anil cheerily, suppressing, he hoped, all traces of a quaver (he hadn't: the man noticed and gave a quietly self-confident smile somewhere around the outer corners of his mouth).

Yes, yes, mused Anil, the volumes spoken by those eyes (brown tending to black, with possible yellow accents, like the eyes of Krishna in that painting on the wall of Arun Day's Camera Shop across from their house in Sandrapore) were tomes of contempt, enriched by clear reading of another's weaknesses: instant, in Anil's case, as Anil sensed rather than saw—*no danger from that quarter,* the man's eyes said, reassuringly, having assessed the tremor in Anil's hand, the quaver in his voice, the sybaritism in his soul (armchair, gin, cigarette). The man dismissed the old-sters utterly, with the briefest and most disadainful of glances. Again, he considered Anil, recognizing in his obvious Third Worldness a possible link, and in him a potential coconspirator.

His English was French, or very meridional Latin: Italian? Spanish?

"Basque," he replied, on being asked. Oddly, Shoots was the inquirer ("Eh, are you a dago, eh?"). But the Basque kept his eyes on Anil.

"Bloody heck," self-swore the latter and said, "Basque, are you?" aloud. "Ah, what's your name? You're probably not Seamus, are you?"

"No. India, ya?"

"Well, yes."

"Hey."

"Hey, what?"

"Hey, I don't have to answer you."

Now what the hell does that mean, wondered Anil. Sinister, all of it. Like one of those bloody boring video-game films they made nowadays, *Mission: Botswana* or *SuperQuest IV* or one of those silly pieces of juvenile rubbish, usually starring Edd Dragonia or that other American actor, Benny Bob, no, Bobby Lee something, or whatever. Speaking of Americans, there was the trace of one of those accents in the fellow's speech somewhere, but judging by the chap's totally un-Yank appearance and his fancy continental clothes it was probably a result of watching too many American films on the telly rather than a stint at Harvard.

"Are you, or I mean, did you, um . . . ?"

But it was no time to ask. Urgency suddenly overtook the fellow's every movement. He strode forward with the easy fluid movements of a fencer or, God help us, a black belt karate *sensei,* and stared forcefully at Anil like a practiced hypnotist.

"Now," he said. "Who's responsible?"

Blankness reigned. Victor hawked quietly. Shoots crossed the room, shoes squeaking, to turn down the volume on the burlesque dance-hall music that was still emanating from the computer.

"Mind if I get back to my computer?" asked Victor. "You fellas carry on, like."

"*Your* computer?" said Shoots.

"Well, he's not taking us hostage, is he?" said Anil. He looked at the Basque intruder.

"Just tell me who's responsible and I'll go away. And you can have fun with your, ah, sex videos. I need the"—he shrugged a shoulder in the direction of outdoors—"truck. Who is responsible for it?"

"Well," and Anil heard within himself the warring warnings of a clamour of instincts all screaming *shut up—but wasn't being a free man the freedom to bloody well jump in with both feet and damn the consequences?* "That's me, I suppose, you know, at least I'm the one who drove it down. The van, I mean. Or truck."

"It's a van," grumbled Shoots, sotto voce.

"So, let's go," said the Basque. "You and me, Gandhiji."

"Go where?"

"Well, first to the truck, then to the port. We got business, I think. OK?"

Instantly, with an irresistible feeling of sanctimoniousness, Anil yielded to his main weakness, his towering temper and deeply seated (and entirely misplaced) self-esteem.

"I say, you, you said you'd go away if we told you who was responsible, well, bloody hell, I just told you, so why don't you bleeding well bugger off back to Basqueland or wherever you come from, you great big junglewalla? Who the bloody hell do you think you are, anyway?"

The Basque in response produced a small gun of efficient matte-black appearance, no doubt containing a compact magazine of many death-dealing bullets. No doubt as well that the fellow could use it like nobody's business.

"OK. I've had enough of this bullshit. We can go now."

"Of course," said Anil mildly, as if there were no gun present, as if he'd just been asked to go for a stroll in a midsummer garden by the loveliest girl in Thirthahalli. "Just coming," setting aside drink, half-smoked cigarette, ashtray . . . Holy Vishnu, self-raved Anil, it looked very much as if all this half-cocked nonsense wasn't over yet, despite what the lawyer Ormlet had said, the silly ape ("Drive it, drop it off, and we'll be there to drive you home with your police record wiped cleaner than your arse, nothing to it Anil, old son"[8]) ("old son" indeed; you see, it's precisely that kind

---

[8]A jackanapes, indeed. Reminds me of another legal arsehole, my second first cousin, distantly related to Monk, a prick named Proinsias or plain old Francie, the one who was a dead ringer for my first second cousin Ossie, Monk's cousin-in-law. What a specimen. Once the most promising young barrister in Dublin, but boys oh boys did Francie Pryor ever have his ups and downs. Wait till I tell you. Actually, he was better onstage than in court. During his long and distinguished association with the Midlands and Ballymuck Musical Society (M&B), he excelled in all the character roles of the Gilbert and Sullivan (G. and S.) repertoire excepting that of Shadbolt in *The Yeomen of the Guard,* for which he knew himself to be physically too small (he never

of smooth-talking *raanti* you'd want to avoid at all costs; it was the same everywhere), and here he was actually being taken hostage, not by a silly twit waving a minicam but by an actual armed man who was also probably an entirely real terrorist.

As they left, Shoots made as if to make halfhearted gestures of restraint and apology but plainly thought better of completing

---

exceeded four foot six inches, even in elevators). But he didn't confine himself to G. and S. He was an honorary life member of the Bohemians, and frequently entertained at their Wednesday night musical gatherings in Burke's Hotel, Dundrum, behind the dais, where he was quite invisible except for the movements of his stiffly combed *chevelure.* His last stage appearance was in *H. M. S. Pinafore,* in which he introduced a four-foot-six-inch character named Parcels who is chased off the stage in Act II by a six-foot-six-inch able seaman named Harold Wilson. But life wasn't all strawberries and cream. One has to earn one's bread, and Cousin Francie's working life was spent in the law offices of the Electricity Supply Board (ESB), which he joined in the early 1940s after studying for a law degree at TCD. He was called to the Bar in 1954, where he excelled—but not for long. His tendency, in court and out, to proffer unwanted and sententious advice ("It is preferable in this life not to whinge," "In our profession we adhere to one motto: Never Apologise, Never Explain—Except to Your Betters," "The sooner you learn that everyone's your better, the better") was exacerbated by a growing array of bizarre personal predilections inimical to peace in chambers. These included: (1) adapting the loud clicking of his dentures to the purposes of performing musical selections (a pursuit not entirely without risk; indeed, one memorable evening while performing the castanet section from the theme to *Iolanthe* he choked on his choppers and had to be rushed to the Mater in an ambulance); (2) introducing himself to clients as "Viscount Thompson, with a 'P'"; (3) wearing masks on the job, his favourite being that of Pongo from *101 Dalmatians.* When he was finally sacked (by none other than the up-and-coming senior partner, one Gerald O'Mallet) he took to the world's highways in a fish-frier's van, and for all I know he travels them yet. Ah, well: life's a funny old bag of oysters, as Mum's boyfriend Mr. McCoy used to say when they pulled one of those trick endings on his favourite TV show, *Bag of Oysters* (RTE19).

any of them. Eventually, his shoulders slumped in a token of submission to circumstances (a lifelong failing).

"Cheerio," he mumbled.

"Arrh," snarled Victor, in the distance.

Words of regret came to Anil's mind.

Oh, Auntie. I am sorry.

16

"*Tiocfaidh ar La.*"

"Sorry, wrong password."

"What the blazes do you mean, wrong password? Did you hear me at all? *Tiocfaidh ar la*, for God's sake."

"Sorry."

The sallow, ill-shaven face—with the glum expression of a churchman, or one deeply hung over—disappeared behind the door, which then closed gently but firmly in Pats Bewley's own blanched visage.

"Well, lads," said Pats.

"Well yourself," said one of the "lads," Mrs. Bashir, a self-described "Libyan comrade" of mature figure and surprising youth. "So much for this caper then, eh?"

"Not at all," said Pats. "I've a trick or two up my sleeve. Eh . . . does anyone have five bob for the phone?"

"No, but you can use my mobile," said Mrs. Bashir. She exuded an air of being a lady of many such gadgets.

"Thanks, Mrs. B. I won't be a sec."

Pats took the phone and himself away to the corner of the street and was soon conversing in a rapid undertone, with alternating expressions of obsequiousness and rage duelling like Scaramouche and the Marquis de Rathbone across the sagging wasteland of his face. Mrs. Bashir lit a cigarette and glanced impatiently at her watch. Her companions, Fuad and Anwar, two alleged Libyan marine quartermasters in their early forties, conferred in undertones. The three of them were dressed for rambling: anoraks, plus-twos, corduroys, Aran pullovers, cameras. Rubescent were their mahogany cheeks, but it was the flush of health, not booze, for the two lads were self-styled teetotalers to a man,[1] nonsmokers, too, and no doubt would be eager participants in such outdoorsy events as Pats Bewley's weekend field trips, of which the present event was but a pallid spinoff. Disguised as an outing to the famously scenic south Killoyle countryside, its true purpose was to arrange a "top secret" meeting between Mrs. Bashir, described in her identity papers as the niece of the Libyan finance minister, and the Soldiers of Brian O'Nolan, a growing republican splinter group always on the lookout for more money. With Mrs. Bashir (and her uncle, the sinister Iqbal Shaw) championing "new, aggressive, streamlined liberation movements," it was as natural a get-together as chips and vinegar, or rice and cardamoms. It had been the work of a simple phone call from the Jocelyn Motors dealership in London (Jocelyns were highly prized in the oil kingdoms, where having the price of constant repairs was a matter of prestige) to Pats Bewley, with the usual promise of a 10 percent cut—"Fifteen percent"; "Twelve"; "Thirteen or I'm not dealing and that's flat"; "Twelve it is, mister": "Oh, all right"—and the meeting was on.

All morning Pats Bewley and his three followers had marched grimly through the bogs and crannogs, stood atop Mount Maher, admired the famously sexy sheila-na-gig and looked in at

---

[1] I've had just about enough of this teetotaling nonsense. In the immortal words of the late great Frank Sinatra, "If that's as good as you're going to feel all day you might as well just stay in bed and put a fucking bullet in your brain. I mean, honestly." I mean, honestly.

St. Oinsias' luxurious stone hammock; sheets of rain had hardly damped their spirits, nor a cruel east wind their ardour—until now, on a side street off the main street of the hamlet of Crawlin, in the heather-covered High Breaks of south co. Killoyle, GHQ of the Soldiers of Brian O'Nolan, when it looked as if they might be denied both their tea and the day's main attraction.

"My good man, do hurry up and arrange this matter," said Mrs. Bashir, left elbow cradled in right hand, cigarette wagging 'twixt left index and middle finger. "I have business to discuss. And I do so want to meet one of those heroes, you know. I mean, they're so strong and masculine. And hardly anyone is anymore, when you stop to think about it. Especially men." And she had, after all, she pointed out, parenthetically, paid good money for the privilege (£50 a head, nonrefundable).

Pats snapped shut the mobile phone. Fuad and Anwar were standing together at some distance from Mrs. Bashir, discussing the economic policies of the Libyan government.

"I mean, look at your trade surplus, down eight point ought three percent in the current fiscal year alone."

"Yes, but if current projections hold, we'll see sustained growth of no more than one half of one percent next quarter."

Pats returned the mobile.

"It was all a misunderstanding, God bless us," he said. "With my accent he thought I was saying 'Please go home,' whereas in actual fact—I just checked with the Erse linguistics department at Killoyle Upper College—the password is 'our time will come,' with a stress on the second syllable: Tioc*faidh*. I was never too strong in the Irish. OK. Let's try it again."

Shoulders confidently squared, Pats strode up to the door and rang the bell. The door opened immediately, as if the owner of the sallow face were (indeed, probably had been) standing just behind, waiting for the bell to ring.

"Tioc*faidh ar la*," declared Bewley loudly, as if addressing a foreigner of limited intelligence and hearing.

"Right-o," said the sullen face, brightening somewhat, and re-treating the requisite distance to yield to the opening door and incoming visitors.

"Ladies and gentlemen," boomed the face, "welcome to command headquarters of the South Munster Brigade of the Soldiers of Brian O'Nolan."

The visitors found themselves in a Robert Adam-inspired entrance hall. A frosted-glass dome dribbled dusty light onto a stylized portrait of Brian O'Nolan, chief inspiration of the movement—shown leaning on McDaid's Bar counter, in 1954, lurching somewhat backward, eyes fixed on a heavenly vision of Erin personified as an auburn-haired demigoddess in flowing toga-like robes, perched amid stratocumuli of a tropical voluptuousness never seen in Ireland.

"Stupendous," said Mrs. Bashir. "Is that William Shakespeare?"

When gently corrected, she said, "Oh, an Irish author? I'd no idea you had them. Or that you lot had so much money."

"All stolen, I doubt," muttered Fuad, or Anwar.

"Fund-raising," growled their guide. "I'd watch it if I was you, clever dick. Starting now."

"Sorry," said Fuad and Anwar in slapstick unison.

The party proceeded to echoing, gabled Clontarf Chambers, the main "ops" room, next door to which were the archives, leading in their turn to the Sean MacStiofain Great Hall, a barrel-vaulted inner sanctum which contained the memoirs and papers of MacStiofain, the distinguished Englishman and former IRA chief of staff.[2] A step or two down and there, in a former parlour,

---

[2]Né John Stephenson in Walthamstow, in his twenty-fifth year he came to the conclusion that he was just too bloody English, if you know what I mean. I mean, his dad was a copper, ex-Royal Marines (Cyprus, Aden), his mum a schoolteacher from Lichfield. Young John attended Walthamstow Comprehensive, sat his A Levels a year early and did quite well in math and history,

was the armoury, with Bukhara carpets on the floor and stained-glass windows in the style of Sir Runciman Petrie (Victorian neogothic, circa 1874) depicting the flight of the earls; and in a shallow basement room across a narrow hall was the commandant's office. The commandant himself, Mr. Finn, whom we have met before in the guise of head librarian at the Killoyle Public Library, was seated at his desk, an imitation Chippendale with clawed feet. He rose to his feet as the visitors appeared. In deference, the sallow young man, whose nom de guerre was Tyrconnell ("charming!" said Mrs. Bashir), retreated into the middle distance and allowed the visitors to proceed on their own.

In any case, Pats Bewley appeared to have a more than nodding acquaintance with Commandant Finn, who greeted him by name.

---

then went up to Thames Poly and got a two-two in industrial design and hardware. Like every other bloke on his street he smoked Embassy Regals in the blue packet, drank Bass bitter, played football with his mates every Saturday, and went on holiday with his girlfriend (Sheila) to Torremolinos. Well, there came a moment in his life, possibly in a Kilburn or Archway pub before or after a Saturday match (go Arsenal), when his Englishness quite simply overwhelmed him; and it happened at a moment when he chanced to over-hear the deliciously mangled syllables of Dublin talk. Well, our John drains his half of bitter and boldly sashays up to the bar and loudly requests "A point of staht." To himself he said, "That's it, mate, enough's enough, they can't force a bloke to be too English." To the world he said, "I'm opting out, hold my coat would you, from now on I'm Irish and you can call me Sean." Well you can imagine the reaction of his mates down the pub. "Irish? You're joking!" "Irish? Do me a favour!?" "Irish, did you say? *Irish?* Pull the other one, it's got bells on." "Oh yeh? And mine's a pint of Watneys." "Right. And I'm King bleed-ing Kong. Darts, anyone?" Well, that left our John (now our Sean) with little choice but to join the IRA, just to show 'em, the snooty superior East End sods. And before you (or he) knew it, there he was, running things at Belfast Republican HQ and throwing bombs at his ex-compatriots like nobody's business. I dunno. Just goes to show. Funny old life, innit?

"Hello, Bewley," said he.

"Hello, Finn," said Pats Bewley. "Mind if we just . . . ?"

"Absolutely. But first things first."

With that, Mr. Finn, who in his present capacity was wearing jungle camouflage and three-pip epaulettes denoting the rank of brigadier general, scratched his bum vigorously and handed to his visitors a form containing a waiver of evidence, should they ever be questioned as to the whereabouts of present GHQ.

"You may say it is located in Ireland," said the form, *"but please obfuscate. We recommend, for example, that you claim to have heard seagulls mewing in the middle distance. Or that the sound of heavy air traffic was quite audible, even inside. Or that crowds stood five deep outside the cinema next door. Have a good day and don't forget: Up the Revolution!"*

"Oh, my sense of direction is quite hopeless," said Mrs. Bashir. "Even if I wanted to direct people here, I'd be sure to send them the wrong way." She trilled the carefully schooled, and entirely sham, laugh of a thousand cocktail encounters, and affixed her signature with a flourish, as if enjoying the ceremony—in contrast to Fuad and Anwar, who signed the document with the grim indifference of those accustomed to hunkering their lives away over triplicate applications and other formulae of the bureaucratic life.

Once these formalities had been dispensed with, Finn locked the forms in a drawer in his desk and put on a display of that bland blend of obsequiousness and stern command that made him (in his mind) no less efficient a brigade commander than a head librarian. It was his pleasure, he assured his guests (his pride leaping forward like a hungry leopard), to show off the state-of-the-art computer center and other ultramodern facilities of the Soldiers of Brian O'Nolan, all provided by the most generous of government grants, he explained, in the wake of the third peace treaty and the recent General Pro-Terrorist Amnesty and Assistance Act.

"Oh, yes, we've done quite well, I daresay," he said. "Heavens, you should have seen us when we started, two outdated IBM computers for the whole operation and no Internet hookup at all. Virtually steam-powered. Primitive times, ladies and gentlemen, primitive times. Of course, that was back in preamnesty days, before we broke away from the mainstream Republican movement, when the prime source of income was robbing banks, hijackings, kidnappings—I'm sure you remember, those stories were all over the newspapers," he enthused, warming to his subject, like a small boy discussing electric trains. "Now, as you can see, we have instant communication worldwide. There's our Gaza screen," pointing, as a cheerful computer operator turned and waved. "That's Seamus," said Finn. "Say hello, Seamus. And over there are our links to Athens, Tripoli—yes madam, would you like to say hello to your friends?—and Teheran. San Sebastian, Chiapas, and Bogotá are in there somewhere." He indicated a low doorway beyond which the half darkness glowed bluely in the soft light of more computer screens.

"Remarkable," said Mrs. Bashir. "So what do you need me for?"

Finn doubled over, like a flamingo at feed, in appreciative pseudomirth.

"Good heavens, Mrs. Bashir, for the field operations, of course," he said, wiping false tears from his eyes. "We're skint. We spent all we have on all this stuff. And a few old Katyushas. And the odd Armalite." He peered intently for a moment, at first laterally, then boldly, straight on. "I say, have we met before?"

"No," said Mrs. Bashir, firmly. "And do you do much bombing and shooting yourself, Mr. Finn?"

Finn neighed delicately.

"Goodness me, madam, we hardly 'do bombing and shooting,' as you put it. No, we prefer to describe our missions as active or exploratory. I *do* occasionally go on exploratory missions, frequently in the company of our overseas liaisons, to learn the lay of the land in different target areas. Last year, for instance, I was in the Basque country. Have you ever been there, madam? No? Are you sure? Ah, you ought to go if you have a chance. Ah, yes, quite beautiful. The Guggenheim in Bilbao, you know. Excellent bathing as well, and the food ... ! Well, here, for instance, we have an officer from the Bilbao command of the ETA-II, a breakaway organization similar to our own: Harry Batasuna, or Subcomandante Harry as he prefers to be known."

The young man who had just entered the room gave a slight start.

"Are you Indian?" inquired he of Mrs. Bashir, with some alarm.

"Libyan," she replied, quickly. "Benghazi."

Harry nodded. He had been to Benghazi, once, and at the mention of the name he had a memory flash of baked beaches, endless Fiats, raucous urchins, old men smoking at metal café tables, and no wine or beer anywhere except in the oil compound, for exorbitant prices.

"Ah. A beautiful city."

Such a lie. God, he only wanted this assignment to be over. He had his Isabella back in Irun, and the two of them had plans for a minirace of heroic Euskadians when the war with the Castilian world was won ... but for now he played the game, and had done so quite well, never so well as over the last day or two; oh, he was in line for the top job now, as Commandant Finn had said: snatching an arms cache from under the noses of the Provos, and kidnapping an Indian courier to boot. Exemplary!

But their plans might differ.

"At first, I propose to ransom the Indian," Harry had said, "and share with you whatever we get, if anything. Then I suggest we divide the arms equally, one-third to Soldiers of Brian O'Nolan, one-third to me, and one-third to ETA-II."

Finn's initial reaction had been less than favourable.

"One-third for you?"

Subcomandante Harry, uninterested, had coughed into a balled fist. "Possibly. It's negotiable. Oh, and incidentally, if no ransom is coming for the Indian within let us say a week or ten days—

and there might not be one, you know, I think he is completely no one, an absolute nullity, a zero, how do you say . . . ?"

"Um, nonentity, I believe."

"Then I propose—"

"Or nobody. We can say nobody."

"—to execute him, OK? Slowly, you know, one piece at a time."

"Oh? Well, OK, I suppose. Not too sure about the one piece at a time part, though. Must check the rules."

No sooner said than done: Thumbing briskly through the rulebook, Commandant Finn had ascertained that prompt or prolonged (for information-gathering purposes) termination of alien entities was indeed standard practice with political prisoners who had outlived their usefulness, although the commandant could not help but think (not for the first time) that Mrs. Finn might not entirely approve. Still, war was war, he reminded himself cheerily, and the missus didn't need to know, and what with her aversion to TV news programmes she'd not be likely to hear about it, would she, and he could always blame it on somebody else, it wasn't as if they hadn't done that a few dozen times. Thank God for the Provos, anyway; they were there to take the heat, weren't they?

And if not, what bloody use were they, apart from providing training and materiel and some of those crackerjack videos?

Finn had also found himself wondering parenthetically if that Miss Burke was up to dealing with the semiannual librarian's retreat that he'd been forced to opt out of . . . but priorities asserted themselves and he had soon returned to the business at hand.

"Subcomandante Harry's a real trooper, you know," he said to Mrs. Bashir. "I don't believe he's slept in the past forty-eight hours."

"Duty comes first," said Subcomandante Harry, didactically.

"Good man," said Pats Bewley, himself an enthusiastic proponent of devotion to the task at hand. "Eh . . . could we have a drop of tea, Mr. Finn? It's been a long and thirsty day, that it has, oh aye."

"Certainly, Mr. Bewley, certainly. Although with your name you ought to be able to summon up the owld pot of tay out of thin air, eh? Ha ha ha ha."

Bewley looked blank.

"Eh?"

"*Salaam*, Harry." Mrs. Bashir floated out of the room. Nice, Harry thought, nice. These Arab women, they are man-mad, as all their men prefer boys . . . odd, she does look more like an Indian . . . meanwhile, speaking of Indians (he reminded himself), there's the Indian courier, the ransom, the broadcast, so much to arrange . . . and this man Finn's more in love with his uniform and the posters he gets free from his government than with the actual day-to-day duties of the commandant of a liberation army. Truth to tell (but not to Finn), Harry Batasuna had been in touch with the Provisional IRA crowd a few times; quite half a dozen or more, in fact, the Soldiers not having quite the same cachet over in Euskadi, at least not yet; but the traditional crowd was the same in Ireland as they were in Bilbao, enmeshed in thoughts of yesterday's wars, contemptuous of the novel and untested, in a word (or two): *old women with Armalites*. So he and ETA-II (of which he was the nominal field commander, after all, a courtesy reciprocated, unfortunately, by ETA-II to Finn) had thrown in their lot with the Soldiers of Brian O'Nolan, and recognition for both was just a matter of time after this latest mission, all thanks to him.[3]

---

[3]Into the bog with this smarmy wee bastard and his ilk and pull the chain good and proper. The degree of self-justification in the human animal is quite boggling to the mind, or worse. I mean, these blokes can go and blow up innocents and sleep soundly the night after, all because they've read Tintin and go about with bright Hergé-scripted versions of the future, which of course

But the Indian was a real shitmaker, it was true. He had to do something about the fellow, and soon, especially if the miserable guy croaked on him, which could happen at any minute (perhaps that iron bar had been a bit extreme, but circumstances in the field were never what you expected them to be, were they?).

Shaking his head, burdened by the heavy responsibilities of terrorist administration, Subcomandante Harry returned to the operations room, sat down at a computer terminal, and resumed his strategizing.

Speaking of the Indian, Mrs. Bashir, Fuad, and Anwar all pleaded with Pats Bewley and Commandant Finn to allow them a glimpse—just a look-see—a peek?

"Oh, all right. But just a peek, mind."

Finn led them down a short flight of stairs and along a dimly lit passage, at the end of which was a door. Mrs. Bashir turned away and with a tiny delicate gilded pencil scarcely larger than a matchstick, she scribbled something in a small notebook she prestidigitated out of, and back into, her right sleeve.

"Here he is," said Finn, jovially. "Oy! Ullo in there!"

One by one they looked through the peephole.

"He doesn't look too well."

"Is he dead?

---

is never anything like what they imagine, the bloody fools. Just think about it: Is this what you thought the twenty-first century would be like, after all those flicks and comic books? Not I, mate. I'd expected a helicopter in every garage and lots of blond birds in red one-piece bodysuits at the very least; but the reality is, given the nature of human nature, as it were, just more of the bloody same, plus mod cons. For instance, I'm sure my dear old da would still be quite at home down the street at Harrigan's, just as he was for forty years, with the possible exception of computer talk and the like, but every age has its fleeting jargon. Why, back in the forties, they talked with many a wearisome nudge and wink of "snappers" and "bridles" as the coming thing, and who remembers that ballocks? Not I, for one.

"I'm not sure; I don't think so . . . of course, he *was* interrogated by Subcomandante Harry, who's nothing if not thorough, ha ha . . . no, there, look, he moved."

"No, I think that was a fly."

"What's that around his head?"

"A turban? Is he a Sikh?"

"Why don't you ask him?" said Mrs. Bashir, through gritted teeth.

"Right-o. I say, there," sang out Fuad, "you there, my good fellow, are you a Sikh at all, by any chance, eh what?"

At the sound of his voice, it seemed momentarily as if the recumbent Indian stirred slightly.

"Oh, no, look, it's covered in blood."

"Ugh. I wonder if he's conscious."

"Hello there! Hello!"

"How's the curry hereabouts?"

"Waiter! Two chapatis please, and a side of mango chutney! Ha ha!"

"All right, that's enough, come along now."

Pats Bewley turned to Finn, with a ochre-coloured smile plastered across his smarmy gob.

"Well, *Commandant* Finn," he said, with what sounded perilously and (to his companions) unaccountably like irony, if not sarcasm: "To business? Eh?"

So he, Mrs. Bashir, and her two lieutenants closeted themselves with the commandant for a good half an hour by St. Wolseley's clock,[4] and when they emerged it was in a fuzzy if not downright

---

[4]Crawlin's local church spire. Interesting thing about that particular hamlet is that it's 100 percent English, despite it's being in Ireland, like. As the local guidebook says, "Note the sculpture of St. Wolseley and the Spaniel. Below this sculpture is a bifora window with a relief of St. Nicholson in the lunette; an oculus surrounded by heads of angels; and, at street level, a pair of crouching telamones." Nice, but it's C. of I., and there's no R.C. church at

furry glow of human warmth and bonhomie, spewing ions of goodwill and happiness.

"So it was Zurich, was it?" said Finn, with a trace of hand-wringing. "Or Geneva?"

"Either one," said Mrs. Bashir. A hint of weariness—at the world, at men, at Finn—crossed her finely sculpted features. "We have accounts in both cities, Mr. . . . . Ah . . ."

"Finn."

"Yes. Good-bye, then."

"We've enjoyed having you," said Finn, with the utmost sincerity, for he did, indeed, enjoy showing off his uniform and demonstrating his talents as an administrator. "And remember—mum's the word!" Eyes twinkling, he raised a forefinger to his lips. "Or we'll come after you and do some professional work on your kneecaps, ha ha!"

"Ha ha my eye," said Mrs. Bashir when they were at the bus stop, out of earshot of the nervously watch-consulting Pats Bewley (he had a test drive scheduled in forty-five minutes, and by gum he'd better be on the premises or they'd likely pass on the commission to one of them newcomers, dodgy lads all of 'em). "I wonder if he meant it," she mused. "About the kneecaps."

"Oh, I should think so," said Anwar, or Fuad. "I don't know about everybody else, but I thought he was a bit narky."

"Absolutely," said Fuad, or Anwar.

"Of course, the man's an idiot of astonishing proportions," said Mrs. Bashir, as much to herself as to anyone else. "Idiocy of such

---

all, and nary a name in the town adorned with O' or Mac. As for the pubs, they all have silly Agatha Christie-ish names like the Fox and Hounds and the King's Arms. Oodles of Smythes, and bags of Brownes, and one or two Worsthornes and Thatchers, and it's rumoured widely that a Union Jack floats lazily above the town hall every queen's birthday, but no one's ever admitted to seeing it. Ideal place for an armed Irish guerrilla group, I suppose you could say.

magnitude is near-genius," she added loudly, as if conscious of coining an aphorism—but it was ignored, the fate of most aphorisms.

"Wouldn't like to run into him on a dark night, eh?" chirped Fuad.

"Not at all, thanks very much," said Anwar. "Ah, here's the bus. Should get us back to town in time for market closing."

"Oh, I don't think so. If we travel at the standard twenty-five miles per hour we'll just miss it."

"Fifty pee says you're full of Bulmers."

"You're on."

And in a spirit of good fellowship, the little party, tired but relatively happy, boarded the cheerful green-and-white (with purple edgings) CIE coach and rocked and swayed jollily, in sympathy with the vehicle's aging but still-fluid suspension, all the way back along the coast road and inland through the bitter marshes of the northern Southern Breaks, past the great sheila-na-gig and so, via St. Oinsias' stone hammock, where now there gathered Japanese tourists united in their desire for the world's most perfect photo album, to Killoyle City—just after the markets had closed ("Rats!" exclaimed Fuad, or Anwar, "I owe you fifty pee")—and the bleak snot-green precincts of MacLiammoir Bus Terminal (alias Busaras). Once there, Pats Bewley hurried off to the Jocelyn works, rubbing brisk hands obsequiously.

"Cheerio, then," he bawled, "and remember: Mum's the word, ah ha ha! But do call if you, ah . . . need anything else, like. Eh?"

Anwar and Fuad discreetly conferred with Mrs. Bashir in the shadowy purlieus behind the bus terminal; then, having pocketed their fees (£5 each), they mounted Anwar's Vespa scooter, Fuad riding pillion, and put-putted away to their respective jobs as headwaiter and assistant headwaiter at the Star of Bihar. As for the elegant and mysterious Mrs. Bashir, she soon threw off her disguise and set to work on a plan that had better not fail, by Vishnu, or she wasn't Rashmi Vashnapuram, newly released pseudomilitant (bail of £1,000 airmailed from Calcutta on Overnight Oberoi Express), globe-trotting troubleshooter and would-be femme fatale—which of course she was, and a budding actress of no mean talent, even if the dopes whom she'd duped as Mrs. Nonexistent Bashir were cretins, as she repeated to herself, of the most thoroughgoing and credulous nature. Like retarded children with a taste for heavy artillery.

"Rubina?" she inquired, later of her mobile phone. "It's OK. He's there. I saw him. We're ready. *Jai.*" She dialed again, then: "Super?" she inquired further of the same source. "We're going in."

Two hours into the darkest recesses of the night a silver BMW 3-series coupe, Rashmi's, driven by herself with Rubina Swain at her side, both of them even darker-hued than their birth tint under burnt cork makeup hastily applied in the interests of ano-nymity—and ready for combat in olive-drab combat fatigues (supplied by Rashmi from a favourite scrounger in Army Sur-plus in Deradun), ill-fitting but oh so stylish—drifted silently, headlamps dimmed, into the night-darkened grove of yew trees behind Armalite Hall—in which only the lights of one room, that (Rashmi judged) in which Anil was being held, were on.

"That's him," she whispered. "I'm sure."

"OK."

Their tactics wers spontaneous but their strategy rehearsed. Their determination was steel-solid but their dependence on the gods (especially Krishna) absolute and unquestioning. Rashmi's instructions were clear and delivered in a strident contralto. With her Nagano 3500S SuperMicroCam hanging from a cord around her neck, she would remain in charge of photography—"We want to be able to recognize these beggars in the police ID parade, don't we?"—and the getaway angle. Meanwhile, Rubina would run into the woods behind the house hefting a Vijay-Boas X240 MegaSound personal stereo/CD/cassette player with detachable subwoofer loudspeakers. Behind concealing bushes she was to assemble the machinery with particular attention to the exact placement, ideally in treetops, of the loudspeakers. Then, after a discreet, whispered one-two-three audio test, into the stereo would go a brand-new digitally enhanced recording of Bhoona Bulbul, the Nepalese Nightingale, rendering her latest hit "Swami Swami O," a hit the length and breadth of the subcontinent from Bhadgaon to Bangalore, a song whose unresolved modulation from G minor to D^5 could only, at sufficient volume, blast the socks off any listener, with concomitant damage to eardrums not at all unlikely. (Rubina was equipped with Styrofoam earplugs of a nice squishy consistency that lent themselves to creative fidgeting when not in use as the manufacturer intended.) Meanwhile, Rashmi and her camera, behind another conveniently placed item of shrubbery, would be awaiting the inevitable sudden front-door exodus from Armalite House of the paltry Soldiers of Brian O'Nolan force (six, she estimated, in all). It would, she assured palpitating Rubina, then be but the work of a moment to run inside and free Anil.

"How?"

"With this." Rashmi brandished a jimmy.

"What's that, a nutcracker?"

"No, silly. Look." And she fell upon a padlock at hand and dexterously, within the space of seconds, split or entire, had defeated the puny mechanism.

"Where did you learn to do that?"

"Calcutta. Labour tribunals. The prosecution had incriminating documents, so they sent me in. . . . But it's a long story."

Rubina gazed openmouthed, with a wriggling tapeworm of anticipatory envy, at her intrepid, dashing young cousin-in-law.

---

[5]Considering the F# as a simple delay of E-natural, producing a dominant seventh in third inversion? Hand me the earplugs.

The loudspeakers were in position and the CD was in the stereo when a curious dog arrived and had to be shooed away with hissed imprecations in Hindi—a language the cur appeared to understand, judging by its reaction on the visual basis at least of drooping tail and uncertain rearward glances. With no further disturbances, at three minutes past midnight GMT Rubina turned on the machine and inserted the CD. A loud crackling came from the loudspeakers; then, ten seconds later, tablas throbbed, a sitar uttered its plangent diminuendo, and the piercing countersoprano of Bhoona Bulbul ripped asunder the plump, velvety Indo-Irish night.

Swami-i-i-i-i-i-i-i-i-i-i-i-i-i-i-i-i-i-i-i-i-i-i-i-i-i-i-i-i-i-i-i-i-i-i-i-i-i
Swa-a-a-a-a-a-a-a-a-a-a-a-a-a-a-a-a-a-a-a-a-a-a-a-a-a-a-a-a-a-mi
O-O-O-O-O-O-O-O-O-O-O-O-O-O-O-O-O-O-O-O-O-O-O-O-O.

Exclamations of manly rage were not long in coming. With camera purring quietly, Rashmi crouched in her olive-drab fatigues behind the bushes, expectant. In Armalite House the lights went on and off and on again. Footsteps pounded. A dog barked in English.

"Come *on*," Rashmi said urgently. "Oh, do hurry up."

Finally the front door opened and six men ran out: The glum young fellow who'd let them in; Subcomandante Harry Batasuna ("Oh, I know you," muttered Rashmi, pointing the microcam, "oh yes I do"); Finn, with gangling motions of arms and legs; a hefty chap wearing a chef's toque; and two sallow youngsters. At first they seemed intent on confounding Rashmi by splitting up and going in separate directions, but to her relief they coalesced and at a rapid pace departed in unison for the Bulbul-melodious woods. Rashmi lost no time. She turned off the camera and slung it around her neck, and inside a minute she was at Anil's cell door, jimmy in hand. But as luck, and incompetence, would have it, the door was open; he was awake, if groggy; and she had him out of the house and safely, if painfully, tucked into the back seat of her BMW before they, or he, could say "Jack Robinson."

Rubina, who had made her way back to the car through the grove of yews, clung to her battered hubby so hard he screamed in pain.

"Shut *up*," hissed Rashmi, maneuvering car and gearbox rapidly into prime departure mode. "We're not out of the woods yet."

"Oh, but we are," said Rubina. "We are." She gazed fondly at Anil, clucking piteously at the bruises and swollen lip that betokened his recent ordeal.

They raced into the night, as behind them the swelling voice of Bhoona Bulbul was suddenly cut off, with a gruff voice snarling,

"There. That takes care of that fucking din. Question is, who's the bastards who put us up to this caper?"

"The Indian!"

"Fuck me, I'll wager you're right."

"Nice stereo, but. Reckon it'll fetch a couple hundred."

"Aye, that'll buy us a gram or two of Semtex, right enough."

"You estupid fools. *Madrecita.*"

"Oy, watch yer language."

"Or you will do what? Hah? Hah? You big impotent?"

"Now, now, come along, lads. Let's go back in and have a nice cuppa. We've work to do."

17

The pint-pulling Olympiad was nigh, and all the world was an athlete. The brewers had assembled their teams and champion barmen were on their way from the four points of the compass. In honour of the occasion Milo Rogers, heir to the great *fili* of Ireland's bardic past, and newly appointed poet laureate of Munster, had penned a neo-Augustan scrap of verse, at no one's urging save that of the foolish old muse within him.

OLYMPIA HIBERNICA

Through stocious *Killoyle* town
Beside the silvery puk'd-upon strand
Abundant *ale* untrammel'd flows
From agèd oaken beerkegs tap't,
By dreams and trembling hands inspired
Boozeward, and beyond.
Ay, thence wends *stout* her copper'd foam,
A Rhine of drink, a Meander in flood,
'Twixt bar and freehold, dusk and dawn,
All amply, abundantly, fully *pissed,*
Till *hangover* shrills her morning horn.

Hey! Hey!

(Milo thought the italics and odd abbreviations gave it a nice Popean effect,[1] but the *Clarion* rejected it all the same, the bloody philistines.[2] "Atrophied rubbish," sneered their poetry editor. "Pure bumwipe," decreed the editor-in-chief, a former friend. *Just as well*, sniffed Milo. *They'd have just spelled everything wrong anyway.*)

So it was in the Balsa Room of the Spudorgan Vacation Inn, under his moist, pink-rimmed, but ever-keen (if somewhat jaundiced) eye,[3] that the poetaster and hotel managing director was supervising the pre-Olympic preparations. It was the first day of the ale festival, first event of the Olympiad, a day that would be devoted to tastings, beer tours, and general drunkenness, it was to be hoped of a polite variety. On the second day would be the tasting contest; and on the third, final day, the world's best bartenders would compete for the title of Champion Pint-Puller. Not since the royal visit of 1828, when His Majesty George IV reprised his smash hit from Howth Harbour, "The King Pukes All Over Himself,"[4] had Killoyle seen such excitement.

---

[1] No Pope here, if you ask me. Just joking. But ask a man about his own work, eh?

[2] First good thing I've heard about them lads, let me tell you.

[3] Thanks for very little. All right, all right, I'll scrub round your more personal comments for now, but we'll take the subject up again later when this silly rubbish is done with. Just you and me, mate, out back, *comprende?*

[4] A tremendous hit, I understand. Tree*men*jous, boy, and I mean not at all. Just look it up in the *Clarion* archives. Actually, it was a disaster—a catastrophe—a *farce.* And on a fine blustery day in March, too, just this side (or that) of St. Pat's, in the Year of our Lord 1828, with the sky alternately a lowering Nordic grey and a ceramic-bright Levantine blue. Great golden beams of light probed the scudding clouds. Rain squirted down in alternating light freshets and vicious downpours of horsepiss intensity. Umbrellas—uniformly black— bloomed like the petals of the deadly nightshade, then folded up immediately, unlike same. A band was playing, desultorily, pops of the age ("Tyne of Har-

Milo was on his second stint in the manager's office at the venerable pile that he had so long served in such a variety of positions, most of them supine. What hadn't he done over the years,

---

row," "For He's a Jolly Good Fellow," "Ranulph Robinson my Dear," "How Cold and Temperate Am I Grown," "Alas! I Cannot Keep my Sheep," "That Time the Groves Were Clad in Green," and other favourites), the musicians' noses red with the wind and the drink. On the dock snapped the standards of the House of Hanover, that of the three then-united kingdoms, the blue Harp banner of Brian Boru, and the sacred standard of the four provinces. There were Burke, Murphy, Smythe, and Smith, the local aldermen; Sir Percival Percy, K.C., the magistrate; Zachariah Snodgrass the lord mayor of West South (as Killoyle was then known, or occasionally South West when the wind was in that quarter); the Munster military governor, Lord Elphinstone; Signore Spinelli, the famous Neapolitan tenor; and various and sundry lords, ladies and gentlemen. Docked and quietly rocking in the swell was the royal yacht *Hannelore,* on loan from the Brunswicks and flying, therefore, not only the Red Duster and the Lion Rampant but also the black and gold of the German princely states and the imperial standard of Prussia; and there, finally, after the assembled dignitaries had been waiting for an hour and a half, huffing and puffing impatiently, consulting their fobs, stroking their dundrearies, open ing and closing their umbrellas, passing around a flask or two of finest single malt: His Majesty King George IV of England, Scotland, and Ireland; prince of Hanover, Saxe-Coburg, and Thuringia; duke of Cornwall, prince of Plattenberg, maharajah of Jaipur, grand duke of Niederwald and Lower Uhland, Defender of the Faith, et cetera, et cetera. "I say," said His Majesty, reeling, "more bloody Irishmen," then, with one hand on the ship's rail, he tilted his leonine head sideways and vomited heartily and copiously over the broad shoulders of Sir Darcy Dancer, the royal equerry. In response to the murmur that rose from the dockside crowd, His Majesty turned and bellowed, wiping his mouth on the waistcoat of a colonel in the Irish guards, "And you lot bloody well shut up, you horrible Irish bounders." Then, without further ado, the king lurched belowdecks, where he could be heard bringing up the remainder of his ill-digested lunch and roaring for ale. The yacht cast off moorings while the disillusioned crowd offered up a pro forma, and quite ragged, rendition of "God Save the King," before dispersing in grumbling twos and threes. Typical, eh? Small wonder we got rid of the bastards.

after all, short of scrubbing the boss's privates?[5] *Jaysus, God, and the fuckin' massed saints of heaven Al-fuckin'-mighty.* First time around, though, his poetic ambitions had been too great to allow him the luxury of the mediocre thinking so vital to a successful career in business (quite apart from which he'd narrowly escaped being assassinated by one of his colleagues[6] wielding a pipe reamer), so he'd been pleased to take a languid sabbatical as a subeditor at *Glam,* the women's fashion monthly, courtesy of Kathy McRory Hickman, star *Glam* reporter and Milo's then-light o'love. It had been a well-deserved break requiring no work at all except making the tea, reading newspapers, and washing one's hands after going to the loo—until, that is, Kathy[7] became editor-in-chief and

---

[5]Right, I warned you—well, true for you, actually. Those would be *les privés de* Carfax, the former jockey, now serving five to eight in Dade County Correctional for money abuse. God, how I hated that bastard. Despite which I owe everything to him.

[6]Wolfetone Grey, as everyone knows (see *Killoyle, An Oyrish Fierce,* pp. 1–241). Once a nutter deluxe, Grey has become one of the power brokers in the East Ulster Assembly. He's OK now, they say, but one thing you don't want to do is ask him about God, at least not when there's a pipe reamer within reach. That old neck tendon still throbs in damp weather.

[7]Ah, quite a gal (*cf., op cit. supra*). Fed up with fellas, Kathy is, like so many women who love 'em. (Whereas the lizzies can't get enough of 'em. *Plus ça change,* eh?) Anyway, it's quite a touching story. Last I saw Kath was in the cafeteria at Peterborough Station. Wait till I tell you. I was leaving the next day for South Africa and a promising medical career, and Kath was going back to her little boy and dull but worthy husband. So there we were, gazing into each other's eyes for the very last time, when wouldn't you know it that fearful old gossip Mrs. Witherspoon sat down at our table and insited on gassing on endlessly about her rhododendrons and the size of the bishop's new bicycle (extra large: odd, because His Grace was a shrimp). Ever the gentleman, I forbore telling her to sod off, so Kathy and I could only exchange moist winks behind her back until finally my train came in and I had to leave. Tears gushing from my eyes, I squeezed Mrs. Witherspoon's shoulders by mistake and rushed blindly out, intent on throwing myself under the express—no, that

got ambition, and that with the zeal of an evangelist. She lost no time in conducting a purge, which included (indeed, started with) booting Milo out. Reasons adduced at their final interview included his incessant smoking beneath now-nicotine-yellowed No Smoking signs (Kathy, a once-ardent fag-puffer herself, was now a convert to healthy walks, tofu, and chain nonsmoking); the tendency of his elastic gaze to adhere glutinously to younger women; his poet's ways (protracted throat clearings, neckscarf, mocking laughter at—indeed, causing—awkward moments); and his habit of "always leaning in the doorway, hands in pockets like some kind of bloody streetcorner lout smelling of beer—but half the time smelling of wine instead."[8]

"Always," she said, her once-gentle sky-blue eyes now glittering cruelly like the crystal orbs of an Aztec god.

---

was Kathy, not me—hang on, I'm getting muddled. One thing I do remember quite clearly—and it was damned rum for a Britrail mainline station, I remember thinking it at the time—is the full orchestra and soloist they had playing Rachmaninov somewhere in the background. Ah, that was quite the day in and out of clover, all in all. But those were different times, ah, so they were. Oh no, I have it—it was a film.

[8]A pose no doubt inspired by a photograph of our fellow poet, the young James A. Joyce, M.A., who never had to put up with this kind of guff—not, that is, until he met sexy Nora B., who never read a book in her life, least of all Jim's. "I don't know what that man does in there," she averred, with regard to J.J's long sequestered absences in the bedroom at Square Robiac (VIIe.) and frequent outbursts therein of shrill tenor laughter, "but I hear him laughin' an awful lot" (only, being from Galway she'd have actually said, "an affa latt," like a Jamaican), and this of course boded ill for old Jems, who had then to slip out after what appeared to Nora to have been yet another day of utter indolence (but chalk up another eight hundred words of *Finnegan*) and down his several *petits blancs* at the corner café while mumbling hard-to-follow non-sequiturs through endless upribboning strands of cigarette smoke (filterless Gitanes *papier maïs* clutched between nicotine-bronzed forefingers and middle fingers—oh, I can see it now) to Sam Balsam or Hank Budgie, coboozers twain.

"Balls," said Milo, true to form, and left.[9]

Alas for the parting of once-fond ways.

The hotel, however, being in a near-permanent state of crisis, had been only too willing to take Milo back, despite those Bohemian tics. In fact it was he who—through a connection made back in headwaitering days with a Chicago businessman named Tony and his slinky wife Trish, both recent appointees to the Vatican of innkeeping, Vacation Inns International in Hoyt City, Florida— had engineered the sale of Spudorgan Hall, as it then was known, to the American chain, provoking a startling effusion of Milo's hitherto unsuspected business acumen and guaranteeing him job security, an office with a view, and a nice pension—*for now.* For at heart he was a poet and pledged to nonconformity; and he ever held the world of bankrolls and business dealings in the most abject contempt.

(So he had it both ways.)

"You there," he barked at a minion, imperiously sweeping the landscape with an outstretched arm, like the statue of Peter the Great in his eponymous city, or Joan of Arc on the Place d'Orléans: *"Desist!"* (Milo was in fine bardic mood, and eschewed comprehensibility.)

The bloke who believed himself to be so addressed had no time for poofters or their *semblables,* even if they were managing directors, and responded in what sounded at first like Afrikaans, but which on closer analysis turned out to be Glaswegian.

---

[9]Squarely in the Rogersian idiom, anyway. "Superb economy of language," as Hector Amethyst-Borges said in his review of *Gobbing in the Gutter* in the *Llandudno Ledger;* and, of course, Tom Doubtfire in *Poet In, Poet Out* memorably stressed the almost entirely monosyllabic quality of the poet's *oeuvre* in a succinct monosyllabic composition of his own. "A. Real. Cod. In. Words (And Do I Mean Words!)" (Well, it takes all kinds, and that includes arseholes, sonny—and by the way, you wouldn't have five bob on you, would you, Misther Newspaperman? as dear old Uncle Francie used to say.)

"See yüü, Jimmie," he snapped. "Whüüüü are yüüü pointing ât?"

"No, no," sighed Milo. "Not you, Jock. Him." Wearily, he indicated a bearded and turbaned cleaner cleaning the Autumn Ale display. "It's *supposed* to look cobwebby," he said. "Turkish, are you? Or just deaf?"

"I'm not deaf," said the cleaner. "And who's Turkish? I'm from Rathgar. Dreamers we are to a man, as you ought to know."

"Oh, well then," said Milo. "Take a break yourself. Give me that broom."

The man nodded and was soon gone to the brief freedom he'd been vouchsafed (a smoke on the top steps outside; a glance at the westering sea and consequent stab of longing for a life far, far beyond mops and brooms and meths clinics; a flash motor; a nice bird . . . maybe he should reconsider bank robbery after all).

Meanwhile Milo, cigarette dangling limply from his lower lip like a clumsy symbol of failed libido, gave the floor in front of the Autumn Ale display a few expert broom passes and stood back to admire. Things looked intact—professional—spic-and-span—ready to go. In the demidiurnal glow of the Balsa Room's six French windows, the beer engines gleamed under their plastic cobwebs like a row of Bugattis in a Champs-Elysées showroom, circa 1937.[10] Softly illuminated behind the pub-style bar, which boasted both scrolled wooden pediment and *faux* stained glass were poster-size photographs of bonnie Scotland (Autumns being

---

[10]Careful, lad. I know those as was there, spring of '37. One of 'em lived in a sixth-floor walkup in Billancourt and couldn't afford to run a motor, much as he wanted to; he biked instead, via the Porte d'Italie. Word had it that he was a Boche spy, though. I never knew for sure, but three years later, as the German panzers rolled into Paris, there he was, moving into a top-floor flat on the Ile St. Louis with Annick, Comtesse de Noailles on his arm, and the pair of them murmuring sweet nothings—or *nichts*—in German. Very suggestive, that, if you ask me.

Kilmarnock brewers, well-favoured in the windy wynds and haunted haunts of Scots academe) predictably displaying touristic shots[11] of Loch Ness rather than Loch Leven; Ben Nevis, not Ben Tulloch; Auld Reekie rather than Greenock; and of course, not Paisley at all, but dear dirty "Glasgae" at the heel of the hunt (where she belongs, God bless her). Pipes skirled quietly, like hungry fledglings, from hidden loudspeakers. Glowering at the Scots from across the concourse were the Germans, pride of the beer-drinking world—unless that title belonged to the Belgians, those for instance of Très Bon-Bon raspberry ale (120 proof) with the bulbous-featured Van Eyck (or Dyck) portraits and quiet scenes of Bruges canals and great mashed-potato cloud banks above flat Flemish fields to vie with the plunging battlements of Mad Ludwig's Neuschwanstein the Jerries had, quite naturally, laid on in the visual department, adjacent to snaps of the Ku-damm at night; Hamburg's moonlit, spire-crowned Inner Alster; a redbrick church of the Lutheran persuasion dozing amid the snug wheatfields of Schleswig-Holstein; Weimar, with its twin boffo boys Goethe and Schiller, both snow-cloaked in the fairytale winter of *l'Allemagne Profonde*; a statue of Bonn's own Ludwig van, glowering; and an aerial view of the deep-forested Harz range full of *walpurgisnachts* and *vogelsingers* and the roving bearded spirit of Frederick Barbarossa. All the foregoing images bore the humble but evocative caption "Deutschland." Von Kneipesmanns and

---

[11]Pause for reflection: Why is it that travel pix of Scotland, no matter how glossy and fresh, always carry with them a whiff of the 1940s or '50s to my mental nostrils, as it were? There's something so unmodern about the place in a way that isn't true of, say, Brussels, or Milan, or even Dublin, these days, with all them mobile phones and minicomputer screens—oh, they have mobiles up the arse in Edinburgh too, of course, but somehow I always expect to see a line of black 1949 Wolseleys and Ford Populars and a plume of steam from the smokestack of the Royal Scot in the middle distance. I dunno, maybe it's just me, and God knows I'm no Scotsman (or woman).

Kleine Ausgabe were the Fatherlandish breweries of the moment, each offering a discount to all who might sample the entire product line of fine beers consecutively, depending on speed of barman output (one imperial gallon per capita per secondum, give or take).

Then there were Americans, mostly hirsute, all West Coasters, all peddling piss; one French-speaking Canadian from Trois-Rivières, Québec ("La Bonne Bière du Tabernacle"); and of course the Czechs were there direct from Plzen and Cesky Budejowicz, three open-faced youths and a maiden with flaxen hair already becoming quite the magnet for resident roués' eyes (Milo's slid, discreetly, back and forth); and the Japanese ("Very Old Tory Gate Extra Special European-Style Drinking Beer") of Sapporo, brewing hub of the Chrysanthemum Empire, braying awkward bonhomie in powerful accents, quite drunk. Italians, however, there were none, despite the brewing traditions of the Alto Adige and Veneto; nor were there French, nor Swiss, and surprisingly the Scandinavians had begged off, but local talent was well-represented, with the usual hefty lads named Arthur and Murphy muscling in on the little man, the littlest man in this case being Killoyle's own Molloys Filthy Bitter Dregs, noticeable primarily for their brand-new, and odd (yet oddly appealing) emblem: a bespectacled white rat elaborately caparisoned in tweeds, plus-fours, Argyll socks, and a Donegal cloth cap, holding a foaming mug of (presumably) Molloys.

"Drink Molloys," pleaded (or urged, depending on your mood) the Molloys advert. "Don't be a rat." Opinions differed as to the efficacy of such a slogan, but the lights were already on, the beer engines were cranked up, and one or two customers (journalists, the poet Rogers noted with disdain) were already queueing for a taste.

"Love that rat," said one of them.

"But," pointed out his colleague, or competitor, "the slogan should be '*be* a rat,' not 'don't be.' Why spend time and money—

and quite a bit of talent, too, I daresay—on creating this appealing little fella if he represents what you're *not* supposed to be? If
you get my drift?"

"I do, I do. And mine's a pint."

Milo passed on with an inward smile, like a king in disguise.
There'd be grand crack this day or he was a true-blue Orangeman.
Indeed. Sunlight splashed onto every hyperpolished counter.
Crisply laundered beermats were laid out in expectation of the
oncoming flood. Detergent-redolent dishtowels and snow-white
serviettes hung limply like the standards of the Queen's Own
Borderers awaiting the arrival of Her Majesty on St. Andrew's
Day. Indeed, the entire hall looked burnished and well-swept, fit
for a class or two above Everyman and his wife, and the world's
press and media would be well accommodated in the press box
at the far end of the room, his own idea and a halfway decent one,
if he said so himself. . . .

"Not bad," self-observed Milo.

"Eh," said the recently irate Scot, approaching once again, but
this time diffidently, with a lopsided gait that gave him the air of
a hard-riding equestrian. "You're the manager hereabouts, are ye,
Jimmie?"

Milo nailed down this dialogue with a yes, repeated thrice, the
third time in a near-bellow, in the interests of penetrating the
Scot's thick skull and/or deficient hearing.

"Aye, I'm a wee bit corned beef," averred the latter. "Ye'll have
to speak up, Jimmie."

The Scot—whose name, as it transpired during the parry and
thrust of name-exchanging—was (somewhat ironically) Jimmie,
conjured up, from behind a curtain, a female companion ("wife,
actually") named Eileen, as Irish as Milo, or Gay Byrne, or the
berries of Dingle. She was, moreover, a Killoyler born and bred.

"Grew up in the shadow of St. Oinsias. But now I'm in Scotland, and I love it so," she gushed. Milo's managing director ar-
mature (not to mention the poet's soul that rendered him akin to

Alighieri and Milton rather than to a long line of mere hotel managers) was proof against accusations of haughtiness or insolence as he sniffed, not unlike an Italian entrepreneur of noble lineage—say, a Tuscan count-cum-shoe exporter, or an Umbrian *principe* in the bespoke-tailoring line. . . .

"Well, I'm *so* glad to see you could bring yourself to come back for a while."

Truth to tell, like many of the Irish race Milo despised the eternal emigré whose grass was always greener elsewhere and who insisted on coming back again and again to tell his or her hapless stick-in-the-mud friends all about it; whereas sound Irishmen like himself knew for a fact that nowhere on God's patchily green earth was there greener and lusher pasture than right here in dear old Oarland, especially with the software revolution hitting its stride and the stock market topping three-thousand.

"Oh," said Eileen, instantly sensing the prickly patriot beneath the bluff exterior, "it's not that I don't like it here. It's just that, well, you see, I got divorced over here last year and I've no doubt that my ex-husband's lurking somewhere about. Where there's beer, there's Mick. Anyway, Killoyle's not exactly the size of London, is it?"

"No, madam," concurred Milo. "Is not, never has been, nor will it ever be."

At least they now concurred.

At least, or slightly more, Eileen and Jimmie had started treating Milo with the respect due the managing director of a great hotel rather than the abrupt high-handedness all too often the common coin of grubby fucking bone-idle so-called poets in the minds of the Mammon-mad. . . .

"Fine layout here," said Jimmie. "Eh. Spiro. Fancy a pint?"

"Nah. Too early. We can do you tea, though."

"Mine's a pint of Autumn's."

"I said no, it's too early for me. How's a cuppa?"

"Aye, a pint of heavy and a packet of crisps. Salt and vinegar."

"Bloody heck. Wallfish!"

The man so named, attempting to pass through in unobserved discretion like the resident ghost, flinched as if struck but hesitated not in obediently running over to his new boss, not as petty a boss as his last one (the late unlamented Goone), but a bit of a headcase anyway, like all bosses, and, like all bosses, he had a good side if you could just find it, but Milo's, Wallfish had discovered, was definitely not in evidence when underlings such as he, Wallfish, were walking about eating sandwiches and trailing bread crumbs, ham shards, specks of mustard, et cetera; nor was the poet excessively fond of defiant displays of squalor of any description, seeing them (accurately) as self-willed attempts to shock the bourgeoisie, just . . .[12]

"Yes, Milo." (As in so many American-owned establishments, a sham informality manifested itself in the use of first names on the part of the underlings.)

"Brew up a pot of oolong for these folks, will ya."

"Absolutely, Milo. Will do. Darjeeling, is it?"

"Oolong. Suffering Jay, is everyone suddenly deaf?"

"Eh?" called out Jimmie.

"Absolutely," said Wallfish as, fishily, he shimmied off.

"*That was Wallfish!*" shouted Milo. "Used to work out at that Emerald Mats place. Didyez hear that story now, what a corker, got everyone to talking, wait till I tell yez."

---

[12]Sorry, can't help meself, but here goes: Ever noticed how it's always the tree-hugging eco-wankers who drive the filthiest, smokiest, old bangers, and who dress the most like friggin' tramps or North Wall down-and-outs in the shabbiest shite-stained ripped jeans and the like? Just goes to show, if you ask me (I know you didn't, but still) it's nothing to do with ecology, it's all me arse and just another way of giving Mum and Dad the old fig. I should know: I used to be one (ah, Marike—Earth Day, Amsterdam, '89 . . . but that's another story).

"Och," said Jimmie.

When Milo had repeated himself *à haute voix,* Jimmie grinned and said, "Och, no, it's the other way aroond, Spiro. I'd wager you don't know the half of it. You see, I own Emerald Mats the noo."

"Do you, really? By the way, that's *Milo.*"

Milo was, indeed, caught with his metaphorical pants down— or "troosers doon," as Jimmie would say (his quaint but irritating dialect being yet another we can dispense with in the interests of clarity and reader-friendliness). First of all, Emerald Mats had always been a proud and proudly Irish institution, and this Jimmie article was a foreigner—not much of one, Celtic cousins and all that, granted; but still . . . Eileen acted as interpreter, having apparently succeeded in striking the precise pitch—a C sharp minor—that rendered her speech comprehensible to Jimmie.

"Aye. Well we're all in the dear old Union now, aren't we?" said he.

Second, well . . .

"How did we manage it?" asked Eileen rhetorically. "Well, we'd agreed to a controlling stake in it before Goone eh, passed on. By the way, that was no domestic quarrel. A professional hit, is what I heard. Certain parties were interested in buying him out and word had it he was getting ready to sell *them* out and move to the Costa del whatever. . . . At least, that's what I heard."

"I heard it was to pay for a sex change for wee Colin, his bumboy," said Jimmie.

"Cornelius, wasn't it."

"No. Colin. Goone had a bit on the side, I heard. This Colin fella. A stevedore from Bristol who was doing his internship in rough trade down on Crumstown Wharf. His ambition was— maybe still is—to open a school for transsexual orphans."

"Cripes," said Milo.

"Ah, well," said Eileen, shrugging the shrug of indifference masquerading as tolerance. . . .

Bloody *hell,* it was an outrage to all civilized standards of conduct (raved Milo, inwardly). . . .

Like his own, highly dubious morals.

But still.

Wallfish, shedding crumbs, arrived with a pot of fresh Darjeeling. When he'd departed, Milo used the wretch's name as the centerpiece of a conversational gambit about the exact sequence of events out at Emerald Mats, but Jimmie, even with Eileen's intervention, had suddenly become cagey, perhaps suspecting espionage, or the inherent gabbiness of the Irish.

"Aye," was all he said, with boring reiteration, except for the occasions on which he said "No." Eileen, however, being one of us, was more inclined to blather, and how. Milo's face, at first aswarm with the nods and winks required by his day job, soon became as if trapped under hardening wax with the rictus of a rabbit hypnotized by a python. It wasn't actually so bad at first, because she started off by filling Milo in on the tales and rumours that were circulating, and that was always useful; but when she struck out for pastures new and started to go on and on *and on* in what Milo might well, in a retrograde moment, call typically female fashion . . .

"So now we control most of Emerald Mats except for that Belfast consortium that holds a percentage and we're looking at linking up with Jocelyn Motors and Aidan's Doilies, as well as looking 'round for good cheap web sites that might be going belly-up, you know the kind of thing, totally mismanaged by young fellas who'd not know a business opportunity if it reared up on its hind legs and sang 'The Owld Triangle' in their ears. But the Emerald Mats deal was a near thing, you know. Goone was planning on double-crossing a lot of people, we heard. Including some prime investors from up North, nudge nudge wink wink."

"How do you know all this?" he blurted. "You live in Glasgow."

"Edinburgh, actually. Ever heard of the Internet? Www dot gossip dot com?"

"Say no more," said Milo, but Eileen said much more. She chronicled a journey through the maze and thickets of rumour and hearsay, starting with the Indian waiter/terrorist/bank robber who'd mysteriously disappeared and whose *wife* and *cousin* had also mysteriously disappeared ("at the Koh-I-Noor, was he? Stuck-up bunch of prats. Oh, I remember him, chief prat, wasn't he? I always preferred the Star of Bihar. Outstanding chicken tikka masala," was Milo's last, shouted comment before being gently but firmly thrust under the warm sea of Eileen blather) and moving briskly on to the cross-dressing clergyman (well, *sex*ton, actually, har har[13]) and the high old time *he* was reputed to be having in the clink, picking and choosing his suitors with Wildean panache. Then, from these topics, Eileen veered to a less germane, that of the reported sightings of ghostly presences coming and going in the watches of the night—and from there she was well away, into total irrelevance reminiscent of a supermarket tabloid, or one of the more obscure Protestant sects:

> Rumours of war and the distant rumble of cannon off the Cliffs of Moher (the year of the French, again?) as heard or half heard in and around Banion's Bar, Killiney;
>
> Grey glowering faces, unshaven to a man, glimpsed in the ill-lit parlour windows of Ringsend and Irishtown, the very same faces gone a second later as if plucked away by a hidden hand (possibly the hidden hand, mused Milo, of opening time?);
>
> Whinnying of horses and galloping pursuit across echoing cobblestoned squares, circa 1897, heard again last Wednesday at 11:30, just after *An Nuacht* on RTE2, with (guess what) *nobody there*;
>
> Wind keening through the chinks in the tumbledown walls of Inishbofin where once monks prayed to the loonybells of their doom-laden God;

---

[13]Well, homosexton, actually. Sorry, just thought I'd . . . sorry.

Nocturnal mewling of curlews in the reedbeds of Lough Neagh;[14]

Chirping of mobile phones amid the ferns and exposed brickwork of Sartre's Food Court (Grafton Street, Dublin 2) as well as the entire menu at that fab eatery, including part of the dessert list;[15]

Cavernous coughing in the cellars of Svidrigailov Manor (Co. Kildare), reported these many years by all who dwelt therein—*and no one there;*

Booming voice in the vestibule of the same venerable precincts, heard late nights and early mornings declaring "Take off your knickers" in stagey old-fashioned accents à la Ralph Richardson or Michael MacLiammoir, with (of course) *no one there;*

Wispy lights of shamrock-green gas (or ectoplasm?) seen flirting with the gables of Mansion House of a moonlit night;

The round-the-clock queue at Princess Diana's grave, 72 percent of them citizens of the Irish Republic, 14 percent of the remainder North Americans, only a tiny minority (10 percent) actual Brits;

Sophie Ashburton's new beau, the Italian actor/model/bestselling author Tadzio,[16] and wasn't he great in the cameo role in *Urinals in the Desert;* well, all right, that *was* slightly off topic. . . .

The Neo-IRA, then, and its expanded web site with links to online booksellers selling hot-off-the-press tomes penned anonymously by former quartermasters, strategists, and other masterminds of that venerable organization;

---

[14]The sweetest of God's musics to me is that. Not.

[15]Baklava, sachertorte, bombe à la russe . . .

[16]Ah, Tadzio. Wasn't he the *Gabinetti da Rapallo* chap? It's in all the bookstalls. And *Bodysurfing for Five?* Or was that the other fella?

And back to the once suspected, now pretty much confirmed (and here the rattling vehicle of soliloquy lurched unexpectedly back onto the rutted highway of relevance) existence of what began, like a cancer, as a cell, and had now grown, or mestastasized, into a full-blown something-or-other, somewhere in south Co. Killoyle, according to the latest reports on gossip.com: the Soldiers of Brian O'Nolan.

"So they call themselves, some believe after a mythical nationalist poet activist of the late forties and early fifties. Never heard of him myself."

"Ah," said Milo, who had.

"And they've a Basque fella with them. Rumour has it the ETA, the Basque terrorists, you know, have declared war on the IRA for having violated the spirit of terrorism by signing the truce, so this Basque guy is over here to steal IRA ordnance and generally chuck a few spanners in the works. At least that's what an anonymous posting on the Gossip dot com e-board said."

"Indeed," semiyawned Milo, thoroughly bored with: (1) e-anything, and (2) the unending bleak intricacies of terrorist politics, in which from one day to the next *this* one's in, *that* one's out, *that* lot's declared a truce, but *that* lot haven't, *those* gawms have allied themselves with the Generic All-Mediterranean Liberation Army—oh no, *they* haven't, it's the other way around! But *that* crowd's finally vanished from the scene . . . no, hang on a sec, there they are again! Bombs away! Ad nauseam. Quite apart from its murderous angle, reflected Milo in lieu of listening to Eileen, the whole terrorist-nationalist-liberationist business was like a lifetime's worth of catechisms plus heavy artillery . . . *such a bloomin' bore.*

Speaking of which, Eileen was far from done. There were also, of course, she reminded Milo, the alleged imminent money troubles over at Jocelyn Motors PLC, with possibly quite dire consequences for the economy of Killoyle City and environs, including that of her ex-husband, explained Eileen, and she launched into a tangential diatribe re: Mick McCreek of such astonishing, filigree-like intricacy and detail—his likes and dislikes, his toenails (irregularly pared), his chest hair, or lack thereof ("none whatsoever, the number of times I begged him to buy a false piece, but oh no, would he listen?"), his drinking, his smoking (both monumental and nonstop), his character flaws parts one and two—that by the time she paused for breath Milo felt, along with that wooziness and lack of focus in his head that he'd previously associated with visits to the dentist or really bad hangovers, that he'd not only known Eileen and her ex for years but had actually lived with them as a lodger for a good part of that time, sharing their ups and downs, their triumphs and tragedies, the monthly arrival of the gas metre man, the bickering over bills and rent, the hysterical passage (Mick down the boozer) through Eileen's two hysterical pregnancies, the somewhat compensatory—successful, at least—six-hour labour of their long-haired pointer Simone (now in Scotland), the confounded noise of the O'Sheas' music next door (that was back in Terenure, of course) . . .

Funny he asked!

He hadn't, actually; it was like the casual scratching of one's head in the front rows at Sotheby's occasioning the inadvertent multimillion-pound purchase of, say, Van Gogh's *Sunflowers*.

"Ahem."

Was Milo married, by the way?

"No, thank God."

"I thought not. But that's hardly the right attitude."

Irish as she was, there was something in the way she uttered this reproach that seemed to Milo pure Scots, Edinburgh variety, even unalloyed Morningside, with an implied hint of cocked pinkies over thin tea and excessively friable shortbread.

"Good tea," said Jimmie.

"Oh, my God," said Eileen. "I knew it. I just bloody knew it. Didn't I say? Didn't I tell you?"

Milo was way ahead of her. The roaring vortex in his head had faded. He looked around. A fortyish man in a pullover and jeans, with long wavy hair and a fleshy, sensual face reminiscent of one of the Romantic poets—Shelley, perhaps, or Coleridge (or was he thinking of Boswell?), was standing by the Molloys' Dregs display, smirkily admiring the rat.

"That would be your ex, I suppose?"

"Spot on. Good God. Look at him. Look at the weight he's put on. As if he wasn't bad enough before. He must be on the sauce day and night now. Look, you can tell, he can't wait to get his hands on the stuff. Come on, Jimmie, let's go."

"Time for a pint, hen," piped Jimmie plaintively, his cringing attitude hinting at the dependent geriatric he was clearly destined to become.

"No, no. No pints, Jimmie. Time to go."

But Mick McCreek had turned, like hapless prey scenting predation. The inexorable process of recognition was playing itself out across his lumpy features: a slow half turn into bland oblivion; a still-oblivious turn away followed by a cinematic pause; a sudden double take; a full-body slew-about; a disbelieving shake of the head; an ingenuous gape . . .

"Mother of God, is it you?"

"It is, God help us."

"What the hell are you doing here? And is this the fella?"

"No. That's the hotel manager. This one's the 'fella,' as you put it. I'm here on business. Funny coincidence, isn't it?" She uttered what can only be described as a mirthless laugh. "Ha ha *ha.*"

"Well, sod me."

"Jimmie, this is my ex-husband, Mick McCreek. Mick, this is my husband, Jimmie."

"Pleased to meet you."

"Fuck off."

Mick shrugged and disdained a handshake, to Jimmie's evident satisfaction. Milo filled the vacuum.

"Milo Rogers. How are you?"

"Oh, you're the poet, arencha? Nice to meet *you*. Poet's right, isn't it?"

"Well. I am that. No bloody Yeats, but you know, that doesn't bother me. As long as somebody gives me credit, like."[17]

"I get you."

They shook hands vigourously, each at first glance approving of the other. After all, they weren't vying for a woman's favours at the moment, and they were both well-seasoned Irishmen on the cusp of middle age with a sense of obligation to the past and their own six senses; and Mick liked the other man's grog-blossomed visage, with its cynical downturn of the corners of mouth and eye. Milo had seen Mick before, as well, not knowing who he was, of course (some poor waster with the face of a welterweight—John Keats, or was it Shelley?) a few times here and there. The same was true of Mick, who'd spotted Milo about, in each case nodding over a glass at Mad Molloy's and known to his fellow punters as "the powett fella" or "the wan up at the hotel, loike"; but Milo and Mick were both men of old-fashioned liberal persuasion and, on the premise of drink being a good man's failing, would never hold the taking of same, drop by healing drop, against anyone. (Certainly, if they did, they would be the world's most gilded hypocrites, considering the number of times beyond counting that they themselves had stumbled out of pubs into the weary, cold universe of *after closing time. . . .*)

Still, it was an entertainment worth the price of admission (viz., one Eileen soliloquy) to see ex-husband and current husbands side by side, a position that neither intended to adopt for long.

---

[17]I know, I know, immortal prose it ain't, but when you're constantly on the edge, as I am, you have to be economical with your words. Payoff? When you do say something, women tend to look at you more closely. Take Penny, now . . . or later.

"Right, then," said Mick. "I'm expected back at the booth."

"Cheers, then."

"Aye. All right."

"You working for Molloys?" inquired Milo. The two men strolled back to the now-bustling service area.

"Not officially. As a consultant, like."

"The rat, eh?"

"How did you guess? Well, you probably didn't."

"You were admiring it in such a proprietary way."

"Prop . . . ? Ah, I'm with you."

"She said you were in the computer line. Graphics, was it?"

"Nah, I'm a car man, really. Test driver, you know? But they sacked me over at Jocelyn's, so I took on this gig at a place called— and don't laugh—NaughtyBoy Graphics, where they put me to work designing the online clothes for some fucking idiotic cartoon character or other, a rat, if you can believe it. . . ."

"Whitney the rat. Aye, my wee nephew watches him on the telly."

"Does he, yeah?"

"You ask me, Whitney looks grand up there. Very dignified. Just the sort of rat you'd fancy having a pint with."

"Oh, no, that's not Whitney. I couldn't use him without copyright permission, like. No, that's a new fella entirely."

"Looks like Whitney to me."

Mick explained how in an idle moment at the office he had cut and pasted the original from a NaughtyBoys web page and how he had deftly added the odd differentiating detail before whisking off the design via e-mail to his old butty Finnucane, Molloys' head brewmaster. Finnucane had delightedly accepted the new design, although having absolutely no authority or right to do so, and probably being langered, wholly or in part, at the time. Still, didn't it look great altogether.

"And please note the eyeglasses. Quite unlike Whitney. And the whiskers a touch longer. *His* name's Roddy."

"Roddy, is it."

"Roddy the Rodent, you see."

"Great stuff, Mick."

"Thanks. Ah . . . is herself still . . . ?"

Mick cast a furtive glance over his shoulder, but Eileen had gone, and with her her Jimmie. What an arsehole, he thought. But what a lucky break for her, he also thought, buoyed by the total absence of Eileen nostalgia in his soul. The man's a wet and needs a wet nurse, and that was something she'd always tried with him, Mick, to no avail, wet only in the ways of the pubward men of Ireland. Farewell, then, Eileen, he said to her via himself, inwardly. Cheers, acushla. The best of Irish luck to the pair of yez. *And stay the fuck away from me.*[18]

"Nice gal, your ex," Milo said, insincerely.

"Ah, come on. You and I know that it's a meat axe you'd be needing once she gets started."

"Well, she does talk a bit."

"A bit, is it? And the pope's a Roman Catholic, I believe."

"So I've heard. I take your point."

They were arranging themselves elbows first on the bar counter when, from behind, came an American voice:

"No fuckin' way!"

Milo turned, startled; Mick turned, recognizing his master's voice, the voice of Denny Tool of NaughtyBoy Graphics, dressed as usual in black T-shirt and jeans and unshaven to the precise

---

[18]And she hears not a word, nor feels the slightest pity for the struggles of he who was once her all . . . ah, God, the infinite sadness of relationships failed, when the quirks once so loved become the odious objects of hate! The once-saucy spirit degenerating into nothing more than flippancy and lies; the easy charm become whorish affectation; healthy boyish appetites transformed over the years into the gross lusts of a Farouk . . . well, that's why they passed the divorce referendum. I only wish I'd taken advantage of it sooner. As for Kathy . . . but you can read as well as I.

point of three-day shadow but not as far as actual beardedness. Next to him towered Ramona, a "buyer" from New York who turned up occasionally, swelling into all tight corners of her sprayed-on jeans and preshrunk blouse. The two of them added a touch of class, or was it sleaze, to Killoyle's artistic demimonde.

"That's Whitney."

"Oh, hello, Denny. No, ah, it isn't, actually. Whitney, that is."

"Hey, Mick. You think I don't know Whitney? That's him. And he looks like he's advertising beer."

"Well, he is advertising beer, I suppose, but it's not Whitney; actually, his name's—"

"Fuck that. You can't do that, Nick. You can't just take one of our clients' logos and stick him up there. Do you have any idea of the copyright issues involved in something like this?"

"I do, actually, Den, and that's why I changed rats. If you look closely you can tell. See, he's wearing eyeglasses . . ."

"Eyeglasses my ass. Hey, if I have to get up on a ladder and squint to tell the difference between them, I can tell you this: There *isn't* any God damned difference between them. Capeesh?"

He was standing with torso canted forward and index finger pointing skyward, a fugitive from the mean streets of the silver screen, daring Mick to meet the challenge. (The "capeesh" was the tip-off.) Mick, himself no stranger to the allure of Hollywood manliness, not after years of watching Bobby Lee Irwin "sculpt his rough-hewn persona,"[19] was sorely tempted to go *mano á mano* with the bugger—although mature reflection would have advanced Denny's twenty-year age advantage, not to mention the inverted-triangle shape of his torso, as reasons to opt for flight, not fight—but his impulses were soon smothered by thoughts of

---

[19]Sounds like a piece I read in *Flick Knife* a while back: "Bobby Lee We Hardly Know Ye" or words to that effect. To wit: Your man doing a good job of balancing offhandedness and shameless arrogance.

the familiar trio of joblessness, the Sosh, and the petty humiliation of it all—until he caught sight of Penny Burke, at which point his inhibitions melted away like butter in the small of a sunbather's back.[20]

"Capeesh, yourself. In actual fact, Den, there is a difference between them. This guy's got glasses and longer whiskers. As you can see."

"Fuck that. Listen, we're talking job security here, or rather lack of it, if you don't take a deep breath and think about what you're saying ..."

Mick had, as he could see from the other's progression from glances askance to full-frontal stare, actually registered on Denny's radar screen as *himself,* Mick McCreek, not as just another faceless formless gormless paddy underling, no mean accomplishment with such a walking, talking monument to self-absorption as Denny Tool; and it was as himself that Mick would go down in flames, or soar into the blue empyrean, that much he (romantically) swore in the gloriously defiant, Puccinian style he had longed for all his life, himself and his adversary silhouetted against the stormy skies above the Aurelian Wall. . . .

---

[20]Ooooooh, sexy. You naughty boy, just putting that in there like that. Shame on you. I'll tell your mother, et cetera, et cetera. Anyhow, it reminds me of Torremolinos, circa 1979, the year when Brigitte and Olympia fell in with me and I with them and all the livelong day, beside the booming Mediterranean surf, 'neath the roaring Mediterranean sun, we rubbed suntan lotion into each other's shoulderblades whilst exchanging glances of heavy significance and conversing along the lines of "Allo, boy, you wanna do it?" and "Allo, gal, you bet yer sweet bumsicle"—ah, yes, it all comes back to me now, the mingled tang of suntan oil; the brash brackish Med; the mewing of the gulls; the silken skin of the twinned Nordic beauties; the wafted aroma of *paella, tapas,* and *vino tinto;* the thrum of four- (or even three-) cylinder engines; the guffawing of burros—no, hang on a sec, *that* was a commercial on the telly for Cosmo's Cosmetics, or was it some Spanish plonk? Ah, well. Never say die. Pen and I'll be going over there next Easter, so who knows . . . ?

Milo sensed disaster and stepped aside, after briefly contemplating, and promptly rejecting, a mediatory role. As for Ramona the New York "buyer," she pouted and, evidently losing interest in the gestating conflict—or envious of its hold on Denny's attentions—took herself off with an exaggeratedly sashaying gait to the Von Kneipesmanns booth, from which emanated the musical flatulence of Des Knaben Wunderhorn brass band from Füssen, Bavaria. Denny, momentarily unmanned, glanced after her. Put off by the tubas and the excessive Germanness of the Germans, she set a course for the Belgian stand, itself offensively loud with popular music of the accordion variety but rich with crêpe scents and the tangy pong of raspberry ale. A seedy bloke in a mac lost no time in detaching himself from behind the German bar and sauntering pointedly behind, hands insolently in pockets and an invisible smirk on the back of his head. Denny gawked.

"Hey, where ya goin', babe . . . ?"

Mick was poised to strike when he was himself distracted: he suddenly realized that a fellow *he'd* casually noticed, who'd seemed to be vaguely hanging about but no more part of his scene than any other of the punters, was actually accompanying Penny Burke, and that said specimen was one of those namby-pamby granola types with a ponytail and, as God was his (Mick's) witness, a pair of eyeglasses the spit and effin' image of Roddy's, which had in turn been inspired (as Mick admitted freely, but only to himself) by John Lennon's, New York City, circa 1980 (poor bastard).

"Hello, Mick."

"So up your bloody rat, Tool," screamed Mick. "And up your bloody company as well."

But Denny only waved brusquely and hurried away after Ramona with a parting "We'll talk on Monday" over his shoulder.

As for Milo, who was watching all this, he was immersed in his first pint of Molloys Filthy Bitter Dregs, with a nice line in left-wing political craic going with the barman, Seamus, ex-curate at the Orinoco Grill in Crumstown, he said—just before further conversation revealed him to be a first cousin of Spudorgan's old curate and Milo's one-time chief nemesis Peter X. Murphy, now serving three years in Crumlin Road for abetting terrorism or arms smuggling or some such rot ("ah you're a dead cert for the pint-pulling prize, Seamus, with the wrist movement you've got on you, and that's as sweet a head as I've seen on a pint of stout since your cousin Petey was presiding"), watched from the Olympian heights of his own detachment (poet, hotel manager) as Penny approached Mick (nice fella, if a bit intense) and made it pretty clear, to Milo, anyway—and hadn't he had a few hundredweight bags of practice in the body language of the avenging female—that Mick had transgressed her standards in some serious, fundamental, even life-threatening way probably completely unsuspected by Mick; or, alternatively, that Mick was simply, existentially, *not good enough*, not as good at any rate as this paragon of superannuated hippiedom she'd picked up from under the table somewhere.

Truth to tell, Milo was grizzled enough to feel like the greying sage of Schnitzler's (via Ophuls) *La Ronde*, or a minor Greek god (say, Hephaistos) shaking his head over the antics of foolish mortals.[21]

"Derek," said Derek. "Mick, yeah?"

"How'r'ya, Derek? Folkie, are ya?"

"Hi. What?"

Derek had an extra pair of free tickets to the Baron of Beef concert down at the auditorium, Penny explained, with a defensive high note in her voice. Would Mick like to come?

"Baron of Beef? Are you codding me, so? You know I can't stand that shite," he said. "All that folk music diddle diddle diddling.

---

[21]More grizzled now, and twice as ignorant. All I know's that I know nothing, as the old Greek said.

And the wee gawms with their earrings and ponytails." He glared at Derek, who smiled.

"I know, but I just thought I'd ask."

"Ah, go on yourself out of it. Ya ballocks. Cheers, then, eh?"

It was Mick McCreek at his best and worst simultaneously, displaying qualities and defects that, taken together, constituted the *echt*-Irishman that Penny Burke alternately longed for and despised and knew she would never find (along, admittedly, with much else) in the shallow soul of gentle Derek.

"Yeah, cheers, then, Mick."

Penny shrugged and left, with Derek loping nimbly alongside. So fuck it anyway, thought Mick, beholding what he thought was probably the devastated end zone of yet another on-and-off relationship. Nice to have his nose rubbed in *two* of them within the space of ten minutes.

"Thanks," he said, addressing himself upward.

Well, well. What was left but the consolations of male companionship and the roasted hop of the brewer's vat, the world's grandest consolations, those. Chalk up another one, self-instructed Mick. Step out—hit the road—onward.

"Will you have another one?"

"I will."

18

Old as the Katyushas were, and some of them predated the Soviet invasion of Afghanistan (1979–1980), like World War II ordnance in London parks and gardens[1] they could never be counted quite out, fortunately for the aim and self-respect of the Soldiers of Brian O'Nolan, specifically Subcomandante Harry Batasuna, whose mission it was to select a target and gain maximum publicity, not for the Soldiers but, paradoxically, for the Provisionals, who'd signed the peace treaty, the traitors. It was only fair to hold their feet to the fire, as it were. And what better place than the great hotel atop its looming escarpment, with half a hundred brewers from the four corners of the world and attendant drinkers and reporters and rumours that the top brass themselves stayed there on occasion?

Subcomandante Harry parked the van on Uphill Street, nodded amiably at a passing traffic warden (Ernie Dornan, twenty-six, father of two), smoked a small Dominican Porfirio cigar, then set up the rocket launcher, aimed it with the precision of the

---

[1]One of which exploded underfoot on me at number 1, Onslow Gardens, SW7, when I was in search of beer, companionship, and/or employment involving same. Scratch two toes and chalk one up to experience, what? I almost met Kathy in the surgery, by the way. Just goes to show.

Pyrenean hunter he was, and fired, and fired again; then he drove off, enjoying the distant sound of wailing human and mechanical, and content that a point had been driven home, an otherwise meaningless life or two sacrificed for the ultimate good: *Askapena!*

(Oh, and *Erin go bragh* as well, as long as we were at it.)

Commandant Finn had already made the requisite phone calls of warning, one to the police and one to the Spudorgan Inn, from his office at the Killoyle Public Library after discussing with the same phone the evening's supper menu with Mrs. Finn (haddock pie, mash, swedes, a pint of Workingman's, a slice of Phelim tart).

"Oh, I don't know. Phelim tart? Must we?"

"That's what you always say whenever I make Phelim tart."

"Oh, all right. But go easy on the fenugreek, will you?"

"Honestly. You're impossible."

Finn hung up on his (much) better half, then dialed the hotel, humming. He quite enjoyed these telephonic roles. He had one or two favourites: The quavering priest, the raunchy blue-denimed labourer. This time he saw himself as a brawny, hard-drinking rebel from the docklands of Belfast, a raunchy, self-made man, a muscular man of the world, a wild colonial boy, a snorting stallion from the emerald pastures of Ulster, a green-dyed nationalist from the toenails up.[2]

"Hello, Vacation Inns, Spudorgan Inn here, this is Maire, may I help you?"

---

[2]Anything, in short, but the pallid reality of who he was, a bespectacled emasculated hemorrhoidal horror of a pillock from Port Laoise Comprehensive, Maynooth and UCD (M.A., library science, '79) who'd done sod-all except take the occasional holiday in the Algarve, Romania, and northern Spain and hang on to a single dingy office job to span the intervening eighteen years. And, of course, found the Soldiers of Brian O'Nolan, the only thing that will earn him a footnote in history—or at least in this book, itself a future footnote. . . .

"Aye, it's the Provos. There's a rocket launcher set to go off nearby the Spudorgan," growled Finn, masking his mouth with a hankie and, for extra protection, turning away from the receiver and covering the hankie, and his mouth, with his hand, then hunching forward and crawling under his desk, there to sit nose-to-nose with the wastepaper basket, growling, "somewhere down the hill it'll be, in a dumper truck, I reckon. A right barrack-buster it is, so 'tis, so ye'd best not be danderin' about. Eight or, oh, ten minutes from now."

"I beg your pardon?" queried the voice, unheard.

"Git yer women and chilu-dren out of there pronto."

"Who is this?"

"Provisonal IRA," said Finn, in what he imagined was a working-class Northern accent. His eyes were closed; he was im-mersed in the part. No longer Finn the librarian, he was fully in command of the part, fully Commandant Finn he was, fighting man of the people, hero of Cuchulainn's army, comrade of Pearse and Smith O'Brien and O'Donovan Rossa and Ireland's martyred dead generations.

He almost forgot the code phrase.

"Shite go bragh. I mean slainte up your arse. This *is* the Rah, you know."

"Do you mean this is a bomb warning?" piped the voice, alarmed.

"Never you mind," said Finn, shaking with silent laughter as he replaced the receiver on its cradle and regained his armchair. He gazed for a while out the window at the library car park in the tranquil sunlight of midmorning. An elderly couple was en-tering, he leaning on her, she leaning on a crutch, the two of them stiffly bent like grasshoppers (poor miserable old articles; they'd come to the point in life where there was nothing more exciting to do than spend five hours reading back copies of *Sewing Circle* and *Geriatric Geographic* in the public library; ah, what a nuisance life was, when you got right down to it); and at Miss Burke arriving (early, Finn noted approvingly) with some long-haired bloke with a ponytail (he noted disapprovingly, but goodness gracious he wasn't her father, after all, and thank God for that) . . . and at a small crowd from St. Aloysius Elementary, a bunch of squealing kids (good thing there wouldn't be any kids at that beer festival)—he felt stirrings of remorse, soon squelched. That lot had had ten minutes to clear out. That was more than *he* got every morning when he entered the near-lethal traffic of the MacLiammoir Overpass. . . . No, he'd done his duty, he'd warned 'em fair and square. It was the usual technique. The guards, not having a clue, as usual, would take them at their word and blame the whole thing on the Rah boys, the Belfast men, the *real* IRA, the bastards who'd signed the truce, and things would go downhill pretty bloody fast after that, and *that* would serve the bastards right, doubly so if they found out young O'Mallet had been helping himself to weapons from the IRA arms caches and selling them at a discount (but still at quite a fair price) to the Soldiers of Brian O'Nolan. Of course, he'd misled them a bit, he'd been lining his own pockets, everyone knew that. (And it wasn't totally out of the question that Subcomandante Harry might have to pay him a visit, just for interrogative purposes, like. Tom O'Mallet *was* a slippery customer, out for the main chance, and Harry was a bit of a miracle worker, the way he could get things out of people, give him half an hour and an empty room.)

Of course there was that Indian gobshite; now, that had been the bit of an old debacle itself, and no mistake. They'd scheduled an execution by the book—taps, blindfold, well-oiled Armalite, 1970s hit of one's choice on the gramophone (personally, he'd have chosen something by the Platters, circa 1959), quiet glade in the woods—but the bugger had escaped, or been sprung, something to do with that caterwauling out back and the Indian stereo player (only worth £35, as it turned out, scarcely enough to

buy two clips of ammo, or a decent fifth of Black Bush) and the
car they'd seen speeding away. *That* was a cock-up, right enough,
oh, you'd not get any argument on that score. He'd called Bewley,
but Bewley'd been shtum.

"A right cock-up, Finn, if you want my opinion."

And now they were getting these mysterious phone calls from
a certain "Hamid" threatening to blow the place up. Harry had
answered once; he swore it was the Indian. But there'd been a
woman's voice, too, and the fellow's wife had gone missing: could
the two of them be hiding in the hills, planning a mortar attack?

Finn picked up the phone, dialed the secret line, rapped out
the curt syllables of authority.

"Finn MacCool here. Any news on the wee Indian? No? Have
you found the cousin? The wife? Well, what the blazes are you
playing at?"

He hung up in high dudgeon.

"What a shower."

They weren't making much headway. The wee bugger's
cousin, too, was somehow implicated, and Finn had forged an
(accurate) mental connection between her and that Mrs. Bashir
who'd come on Pats Bewley's group tour—well, of course it was
her, bloody obvious, wasn't it?—because they'd sprung him,
hadn't they, coming in through the conservatory the way they'd
done it, the way only someone who'd actually been *in* the house
would have known about . . . and as for those two chaps who'd
come with them, they were Criminal Investigation Division
(CID) or he, Finn, was a unicycle-riding, concertina-playing, one-
man band like the one they showed on the Eurovision song contest from some small town in France, the eejit with the monkey
and the flowerpot on his head. . . .

And he wasn't.

Oh, they'd learned their lesson, but. No more guided tours, oh
no. They weren't quite grand enough, or sinister enough for that,
nor did they have enough friends among the media-savvy, or

American television journalists. No Omar Ben Salaad, he![3] No, such resources as they did possess would have to be severely husbanded (he liked that word: *husbanded*), and what better husbandman than himself, a regular Charlemagne or Cosimo de Medici, a warrior-scholar with the best of 'em:

"Oh, aye. Just call me Cincinnatus," said Finn, with a giggle.

But it was true, wasn't it, in a way? On the one hand he ran the great Municipal Library of Killoyle, which was humming along as it hadn't done for years, with half a million volumes on the shelves, a new computerized cataloguing system, and a full complement of book orders, seminars, and games for the kiddies. On the other hand, Finn was the commandant of the army council of the Soldiers of Brian O'Nolan, Ireland's newest and most effective militia (as the slogan on their web site had it), staffed exclusively by professionals, discreetly subsidized by the government's Peace Ahead secret grants to self-styled "liberation movements," but those were mere stipends, sufficient only to furnish the place and put a carpet on the floor and buy the odd computer or two. The real hardware was being discreetly financed by what Finn colourfully called (ah, he was the two ends of a wag itself) "hands-in-pocket" operations like phone pledge drives and Mrs. Finn's charity fund-raisers for immigrants and the odd book sale—in fact, they'd bought their new Armalites with the proceeds from an especially pristine set of P. D. James first editions,[4] thanks to the negotiating skills and Continental contacts of Tom O'Mallet.

Time for tea, Finn said to himself, reinforcing the sentiment with brisk palm-rubbing, followed by a cosy old tea-anticipating yawn,

---

[3] A forgotten flunkey of the opposite religion, circa 1990s. Also quite a bomb-thrower and beard-grower, in his spare time. Not big on people, though, like the rest of them.

[4] There's that name again (*qv., supra*).

while in the distance the comforting crump-crump of rockets hitting their targets could be heard.

Mick sat down at the bar at the precise moment at which Milo wandered off to admire the beer machine at the Guinness booth that could, it was alleged in the drinking fraternity, automatically fill a tray of thirty-two pint glasses in three seconds flat, just before the first rocket crashed through the French window at the far end of the hall and exploded behind the Czech display, demolishing a fine porcelain model of Hradcany Castle.

"Fuck," gasped Mick, holding his head in both hands like a Gaelic football. Flakes of plaster and soot rained, or rather snowed, down on his shoulders as he sank to the floor.

Kaaa-tsuuuuuuuuuu.

Boom! (Actually, it sounded more like a hundred cats hissing.)

Tsssssssssssssssssssssssssssssssss.

Pow.

The second and third rockets made it most of the way inside before blowing up and showering shards of glass, china, burled walnut, et cetera, over the bloodstained, although still twitching, figure of Milo Rogers[5] and the recumbent—indeed, quite dead— bodies of the four young Czech attendants, none of whom had ever left the confines of the Czech Republic before, except to visit Slovakia and Germany on day trips.

---

[5]Ouch. To say the least. And feeling at first like some great big gangling galoot had just tackled you from behind on a sideways throw (in rugby terms, or Gaelic footer). Then feeling all shivery-like, as if someone had just turned down the temperature. Know what? Avoid it if possible; that's my advice.

19

The faint disc of yellowish light from Tom O'Mallet's torch bobbed up and down and sideways before going out completely.

"Fuck it. Hang on a sec, I can't see a thing," he said. "Seamus, hang on there a mo, won't you, for the love of God. Me torch went out and I reckon I've sprained me fuckin' ankle, as well."

Tom fell to hobbling as Seamus crunched stolidly through the bracken somewhere ahead of him. Tom stopped, then he heard Seamus's voice and what sounded oddly, and unexpectedly, like a low laugh, unless it was the throat-clearing or mating call of some wild woodland creature.

"This way, Tom."

"Who the fuck's that? Is that you, Seamus?"

"Oh, aye. It's me. The man from Sarajevo, yeah?"

It was Seamus, right enough, but his voice sounded different, more knowing and amused at the same time, as if it contained a response to a question Tom hadn't heard; as if your man had just run into an old friend, and the two of them were up to no good. It was just like high jinks at school again, only a touch more serious, with a million quid's worth of ordnance up for grabs and the cold bloody drizzly darkness of south Co. Killoyle all around. . . .

Not to mention a life or two at stake; Tom's own, for a start. He paused and heard a tiny moan, at first identical to an imagined cat, say, or a stranded fox cub, or even a power drill, far far away; but when he heard it again he recognized it as a faint wheeze threading itself into the even pattern of his breathing. A hint of asthma on top of everything else. He'd always been susceptible to asthma, especially on damp nights like this, with buggers smoking, as they would . . . in fact, he could swear he caught a whiff of cigarette smoke now, somewhere up ahead.

"Ah, give over the fags there, Seamus, can't you wait till we're done?"

There was no reply. Things were turning a litle too ominous for Tom's taste, which ran to safety interrupted by purely cinematic danger, of the kind routinely faced by Bobby Lee Irwin and the like. A cold rivulet of sweat trickled its way down Tom's spine. All he could see in front of him was the faint outline of the hilltop, or the brush of trees and bushes that crowned the hilltop, against the distant glow in the night sky of the lights of Killoyle City, five miles distant (might as well have been five hundred). Directly in front of him he saw nothing, or rather an assemblage of indistinct dark shapes that could have been anything apart from what they probably were; that is, furze bushes or gorse or some such, rather than piles of . . .

Piles of . . .

Say, hand grenades, or loose ammo, perish the thought. He kicked out at one; it rattled and loosened into several pieces, like scree.

"Shite," said Tom to himself. This was turning out not to be a very good idea after all, and he had only himself to blame, fucking bone-headed eejit that he was. He was the one who'd insisted on coming alone, rejecting Bettina's pleas, not to mention the Da's.

"Fuck it, boy, they'll take the guns and the money and shoot you for a lark," the judge had said. "Things are too volatile now. Best lay low for a while, eh?"

"Sod that." Yes, that was what Tom had said to his father, earlier that evening, in fact a scant hour and a half previously when his surroundings could not have been more different from his current ones, could not possibly have been more familial and secure: his father's dining room, where they'd spent so many long nocturnal hours debating and haranguing and sometimes just talking . . . in an access of juvenile bravado, he'd said he'd see it through, he'd take care of it, oh, Tom O'Mallet was the wild Irish rover, he was the lad, wasn't he, he wasn't afraid of man nor beast—nor even the Provos. And anyway, for fuck's sake, the Provos were on *their* side, weren't they? McArdle had said so. It was the other crowd, the Pure IRA and God knew who else . . . maybe the Basques, some of them anyhow . . . it was that lot they had to look out for. *This* was a simple exchange of merchandise for money, a straightforward business deal of the kind Tom O'Mallet had brokered by the dozen in his not-so-long and not-very-distinguished career.

But now he was lost.

"Ah. Seamus?"

He had arrived in a clearing of some kind, and the contours of the ground had changed, solidified, turned to asphalt, firmer underfoot at least, like a car park, or a loading bay; but no cars were in sight, and the shapes Tom thought he could make out were too irregular to be buildings. Trees, more likely, and men, that low laugh again followed by a loud hawking of phlegm . . .

"Ahhhhhhwwwkkkkkkkk. Ahem."

Now he knew that sound; of course, it was the so-familiar music of Ireland, but that particular sound, with the terminal, somewhat prim "ahem," like a reflexive memory of a proper upbringing ("cover your mouth, child!"): that was a lace-curtain Belfast cough; it was McArdle.

Ever the gambler, Tom threw his all.

"Is that yourself, Martin? Sure I'd know that smoker's hack anywhere this side of the Lagan Valley."

But there was no reply. Now Tom mutely gave himself permission to worry. The air was tense with menace. He wondered about taking off, just running blind, back down the hill . . . but he'd been depending on Seamus to lead the way, more fool he, he hadn't a hope of retracing his steps in the dark, not after zigzagging uphill for what had seemed like about an hour and a half.

He looked at his watch, a luminous model, mock-Swiss made in Thailand: it read ten after ten (ideal watch-time of adverts). Only twenty minutes since he'd parked on the Crumstown Road? *Twenty minutes* to fill up an entire eternity and then some?

And just an hour since he'd left home?

And where was the Basque contact they'd been talking about? Was that the fellow he'd heard laughing? (If indeed he had heard somebody laughing?)

"All right, yez bastards," Tom bawled, "show yourselves like men, if men you are, which I doubt, yez fuckin' cowardly shites. . . ."

"Now there's no call for language like that, Thomas."

These words were spoken in the rich, rubicond, and blandly reassuring West Belfast tones of the brigade commander himself.

"McArdle, it *is* you."

"Oh, aye. Just supervising things, like. Holding up my end of the deal, you know."

Tom heaved a sigh of relief.

"Grand. Grand. It's grand to hear you, Martin. I don't mind saying, I was well on the way, a second or so ago."

"Aye. It's no so good an idea to have these transactions in the middle of the fuckin' night. I don't know why; we've always done it like that. Now. To business."

"Oh, I'm all in favour of that."

"Soldiers of fuckin' Brian O'Nolan, is it?"

"Beg pardon?"

"Them bastards lobbed our rockets at the Spudorgan Hotel. My question is, how did they get hold of them. Eh?"

"Pissed if I know, Martin."

"Ah, none of that, boy. This is your chance, Tom. Now or never."

Tom was sweating and conscious of a fluid rubbery kind of feeling connecting his suddenly sagging lower intestine to his knees; but he was an O'Mallet, and O'Mallets gave the rest of the world the fig, even if . . .

"Sure, business is business," said McArdle.

"It is that?" said Tom.

"No hard feelings then, Tom. Eh, lads?"

Tom's relief was so great that it took him a minute or more to realize that there the "lads" so addressed numbered five or six and that they had already somehow managed to surround him, and a further half-minute or so to correctly identify the smooth plastic-sounding click-and-shut noise he heard as the release mechanism on a semiautomatic pistol; and by the time he'd come to the correct conclusion regarding the use to which the pistol was going to be put, and its relation to his immediate, and eternal, fate—for whatever his faults, let it not be said that Tom O'Mallet was by any means a stupid man—it was too late for second thoughts or third ones or voiced regrets or offers of marriage or threats of exposure based on sealed documents in safe deposit boxes or any other course of action or indeed anything at all, and the great roar of the weapon elided into a blinding red-and-yellowish flash and he was dead.

And therefore in no position to hear Martin McArdle chuckle coldly and say, "Search the body, lads, just on the off chance he was wearin' a wire. Then dump him in the fuckin' ditch."

And it's the Mafia they say are the hard men.

20

Anil's body was on the mend, but not his temper. Recent events tended to replay themselves ad infinitum on the cinema screen of his brain, with the result that several times a day he would sit up in his bed and scream hollowly, his voice encrusted with ire, "Give me five minutes with that fuckwallah and there won't be anything left of him except his scrotum, which I will personally feed to the jackals of Rajastan, I swear it before great Vishnu himself," or words to that effect.

Rubina's response to these ravings was always the same.

"Calm down, Uncle. You need to rest."

"And that Awmley fuckbastard. The solicitor. He's the one who set the whole thing up, you know."

"He's dead, Anil," said Rashmi, who kept herself *au courant* of events. "Found shot in the woods, execution-style, it says in the newspapers.[1] Probably IRA." IRA definitely, she self-asserted (being rather more in the know than she cared to let on). . . .

---

[1]Reported by the *Clarion* under the headline, mistakenly transposed from page six, "It's a Great Day for the Irish." On page six, above the hot-off-the-press news story about Ireland's victory in the Five Nations Tournament at the Parc des Princes, hovered the errant headline "Bod in the Sod: Mysterious Death in the Hills."

"Good," said Anil. "If only I'd done it myself. Good riddance to bad rubbish, I say. By the way, behold how my enemies perish, eh? First Goone, then that Ormlet chap. There's some justice somewhere, you can't deny it."

"Shut up, you incredibly silly man," said Rubina. "It's bad luck to talk like that."

Anil brooded.

"Ormlet's father was a judge," he muttered.

"Good-good," said Rubina. "Now lie back and watch the telly."

Anil grudgingly obeyed, but when the ladies were asleep, or out (Rashmi had a constant schedule of comings and goings and mysterious mobile phone chats in the next room, or in the car park), he gingerly rose from his bed and stole a quick peek at the phone directory, in which he came upon no Ormlets or Awmleys, but finally:

"O'Mallet, Gerald F. D. C. Judge. Squarestairs Mansions. 321 Volt Avenue, Killoyle E. Tel. 987–6543."

He made an exploratory call, but only reached a chilly recorded voice inviting him to leave a message. This he did, with valiant efforts to disguise his subcontinental accent, to no avail; still, he reckoned "I've got you in my sights," spoken by a stranger named Hamid over the phone in any kind of accent, would be enough to put the wind up any number of old bastards.

Rubina sat by Anil's bedside throughout his protracted convalescence, at least during the relatively brief waking hours when his attention detached itself from the TV. Fugitives, for all they knew, from both law and lawless, they were staying under assumed names ("Mr. and Mrs. O. Henry," after the author of one of Anil's favourite stories, "The Necklace"[2]) in a king-size double-

---

[2]Well, that's not quite it, is it. A slight to the memory of the great Maupassant, that is. Ah, the old roué, dead of the clap at forty, no less, no more—and who once (stop me if you've heard this before), after an hour's worth of heavy ogling,

queen master suite ("The Im erial," with a missing "p") in the
Mascara Motel on the main Killoyle-Crumstown Road. Anil, with
two broken ribs, a bruised clavicle, and a spavined elbow—and
lucky to have suffered no worse, as Rubina reminded him—
needed a few days in bed, after being tended to by their family

---

requested his luncheon companion, who happened that day (at Simpson's on
the Strand, during Guy's only transchannel venture) to be Henry James, who
had been droning nasally on about his digestion and the plotting and struc-
ture of his latest epic of upper-class ennui (*The Golden Bowl*), two subjects in
which you can be sure Guy was about as interested as he would have been
had you or I been there and started blathering on about, say, the workings of
the latest roller blinds (less)—so anyway, Guy interrupted boring old Henry
by loudly asking him, with many a heavy wink, to "get" for him a lady (married, accompanied) at a neighbouring table. "I say," blurted Henry, shocked,
and dabbed his lower lip. "Get her yourself, you bloody Frenchman." "Very
well, then, *mon ami*," said Guy, and bold as brass he whipped his chair around
and introduced himself and before you know it he and the lady (Lady
Samantha Fortescue-Bolton of The Rubbings, Osprey, Beds.) were making
dates for that year's Henley Regatta, oblivious to: (1) the purlings of poor
Henry, and (2) the spluttering of Lady Sam's husband Denys. *Touché*, Guy!
Poor bloke was dead as a doornail six months later, not that Henry cared much
("Lecherous bloody Frog," he muttered. "God, I wonder how many women
he slept with. Lots, I'd guess. Crikey. I wonder what it's like. Well, too late to
ask Guy. But that Zola chap's still around. I wonder, if I sent him a tele-
graph . . ."). Anyhow, to pursue the matter a little further (no worry, it's my
round next), the mere mention of Victoriana evokes in my mind at least
images of musty boudoirs stiff with heavy hangings and gloomy draperies,
blood-red to an extreme and antimacassared half to death, with of course a
piano or pianola, survivor of many an infinitely dull evening recital squatting
in one corner, topped by a potted palm, the whole lightly dusted with dust.
Only funeral parlours today have that feel, which explains—to my satisfaction, anyway—the obsession with blood (vampires, Jack the Ripper, Barbey
d'Aurevilly) and death that permeated the Victorian age. Bunch of necrophiliac
buggers, if you ask me, and that's flat. Actually, my Galway cousin Monk used
to live like that, now that I think of it, in a draughty old pile near the Spanish
Gate. For the longest time he never went out save by dead of windy night,
and traveled in a charabanc to boot. Monk was an odd lad, oh, he was that.

friend Dr. Roybal ("tsk, tsk, Sri Anil, when *will* you stop acting the goat?"); and anyway, Rubina herself needed time to think things through. What would she do? What was becoming of them? What did this madness mean? Whom was she married to? *And why?*

Money, at least, was no problem for the time being. Cousin Rashmi, in customary high-energy fashion, took care of it via urgent mailings from London, Geneva, and Calcutta. Yes, Rashmi, scarcely twenty-eight years old, was coming into her own. By golly, Anil thought, she thrived on all this bullshit. Tall, well-proportioned (in the mornings Anil peeked and looked away, glimpsed, alas, by his wife), and light-skinned,[3] her features marred only by the scar across her nose ("from a police cavalry

---

For the longest time he always said he'd been having a recurring dream that he was just standing about minding his own business when presto, a house fell on top of him; then what do you know wasn't he out for his nocturnal constitutional, cape aflow around his shoulders, hair tousled in fine Gothic fashion, when No. 145b, Plunkett Place, just off Eyre Square (S.), suddenly trembled from chimney to cellar and collapsed atop old Cousin M., pinning him beneath its rafters. The occupants, the MacShanes, Sid and Molly, apologized till they were blue in the face (it was a cold night), but to no avail, as Monk simply lay there, speechless, peering through a gap in the bricks, weighing up two of life's innumerable little ironies: there he was, with, on the one hand, the satisfaction of having foretold his own fate, no mean feat; but with, on the other hand, four broken ribs, a fractured skull, and six months in traction. Then he was OK, though, and thereafter drove a motor (a Honda 800 automatic), sparingly, with headlamps firmly in the On position, and at pedestrian speeds through the narrow night-time streets. Sorry: Carry on.

[3]Crikey, she sounds a corker. You had me sobbing me old eyes out there for a mo', mate. Your gal's the spitting image of Dolores. Ah, Dolores, or "Dolly" as I called her. I met her in Youghal, at a yachting convention. "Fancy a quick one, hon?" says I. "You bet, buster," says she, and before you could say Upsy-daisy we were off, or up, or down, or all three, and Gran's doilies were never the same again. Nor were the vertebrae in my lower back, if you take my meaning (Austin Seven, fading light, ever-present danger of: (1) the gearshift, and (2) voyeuristic passssersby).

charge on Connaught Circle, must tell you about it some day, oh, is that the time? Must dash"), she carried a queenly presence around with her. Still proud of the success of her Mrs. Bashir caper, she decided to try on a new identity, that of one Layla bin-Hammas of Damascus, Syria, continentally coiffed and turned out with mobile phone eternally in her palm, or at her ear.

"You're good, Rash," murmured Anil in robust admiration.

"Just remember, Cuz," she said. "To the Irish, all we dusky foreigners look alike. You could probably walk into that Judge O'Mallet's office tomorrow and tell him you were Vijay Amritraj and get away with it."

"Vijay, eh?" said Anil. "Why, do you think I look like him?" Coyly, he revealed his crooked teeth in a smile meant to be whimsical, winsome, even seductive. "Quite a good-looking *chikna*, isn't he?"

Once again easily interpreting the role of the no-nonsense harridan in a shopworn domestic farce from the overworked studios of Bollywood—*Pestonjee's Travels,* for example, or *Ranji's Neck*—Rubina leaned forward and applied firm pressure, once, to the area surrounding his left earlobe.

"*Kaan kay neechay rappak lagaoonga.*"[4]

"Ouch."

"Stop it, you two," said Rashmi. "We have business to discuss."

Oh, she was indeed more than adequately prepared for her new role as Layla bin-Hammas, "active liberationist," her term for *good* terrorist, as opposed to "baby-killer," or *bad* terrorist. Their overriding enemies, she explained, were two, apart from the system itself: the Soldiers of Brian O'Nolan, because of what they'd done

---

[4]Eh, you say? Well, when I heard this in the backrooms of the Taj on Beaufort Terrace, it meant "I'll slap your silly mug" or words to that effect, but I wouldn't swear to its meaning now.

to poor Anil (who had, at least, undergone his baptism of fire as a soldier of the revolution); and Emerald Mats, PLC, arch-exploiters of the weak, oppressed, female, brown, black, handicapped, dull, sexually ambivalent, et cetera.

"Never mind Emerald Mats," shouted Anil, weakly. "It's that Spanish fuckbastard I want to go after."

"Syria? Try Palestine," said Rubina, not relating at all to Ms. bin-Hammas.

"No, too many associations. The Irish are all pro-Palestinian, out of some half-baked idea that what's happening there is like their silly Easter 1916 revolution or some such rubbish. No, Syria's better. No one here could even find it on a map, I'll wager you a pile of rupees, Cuz."

It even transpired that she had a contact or two here and there, as Anil put it, or rather that she was a member of several less-than-respectable organizations, some of which actually had— indeed, specialized in—guns, grenades, and the like.

"But they usually don't get this far west," she confided, leaning forward to adminster a dose of *chai,* her long hair swinging like curtains above Anil's screwed-up monkey-face that was, in fact, utterly unlike that of the distinguished Vijay Amritraj. "Kashmir, mostly. And the Trincomalee area, for the Tamils, you know. I daren't say more than that."

"Bloody hell."

"Oh, bloody hell, indeed," said Rashmi. "I think this lot who buggered you about went way beyond the bounds, you know. Not active liberationists at all, no, by gosh. Why, our outfits back home survive quite nicely by just setting off the odd bomb in the odd barracks and taking potshots at Gurkhas, not by harassing civilians. Or launching rocket attacks in broad daylight."

She was, of course, referring to the assault on the Spudorgan Vacation Inn's beer festival. The night of the attack, all three had eagerly settled back, popcorn at hand, washed down with a quick orange juice or soda, and watched the news on RTE6, Anil's favourite channel.[5] Quick-cut shots danced from one end of the screen to the other: ambulances, medics holding aloft drip tubes, Milo Rogers on a stretcher, eyes staring fixedly aloft, followed by the recumbent forms of the dead Czech youths, entirely covered by blankets: "However," pulsated the narrator, a youngish johnny in a sporting vest and hornrims, "the organizers, with the approval of Hrçko, the Czech brewing company, have announced that the festival will resume tomorrow morning with the theme 'Life Goes On.' The hotel manager, Myles Roberts, although quite seriously injured in the blast, consented to say a few words to reporters."

"Leave me alone," Milo was heard to say weakly, beneath a tangle of tubes and wires and the heaving shoulders of medics and security personnel and one or two TV types. "Sod off, you stupid bastards."

"Robert Myles, speaking from his hospital bed. The general impression," cliché-crowed the news reader triumphantly, "is of a community bearing up bravely under extraordinary pres-

---

[5]Quite the telephile, isn't he. Well, more power to the lad is what I say, after half a lifetime's arguing with pseuds about the desirability or not of even having a television; I mean, I think the issue's beyond dispute by this point in time, but there are still those, usually young, leftish would-be artists, who reckon it's somehow superior not to have one, that it enhances their incredible native creativity so they can turn their attentions to fashioning ceramic pots or necklaces of Tibetan prayer bells or tending their fields of tofu. Question is, how do they know it's so bad if they haven't watched it? And if they have watched it, how have they escaped being poisoned, tainted, infused by the cultural toxins that kill everybody else, according to these smooth-talking snobs (and one of them served me breakfast this morning, disdaining even to turn over the egg sunny-side up)? Balls to that lot I said then, and balls I say to them again now, and they can queue up to smooch my royal Irish arse. Q.: Join you for an antigovernment protest next Tuesday, outside the president's house? A.: Sorry, I see by my calendar that I'm watching TV that night.

sure." Various community dignitaries were then permitted a ten-second televisual appearance in which to briefly summarize their reactions: the outgoing lord mayor, Ben Ovary ("a despicable, cowardly act"); the Superintendent of Gardai, Pat Talbott ("A cowardly, despicable act"); the housing developer and philanthropist Dr. Thomas Maher ("Arrhh arrah that's a right crowd of despicable cowards so they are God help the rest of us, specially the ones with deafness in one ear or the bit of a kidney problem like oh let us pray to St. Jude to intercede for them, it's all right, I've named one of 'em new housing estates after him—St. Jude, that is—St. Jude's Emerald Acres, it's called, out on the Derrydingle Ring Road, all mod cons ya can bet yer arse, boy, as well as guaranteed twenty-four-hour security against the likes of 'em bastards—and wait till I tell youse—Tim, is it? I can tell ya if I catch a single one of 'em murderous bastards anywhere near me own snug domicile, not to mention any of me dear owld housing developments, well the jig is up and then some, I'll give 'em what-for, be all the massed saints of paradise itself, and be the way Tim so long as we're at it like allow me to compliment you on that scarf, looks like a college one, Trinity isn't it, a Trinity man are ya, well, well, it's a smaller world than the inside of your Y-fronts as me old gran used to say; of course, she was from Sligo ... and sure in the sight of God amn't I a Trinity man as well, just like yerself, well all right, no, I'm not, not really, honorary doctorate, you know, like, but be janey just between you and me and the dustbins I'd have made a first-rate TCD student believe you me," etc.); Kathy McRory Hickman, editor-in-chief of a prominent local periodical, *Glam* ("Oh, poor Milo, my goodness, back in the hospital again, oh it's just awful when this stuff hits home, despicable cowards, aren't they, now if you'll excuse me," then "Strongbow! Shut up!" to a barking off-camera dog); Charles Carleton McShaunessy Finn, director of the Killoyle Public Library ("Oh, I don't know what to say, I mean there they were, eh? I mean, I suppose they had a warning call ten minutes or so before it happened, didn't they, so they *did* have time to get out, if they'd really tried, but people are hopeless, aren't they, the despicable cowards?"); Eileen McCreek Cashman, managing director of Big Jimmie's Emerald Mats PLC ("Oh, it's a despicable and cowardly act right enough, and it reminds me of three things . . .")—

"Stop!" shouted Rashmi. "That was him! He!"

Other VIPs came and went but Rashmi was transfixed by one and one only: the nasal, patronizing, nodding presence, gone so soon, of Finn the librarian.

"It's him, all right," she said. "I knew it. Don't ask me how. I mean, apart from actually having met the man . . . didn't you recognize him, Anil?"

"No, no. From where should I, bloody hell? I don't go to the library except on Sundays to rent videos, not that they have very good ones there, and I've never seen this man on the telly before, no not at all, I'm quite sure . . ."

Well, Rashmi had to steer her cousin's meandering thoughts back onto the straight and narrow, spelling out the dread reality of the matter in the vivid and militant fashion she had claimed for her own; and once she had, neither rabid dog or bat nor bloodthirsty crusader at the Krak des Chevaliers in, say, the year of our lord 1275, could have rivaled Anil Swain in production of sheer foam from the mouth and amplitude of righteous desire for vengeance.

He rose from his bed, majestically, and flung out a commanding arm, resembling ever so briefly the equestrian statue of Lord Cavendish on Connaught Place in New Delhi.

"Give me a gun," he said, grimly, "and I'll shoot him between the testicles." He paused, eyes busily searching. "If it is him, in fact. If you're quite sure. I mean, the head librarian, a terrorist? It's pretty bloody silly. Librarians aren't terrorists."

"Of course it's him. I had tea with him yesterday. And you were lying there. I even wrote out a cheque for ten thousand pounds to his stupid organization."

"Golly, I hope it was a make-believe cheque."

"So do I, actually. It was on one of our Swiss accounts in the name of... well, whatever. Well, if it isn't, they can always write in to cancel it, or something. But never mind that. We haven't the time to dither about. Action stations, girls and boys!"

And so a quirky, unexpected, absurd and risible yet utterly dedicated counterterrorist force was born, with Anil gamely tagging behind, walking stick in hand, and his foolhardy but superbly stacked cousin Rashmi leading the way like much less sexy Mohandas Gandhi on his salt march to the sea. It was a crusade that others joined when enjoined telephonically so to do (some enthusiastically, others not so): Fuad and Anwar from the Star of Bihar ("I told them it was my budgie's birthday, so there was no problem shutting down"); Sylvia and Adrienne, burly union organizers over from Llandudno; Thackeray Singh and Pedro from the currently shuttered Koh-I-Noor, arm in arm from the neck up; Prait, an intense intellectual from Dublin of Mumbai origin on his mother's side (as he explained, briefly). He looked at Anil and said, "Parsee?"

"No," said Anil.

Once the tally was complete, the group assembled in Rashmi's rooms off the Strand. A stereo played the sarangi quartets of Hanuman Mishra.[6] Through the tall French windows drifted a breeze, stroking the curtains and the fevered brows of the assembled militants. Beyond the balcony, the moped-echoing street, a row of shops and the Michael Collins statue, roiled the grey scrotum-tightening sea.

"Just like Kerala," as Rashmi enjoyed saying, "except for the sun, the sand, the palm trees, the smells, the climate, and the tem-

---

[6]Ah, them's the lads to set the toes a-tappin', right enough. Nothing like a splash of Paddy's in the glass and one of old Hanuman's quartets on the old Victrola to round off a perfect soirée.

perature. And the sea here's grey, whilst back home, you know, it's quite blue."

She repeated the pleasantry to her assembled comrades, but none so much as smiled. Thackeray had Pedro in an affectionate hammerlock, and Adrienne and Sylvia stared glumly at the floor, breathing heavily, lust-besotted by each other's nearness.

"Bloody hell, Rash," said Anil querulously, "here we are about to go off and assault a bloody IRA outpost and all you can do is sit there and make silly jokes. Well I don't know about the rest of you but I say sod that."

"Aye aye," said Prait. "Hear hear. What ho."

"Oh, do shut up."

The point, however questionable, was taken, and seriousness characterized the remainder of the group's deliberations, revolving initially around the name by which the strike force would be known. Anil's contribution, promptly rejected by the non-Indians among them, was the Swayamsevaks, or volunteers. Soldiers of the Goddess, proposed by Sylvia and Adrienne, died a timely death. The Irish Foreign Legion met with dubious snorts and chuckles. Finally, the Avengers, time-tattered that it was, came in as the odds-on favourite, conferring as it did a spurious air of John Steediness to the men and Emma Peelery to the women.

"Cool," said Prait.

"Now we already did a recon," said Rashmi, smartly. "So we know the general layout. But this time we're going for the kill, boys and girls. And fear not: Right is on our side."

"Not much good if you're dead," muttered Prait, dubiously.

Distribution of ordnance and the assigning, and acceptance, of various tasks, took up the remainder of the evening. Voices were muted in comradely harmony, and the small chimneys of cigarettes were soon chummily bluing the air with their ribbons of smoke. It was congenial, cosy, a near-love-in reminiscent of the glories of Greenham Common and Woodstock, not to mention

Dresden '48 and Paris '89 (and '68[7]). Most of those present had been involved in militant organizations or militias one way or another, from then-Major Thackeray's service against the Hillside Pushtuns in the elite 249th Kashmiri Rifles to Anil's unremarkable yet memorable eighteen months in the First Orissa Fusiliers to Adrienne's womanning of the antiman barricades at the infamous Siege of Radcliffe Hall, summer of '69. Prait Cunningham, too, had scented battle before, having once gone after his landlord with a hammer. Ever since, he had considered himself an expert in the art of tracking and reconnaissance. All present had been, therefore, to a greater or lesser degree, tested in adversity (Rashmi herself, of course, bore the scars figurative and literal of many a nameless confrontation), and were

---

[7]Oh, get '68 in there, by all means. I was there then, or was I? No, I'm quite sure I was. I remember coming out of the Parc Monceau metro station with a few Pernods in my tum, and before you could say "Hail fellow well met" there I was retreating in a hail of rubber bullets and clouds of tear gas all because the bloody CRS had apparently mistaken me for some napper called Danny Le Rouge. (I later received a full apology, signed by M. Le Rouge himself.) That was all right, but. It led in a maze-like way to dinner at Jo Goldenberg's in the Marais, the night of the Billancourt work stoppage: klezmer music going full tilt, the scent of fresh pierogis and blinis floating out of the kitchen, a fine bottle of Château Manischewitz '64 on the table, and me arm in arm with six or seven hearty Renault assembly workers, thick as two short planks they were to a man but goodhearted for all that, and stalwart souls to boot, as we swayed back and forth and hummed (none of us having the exact words) the *Internationale,* bunch of right friggin' cafflers that we were ... hang on a sec, sure wasn't it there that Kathy walked into my life for the second time? "Hallo boy," she said, then turned and walked out, her slender back and swaying hips challenging me to follow, against the background of knowing mockery from my Renault assemblyline chums: "ouf!", "oh-oh", "oui oui!", "Are you a man or a woman?", and the like. I didn't follow her then, but most definitely did so later. Odd, that we kept on nearly meeting like that, then broke up when we got together. But *plus ça change,* as the French have it, eh?

unanimously ready for further combat in a just cause. Everyone agreed that the Soldiers of Brian O'Nolan were: (1) an obnoxious impediment to Killoyle's growing reputation and a decided obstacle to the efforts of the Bord Failte to encourage tourism with its consequent upside for the local economy, waitresses, taxi drivers, diversity, et cetera, and (2) an actual threat to their own livelihoods, not to mention lives.

Yes, it's true to say that all in all they were as eager as a bunch as the Kim Il Sung battalion on the Yalu River in November 1950—and quite sober, being non-Irish.

The attack started at midnight, after a high-spirited yet hair-raising drive in three vehicles: Anil's Escort, an invalid increasingly hobbled by infirmities and rarely out of second gear; Rashmi's BMW, rarely in second gear; and a Bedford farm van decaying from the underside up, owned jointly by Sylvia and Adrienne. This caravan of disparities arrived at Armalite Hall in a state of near-hysterical excitement that boded ill for their offensive.

"Now calm down," said Rashmi in a hoarse stage whisper.

"Yessir," chorussed her obedient footsoldiers, as one, sotto voce.

When the Avengers launched their assault it was done *desi*-style, or *a l'Indienne*, as Rubina observed, with tirades of half-coherent speech forgotten amid much bonhomie, scattered prayers to Vishnu and sundry avatars, familial squabbling, and the imaginary aroma of tandooris and coal smoke; but as Prait, Indo-Hibernian intellectual *par excellence*, observed, "It's not how it was done, but that it was done at all, that will set tongues to wagging from here to golden Samarkand."[8]

---

[8]Golden Samarkand? The restaurant? It used to be my favourite, but once they got that termagant of a chef in, I stopped going, thanks very much, the one with blue hair and adhesive sparkles across her cheekbones, what was her name, Buddy? No—Bud, not Buddy, that's it.

At one A.M., a Rover 175 belonging to Finn (its windscreen bore a telltale Killoyle Public Library roundel) was torched, but without Finn or anybody else in it—"Or at least I don't think so," said Thackeray Singh semidubiously, as Pedro squawked for breath in the crook of his burly right arm. "But there is a bit of a mess on the floor. Still, it doesn't smell like meat," sniffing. (Rashmi wrinkled her scarred nose fastidiously.) A grenade, lobbed by Anil through an ajar scullery or pantry window, took its sweet time to ignite, incurring the anger and curiosity of the troops, as in any number of lamely predictable war flicks: "I'll go and see what's wrong"; "No, don't, are you mad, come back, no, NO"—then exploded just in time—*paaaaaaaaapppppbbbbbbbbbbbbssss* causing much damage, as far as could be aurally ascertained from the *crack shatter tinkatinkle*, primarily to objects made of glass and china and allied materials, as well as to (of course) windows and their cohorts: skylights, glass-paned doors, cabinets, et cetera. An alarm bell suddenly but not unexpectedly embarked on a hysterical metallic soliloquy: *shre-e-e-e-e-eeeeeeeeeeee(iiinnnnnngggg)*. Lights went on in the nearest neighbour's house, about a half-mile distant, behind the copse of yew and an old waterbasin. Somewhere in the darker distance, from that house or another, a scratchy yet remarkably potent aged-in-the-wood Munster voice embarked on a monotonous verbal bastonnade that rose and fell in intensity with the vagaries of the nighttime breeze; but prominently above the wind rose the word "shite" and its cousins "shit" and "ballocks,"[9] with the occasional "bugger" and "sod" for good measure. Dogs, of course, hurled their yapping invective at the incomprehensible night. Even a fox joined in, coughing quietly in the undergrowth. The neighbourhood, in short, was on the *qui*

---

[9]Sounds like Victor. Hang on a sec, you don't think . . . ? Sure, I'd recognize the old culchie anywhere. He's probably visiting that bint old Shoots told him about.

vive. Before long, uniformed representatives of the civil authority would be on the scene, and vengeance as a motive for bomb-
tossing carried scant weight in the courts of the Republic. Worse,
it was more than likely that this clumsy act of retaliation would
attract other such acts, from sources far more experienced in the
art of lobbing a few at innocents.

"We've done what we can," whispered Rashmi into Anil's ear,
imbuing his little corner of the night—of the world—*of the cos-
mos*—with mingled scents of ripe womanhood, sandalwood, as-
tringent perfume, and chives. "Let's go." Suddenly, beneath his
exhaustion roared desire; the miserable wretch wished she was
talking about the two of them and nobody else. Oh, Rashmi! She
was Woman, she was the spirit of the Ganges, she was India itself. She was silver screen goddess Madhuri Dixit, she was mythical goddess Lakshmi, she was goddess Parvati, wife and lover.
Anil's heart twisted itself into a sudden knot of nostalgia and longing for—well, yes, Mother India, and Sandrapore, and Home, sans
annoyances (that bugger Pal, the caste system, crowds, Muslims);
but also, sad to say, for his cousin Rash, and his wife Rubina, sharp-
eyed as a sparrowhawk above the rolling plains of the Deccan,
didn't like it one little bit.

"I think I've had enough of this nonsense," she said, with a firm
grip on her husband's left arm. "It's time to get a normal job, Sahib
Anil Swain. No more of these antics. Let's go home now."

Hurriedly, the Avengers returned to the bejeweled streets and
dark gardens of Killoyle City without incident. The three cars
took their three separate ways to allay suspicion, or rout the
enemy (all except Anil's, which backfired with such mightiness
just outside the Continental Ferry Docks in Crumstown that
lights went on from there to the gardai post just up the hill on
Pewterpeter Place). Within the hour the Avengers had disbanded,
and its members were asleep or awake in their respective dwell-
ings, alone or together, and in some cases, already snorting with
long-bottled-up lusts (no names, but their initials can be found

somewhere between A and Z). In short, all was well that ended well—from a *human* perspective, but from the point of view of a certain burrow of moles on the eastern side of the main Killoyle–Crumstown–Youghal dual carriageway it was a night to mourn, for, a mile or so outside the city, Sylvia and Adrienne, in their rust-cancerous Bedford van, almost obliviously (*Crunch:* Adrienne frowned) ran over a young father mole, a wee timorous year-old beastie who had chosen that selfsame unfortunate moment to leave the close confines and gamey odours of a snug two-foot-wide burrow and proceed blindly, nose-guided, at an infinitesimal pace across the road to a fresh rubbish tip on the other side in search of a midnight snack for the family, the little ones having been mewling and whimpering something terrible. Dead instantly, he twitched once, then lay still.

In the burrow, now inhabited by a mole-widow and two half-orphans, silence reigned, as if the sensation of loss had visited them in person with a warrant, a police photographer and three witnesses.[10]

---

[10]Sounds symbolic to me (you know these author johnnies), but of what? The risk of depending too much on your nose as a vademecum? The dangers of crossing a road at night, blind, at a speed of three centimeters per hour? The essential moleness of all of us? The sanctity of the burrow? The fragility of life? Well, the last one's an old favourite in yarns like this, so I suppose I'll have to settle for it. Pity about the wee ones, though. Makes you want to drive out there and scoop 'em up yourself, with eyedroppers containing milk.

21

Confusion and anger roiled Mick McCreek's heart and bowels. Once returned from the loo, his only solution was to hold up his foam-flecked pint glass and wag it suggestively from side to side in order for the curate to provide him with his third—well, third and a half, as he'd started off with a chaste half-pint, determined not to yield to age-old temptations, not today, not on the day when he'd had to start setting about pulling himself together and his socks up, boots on, et cetera; not on the day on which *he'd been fired—again—yes, twice in one month—going for a record.*

Adding insult to injury, or permanent intestinal damage to the parlous, beer-lashed state of his innards, had been breakfast at My Three Buns consisting of unshaven chunks of pig flesh masquerading as bacon beneath a more-or-less uncooked egg in which the orange embryo of the chick that might have been was still visible. Mick's stomach rebelled; his lower guts strained to process the sludge. Only half-jokingly, he'd accused Devereux of trying to poison his customers.

"Not all of 'em," had been the gnarled gnome's gnomic reply. "You mark my words, boy. Not all of 'em."

It had been, therefore, with much acrid belching and fierce intestinal chortling that Mick had tackled his destiny in the person of Denny Tool in Denny Tool's third-floor penthouse suite at nine A.M. The interview had been short and sour, much like Mick's breakfast.

"That rat of yours?" Denny had said, busily punching out numbers on a minuscule mobile phone, his back to Mick, his attention captivated by the car park below, whence Ramona was emerging, having just sinuously climbed out of her red Ford Octagon. "It's history. I've been on the phone with the beer people and they've agreed to take it down. You bet they agreed, because I told them it was their ass or the rat. Man, that didn't take them long. Hello? Is that Ken?"

"Ah, for the love of God put down the bloody phone for just a minute or so," said Mick, pleasantly. Denny swivelled around with the phone yet clinging to the side of his face like an ear-invading alien parasite from a sci-fi thriller.

"Hey, Ken, it's Den. Hey, man. Cool. Hey, can you hold for a sec? I've got a situation here. OK." He held the phone in one hand as tightly as a beaver might clutch a fish and gave Mick a halogen stare that would have done credit to the late Tom O'Mallet but which had no effect on Mick, who was primarily concerned with the imminent possibility of intestinal eruption and/or rupture. "You're fired, buddy," declared Denny crisply, "not just for your attitude—I've always considered you a slack-off son of a bitch, and I really don't like your clothes, like what's the idea, wearing a tie every day?—but also, and mostly, for violating company confidentiality, not to mention about half a dozen international copyright laws, in this country and the States as well as just about everywhere else around the world . . ."

"Ah, shut yer hole," Mick had said, in the same relaxed manner, as if doing a deep body stretch in a tantric yoga class, or raising a jar with mates. "Send my check along PDQ. Everything else you can stick up yer arse. Starting with your mobile." Enjoying the momentary plain-as-a-pikestaff dismay on Denny's face, Mick rose and walked out, holding himself as erect as the crick in his tum would allow.

"Good on ya, lad," he murmured to himself. "That was telling him. The bastard. The bloody corner boy." He was chuffed.
He'd done the best. True, he'd lost his job, but for once he'd
told a right caffler where to go. But it would have been harder
(he reflected) if Denny were an Irishman. Somehow his being a
Yank made that kind of abuse all the easier, not to say downright tempting . . . back in his office Mick completed his exit
from the ludicrous farce of NaughtyBoy Graphics by hurriedly
removing from his desk those few props that were his (*The History of the Bagiotti Coachworks,* by Count Vittorio di Poggibonsi; a
packet of Gitanes papier maïs, unsmoked; *Wagner's Operas,* by
Franz von Tanzmann (foreword by Harald Graf Rowohlt); a coffee mug bearing the coat-of-arms of the McCreeks of Glenbarry
(one lion rampant above two gueules argent flanked by sable
arms) as well as several that weren't; sixteen floppy disks, unused;
one copy of *Poodlestein* the interactive video game, unplayed; a
chrome-plated souvenir ashtray from Singapore, long disused;
a clutch of auto magazines, new and old, overread). At the adjacent desk Victor Hasdrubal-Scott, coughing and grumbling,
was peering at his computer screen, myopically indifferent to
Mick's presence, absence, arrival, departure, or existence itself;
indeed, as far as he was concerned the person cleaning out his
or her desk next door might have been anyone, or none, of the
following (a random sampling):

1. Hamid, grand vizier of Stamboul under the later Ottomans;
2. Adolf Eichmann;
3. Madonna, the half-nude pop singer;
4. P. D. James;[1] or

---

[1] There you go, you see, what did I tell you? Well, as they say, some
paranoiacs are right on target. They really *are* being persecuted. I tell you, if
it happens again I'll call the guards.

5. Vic's old and despised Clongowes Gaelic football coach Monty McFee.[2]

"Cheerio, then, Vic," said Mick.

"Bugger off, you ballocks. How many times do I have to tell you that my name's not bloody Vic, you silly ballocks."

---

[2]Mine, too, would you believe it. Hang on till I tell you. Monty taught at my old school, the Sub Rosa Academy in Ballyblasket, before briefly ascending to the empyrean of Clongowes. (Mother of God, is Victor in my age bracket? Stop the bus, world, I want to get off. Know what I mean?) I was a senior staff boy in sixth form, and Monty took a shine to me. A hopeless judge of character, he reckoned he saw leadership potential beneath the sempiternal sickly adolescent pallor enlivened by gigantic red pimple eruptions that only seemed to worsen when I sought release in extended investigation and practice of the science of Onan . . . but I digress, just as Monty did. I became, as I was saying, a frequent visitor to his horrible snot-green wee wet-wool-smelly suboffice behind the boys' locker room, as well as the object of his interminable anecdotage, which contented itself not in hewing to one narrative path but invariably (in the style of the greatest bores) sought the tangential byways of subanecdotage, e.g. (off the top of me head, like) "Nice to have you here on Sports Day, lad. Pity you came in last, but I'm wise to your strategy, O'Donnell, oh aye, I am that." (He called me O'Donnell.) "Was that your da I saw with you just now? Fine-looking man. You know, that reminds me of a story. Back in Cyprus"—too late to serve with Big Monty in the big one, wee Monty'd been in the British Army in Cyprus—Royal Welchers, I believe, or Queen's Own Ulsterers—"we had a lorry driver, big bloke, Bedfords mostly, with the odd Transit van, well perhaps the odd Humber, his name was George, he looked just like your dad—which reminds me, General Grivas had a dad, as well, and I met him once, there we were at a suspected terrorist hideout just south of Limassol—that's on the south coast, real shitehole let me tell you boy (it *is* boy, isn't it, ha ha, despite that long hair of yours?)—having a drink (lemonade for me, thanks very much, and you can believe I made sure my lads had the same) in a caff on the main square, Makarios Platz—and I knew him right away. 'Man, you're the spit and image of that Grivas chap,' says I, boldly. 'Eet ees because hee ees my son,' said the old fella, disclosing toothless gums. Mind you, he showed a fine clean pair of heels when I set the lads on him. Took off like a cheetah, he did. We never did catch him, far as I

"Too right, old son. Well, enjoy your old newspapers."

"Comeinandlearnallaboutitdotcom," harangued Victor. "Not old newspapers. It's a new web site now."

"Whatever, Vic."

"Victor to you, sonny."

"Aye."

Even his five-year-old Jocelyn GTS seemed to be in better spirits after that, Mick observed, still prepared for the worst—that is, dismissal, embarrassment, looming poverty and its possible corollaries, eviction and/or disgrace—to descend in ever-narrowing spirals to the *even worse*—for example, a myriad of fresh irritations along the lines of recalcitrant car ignitions, leaking shoes, more bowel trouble (ominous groaning from that

---

know. But we went back to that caff oh, twelve or a dozen times altogether, now I was no saint in them days, lad, but be gum and gorrah the girls there could kill at twenty paces with a look, there was one I remember whose name was Mario—odd, isn't it, she being a lass and all and going about with a lad's name, well, the Greeks are a rum bunch, lad, and that's all I can tell you, although just between you and me and the yew tree although she was quite heavily bearded for a girl she had a damn fine pair of—where was I, now," and of course in me, a poor timourous wee sixth-former, Monty had a captive audience, as he well knew; I'd have had to sit there until the moon shattered into slivers of ice over the Maamturk Mountains if that was his fancy. (Schools were strict places in them days.) But in the end things worked out quite nicely: accused of self-aggrandisement, Monty resigned from Clongowes (as I heard, or read in the *Church Times*) and was later shot trying to climb up, or down (accounts differ) the walls of Derry during an Apprentice Boys March, whether to praise the Orangemen or bury them we never knew. I don't know what his tombstone reads, having never seen it, but I know what it should say, in my humble opinion: "Here lies a nutter." For one thing, he was strict tee tee—yes, another one. For another, he always eschewed the camera, and not a single photograph of the man survives, bar a fuzzy b-and-w (as they say) long-distance shot of him leaning out the back window of a Morris Minor in the early spring of 1949, en route to Skibbereen. He's buried on Magilligan Strand, in sight of the golf links he loved so well.

quarter, as of a long-endungeoned soul), public mockery, lawsuits, tripping over your shoelaces, et cetera; but the car started with one easy flick of the igniting wrist, and Mick McCreek, ex-computer graphics designer—ex-car tester—ex-husband—ex-optimist—ex-youth—drove away without a backward glance, indifferent in his soul to the opinions of others (say, Penny Burke, she of that damn barking barking barking dog and array of braying donkeys back in Galway or wherever it was and worst of all that fucking long-haired folk-music wanker) yet solid in the conviction that his departure was being witnessed, hollow-eyed, by an already conscience-stricken Denny Tool, standing at his office window. (Whereas, in fact, although he was indeed standing at his office window, Denny had already forgotten the name and existence of Mick McCreek and was at that moment conversing blandly but loudly over the mobile to Ken Kim in Seoul, Korea, whom he and Ramona were to meet next week for lunch at Spago's in West L.A., while in the background of Denny's black-leather-adorned penthouse suite Ramona did a bump-and-grind to the thumping and drooling neomusic of the Techno-Hüren, a band from one of the less salubrious industrial slums of the former East gone West. . . .[3]

"Cool, Ken," said Den.

Thumpabumtsss! Thumpabumtsss! Thumpabumtsss! Thumpabumtsss! Thumpabumtsss! Thumpabumtsss! Thumpa . . .)

Mick had first gone home on the wild off-chance that compensatory good news (*a job offer from Jaguars—the winning prize in*

---

[3]Quite successful, topping the charts in Magdeburg, Rostock, and Leipzig, and coming damned close in Hanover and Weimar. Of course, their group suicide had something to do with it, I don't doubt. Gruesome folk (or should that be Volk?) the Jerries, but man oh man do they ever do a delectable currywurst. *Noch eins, Herr Ober!* (Beethoven's not bad, either, except for that "Wellington's Victory" blatherskite. Poor deaf old lad. I raise a glass to his memory. Cheers, Lud.)

the Sweeps—a signed photo of Princess Arabella Torricelli, reigning hearthrob of Cinecittà—the freedom of the City of Paris) awaited him in his letterbox; but in his deepest heart of hearts he knew that there was about as much chance of that happening now or ever as there was of him suddenly speaking fluent Yoruba or sprouting horns and mounting a ewe in a field—or both consecutively (or simultaneously).

(*Less.*)

Later, after putting in a call to the Sosh ("According to our records you've never been employed . . . what's your name, again? No, you've never had a job as far as we can tell . . . now don't take that tone with *me*"), he hied himself in most urgent need of a jar— determined to display solidarity through drinking on the battle-field—to the semirepaired, ladder-strewn, and hammer-echoing premises of the Pint-Pulling Olympiad at the Spudorgan Vacation Inn, now, thanks to the rocket attack, a major tourist draw equalling the Martello Tower at Sandycove, Yeats's grave, or Glendalough ("great to actually *be* where the IRA fired a rocket," remarked a passing Aussie, lit up on his own national brew; "just imagine, the *IRA!*"), and by the way Mick was mildly curious about what Molloys were planning to do with Roddy the rejected rodent.

He soon found out. In Roddy's place hung a towel with a Claddagh ring stitched upon an imitation scroll above the mock-Erse slogan Cead Mile Failte. As if that wasn't bad enough, the bartender on duty was none other than the scumbag Francis Feeley, ex-victim of Mick's traffic misdemeanour, freshly released from the lockup in Wales or Man or somewhere over the rolling main.

"Thanks for the rat," snarled Feeley, a decrepit specimen of a man with eye pouches deep as the tarns of the trackless Wicklow hills and tufts of hair sprouting on his cheekbones as abundantly as wild grass on the outcrops of Slieve Donard. "And no thanks, we don't need no more of your bleeding artwork, rat or no rat. Rat me arse. Run anybody else over lately?"

"I'll have a pint, then."

"Not here you won't."

As if to celebrate Mick's humiliation, the German brass band deafeningly struck up "Berliner Luft" from nearby.

"You're a sorry sod, Feeley," bawled Mick, "and a veritable walking sack of shite."

"You watch it, McCreek, or I'll."

"You just try."

Seething, Mick moved over to the Autumn's booth, already teeming with eager drinkers and their freeloading satellites.[4] A half to douse the flames led to a full and before he knew it he was lean-

---

[4]Ah, they touch my conscience, do those words. A freeloading satellite was I, once, oh aye the merry o. Never more so than in the company of another, more expert freeloader, one James O'Joyce, barstool climber and social climber from the rainy verge of Ranelagh. Indeed, a rainy day was it when first we met, O'Joyce and I, each attempting a free load from the other somewhere near the snuggy part of shady Flanagan's Bar out Sandymount Way, but a hop, skip, and jump from the sandy strand and the shifting bowel-loosening sea; aye, touchers twain we were, he and I, and recognition of our mutual weakness and strength soon dawned in our otherwise blank and expressionless eyes, upon which occasion we called it quits, arms mutually akimbo, and joined forces for the best results. And results we had, better than the best, yes by janey oh by the rood did we ever, with himself passing as quite another, slimmer (and then-dead) Joyce (sans O') (yes, *him*) and myself as his sad sidekick Sam, as in Bludgett the rugby fan, dear dead Sammo for aye; for aye, 'twas Sammo O'Bludgett that I styled me so, with mellifluous attention to the singing lyric of the vowel, a double diphthong's pleasure to be had as the "o" in "sammo" elided neatly into the "o" of "O'Bludgett, o." Oh, singing for my supper, I haunted the wynds, o. Declaiming à la Parnell, he, too, hunted for grub, and together we formed quite a team, such a one in truth that we were mistakenly awarded the bronze medal for civic-mindedness by one Theo Tafferty, self-styled mayor of a so-called townland too far South to matter, let alone make it onto the maps. . . . Mr. O'Joyce was a pot boy once, you see, and attributed his spiritual formation to the influence of long having been under the influence of pubs themselves, as well as of their wares. He was a joker, was Mr. O'Joyce. A joker and a card and wasn't he somehow the two ends of

ing on the counter, head tilted sideways like the stem of a church-
warden pipe, saying to a neighbouring bottlenose, "Twice in one
month, would you believe it? First because I had a bloody car accident and now because of some bloody dumb bunghole of a Yank.
Yanks, eh? God, they're everywhere, aren't they? Don't seem to
get any smarter, either, do they? I mean, good God, what do they
teach 'em in those schools of theirs, baseball, I imagine, or that
fucking game they call football, don't make me laugh, football?
Anyway whatever it is it's certainly not history or geography, between the two of us I'm tellin' you that ninety nine point nine percent of them couldn't find Europe on a map, let alone . . ."

"Well, I could. And I'm from Cleveland, Ohio."

Mick sought refuge once again in a quiet cubicle in the loo.
S(h)itting there, he overheard a conversation at the sink between
two employees of the Spudorgan Inn, both heavily bronchial, both
Liffeysiders.

"Poor man, your man Milo. Depressed, so he is. Ahaaak
ahawwwwwkkk."

"Haaksss. Hwwwwwwwkkk. Well now that'd be because of him
being a poet, would you not say so, Sean?"

"Poet me arse. He got near blown to bits, man. I'd say he had
the right to feel the tiniest bit off his feed."

"Well, all I know's he's not a bad fella to work for at all. Did
you go and see him yet, yeah? Haaaaakkk?"

---

a wag altogther at the same time and simultanous with the foregoing . . . ? But,
sad to say (sniff), he succumbed to the inevitability that lurks just 'round the
corner for us all, and hey presto, halfway through the third round I had a dead
man on my hands one blustery day this side of St. Pat's, and his name was
James O'Joyce of no known abode-o. A-beggin' then went I no more, but I
did rifle his pockets on the way out. Now it's respectability for me, o thank
you so, and as for him (whatever *was* his name?) none knows where his bones
lie, the merry-o, nor if they're visited nocturnalwise by milkmaids or moguls,
or plain old ghouls, o hey ho the nonny-o. (Whew.)

"No, I'm doin' that tonight during the late visitin' hours. I'm on here till six. As you know perfectly well, seein' as you come on directly after."

"I'll be takin' him a bottle of Powers when I go, I reckon. Huuuuwwwkkk. I can get it cheap down at Madame Walewska's."

"Just so long as he don't think it's a bribe, like. Haaaaaaak splatt."

"And if he does, so? 'Tis a bribe, man. I want to get off this bloody horrible old graveyard shift of mine and I know Milo likes the odd drop, the old gutty. I'll share it with him, but. The way he'll not give a toss anyhow. Ahuuukk. Ahaaaaaakk. AHAWWWWWWWKKK."

"Aha. Good thinking there. Good man yerself, Wally Dalton."

"Haaaak-*splat*. Bah. Spare me blushes Sean Henry. Sure 'tis nothing at all but the simplest analysis of human nature, just."[5]

---

[5]Sure that's never Wally Dalton. I knew the man in his French days when he worked like a Trojan twelve hours a day sandblasting walls and polishing floors all for the few francs that would buy him the consoling glass and slice of brie at day's end. A relative of Cousin Monk's, he was, if I recall right; his murderer, too, you might say, albeit indirectly. Indeed, over a cheery glass of sherry one evening down at Traynor's Bar he offered to refurbish Monk's old Galway manse from rooftop to cellarage if Monk let him live there thereafter rent-free. Well, you have a pretty shrewd idea of me dear cuz's reply, I daresay. "Get out!" he screamed, his face mottled with rage, in one hand clutching the latest *Irish Times* interview with Edna O'Brien (God bless and keep her lovely face). "Get out now!" 'Twas only much later that he realized that he was in the pub, not at home, and therefore in no position to order people about; but the damage was done. By then Monk had shouted himself into a stroke and had to be rushed to the Lady Gregory Clinic at Coole. While he was there Wally, behind his back, as it were, went ahead with his plan, transforming Monk's gruesome pile into something lighter, airier, all-natural, with no artificial preservatives, real nouvelle cuisine in bricks and mortar, done in the pastel shades of other climes. Well, wait till I tell you. When Monk returned, in a shawl and muffler enwrapped to guard against the treacherous Atlantic wind, he discovered his once-grey house to be a deep shade of St. Tropez aubergine, with pinkish-white accents. His own face colour-coded to match,

After the two stalwarts had gone, Mick emerged chastened from his stall. What with the onrushing juggernaut of his own demented fate bearing down on tiny insignificant him he'd forgotten the parlous condition of another, one wounded in battle— one he'd determined he quite liked, actually, and there were damned few such about, living or dead—and it was by purest blindest luck, or divine intervention, or both, that the man in question wasn't, in fact, *dead*—that person being of course none other than the poet/manager Milo Rogers, injured in the rocket attack and even now abed at the Mater, not even in his own private room but lying adjacent to older, less battered valetudinarians with, at least, a view of Killoyle Harbour. . . .

But Mick wasn't to know all that just yet. He finished his pint at a safe distance from the American drinker, who eyed him malevolently through the shifting crowd of alehounds and once silently mouthed in his direction what Mick lip-read as "Ahma gonna killa you." Mick snarled back, turned away, and weighed the options. One more pint seemed about right, and the Czech booth was of course reaping the benefits of sympathy custom: draped in black, with black-bordered photographs of the dead young heroes, manned by women of buxom stance flown in from Prague and Brno, offering for sale a special Bohemian brew brewed only in grim or ceremonial circumstances; for example, the inauguration of a new president of the Czech and/or Slovak Republics; War Victims' Day and St. Bohumil's Day, annually celebrated by deep, solemn woodwind music matched by equally deep and solemn drinking; Smetana's birthday (but not Dvořák's, the old Yankee pirate) . . . of course, amid grief profit was not despised, and the special brew had its price, at two quid fifty a

---

he dashed about breaking windows, then dove onto the greensward, there to lie dead for a while. Still lying dead, he's buried by that tall fellow up in Sligo somewhere.

good twenty pence dearer than, say, Autumn's finest, not to mention Molloys' filthy; but Mick gladly paid the balance and sipped his tincture as appreciatively as an oenophile might savour a fine Médoc, while (he couldn't help himself) glancing with equal appreciation at the sturdy chests and round thighs of the barmaids, Ulrika (ex-Karlovy Vary) and Nadya (a Prague gal first and last).

"Hi, big boy," said Ulrika, simpering.

When Mick got to the hospital he was as pissed as he'd been in a good while. His face was high burgundy in hue, his hair as tousled as if he'd just stepped out of a wind tunnel (which in a way he had, what with the currents going down Uphill Street in the autumn). The sister on duty at the front desk looked him up and down and, being an Irishwoman, she pegged him with dead-on accuracy as a flewtered wee waster without brains or prospects but harmless enough, when all was said and done.

"Arrah, sister. Top o' the day to you. Milo Rogers here?"

"Begging your pardon?"

Wheedling always worked, even with virginal grimness incarnate like Sister Theodore who, notwithstanding her sworn obeisance to the Lord, had known her fair share of feckless Irish males, notably far too many brothers, an uncle or two, six to a dozen cousins, and of course the dear old Da who was carried offstage on a shutter lo these many years . . . a few stray tears never hurt, either. By the time Mick reached Milo's ward his arm was around Sister Theodore's shoulders and he'd woven for her a weepin' wild and wondrous tale of himself and his poor darlin' cousin Milo his mummy's sister's son struggling to bring up eighteen children in the absence of brutal fathers on their Celto-Iberian rounds of hostelry, mistresses, and the nags; oh God, oh God, whimpered Mick, and I'm that afraid the poor lad's doomed and at this very moment the massed angels of heaven are standing around his poor wee bed. . . .

Angels there were none, but at Milo's bedside stood a red-haired woman of full figure.

"I'll leave you now," said Sister Theodore. "Mind you don't fall out the window or slip on the floor or something."

"Anything," roared Mick. "For you, sister, anything."

"You're potted," said Milo. "Nice of you to come see me, but." He smiled up at the redhead, who turned her strangely alluring gaze—green, liqueous, shimmering—upon Mick. (Or was it just the beer?)

"This is Kathy McRory Hickman," said Milo. "My ex. There here's Mick McCreek, darlin', a fella I only met the other day but I feel I've known for half me life already."

She smiled: no longer young, not yet old, she was passing into the burnished maturity of middle age. (No, it was more than the beer.) Mick made a conscious effort to straighten up, smooth down his hair, focus his gaze: *Ten*-hut!

"I can see why," said Kathy McRory Hickman in no-nonsense tones. "And what's your line, Mick McCreek? Apart from getting legless?" Her bold badinage violated no decorum. She, too, felt she'd known Mick for years, or someone very much like him—her dead husband, for one. In fact, when Mick had entered the room it was for a second as if the ghost of Phelim Hickman had entered in his stead: the same swaggering gait, the same mess of Irish hair, the same rueful twinkle in the eye—and Phelim would have been just the same with that old sister. Old Ireland's men were all the same at heart and by Jesus she loved 'em, so she did.

"Ah, sure now, God bless you," said Mick, "I'm not legless sure if I were wouldn't it be the first thing you'd notice."

Milo looked on, beaming. "Legless or not, Mick used to test-drive cars," he said. "But they sacked him when he drove into a couple of other cars and a pedestrian simultaneously. I have that right, don't I, mate?"

"Ah, get out of it, Milo," gruffly grumbled Mick, the faintest tint of an old blush on the uppers of his eyebones (noted Kathy shrewdly, manless herself these six months and counting).

Vigorous of voice and ruddy of cheek, apart from his being on his back in a hospital bed and having a tube entering and exiting his left arm, Milo's appearance had in it none of the decrepitude or anguish one might expect would result from being struck by the shards of a Katyusha rocket.[6]

"A Katyusha? That's what the Russkies used in Afghanistan, wasn't it? No mean rocket, then. Such an honour. Less of an honour for those poor Czech kids. I sent flowers. I'd have gone if I could. No, I'm OK. It was just a scrape, really, but a scrape across the side of me skull, you see, so they reckoned I'd best stick it out here for another day or so. But I hate missing the Olympiad, so I do. So I hereby delegate the two of youse to go in my stead."

"I've been, actually," said Mick.

"Well, have a coffee and go back. The pint-pulling semifinals start at four. Not as if you've anything better to do, eh? Or you wouldn't be here, would you."

"Ah, I'll take care of him," said Kathy. "And we'll do you proud, Milo. Won't we, Mick?"

Mick found himself pulling himself hand over hand up the slippery ladder of sobriety with unexpected alacrity, stirred by desires still unforgotten and old pop-song lyrics of a foolish appropriateness undiminished by time:

Something in the way she moves . . .

"We will, Kathy," he said, firmly. "We will, indeed."

Something in the way she wo-o-o-o-o-s me. . . .

Or was it the drink?

---

[6]Easy for you to say, clever dick. You should have seen it from my end.

22

After eleven days of being dead Fergus Goone, or whatever remained of him—a substantial chunk, actually, minus this and that (an eyeball, a testicle, both vied over by mangeflies and maggots: a veritable smorgasbord for vermin, as are we all in the end[1]) was lowered into his native stone-strewn soil in the churchyard of the Dundreary United Free Presbyterian Church, three miles northwest of Coleraine, county of

---

[1]Speak for yourself, sport. I'm going to have myself cremated, so I am, and the old ashes scattered under the number twelve bus en route to Ballsbridge, somewhere in the Ringsend area, or Irishtown at a pinch, near where Bolands Mills used to stand, maybe, or across from Mrs. Ryan's Hair Salon. Ah, 'twas always my favourite, was the old number twelve, lurching and swaying up Dame Street of a crisp, sweet autumn morn and groaning to a halt at the corner stop past Waterhouse's clock; ah yes, *yes,* as God's me witness, especially back in the dear old Cuba Car days (that was when we up and sold to Cuba the buses we'd bought on the cheap from London Transport, then the Cubans waited awhile and, a bit like your man Hugh Boylan and his twice-sold horses in J. J.'s guidebook to Dublin (including Howth Castle) and environs, sold the old buses back to us at a mark-up, thereby netting Fidel a handsome profit and screwing you-know-who, alias Poblacht nahEireann, alias Muggins, for about the nine thousand and fifty sixth time in the seven hundred years of Irish martyrdom when I was a nipper trying yet again to get meself a college degree but running out of colleges (I ended up in Roscommon, more's the pity).

(London)Derry, Antrim District, Province of Ulster/six counties, United Kingdom/occupied Ireland, on the brisk and overcast twenty-second day of September last, typical weather for
that part of the world at that (or any other) time of year. It was
an event that had received some notice locally. The local TV
news channel, Red Hand Channel 1 from (London) Derry City,
had misreported the death of a Mr. Boone, "local philanthropist and supporter of liberal causes like guy rights." The fustian
and almost totally unread local right-wing tabloid of record, the
Orange Order-owned *Orange Horn,* attempted to outdo its own
headline reporting Goone's murder—"Bugger Shot"—by gild-
ing the lily with "Bugger Buried," and so the header would indeed have read, had the *Horn's* typesetters (for reasons of tradition
and cheapness, the *Horn* still used the old-fashioned hot-type
method) been awake, alert, and properly on the job; but it was a
well-known fact in the windy byways and sidestreets of
Dundreary, population 1,221 (give or take an even or baker's
dozen, especially when the Walters clan is away in Majorca), that
those printer's lads, Sammy Anderson and his wee brother Billy,
had a longstanding habit of sloping off in the first days of autumn,
with concomitant decline in concentration and accuracy of
printed matter; result—typos galore. To make matters worse,
the paper had, alas, long since retired its only copy subeditor,
old and blind Manny McBurns Bushcastle, now an ever-farting
OAP at the Lilies of the Field Nursing Home in Cookstown,
Co. Tyrone; consequently, the banner headline of the *Horn* on
that significant day now trumpeted "Bugler Buried," causing the
paper's diminishing readership to search in confusion for an
accompanying story appropriate to the subject, certainly not one
about the obsequies of a semiobscure local dignitary . . .[2]

---

[2]Unless right-thinking liberally outraged sabotage was the culprit, not an
impossibility even in the medieval fens and glens of the Province of the
Orange-Utan.

It had taken place on said brisk, pigeon-grey morning some eleven days after the murder, from the revelations of which Dundreary had yet to recover. Once the subsequent tabloid reports of the kind of life the late Goone had been leading (a perfectly tranquil kife of standard two-person domesticity, when you thought about it[3]) was bruited about, the name Killoyle—already steeped in the infinite sins of presumptive Popery, what with the Shrine of the Invisible Virgin, priests, it being in "tha Ropublic," et cetera—became synonymous with, say, a virtual Sodom-on-Sea to the stern Presbyterians of Dundreary, many of whom were blood relatives of the late Fergus, and all of whom, like the deceased, had glittering Celtic-blue eyes, thin lines in place of mouths and the facial ruddiness of lifelong heavy tea-drinking and raised blood pressure at the thought of all those Papist poofters lurking nearby. . . .

"Aye. You nuver know what's gonna happen next dine Sithe," philosophized their Elder, the Very Rev. Patrick Pinnup, DD (Edin), a wizened male crone of some eighty-three winters, few brains, and no wisdom. "Ut's a lond of Romans."

The wind blew in from the Nordic seas and stirred up tiny rustling eddies of leaves at graveside. The wind smelled hollowly of decay, autumn, Halloweens come and gone, and the transfiguration that awaits us all. It was a grey autumn wind, an Ulster wind, a medieval wind, evocative of gloomy plains and boggy boreens and ruined keeps like the craggy remains of Dunluce Castle, not twenty miles distant, beetling above the iron-grey sea across which Vikings and Manx marauders were wont once to roam. The gusts blew cold and damp and chilled the five mourners standing in a line at the graveside: Linda Darnell-Goone, mother of the deceased, known throughout Dundreary and adjacent precincts as "Linda," or "Lynn";

---

[3]But not too much.

Veronica Goone-Lake, daughter of same, sister of the late Fergus; Richard E. ("Ricky") Lake, husband of foregoing and, therefore, the deceased's brother-in-law; Angus MacGillivray, treasurer of the Dundreary Democratic Unionists, who'd never once, to the best of his knowledge—well, maybe once, inadvertently, on a bus going to Limavady in the early spring of 1973 ("d'ye have the tayme?")—spoken to a Papist ("aye; hof-three"); and Ewer Burk, headmaster of the Samuel Lever Secondary School and local chairman of the Ulster Swan and Eco Party, total membership nine, with one undecided, just coming in to make the coffee and give the desks a wee dusting, like.[4] Ewer Burk was the late Fergus Goone's oldest childhood friend and a self-described "progressive democrat" and "bleeding heart" and "sticker-by through thick and thin" who'd declared himself, perhaps a touch too loudly, as being quite unfazed by the details of the ménage à deux as revealed by such broadsheets as the *Horn* as well as the *News of Everything Everywhere* and the *Absolute Truth, Belfast Style* and who, furthermore, enjoyed nothing more than seeing quivers of embarrassment and disapproval chase themselves up and down the gelatinous jowls of Dundreary's Presbyterian notables like squirrels on treetrunks.

Ewer was C. of I. himself, quite high church actually, but of course freer thinking than that implied—if not entirely nonthinking altogether.

---

[4]Ah, I'm catching on here. "Swan" hints at ancient Irish bardic traditions, that of the legend of De Danaan in particular, without being too specific about it and thereby getting up Prod noses; and "Eco Party" rather than "Green Party" because the colour green and the forty thousand shades thereof have such permanent associations in dear old true-blue Ulster, being identified as they are strictly in politico-religious, that is, moronic, terms with the eternal opponents of the Orangemen, the little green men, those inebriated Papist-Republican leprechauns jigging round their little brown jugs at the country crossroads and waving their shillelaghs by the light of the verdant moon.

"Och, many's the time I visited Fergus and Cornelius down in Killoyle," he would say, casually, as he leaned back in his Queen Anne armchair, reveling in his role as Resident Liberal Free-Thinker, gloating over the grimly pursed lips and downcast eyes of his interlocutors at the mention of the names "Killoyle," "Fergus," and "Cornelius," mention of which Ewer therefore insisted on making as often as context would bear. "A fine couple they were, Fergus and Cornelius, most well-matched, so I thought, and quite plainly deeply in love and quite happy to be in Killoyle. Although admittedly young, Cornelius struck me as a wee bit extravagant for a church sexton, with his Balenciaga gowns and falsies, even considering the relatively liberal attitude they have toward things down in Killoyle. God, Fergus hated those falsies, but," as the light of reminiscence genuine or manufactured glowed in Ewer's eyeglass-magnified eyes, "almost as much as he hated you," the magnified eyes coming to rest like plump doves on the person of the elder.

"Weel, forguv and fergit's my motto," said that worthy, sanctimoniously. He said a good deal more at the grave, it having fallen to him to deliver what was still quaintly called, in these rural precincts of darkest Ulster, the "funeral oration."

"Sunners all are we, oh aye, sunners we are all, so we are, all of us, and wasn't it true enough as mony of ye have said yon Fergus Goone was a sunner too, aye right enough, but aren't we all, and the veriest sunner among us leaves behind loved ones, even Hutler, for goodness' sake...."

"Hutler?" muttered Mrs. Darnell-Goone.

"I think he means Hitler," said Ewer in a stage whisper intended to be heard. "The old fool's comparing Fergus to the führer."

"I say, that's a bit much," said Mrs. Darnell-Goone, pirouetting to her feet in violent indignation. "Stop that this instant, do you hear?"

"Och away, Lunda," declaimed the Very Rev. Pinnup in ringing tones. "Sut dyne and shut yer mythe. No offense untended.

Only inasmuch as we are *all* sunners, whether we're Hutler or not, d'ye see? I doubt there are those among us whuu're every but as sunful as puur wee Fergus, oh aye. But ut's not for the laykes of me tae judge, och no. Tha's God's terrutory, aye. As the goo' book says on page forty-two: 'Share thou thy firkin, cleanse thou thy jerkin, keep an eye on yonder welkin, and spare thus thy noggin.'"

(Here ends the dialectical transcription. Once again such quotations in this work must bear the following warning label: All locals, however folkloric, will be represented as speaking a brand of standard, if oddly turned, English.)

"What good book's that?" querulously demanded Mrs. Darnell-Goone, flutingly, her voice hinting at the near-crack of hysteria. "Doesn't sound like the Bible to me."

"Never mind, Lynn dearie," boomed Ewer Burk. "It's another good book he's read. Surprised to know he's read more than one, the old oaf. Anyhow, it'll all be over soon, then we can go to the funeral tea. They said they'd have sausages. Yum yum, eh?"

"Oh God," blubbered the mum. "My poor wee Fergus."

"Aye, Lynn girl. Aye." Ewer squeezed her elbow in earnest of companionship, stealing a sideways glance to comfirm his status in the eyes of onlookers as Good Old Broadminded Burk, Friend of Dead Homosexual's Mother.

"Lord," intoned the Rev. Pinnup, "hear thou our prayers in heaven thy dwelling place. But first allow me to take time out for a brief message from our sponsors. To the congregation. Aye. For those caught between sin and goodness, I have a word of caution, or even several: Don't do it! It's no' worth it! Seven words in all, unless you count the contractions double." He yawned and stretched and leaned forward, one hand bracing himself on the tombstone, looking for all the world like a somewhat over-aged Placido Domingo on the cover of his latest Firelight Romantic Hits album, preparing to ape nostalgia and intimacy while remaining, at bottom, utterly indifferent. "You know, back when I was a lad there was a cartoon series, this was back when I was a lad, of course, called Desperate Dan, so it was, oh aye, the things I was up to back when I was a lad, some of them would hardly bear repeating in such distinguished company, och. And one of 'em, I'm sorry to say, was the spurious extraction of what passed as *wisdom* from such suspect sources as the *Boy's Own* paper, the organ in which Desperate Dan performed his desperate deeds. I remember once . . ."

At length the train of his oration groaned to a halt, but not before clattering over the myriad points of reminiscence, sermonizing, feeble humour, anecdotage, and just plain old dotage. Ashes to ashes, dust to dust: The mortal remains of Fergus Goone, sinner, lover, tycoon, and sycophant, were finally laid to rest for all eternity, or until the churchyard was dug up to make way for a new Orange Hall or the Mid-Ulster Marvellous Mall and Worldwide Shopping Precinct,[5] whichever came first.

The main event of the week was, of course, the will reading, held the next day at Dundreary Town Hall, annex three, in the law offices of Claude Quiller, Q. C., presiding attorney, the town's only remaining bigwig now that Fergus was gone. Actually, Q. C. Quiller, a barrister much in demand, was usually away in Belfast or Cork or London opposing tort reform and raking in

---

[5]Oh, orange halls are on the way out, take my word for it. This'll be a shopping mall, don't you worry, one featuring (and I know, I've been there in my dreams, right turn just after Manderley) emporia offering for sale seven varieties of clothing and footwear; a pet shop; a video arcade in which the latest Hi-Grade Doc and Drooley Twins Super-Rama Elimination Games will be a special attraction; a Roach the Chemist's; a W. H. Smiths; Samosas, an Indian wine bar and restaurant not of the ex-Goone empire; a Spar or Tesco market; an English-style pub with nonmilitant name conjoining, say, canine (Dog) and avian (Duck) to obviate warring factions claiming, say, Murphy's Bar or Taylor's Public House as their own . . . oh, and a fag shop, cheapies only (Players,' etc.), run by two Lebanese brothers, one glum, the other a bit too jolly.

the wherewithal for the maintenance and adornment of his hill-side condominium in sunny Ibiza, whither he was shortly bound; but for the time being he was (for him) at somewhat loose ends. Moreover, he'd been piqued by more than idle curiosity to pre-side over the will reading: He wanted to know if there was any-thing in it for him. He'd taken Fergus's side once during a football brawl (Linfield versus Ballymena United), and he thought the old bugger might have remembered; but Q. C. Quiller wasn't born yesterday, and he hadn't come into silk by believing in the man in the moon, or in the generosity of so-called old friends.

"Old friends me backside," he was wont to say, ideally (if he were in the street) with a sideways spurt of sputum. "Let's see the colour of your money."

Disillusion, therefore, was impossible, if surprise was not.

"Are we all present?" inquired Q. C. Quiller of the audience, who were indeed obviously present, as opposed to the many others, including most of humanity, who were absent. "Good. No time to waste on bowing and scraping and 'How're ye doin's' and all that rubbish. You know who I am and I know who you are, God help us all. So let's begin."

Now, everyone in the room was aware that, given the abrupt nature of Fergus's departure from this life, and the corollary lack of urgency, prior to his death, to modify the will or add an exclu-sionary codicil thereto, it was Cornelius Regan, Goone's mur-dering widow, who stood to inherit a bundle. The fate of Goone's business ventures was in the hands of Killoyle magistrates, Scot-tish venture capitalists, Belfast businessmen, and Q. C. Quiller's cunning Southern counterparts. Apart from that slim certainty, exactly what and how the bereaved relatives themselves stood to gain, was Unknown Factor Number One. But to give her her due, Mrs. Darnell-Goone was genuinely grief-stricken and for the moment at least entirely devoid of the greedy gilt-edged dreams of (for instance) Veronica and Ricky Lake. *That* pair had already gone on a wild mental spending spree with the late Fergus's gelt,

blowing it all on such sundries as a vacation hideaway on one of
the Greek islands, probably Patmos (cheaper, less developed than
Mykonos, and oh those ceramics!); a pebble-dash mock-Tudor
minimansion in one of the leafy byways at Nutts Corner with a
thirty-nine-inch Watanabe SuperScreen TV and a landscaped
half acre out back (not sure about the gazebo, yet, but you can
bet your butt Ricky'd have his potting shed-cum-workshop, oh
yes); a cobalt-blue Range Rover four-by-four to spiff up the drive
and impress the neighbours; matching sets of his and hers golf
clubs with lifetime membership at Owen Parsley Hills Orange
Golf Association and Clubhouse, a fine Christian sports venue
for fine Christian folk, nae Jews or Taigs need apply (well, they
can *apply*, right enough, but there's a recycling bin at the rear of
the main clubhouse—and anyway, they've their own bloody Jew
and Taig clubs, haven't they, for goodness' sake?); a trial membership in the Billy Herron Memorial Swimming and Athletic
Society on the Ormeau Road in scenic East Belfast; an elegant
sofa throw with Frank Lloyd Wright designs, like the one
Veronica had seen in that museum in Tulsa, Oklahoma, when
they were in America last year for the graduation of Ian, their
wee boy, from the Billy Jones's Locker State Bible College in
Noddy, Oklahoma; a DVD player with digitized trailer skip; and
God knew what all.

"To my sister Veronica Goone-Lake and her husband Richard
E. Lake: nothing," intoned Claude Quiller, Q. C. "Fuck-all. *Nada.*
Not a penny. Sorry, Veronica and Rick. Better luck next time."

"The wee pervert," stormed Veronica, flouncing towards, and
through, a door marked "Exit," and thence to the street, but not
before turning and biliously bellowing "The wee cheapskate
poofter bastard!" to the remainder of the assembly.

"Aye," said husband Rick. "She's right. He was a right old catch-
pole and brown-hatter, was Fergus. Always said so, dinneye?" He
followed his wife out the door. With the lugubrious Lakes gone,
the atmosphere lightened momentarily, then darkened again.

"Sod-all to you, too, Lynn, I'm afraid," said the lawyer. "Zip. Zero. *Nichts*. But at least he added an apology, sort of. Here it is.

"'Sorry, mum, but you just weren't there for me. Bye for now.'"

Linda emitted deep, precisely enunciated stage sobs, punctuated by coughs.

"Uh huh-ha-huh-ha-huh," she boomed, basso profundo. "*Aah huh-huh-huh-ha-hah-ha-awk-awk*."

"Shaddup," hissed Angus MacGillivray from behind, in what he deemed a sufficiently low voice to not be overheard, but Ewer Burk slewed around angrily and skewered him with a reprimand, thus: "Another word out of you and I'll give you what-for."

"Ah, go pull on yer willie, ya pape."

"Now gentlemen," bayed Claude Quiller, radiating the bland authority inherent in his silken status. "Hush, the pair o' youse. We're not done yet. But we might as well be, to tell you quite honestly he left bugger-all to anybody else here, either. Cornelius Regan, of course, picks up quite the bundle, a bit ironic, that, eh? Jeez. Thirty grand, not a penny less. And hello, hello, what's this, then? Guess what? Old Fergus also left the amount of six thousand pounds sterling, as converted from punts—a wee bit less, then, after taxes, but still—to the *Orange Horn* newspaper 'on condition that they change their name to the *Gay Orangeman*, hire five openly gay and lesbian journalists and a competent typesetter, and open up a column for the local Roman Catholic parish news, and adopt more progressive attitudes generally.'"

"Fuck me," said MacGillivray.

Q. C. Quiller, clearly a busy man, glanced at his watch. "Aye. So there you have it. Thanks for coming and don't let me detain youse any longer. The door's over there. Hullo, doctor, sorry to keep you waiting," into his desk phone. "Just another of those silly old rill weedings, I mean will readings, sorry. Lunch at one? Wally's, on Donegall Place? Grand."

As Ewer Burk escorted Linda out the front door of the barrister's office, Veronica and Ricky drove by in their lime-green

Renault Cabane minivan. Ricky was at the wheel, so it fell to
Veronica to turn as they passed and raise her fingers—to her own
mother and her dead brother's best friend, no less—in the familiar "V" formation of the fig.[6]

"Fucking sods!" she screamed, muffled only slightly by the
closed windows of the car, which swerved slightly as if startled
and disappeared around the bend in the road to Bushmills,
Ballymoney, Ballymena, and Belfast.

"Good riddance," said Ewer. "It's not as if we snatched the
dough from their hands, for Christ's sake. And now for them sausages, eh, Lynn?"

"I've lost 'em both," muttered Linda. "One after the other. My
boy, then my girl. Oh my, oh my."

Well, that was an uncomfortable thing to have to think about,
and Ewer was nothing if not upbeat about things generally, "high
on life," as the expression goes (or went), so he merely grinned
in neutral nonassent and took her arm as they crossed the street;
perhaps significantly, however, she drew away from his grasp
whem they reached the other side.

"Thank you, Ewer," she said. "But I'll manage on my own now."

Well, sod that, said Ewer Burk to himself, banishing his disap-
pointment with brisk anticipatory palm-*frottage* and the jocular
query, self-addressed: "Now then! Where's them sausages we've
been hearing so much about?"

---

[6]Or goose.

23

"Hello, Judge Ormlet? It's Anil Swain."

"Swain? Not Hamid? The fellow who makes those late-night calls? 'Hello, I've got you in my sights?' That line of country?"

"Aha. Well, judge. OK. You recognized my voice. So what?"

"Not until just now. But suddenly it was unmistakable. And wasn't I after saying to meself after that last call last night that your voice sounded that familiar, so it did, what with the accent and all. But never mind. Never mind it's being two in the bloody morning, either. I'm not sleeping much these days, anyhow. So what can I do for you, Swain?"

"Well, quite a lot, I think, judge; well, I mean, for a start, according to your plan I'm supposed to be dead, aren't I?" Anil's voice rose to a shrill pitch (approaching high C—what if he'd studied in Milan! What a *bel cantore* our Swain might have been![1])

---

[1] What if, what if. "The terrible 'what ifs' accumulate," as Cousin Monk used to say while admiring his reflection in the shaving mirror. So what if Swain had been born a miner's son, you ask? Oh, it makes you wonder, right enough. He's got the grit but not the style, you might say. I mean take those miners in Wales, you know, Jones ap Jenkins and the rest, excavating shite with their bare fingernails eighteen hours a day bar Sundays when they're expected at chapel and no pubs please we're chapel—and every night coming back to their non-centrally-heated redbrick rowhouses each supplied with a coal cooker,

and hovered there, anguished. The judge held the receiver away from his ear for the duration of the vocalizing and continued his slow, head-shaking perusal of Tom's letters. "And I *would* be dead, too, by golly, you old murderer," continued Swain in a lower

---

a water basin of iron, a fireplace in which to combust materials injurious to the health—viz., more bloody coal—and a communal chamberpot for the twelve to fifteen children required per couple (the missus grey-haired and raw-boned and tubercular by age twenty-nine), all blackened and smeared with coal dust and coughing their puny lungs up. Humble morons, you'd say, eh? Stalwart working folk of limited brainpower? Low-level cretins who pretty much get what they deserve? Well, think about this for a sec, Mr. or Mrs. Hollywood: How many of those guys and gals, themselves the youngest of, say, eighteen, ever had the chance to show the world how good they might be as writers, composers, grammar editors, archers, book reviewers, movie starlets, equestrians, and the like? Piss-all, that's how many. No chance at all to do anything but wash off the coal dust and bury the old grey fella when he's coughed up his last wad of coal-thickened sputum, then pick up the pickax and away you go to cough your own way into an early grave—and as for youse lot with your fat arses in the pews of your smug upper-middle-class C. of E. or I. or R. C. churches, giving plummy thanks to the great toastmaster in the sky for so thoughtfully looking after the waterproof paint job on your secondary residence in the Chilterns or the Dordogne or giving a bit of a boost to those new Hong Kong stocks your broker just acquired! While those poor coal-mining bastards are casting off their moth-eaten blankets and heaving themselves out of their narrow rat-chewed mattresses in the cold black predawn hours of another wet Welsh winter's morn, doomed never to move up socially or culturally, except maybe (if they're *very* lucky) to the position of shop steward or miner's representative with a Ford Ka in the garage and a wee grey garden in back. . . . Tell me this, O Lord: How many potential Senecas and Victor Hugos and Puccinis toiled away their lives in those unforgiving tunnels of black? How many bright wits and stout hearts were wasted utterly down there in hell's anteroom? How many, O God, if you care . . . ? Well, never mind. Most of 'em are dead now anyhow, and those that aren't are sitting at computers looking at naked tits and bums or reading the latest social gossip or ordering CDs online. Brave new world, indeed. Not for me. Mine's a pint of Old Hat, please, with a side order of Christianity for arseholes.

register, "if it wasn't for those bungling idiots who call themselves the Soldiers of Brian O'Nolan—*your* lot, judge. The ones you set me up with. I say, you know, I know all about that bloody silly plan of yours. Well, it backfired all over the place, you know. I mean, your son got himself shot—and I suppose I'm quite, or rather sorry about that, well, I'm not really, you know, and I'll tell you why if you like—"

"Never you mind being sorry, Swain. I haven't slept for ten minutes since it happened, I'm that narked at the stupid young bastard. How many times did I tell him to have nothing to do with that shower—"

"My goodness, there you go calling your dead son a stupid young bastard, now that's a major cultural difference between Ireland and India, I'm telling you, because I can assure you in no uncertain terms that back in India a father talking about—"

"Oh, do shut up, Swain. Come to the point or I'm ringing off."

"Shut up? You're saying 'shut up' to me? *You!?* All right then, very well, bloody hell. The point is this, and this may apply to more people than just me, you know: that chap Mick McCreek, for another; my wife, for a third; not to mention others. We could be looking at colossal litigation here, judge."

"Well, the Irish, they are a litigious race. I didn't know the Indians were as well."

"The point is, I know all about the bloody stupid I don't know what you'd call them—*conspiracies?* Well, yes, conspiracies, then, that you and your son were getting up to, by golly. And I'm quite happy to tell everybody about them."

"Unless . . . ?"

"Unless what?"

"Well you must have some kind of blackmail in mind, otherwise you wouldn't have called."

"Well, all right, you're right. But not blackmail, you know; just tit for tat, OK? I never said you were a stupid chap, judge, and by golly you're not, you know. The idea is this. I know you're in a position to change titles to this and that and reassign ownership of say A to B . . ."

"Now hold on there, boy. I'm no flamin' Indian satrap, you know. I don't know what circuit judges can do in India, but here they're severely restricted by something called the constitution."

"Rubbish. You can do what you like. You sort of stretched the rules when you were trying to get me killed, didn't you, getting me out of gaol and whatnot, just so I could drive that van and get blown up by that Spanish lunatic. So here's my proposal. You get me the title and deed to the Koh-I-Noor restaurant on Bundoran Street here in Killoyle City and I'll say nothing about your shenanigans."

"Except you can't, because I have insurance of my own."

"Insurance?"

"Right. Insurance. I know all about that caper of your cousin's the other night, launching a grenade attack on Armalite House. They had security cameras running, you see. Oh, a right lot of halfwits and throckmabawns they are and no mistake, I'm with you there—with the brains of garden slugs and about as much concern for frigging Mother Ireland as the apes of darkest Africa. But they did have the good sense to install a camera or two, containing security tapes which they then handed over to the authorities. And with my contacts in the gardai it wasn't hard for me to sneak a peek. And guess what, Mr. Swain, there she was, plain as day under the charcoal makeup that was a little, shall we say, redundant, if you don't mind my saying so? Boys oh boys what a specimen that one is, more there than meets the eye if you ask me. And your wife as well, I was quite surprised to see. Good God man, running about throwing bombs left and right is bad enough, but do you have to drag the missus in?"

"Nonsense. It's all lies and rubbish."

"Sorry, Swain. It's all captured on celluloid."

"Whose cellulose?"

"Celluloid, not cellulose. For Christ's sakes. I mean, we've got it on film. And we'll use it."

There was a momentary silence, during which heavy breathing prevailed at both ends of the wire, as if two obscene phone calls had collided; then Anil spoke, sharply, imbued with sudden confidence. "No you won't use the film, judge, and here's why. You're a judge, you see, and an important person locally, but what am I?"

"Well."

"That's right, very polite of you not to say it but I'm nothing but a poor bloody forgettable pipsqueak of an Indian waiter, and God knows they're an anna a dozen, like tax collectors or cockroaches, by golly. And we Indians all look alike, don't we? So go ahead and show the film. I'm only a poor bloody insignificant insect of a waiter, made to be trampled upon, crushed, and exterminated. And a foreigner into the bargain, and we all know what a queer lot they are, don't we, eh? But consider this. If I tell people, 'Hey, this judge, he was involved with terrorists, and so on, and he and his son tried to have me killed,' well, what do you think people will say? What a horrible judge *he* is, that's what! We don't want a judge like that saying 'sit down and shut up' to innocent people in the courtroom, no we don't, by Jove. Not to mention 'you're guilty' and 'you're innocent' and 'go to prison' and so on. So then it's bye-bye to your job, I think, judge. And oh what a stink, eh? Maybe even a national scandal. There was a case like that back in India, in Bihar, actually. The judge, Mr. Patel, a distant cousin of my wife's, was caught in bed with some dacoits and ended up being sent to prison for about fifty years."

A rich baritone snore from the other end of the line (it *was* 2:15 A.M., after all) signaled the transition from dialogue to monologue. Judge O'Mallet was suddenly, profoundly asleep, telephone moribund on his chest, eyeglasses askew, mouth droolingly agape in pathetic elderly-person fashion.

"To hell with him if he doesn't care," muttered Anil. He rang off. "I could go on talking until I'm blue in the face. Well, I'm ready for him, by jiminy. Hello?"

This last was spoken to a telephonic voice that soon proved to be a recording informing the caller that the Finns were unable to come to the phone right now but that he or she, the caller, might leave a message after the tone. . . .

"Oh, I'll leave a message, don't you worry," railed Anil. "Never mind the tone, my jolly old johnny." Oh, he was in good fighting trim, he was loose, he was ready, he was *back;* oh, his Irish was up, all right. He was out for vengeance with a vengeance. He'd show the lot of 'em. Especially Finn, the *hajaam.*

Smoking cigarette after cigarette to endow his voice with a slight menacing rasp à la Jimmy Cagney, his eyes prominent with emotion à la Donald Sutherland, Anil Swain was, he hoped, master of his fate, at last—at least at home, where he dwelt once more, amid the glitter of Rubina's reestablished collection of glass animals. She, too, was there, next door, in the bedroom, asleep, dreaming dreams of desperate normality. At Anil's feet, or rather knees (he was sitting in the tantric yoga lotus-flower position), sprawled the telephone directory to Killoyle City and County, last year's edition (September back-to-school special, with the new red-brick B. Ahern Inner Comprehensive School on the cover).

"Hello Finn, how are you? Your time is up, you old phony. I know all about you and your silly gang of murderers, especially that Spanish guy. I'm calling the police."

Boy that will give him the scare of his life, mused Anil after replacing the receiver with a soft "click." Boy, will it ever.

It did, actually. Ten minutes later, over at number 115A, Anchorite Avenue, Finn was still crouching in the dark next to the phone, bent double like a defeated boxer, replaying the message, hissing imprecations through his false teeth while attempting a mental exegesis of the phone message. On the table his fingers danced the nervous finger-jig of a condemned man about to be led to the scaffold.[2] Between the imprecations expressions of pain,

---

[2]Sidibou Sayyid, for one (if you'll permit me a slight digression, but after all that's what I'm here for), the Franco-Tunisian high-society rapist/strangler known to the Parisian yellow press as "Le Chatterley Arabe" for his modus operandi, viz., to hire on as a gardener and promptly lure his *châtelaine* into the potting shed with bland questions about the operation of a mulching machine or the number of hoes required for ditch-digging (none), guillotined in St. Gilles (Gard) on December 31, 1954 whilst puzzling over a satisfactory *explication* of his evil deeds: "I am Satan" was deemed less than satisfactory by Me. Henri-Rousseau, the *juge d'instruction;* "You are Satan" even less so; "I am God" *idem.,* and blasphemous into the bargain; "I am Casanova" was turned down flat, and "You are bullshit (*Vous êtes de la merde de taureau*)" was reckoned to be tolerable only in a Sartrean context—i.e., a sense in which one might well be bullshit while being simultaneously (with no intervening principle coming between nothingness and absurdity) the pope, or Taoiseach, or the chairman of General Motors—but insufficiently persuasive to stay the executioner's blade. The executioner, M. Gaston-Marie Châtillon—himself executed shortly thereafter while strolling across the dark and deserted (but for his executioner) compound of his bungalow on the edge of the Guyanan jungle—oiled the runners of *La Belle Guillotine* and honed and polished her blade and gudgeons with loving alacrity, keenly (as it were) aware of the honour that devolved upon him as the official dispatcher of the nemesis of high-society ladies—not all of whom, by the way (see *Le Petit Parisien,* Volume sixty-one, number three hundred thirty-two, December 24, 1955) were entirely distressed to have been at the receiving end of Sidibou's attentions, provided they survived his subsequent attempts at strangulation (most of which, frankly, were performed with no discernable degree of competence); indeed, some eight months after M. Châtillon loosed the chop of death upon Sidibou's neck, one such *belle dame avec merci* (la Comtesse de Levallois-Perret) bore a son who so closely resembled the late, mostly unlamented Sidibou that the lad was dubbed "Eh! Toi! Bougnoule!" by his schoolmates, whom the brave boy took on and thrashed one by one—but that's a different story for another fireside, especially in view of the fact that said lad, now forty-four, is currently

too, erupted: Finn's hemorrhoids, which had subsided during all the recent excitement, had suddenly declared themselves as decisively as Mount Pinatubo (or Vesuvius).

"Bastards," he muttered, adjusting his position to a gorilla-like squat, haunches akimbo. "Now let's see what he said."

"Hello Finn, how are you?"—hard to read much into that, more of a casual courtesy than anything else, such courtesy as it implied being of course utterly cancelled out by the towering *neck* of calling at half two in the bleeding A.M. (and speaking of bleeding, he had to absent himself for a short but intense visit to a place of white tiles and gentle plashing, returning to his ruminations soon enough) and of course the informal, even insolent use of his surname rather than any courteous title such as "Mister."

"You old phony," would be more by way of manly insult than anything else, the way you'd clap a mate on the shoulder at the pub, if you were inclined toward that kind of macho carry-on, well he wasn't and had never been. . . .

"Especially that Spanish guy" was somewhat less problematic, referring as it must to Harry Batasuna, man oh man how Harry would do his nut if he heard himself referred to as "Spanish," he he he he he (ouch).

"Call the police." "Police," not "guards"—well that's the bit of a dead giveaway, isn't it, proves the fella's a foreigner, for a start. . . .

Of course it's no surprise he's a foreigner, not with the accent he has on him, odd sort of accent. Welsh, is it? No, hang on a sec, Greek? Arabic—

Indian!?

---

running the president's fleet of Citroëns at the Elysée Palace, and is widely spoken of as being himself a not-so-feeble contender for the highest driving office in the land—once he passes the old *examen de conduite;* that is, if you'll pardon my French.

It was. Of course.

Finn staggered upright, bathed in sweat. It was all over. If that poor-mouth Indian galoot was on his trail as well, then they all were, not just the old guard of the Belfast Brigade, who weren't best pleased at seeing their investments at the Pint-Pulling Olympiad blown to shite (nor did they have to think twice to determine the origins of the Katyushas), but the guards themselves, of course, and the inland revenue boys, and the library police, and Interpol, and M.I. 6, and . . . well, *everybody.*

"Fuck's sake," he whimpered, quite overtaken by fear. "Hello, God, are you there?"

No answer came, not for the first time. Truth was, Finn had nowhere to turn. Unless he up and fled the country. Pats Bewley had obstinately refused to answer his phone, and of course he couldn't tell his wife. There were fellows overseas who might help (but he couldn't be sure). Oh, things had been going well, ah, they had, but now the dance was over, so it was. Over, boy, and no mistake. The Soldiers of Brian O'Nolan had attracted altogether too much attention, and disgraceful lapses in security the size of an elephant's bunghole had shone the unwelcome spotlight of TV publicity and rumour: Those silly guided tours, for a start (not his idea, but still), as well as an advert in the local rag and a special feature on the *Monty Montgomery Show* (RTE5, Friday nights at 20:15), even down to the breed of cat (Abyssinians, to obviate cat-hair[3] allergies) favoured by the company cook (Mr. Hamless). Armalite House had had to be turned over to the Crumstown gardai, and they were even talking about shooting a commercial for Quest? bluejeans in the foyer—with no offer of compensation, of course, the ratbags.

---

[3]Precisely. Reminds me of the dangers aboard your average Dublin city bus, bound for the centre.

Worse, questions were being asked in the Dail by disgraceful right-wing Fianna Fail and Gaelgeoirg types who had probably all been secretly bankrolling the lads up North for years.

As for Finn's career as a librarian, ditto: deep-sixed, done with, all over, *finito, kaput, adios, do svidanya,* et cetera. I mean, could you imagine him striding briskly into his office, caroling—with all the hearty condescension of any chief executive towards his underlings—"Good morning!"—while on his sloping shoulders slumped, slothlike, a burden of guilt and pretense so great that Atlas himself would collapse beneath it? For gossip, too, had been swirling, or circulating, with vicious consequences. Finn was said to be (judging by graffiti daubs in the vestibule, vestiaire, and beyond) a "Philistinian [*sic*] terorist [*sic*]," a "wartless [*sic*] womaniser," a "West Britt [*sic*]," a "fat Protystant [*sic*] Fuck-Pig," and just plain "sik" [*sic*]. Many of these sentiments might have been siphoned off from the deep wells of illiteracy and resentment that exist on the lower strata of any community or organisation,[4] but a personal note

---

[4]'Tis true, 'tis true. Businesses should mind their own hierarchies, and ensure that no one elbows his way in uninvited. Case in point, now that you mention it: Just the other day I was making my creaking way across the ancient wooden floor of the haberdashery department at Clery's, treading as softly as I could, like, so as not to draw attention, like, et cetera; but as the dimmest lightbulb knows, the surest way to attract unwanted attention is to try not to draw it. "Oy!" sings out the self-described house dick, a Welshman named David ap Rhys from the township of Llareggub (yes, we're off to mystical Cymru again). "You there! Man bach!" Well, I don't know about you, but I have deeply ingrained within me a rabid fear of Welshmen, as well as of authority figures in any guise, not just guards and teachers and customs and excise men and bus conductors and the like, but store detectives, textbook editors, and even Mrs. Mulligan, the lady behind the counter in the corner sweetshop. My instinct is never to linger, always to flee, discreetly if possible, screaming if not. In this particular situation, having been sighted by Taffy the House Shaymus I was, accordingly, preparing to bugger off at top speed and volume with my perfectly legitimate purchases (a towel; two Mockingbird

of sinister directness had entered this particular colloquy. Penny
Burke, of all people, had snubbed him cold in the hallway the other
day (yesterday) while conversing with that ponytailed hippie-

---

cigarette lighters; a mother-of-pearl paperweight; a miniature print of the
Pyramids at Giza, ensconced in a mock-gilt frame) clutched in my left hand;
ergo, I chose as my most promising route—a doorway marked "Exit"—and
accelerated to a smart pace; but as the poet said one braw bricht moonlicht
nicht down Ayrshire way, "Och." (*Then* he said, "The best-laid plans of mice
an' men sometimes gang agley, och aye the noo. And mine's a pint o' heavy,
Jimmie.") In a trice wasn't I decked, and didn't I find meself sat upon by not
one but three Welshmen, all of them (as I later learned) former Wales rugby
centre forwards, and weren't the three of them going through my bags and
pockets with great method and thoroughness, albeit asexually (thank God)?
And 'twas their dialogue that was charmless, vulgar, and utterly of the old
school. "What's this then, bach?" "Give me it then, bach." "What's that when
it's at home then, bach?" "Is it a fucking picture, then, is it, bach?" "Is it blind
you are then, bach?" "Sod off then, bach," and so on. Eventually the supposed
manager, one Mr. Bach—an epicene gentleman in his mid-forties—arrived,
summoned by a distraught so-called lady shopper, coincidentally named Mrs.
Bach, who fancied, accurately, that she had detected the first signs of asphyxi-
ation in the ever-more-verdant hue of my barely visible features when same
were placed sideways floorwise beneath the muscular haunches of Taffys two
and three (cousins, as it later turned out over dinner and dancing at the Sa-
voy). Reluctantly, when asked to do so by Mr. Bach, they let me up, and by
way of apology explained that the entire Clery's detection staff had been
observing a state of high alert for three weeks, ever since that stick-up in
Perfumes and Ladies' Wear. The culprit, they explained with a show of regret (one even apologized and followed up with a ludicrous foot-shuffling "aw
shucks" routine that culminated in his giving me a business card belonging to
someone else), answered my description exactly, being neither tall nor short,
plump nor slim, young nor old, ruddy nor pale, blond nor brunette, bearded
nor beardless, toothy nor toothless, drunk nor sober, dapper nor down-at-heels,
sad nor happy, stupid nor smart, charismatic nor gormless. Well, it ain't me,
said I, and flounced off in high dudgeon. Later, when I discovered that my
wallet, the onyx paperweight and the picture of the pyramids at Giza had all
gone missing, I realized *the whole thing had been a put-up job*. Sure enough, the

beatnik-tinker class of fella she'd been hanging about with, just turning her back on him when he appeared and guiltily essayed a half smile, pushing ahead to the full treatment when she showed no sign of recognition; then, the snub, as if he'd been a mere pot boy, or itinerant Mormon evangelist . . . imagine, treating him, Finn, like that! It was corrupt, decadent, insulting! Not to mention *unimaginable*, a scant fortnight ago.

And as if all that weren't enough to give the cheeriest of Panglossian lads a pain in the arse, so to speak (ouch), that Hasdrubal-Scott woman had been leaving messages on his office phone, including one that sounded like a drunken invitation to libertinage of uncertain degree—or maybe he'd just misheard, what with her Gibraltarian accent and occasional use of Sephardic-Jewish dialect (or was that Spanish? "*Ay, cabroncito*"?) . . . nonetheless, litigation was proceeding apace, that much he understood, even in the permanent absence of the senior partner of O'Mallet & Ryan, Solicitors. Ms. Mary Rose Ryan had taken over the portfolios of her expired partner with the greater alacrity and determination one must always expect from the female of the species, especially a booming broad in jodhpurs. Mrs. Hasdrubal-Scott (herself no shrinking violet) was out for her pound of flesh, right enough, all because of some silly bloody imaginary insult to that raving coot of a husband of hers. . . . No, Finn, by God, Finn, said Finn to himself (by now returned to his bedroom and gazing at the recumbent form, so much like the undulating outline of the Knockmealdowns

---

very next day, didn't the *Independent* run a profile of the Welsh Triplets and their sallow accomplices Mr. and Mrs. Bach? Gimme a break, snarled I, and snuggled deeper into my armchair with a nice box of Ovaltine in me strong right hand, and to warm the cockles of me owld heart the saturnine yet comforting image of Gaybo on the telly. Comforting it was, too, to know that the key (turned) in the lock (locked) of the front door (closed) spelled security from the outside world's incursions (false: I forgot the kitchen window and the silver hammer lying so close to Maxwell's hand).

at sunrise, of Mrs. Finn, long-suffering martyr in the Irish tradition of martyred Irish wives that she was); no, Finn, there's nothing left for you here. On yer bike, son. Time to pack them bags, me owld spalpeen bawn. Time to bid fare ye well (he turned again to his wife) mavourneen, acushla, darleen. You'll never miss me, no you won't a bit. You'll find another fella. There's that darkie down the street, for one, you've been eyeing him for years, don't think I didn't notice (Egyptian, is he, the wanker?).

As for his loyal companions and fellow combatants, the NCOs of the Soldiers of Brian O'Nolan, henceforth disbanded, defunct, rendered void: frig 'em. Ex-Commandant Finn had no sense of responsibility for that shower, with their silly uniforms and play rifles and video war games and running about shouting "Boom, boom!" They knew it was a risky assignment; they'd known it from the first. They'd land on their feet, no bloody fear. And Harry Batasuna had his Basque butties and battles back in Spain or France or the Basque country to go back to, and plenty of Spanish or French people to maim and blow up in the interests of Greater Euzkadi; and as for Paddy and Seamus and Turlow and the rest—sure, they'd be as easy queuing up in the Sosh for a touch of government nicker as they would, later, leaning on the bar at Molloy's and spending that very same nicker on a round or two of pints of plain.

Finn removed folded trousers from the armchair in the corner of his bedroom and sat down and sobbed quietly but bitterly for a few minutes (six), half concealed by the enveloping folds of the window curtains that kept out the fluorescent glare of the streetlight above the wall that illuminated a gate, a brace of bikes, the redbrick back wall of Moynihan's Cycles, a stunted garden. . . . It was the peace of the known and familiar, but Finn turned away as if presented with a spectacle of horror. Indeed, at about that time a parade of his life's failures was strutting pigeon-chested across an imaginary stage before his mind's bloodshot eye. One by one he enumerated them: *College.* Ha! Four years of gibberish, two or three lukewarm affairs, a fair amount of beer but never admission into the inner circles of laddishness, much as he tried. The upshot, after desultory exams: A gentleman's third, with Failure a dead cert, just round the corner. Then *marriage*, almost as preordained as one of those Arabian or Iranian setups (they'd been neighbours growing up and had once, with their parents away at a Kilkenny hurling match, played doctor). It had been a thin-blooded business to start with, and was entirely bloodless by now. *Family?* Well, they'd had a son, Spike, wasn't it—no, Spike was the Yorkie she'd had for a while. The boy was Spark, that was it. He seemed as old as, if not older than, they, but he was in fact their junior by twenty years. Divorced, he lived now in Winnipeg, down the street (Elm) from his own elderly-seeming son, Skip, and across town from a job in the records office of the Royal Canadian Mounted Police. Hemorrhoids ballooning across the generations! Chalk that whole business up as an utter haimes as well.

Like a squirrel, Finn nervously chewed the inside lining of his cheeks. *Career? Ha!* Once a self-ordained chronicler of the nation's fated struggle, a revolutionary poet à la Neruda and Yessenin, he'd come a cropper, predictably, unpublished, unsung, unknown, yet widely despised. It was no good, it was never any good: he'd just never had the *nous,* the manhood, the balls. So he'd become a librarian at a succession of public libraries—Sligo, Athlone, Monaghan, Skerries, Dundalk. Then came the assistant director-ship at Killoyle Public, plum of the Munster library system: O wondrous opportunity spent, gone, blasted away like so much else! Like the Soldiers of Brian O'Nolan, that (as they'd thought, at first) force of noble fighting men and women dedicated heart and soul to the final overthrow of British tyranny in the North and the reunion of the thirty-two counties under the banner of en-lightenment and brotherhood! And never mind if—before the Aid to Terrorists Act—they'd had to divert the odd library grant or embezzle auction proceeds to buy guns and step on a few toes along the way—well, all right, blow up a few people here and there, just to make a point, but a valid one! And it was what the heroes and martyrs of the past had done, wasn't it? Spartacus, Washington, Bolivar, all terrorists at first, eh? Just ask the historians, for fuck's sake. And Finn had been decisively inspired by a biography of Menachem Begin that had crossed his desk at the library, inscribed "To my dear friend Anwar" (later sold at auction for the price of a few grams of ammonium nitrate fertiliser, sugar, diesel, and Semtex): Begin, vilified as a terrorist, later enshrined as a hero, slight and bespectacled yet undeniably manly (an equation forever denied to slight, bespectacled Finn), later prime minister of the nation his "terrorism" had brought into being . . . and Arafat?

And Collins, and Connolly, and Pearse, and Plunkett, too?

And O'Higgins, God bless him, and Kenyatta, and Nelson Mandela . . . ?

But not Finn, oh no, he was not—he had never been—nor would ever be—of their exalted company!

Finn's sobs probed his lungs like a sudden onset of fungus, and soon he was wheezing like a grampus in the mild waters of the Caribbean and belling like a lustful moose in the backwoods of James Bay, with pauses only to expel mucus noisily through first one, then the other nostril, much like an elephant taking a swamp shower in the still side waters of the Ganges basin. It was a din destined soon to be heard, and was. Alerted instinctually to the unorthodox uses to which the deep watches of the night, traditionally reserved for R.E.M. sleep, were being put, Mrs. Finn: a) groaned, b) awoke, and c) sat up.

"What's the matter? What time is it? What are you doing over there?"

"Piles, dear." Finn sniffed.

"Well, why don't you do something about them instead of blubbering in the dark? Have them removed. Piles are expendable."

"Good idea."

"I mean, honestly!"

"Yes, dear."

"Are you coming to bed?"

"No, dear. I mean yes, dear."

Mrs. Finn reversed the order of her awakening, thus: She lay back, groaned, and resumed sleep. Finn waited breathlessly for a minute or two, then padded softly about, collecting this pair of underpants, that shirt, those socks, that bankbook containing of all of their worldly assets (bar the trust fund; that was hers to do with as she chose); and quietly (except for another attack of sobbing that hit him for a scant ten seconds when he thought of their vegetable garden which *she* had always neglected and which would now have to fend for itself, poor defenceless little marrow plants! And as for the squash, oh, sob) gathered together these essentials in a traveling bag (a gift from Subcomandante Harry's boss Lisalotta, the old flirt) of soft Connolly leather with a shoulderstrap. It was half three. He closed the bag and went downstairs. In the kitchen he found a notepad and scribbled a message for his wife.

"Sorry, ducks," it read. "Cocked up all along, didn't I? I liked you once, *really* liked you. Know what I mean?"

At half-three he left, never to return. His hired car, a Toyota Corolla, sat at kerbside, streaked with the chill moisture of predawn dew. A cat, illuminated briefly by the streetlamp, dripped like molasses over the wall opposite. Distantly a foghorn sounded from the great expanses of the sea. Finn looked around one last time—the emptiness of Anchorite Avenue, with the gasworks at one end and the forlorn spire of Laddi's Disco at the other; his gate, once painted green, now a peeling grey; the letterbox reading "No. 115A," adorned with a plastic shamrock; Spark's old bike, eternally propped up against the side of the house ("this weekend I'll walk that bike over to Moynihan's and have it repaired; that way I can get some decent exercise"); peeping timidly round the corner, dimly lit by the streetlight, the vegetable garden (sob)—then he took a deep breath, seeing himself in the film of his life, in which this scene would come somewhere around the closing credits, with camera pulling back for a sky shot, and he flung the suitcase into the boot of the car with great flair, then instantly cringed in fear of the echoes and inquisitive faces (was that a curtain twitiching at Mrs. Malone's window?).

Taking care not to slam the door, he got in and started the engine, then waited precisely fifty seconds for the engine to warm up (an old habit, timed by his watch) and slowly drove away without so much as a backward glance but with a slight snick when shifting from first to second. The docks at Rosslare were his destination, and from there a car ferry to France; and from France, Spain to Bilbao, and the Pyrenees, where he'd seek refuge with his excellent comrades-in-arms—those tried and true fighters for freedom—those stern yet just men of the mountains—the revolutionaries of Euzkadi (and their flirtatious *Pasionaria,* Lisalotta)! And if all else failed, he could always teach English at Berlitz, or commit gorgeous suicide somewhere on the heights overlooking the Bay of San Sebastian. . . .

Once Finn was on the Ring Road heading northeast, with little or no traffic in sight, he felt oddly ebullient despite the extreme circumstances (and his piles, for the moment of little consequence); accordingly, he failed to notice, through the roseate hue of his sudden, unjustified optimism, that he was being followed at a distance by a dark-blue Ford Mondrian driven by a man of bulk and heft whose features at that distance were indistinct.

But if we—you and I, that is, dear reader[5]—wait for a while by the side of the road, in the placid light-pool of an illuminating streetlamp, and if we then jointly crane forward to get a glimpse of the mysterious driver

---

[5]Dear reader, me old gran. Who do you take yourself for, Charles bloody Dickens? Smarmy talk like that always has me making sure my wallet's still there and my underwear hasn't been interfered with.

*as he speeds by, steering furiously with one hand on the gearshift prepara-
tory to downshifting for greater momentum, he will fleetingly come into focus
as (as we thought) himself, Martin, yes our old matey Martin McArdle,
erstwhile brigade commander and now a roving avenger, a free lance, a*
ronin *of Ireland. Martin's emotions, verbally expressed, will no doubt be
momentarily audible through the quarter-open car window before the onrushing Finn-McArdle Express passes by forever (and a day).*

"I'll get ya, ya shite, ya."

24

Charles Finn's fugue occasioned small talk not only at the library. Heads were put together at gardai headquarters, separated, and put together again when word came that McArdle had fugued off, too.

"Damned rum," muttered Superintendent Patrick Talbott, suspecting more than coincidence. On the horn with Commissaire Patrick Taillebotte, his French counterpart in the Breton coastal town of Killouayle, the super learned that both fugitives had been spotted there, one ("the fat one, yes?") following the other ("the thin one, yes?") and that they had twice been seen in local supermarkets: the Hyper-Champion at Killouayle-Nord and the Carrefour at Bonbec on the road to Quimper. The second man ("the fat one, yes?") had purchased at the Hyper-Champion a package of spicy sausages, a loaf of wheat bread, a Michelin road map, a packet of English cigarettes, and a bottle of Zesti-Cola. The other man ("the thin one, yes?") had bought nothing in either place, but Jacques Kerouac, the eagle-eyed manager of the Carrefour rôtisserie department ("the best in Finistère, if not all of Brittany, *ah non, eh oui*"), suspected him of shoplifting a roast chicken.

"Yes," explained monsieur le commissaire, "because one minute she is there, the next minute, pouf! She is gone! And so is your friend, the thin one, yes?"

While these *pourparlers* were under way at the highest levels of European law enforcement, Penny Burke was awakening into the high and heady realm of her new life, the life of the director of Killoyle Public Library at a yearly salary of IR£35,000—on a protem basis; that is, temporary until confirmed, but that shouldn't be much of a bother, with those old dears. At first, after the phone call ("Finn's gone. Would you like his job?") she'd nearly screamed, in joy or despair she couldn't say. "Thirty-five effing grand," cried she, to whom an annual ten g's had been a small fortune.

Well, she'd been the obvious choice, said the Libraries Advisory Board chairperson Mrs. Sabre at the board meeting. Penny smiled.

"An excellent c.v. and a good attitude. You know the library system, you have a good degree, impressive Irish-language skills, and you've been on board for quite a while—what is it, five years? And we couldn't find any absences in your attendance record. Note has been taken of your blue jeans, however. To the effect that they could be a little less tight in the hip and inseam areas."

But I want to be a writer, Penny screamed inwardly, *and for that I need tight blue jeans and a marginal, half-subservient low-level job I can despise in good conscience, not a business suit and a well-paid well-padded prestigious number with perks that I'll actually look forward to every morning!*

But she said nothing, only smiled again. It was this misperceived enigmatic quality, this Mona Lisa trait implicit of modesty, thoughtfulness, and dependability, that had propelled her to the forefront of the candidates. How absurd! But such was life. And life had a way of suddenly making the hard parts easy, especially if they were the wrong parts, and nothing could be easier than simply stepping into someone else's shoes. It was like dynastic succession in Morocco or someplace. Oh, they'd have to run a pro forma search, of course, and the usual adverts would blossom in the local papers like dandelions in a pasture, but all prospective applicants would be gently turned aside with a routine "Your name will be kept on file should further opportunities open up," blah blah blah (and so on); and anyway, Penny was well in the door thanks to her own hard work, the utter mess Finn had made of things, and God having made her what she was, viz.: a girl with brains.[1]

So she was a professional success, quite unexpectedly, and she now sat in a leatherette swivel chair with reclining seatback and handy PVC footrest.

---

[1]Sounds narky, but inheriting positions of employment is the hiring practice that dare not speak its name, in Ireland as elsewhere, and not just Nepal and Syria. Yours truly, for one, attained glory at Spudorgan, despite morning flatulence and a right bolshy attitude, thanks to the emigration to Italy of ex-boss Emmet Power and the subsequent upheavals, connected with fraud and embezzlement on a monstrous scale, that would have made an actual candidate search a long, costly publicity ordeal (see *Killoyle, Unirish Fest*, pp. 1–2 passim); Sally O'Brien, for another, distinguished chairperson these many years of the local branch of Duchas, the National Heritage Fund, had succeeded to the position upon the death, from his stubborn insistence on consuming (despite warnings) oil-slicked mussels one tipsy night on the Strand, of her predecessor, Sir Errol Giggleglass. There were other instances, most of them success stories (Superintendent Talbott among them). Furthermore—and notably—this quasimonarchical system eases the selection process, reducing man- and womanhours devoted to such mere profitless nonsense. Yes, most of all *it saves money*, an insurmountable argument in nine organizations out of ten. Cousin Monk briefly got ahead in this fashion, too: his boss Dave McMole, fifty-six, fell dead of an aneurysm while straining at stool one busy morning between meetings. Now, Dave had been young Monk's mentor at Antelope Pens, Ltd., of Rhombus Street, for a number of years (three), and his sudden demise threw the organisation (eleven employees, all male, all of a certain age) into dithers of uncertainty. Worse, a government inspector was due on the premises any minute, and all knew of the severe penalties imposed on firms bereft of managing directors; so Monk, with his savoir-faire, was duly appointed to the post by unanimous silent vote. "A-One operation, Dave," the inspector said to him, shaking hands vigorously and staring keenly into Monk's face in that Mediterranean way of his. "The name's Monk," said Monk. "Very good, keep it up," shot back the inspector, turning smartly on his heels and heading for the door, where he paused with one hand on the door handle, glancing back over his shoulder. "And oh, Dave?" "Yes?" said Monk, suppressing a quaver of despair. "The goatee, old man." He shook his head. "No go. I'd try for the full frontal nudity, chinwise. Of course, that's

"Sod this for a lark," she said, "but I could get used to it, more's the pity."

All the more so as Derek was gone; he'd left in a storm of reproach and bile after she told him the good news.

"You're selling out, Pen," he'd muttered, glowering, adjusting as he did so the volume on his headphones of "Pork Pie Me, Pork Pie You," the newest hit by the Antwerp megametallic star Jan Opdijk.[2]

"Get out of that, you," had been Penny's indignant reply. "If that's the best you can muster. Why don't you get a decent job yourself?"

---

just me." And with that he was off, leaving behind him an aura of Old Spice, confidence, and exactitude. (What a man! 'Tis true that we shall not look upon his like again.) Perhaps, needless to say, it is that Monk promptly followed his advice, the matter of a few seconds' work as the goatee in question had been purchased at Fun Fair Ltd. on Corner Street and was attached by spirit gum. Goateeless, Monk surged ahead. Before he knew it, he'd been promoted to assistant senior associate executive director-manager of Fountain-Pen Marketing Research and Development, upon which he resigned and took to the byroads of Connemara in a jaunting car. Still, advice is advice. As Uncle Francie used to say, "God rest his soul in His eternal bosom: The sky's your oyster when you're young, but keep an eye on them pigeons."

[2]Oh, I know that one. Not that I'm an admirer; just that the kids next door keep us up with it sometimes, and we saw it on Eurovision the other night. It goes like this (stop me if I'm mistaken): Bumpathump bumpathump bumpathump bumpathump bumpathump bumpathump bumpathump bumpathump bumpathump bumpathump bumpathump (wail) *eeeee*-oohhh bumpathump bumpathump bumpathump bumpathump bumpathump bumpathump bumpathump bumpathump bumpathump bumpathump (louder wail) *eeeee* (lyrics, sort of) pawk pah meee bumpathump bumpathump bumpathump bumpathump bumpathump bumpathump bumpathump bumpathump bumpathump bumpathump bumpathump (wail) *eeeeeee* (more pseudolyrics) pawk pah yewwww bumpathump bumpathump bumpathump bumpathump bumpathump bumpathump. . . . Well, you get the drift. Music? Certainly, if the sounds of hard childbirth or the drilling of macadam pavement count as such, and they do not.

"Decent job? Listen to you. How bourgeois can you get?"

Seething, he'd tucked his hair behind his ears with nervous index fingers, but Alf had chosen that moment to start barking. Yelling "Fuck . . . *off,*" Derek had unwittingly (but subconsciously) performed his own coup de grâce by giving Alf a swift kick in the rump. The dog yelped but retreated not; rather, he renewed the attack and sank his fangs into Derek's ankle. Derek screamed. Things fell to the floor, as did Derek. In the melee Penny managed to score with her knee in Derek's crotch, and shortly thereafter she closed the front door of her flat, and the figurative page, on Derek and all his works and ushered in, she reckoned, an age of retrenchment, isolation, and celibacy. Well, good enough. To blazes with it anyway, self-swore she. She'd had the bit of bad luck with the boys. Mick? Not he. Derek? Cute enough he was for what he was, and what she needed, and they'd had good crack now and then oh they had, and the bed music they'd made was on occasion sweeter than the piping of bitterns on a wintry morn in the reeds of a Wicklow tarn; but sex wasn't everything, and Derek had, sad to say, a brain better suited to adolescence, or a sea urchin, and what was worse, he played that musical pap of his day and night . . . dear God she'd almost preferred Mick McCreek's nonstop diet of Verdi and Puccini and Hooverini; it was grown-up, at least . . . *and let's face it,* self-admonished she superbly, *the director of libraries couldn't be seen going about with a chancer like Derek on her arm.*

Or Mick, for that matter.

All credit where it's due, she did experience a slight tremor of guilt as the vision fleetingly passed before her mind's eye, displacing the long-revered, indeed iconic, image of herself in jeans, leather jacket, and beret, of herself in a Chantal business suit, cool, ironic, and irenic; but the pang of guilt was instantly supplanted by a warm, ever so slightly smug feeling of anticipated success and prosperity that in turn unfolded mental images wondrous beyond the telling of them, of pleasure palaces atop smooth, green lawns and white vine-bedecked housewalls and lean bronzed bodies silently cleaving topaz waters and humped grey-brown islands on the horizon and gleaming Jags and Mercs in fantasy carriageways and not far off a driver's limp white gloves, containing driver's hands, deferentially busy with wax and chamois. . . .

Hold on there, girl, self-admonished she. *It's only head librarian you'll be, not bloomin' Maeve Collins.*

Still, thirty-five grand was thirty-five grand, there was no gainsaying it.

"I *could* get used to it, you know," she repeated later to Alf, as they descended the outside staircase at the Hoardings, she with all the confidence of a biped newly validated by her peers, he with the uncertain, swarming gait of a quadruped for whom staircases were yet another concept, like static electricity, televisions, and gas heaters, designed by humans to confuse dogs.

Yes, Penny thought, surveying the Hoardings. Someday all this will be somebody else's. One day soon she'd move out of the place with its cheap lighting, paper-thin walls, imitation pebbledash exterior, and leave it to the night students, immigrant waitresses, and lorry drivers who so richly deserved it.

The surface of Uphill Street, at the end of Thomas Maher Mews, gleamed under a sheen of nearly invisible drizzle. Penny stopped and waited as Alf buried his muzzle deep in that olfactory bulletin board of messages from other dogs: a small clump of moist grass, thoroughly urinated upon. Cars drove by. A plane flew overhead, lights blinking. Across the road the Koh-I-Noor Indian Restaurant stood dark and silent. A sign in the window read, "Closed for Repairs," but no repairs were in evidence. Alf overwhelmed all other scents with his own, lifting a leg, then righting himself; then his ears stood straight up and his body went rigid.

"Alf!" he declared in the tones of a dog who has spotted something, or someone, of potential interest. This turned out to be, out of the mist, a man, a woman, and another dog. The dog returned Alf's interest with interest, and soon the damp air was full of the raucous greetings commonly exchanged by unacquainted dogs, and the fruitless pleadings of their owners.

Rararararararararararararararaf.

Alf! Alf! Alf! Grrrrrrrrrrrrrrrr . . . Alf!

Rrrrrrraarrararararararar . . . Rarr!

ALF! ALF! ALF!

"Ah, leave off, will ya?"

"Come here, you damned tyke."

"Shut up, for God's sake."

ALF! ALF! ALF!

"Sit, Alf! Sit, sir!"

"Strongbow! Bad dog!"

Rrrrrrraarrararararararar . . . Rarr!

"Oh, hullo, Penny."

"Oh. It's you."

Rarr!

ALF!

And indeed it was Mick McCreek, a touch better groomed than previously, his hair under control a bit bar the sides (Romano gel? He'd never get it right) and wearing the same old bomber-jacket-and-T-shirt combo she remembered so well; but lo and behold, he was in the company of a woman mature, even elegant, in all visible respects. Her stature, coiffure, figure, dress, were damned near Avenue Montaigne, or Regent Street, at least (well, maybe Grafton, in a pinch). Her appearance defined Upper Upmarket, anyway. She was what Penny would become after a while at this head librarian carry-on, thought Penny; and the thought was good, or at least not as bad as all that, even with the prospect of ongoing publisher's rejections. (Who needs another writer, anyhow?)

"Ah, Pen, this is Kathy McRory."

"Hello, Pen. Penny, is it?"

"Hiya. Penny Burke. Nice to meetya," said Penny, in her ordinary-gal-on-the-bike-down-the-street style.

"*ALF!*"

"He's a cutie," said Kathy McRory. "Or she?"

"No, he. He's a cutie, too," Penny said, boldly enveloping Mick in a female conspiracy of who had the better fella—or rather, who'd lost him. Kathy laughed, a clear and distinct, Ha! Ha! as if she'd studied laughing at RADA, a signal to Alf and Strongbow to resume hostilities.

"*Alf! Alf!*"

"*RAAAR! Rararararararararaarrr . . .*"

The dogs, although irritating in the way of dogs, were a welcome distraction from the awkward necessities of dialogue. Mick, not an avid dog fancier—"they're all right, but, prefer 'em to cats, know what I mean?"—made inept comments about Strongbow's spikey pelt as against Alf's curly one. This provided the women with a moment of united condescension towards the foolish man in their midst, and latent hostility evaporated like the dew of a summer morn.

So she was the one he'd told her about, thought Kathy. Last night after the pub. When they'd gone back to his flat. And he'd proved himself worthy of a place in her life, and her bed.

Aha! thought Penny. A good catch for him if not for her, although (and here she hit the mark) *she's forty if she's a day*, and over forty you can't be too choosy (reflected the twenty-seven-year-old director-to-be of libraries). Something sagged in her heart nonetheless. Not that she missed Mick, particularly; nice fella and all, but they weren't well suited and that was that. Cars, laddishness, and Italian opera, not her cuppa. But still. Beyond him (and Derek) stretched loneliness, except for Alf.

"*ALF! ALF!*"

"*Rararararaaar!*"

Smart tugging of leads restored a semblance of order, but uneasiness—the real thing, not a semblance—was creeping in like the ambient autumn fog. Penny opened her mouth to utter a banality indicative of departure—"Well!" or "All right then" or (with inflection rising on the false diphthong) "So-o"—but Mick stepped in with a blurted remark.

"Kathy's the editor of *Glam*," he said, proudly, as if reluctant to bring the encounter to a close without announcing the fact. "She's my future employer, actually, isn't that so?"

"It could well be," said Kathy. She smiled, first at him, then at Penny. "I've offered Mick a job as motoring correspondent. I reckon he's got the qualifications."

"In spades," said Penny. "Motoring correspondent, is it? Boy, you must be right chuffed, Mick."

"I am. It's not a bad gig. I'll get to drive a different car every week." He paused, aware of how boyish—nay, laddish—he sounded. "And do a spot of travel on top of it, she says. Eh?"

"Maybe. If you're a good boy. And promise to translate those Italian menus for me."

"Paradise for some. Hey," said Penny, engaged in making as if to leave, impelled by lateral inching away by suddenly eager Alf with urgently swimming forepaws, "you should come to the library and give us a little talk someday. About the mag, you know, and all that. Journalism, whatever. I run things there now, you know."

"Oh, we know," said Kathy. "After the story of that man Finn, it's incredible. What a farce. We'll be doing a piece on the whole sorry business."

And so they parted.

Mick and Kathy walked on in silence, beneath an awkwardness the size of Gibraltar. Quite apart from the fact that they'd run into Mick's ex-girlfriend on their first walk together, each had seen the other in a social setting for the first time. Each, therefore, was busy analyzing the meanings of this and that, repeating mentally all that had been said, revisiting this look, that allusion, those references to things and hints real or imagined (imagined, all of them); but each also felt an urgent desire to reassure the other, so naturally both spoke at once and inflated the overhanging cloud of awkwardness to thunderhead dimensions before laughing in mutual recognition that life was a funny old bucket of shit and coming out, with, respectively (Kathy first):

"So that was Penny, was it, now?"

Then Mick: "It was."

Kathy once more: "So we're going to Italy, yeah?"

Then Mick again: "Yeah."

"Good thing we just happen to have an office in Milan."

"Bloody good thing, acushla."

Then Strongbow, who had spotted what he could have sworn was a cat:

"Rarrr! Rararararararararararrrr. Rarararr," but which turned out to be an empty onion-scented carrier bag from Toolan's Markets fleeing a step ahead of the night's chill breeze.

"Rrrrf," Strongbow mused, acerbically, but his humans heeded him not, interlocked as they were in a spectacle that was cinematic to its, or their, toenails, even in the absence of a decent soundtrack by, say, Jerry Goldsmith or John Williams; but they went ahead and kissed all the same, oblivious to the paltry real-life soundtrack provided by approaching electric milk floats twain—one piloted by Tony, the other by Colm, both of Brosnahan's Dairies—and of course the ever-hooting ships at sea; and so, meanderingly, to bed (his: more convenient).

Ah, Mick! Ah, Kathy!

Ah, sex! Ah, youth! Ah, middle age!

Fade to black, or a pearly grey.

25

Once again, our fair city was on the front page of much of the nation's press, and not for its tourist attractions. Although the *Weterford Osprey-Gazette* did take time out to mention "the lovely surroundings of the Shrine of the Invisible Virgin" and "the nonpareil shopping to be had at the shops known as 'The Shops,'" as well as "the unique attractions of dancing at Laddi's Disco, where once priests sermonized on the evils of dancing, et cetera," other broadsheets dealt more directly with the events of the moment.

"Splinter Group's Desperate Attempt to Destroy Peace Process," solemnly burbled the *Tir-Na-Nog Times*'s leader; "Mad Librarian Decamps," shrieked the *Clurichaun Chronicle;* "Ex-Terror Chief Bags It," bawled the *Innisfree Independent;* and as for the *Hiberno-Manx Herald*, nothing less than "Marbella Still a Haven for Tanners in the Off-Season" would suffice—oh, and in the left-hand column at the bottom of page three: "Bad Boys Bomb Beer Bash." Other papers and magazines turned their rheumy gaze outward to world events of repetitive monotony, such as the perpetual ructions of the Middle East, Southeast Asia, and Africa, events and locales that would still be of no interest whatever to 99 percent of the great Irish nation, were a million to die and a million more fall ill . . . yet more bulletins of record concentrated their limited resources on front-page blarefests anent regional sports events, for example, "Will Laois Upset Offaly? Full Day and Night Coverage" or "A County's Pain: Millions Mourn Kilkenny's Loss at Croke Park," or celebrity gossip of the "Deandra Drake Lands at Shannon, Takes Off Again" variety. One or two even ignored all the above and chose to prate breezily on about the price of bovine foodstuffs or the properties of Easi-Fert fertilizer.[1] Of course, had there been a televised trial, or a widely publicised arrest, or a *really massive* bombing, the attention of the press would have been unanimously riveted; but days went by and nothing happened. News trickled in, then dried

---

[1]Ah, those would be the midlands farming journals, seed-and-feed rags from Longford and Leitrim mostly, with a heavy dose of Roscommon-or-garden farm husbandry, as it were. And now that you mention it, I'm reminded that early in Cousin Monk's snail-slow career he worked as an assistant subeditor for the Longford Breed Record. He did quite well at first, being an apt class of man when he put his mind to it, but over the course of a few days he realized that reading about manure and cervical sacs all day put him off his dinner, so he quit. With back turned and hunchbacked shoulders aslant, and displaying an expression of rage and anguish on his averted face, the editor, one "Quasimodo" Fitzpatrick, gave his grudging assent, but later that night the very same Quasi had at poor Monk with crossed marlinspikes and a brace of staves, in the alleyway behind Gill's Bar and Grill from which Monk was emerging replete with Shannon trout, several little brown jugs of porter, and the pleasure of his own good company. Unexpectedly for Quasi, old Monk proved to be one of those fellas who are slow to anger but quite formidable in the lists once aroused; and his unexpected knowledge of *Kentnagano,* the ancient Hokkaidoese martial art of stave-wrestling, came in very useful. He soon had Fitzpatrick pinned to the ground praying for peace and a second chance to lead a wiser and sadder life. Amen, Quasi. (He's doin' the best, the gossoon. Last we heard he was second ghillie on a Dumfriesshire estate once owned by James Boswell; in fact, word had it that he'd changed his name by deed poll to Quasimodo Boswell.) You can read all about it on Victor Hasdrubal-Scott's new old newspapers web site, now owned by Emerald Mats Worldwide PLC, at www.goodoldvictorhasdrubalscottsnicebignewoldnewspapers website.com.

up, then trickled in again. From France came word that two men answering to the description of the fugitives McArdle and Finn had been sighted near La Rochelle in a Codec supermarket where the one—"*un gros, oui?*"—had bought a bottle of Wild Space aftershave, twenty Obélix filterless fags, a liter of half-defatted milk, and a family-sized package of a hundred spicy sausages; and the other—"*un mince, oui?*"—had spent some time loitering in front of the women's WC, trying on several different pairs of sunglasses. The first man was seen again later on the side of the Autoroute, banging his fist on the bonnet of his car, a Ford Mondrian; but the thin one vanished, unless he was the man whose "*voiture étrangère*" broke down near Biarritz and who flagged down a passing motorist only to run behind a bush when the highway Samaritan got out of his car—and got in again when shouts of "*Allez vous-en!*" in a strong "English" (as the gentleman said, having never left France) accent could be (and were) heard coming from behind the bush.

"I assumed the English monsieur was having an Anglo-Saxon joke, or that he was suddenly in need of physical relief. You know? So I left."

"Physical relief indeed," muttered Superintendent Talbott. He hung up and gazed out the window at the schoolyard next door. A small boy was dribbling a football there: whack *plop*, whack *plop*, whack *plop*. That small boy had once been he, mused the super.

"Well?" said his visitor in a voice more feminine than the super's, in a woman's voice, in fact, with a funny accent—Welsh? Arabic?

"Well, they're out there somewhere, that's all I can say."

"Well, I'll find them then."

Indian, by gum!

"Well, off you go then."

The super swiveled around in his swivel chair, his hands nervously fashioning the desk denizen's widely imitated finger-chapel, denoting thought and/or a determination not to fidget.

"Your people gave me a call last night, Major," he said. "A fellow called Nahveed, from New Delhi?"

"Oh, him," said the super's interlocutrix, sitting back in her chair, quite composed as she reveled in the identity that was the most essentially truthful of her sundry selves, that of Major Rashmi Vishnapuram of the Indian Intelligence Service, Research and Analytical Wing (RAW). "He's a midget."

"Ah. You mean a low-ranker? A starting monkey on the greasy pole? Ambition personified?"

"Ambition personified is spot on, but no, he's an actual midget. Three-foot six, I think. But what an intellect! And he makes a divine Manhattan." For a second or so the fiery lass rode that thought out the window like a stallion across the pastures of a distant dreamworld; then she tossed her tumbling raven tresses back, smoothed out her khaki skirt, and was suddenly all business (as the super sat up with a start). "So what did he want?"

"Oh he . . . ah . . . I . . ."

"Because I can tell you that Nahveed doesn't mess about when he's on a case. Whatever he wants he gets, or there's hell to pay. So what did he want?"

"Me to fax him a report on the whole operation, actually. Your cooperation with us, our cooperation, or *their* cooperation—or total lack thereof, actually—with G2, and of course the whole Emerald Mats mess and the Belfast Brigade's involvement—their 'hidden hand,' as he put it, rather imaginatively, I thought—everywhere."

"Yes. Even in Pushtoonistan, for heaven's sake."

"Aye." Wherever the blazes that was. But the super remained, outwardly, composed, stern, manly. "Oh, those Pakistani employees of Emerald Mats masquerading as Indians? The dear knows they may be deported when all this is over but I can't promise anything, that's up to G2 and their toadies in the Foreign Office."

"Too bad. I was hoping for trophies. I wanted at least to take back the organizer of the European branch of that Kashmiri-

Punjabi coalition cell, that Jamal Jaffrey fellow—I mean, that's
why they sent me in the first place, isn't it?"

"To catch this Jaffrey person . . . ?"

"No, no, to blow their cover. To uncover the links between
those guys and the IRA, the Basques and the Mongoose subfaction
of the Tamil Nadu independence movement."

"Crumbs," said the super, thinking not for the first time that
Major Vishnapuram was a damnably attractive woman but that
she might be the bit of a pain in the arse to deal with on a daily,
or domestic basis. . . .

Still, who wasn't, or what . . .

(The super was fifty-four, unmarried, down to earth, a pro to
his toenails, and normally unflappable, but a man had his needs.)

"Imagine thinking my poor cousin Anil had anything to do with
that! The silly wretch!"

"I know. Poor bastard. Oh, sorry. But not to worry, we're making amends for that appalling Special Forces screw-up. Too much
in evidence when they're not needed and not there at all when
they are, eh? So we managed to get all pending charges dropped,
you know, that kind of thing. And something about a catering
license? Our legal people are working on that."

"Fair enough under the circs, I mean, poor old Anil, for one!
But after all it turned out to be a real old hotbed, didn't it? Not
only all those others we talked about but the Kashmiri Muslim
groups as well, and of course last but by no means least, how could
I forget, those silly Soldiers of Brian O'Nolan . . ."

"Who turned out to be little more than a front operation for
the lads in Spain, run by a barmy old coot who liked to play soldier. Now that caught me unawares, I will confess. Especially
when we saw the film you shot during that mock raid—and by
the way, congrats for pulling that off. That took, um," he cast about
for salubrious alternatives to the word, and concept of . . .

"Balls?" said Rashmi. "Thanks." She chuckled. "Actually there
was nothing mock about it. It was a real raid, and it went off bril-

liantly. No question that it would've fallen apart if I'd taken your advice, no offense, and gone with the Special Services Unit. No thanks, no pros. If you want something done right, hire an amateur, that's my advice."

"And I wanted to commend you on your undercover job in prison ... well, city gaol. That took buh, buh, guts as well."

"Ta very much, Mr. Policeman! All part of the job, you know. Actually, I had a high old time in there with the prossies and cross-dressers. They thought I was one of them at first. I only realized later that those Kashmiri tarts really were part of an international prostitution ring. No lead there, but you never know till you've tried."

"Yes, well. We learned a lot from that. And from the raid. And I can tell you, half the lads in the room were onto that Harry Batasuna as soon as they saw him in your film. Bad miscalculation on his part to run outside without a disguise. But our lads spotted him like, well," the super made as if to snap the middle finger and thumb on his right hand, but adherence was absent and he produced nothing but a dry friable sound. "Just like that."

But Rashmi was gazing into the middle, or upper distance, past his shoulder, where light and shadow met at right angles on the bare brick face of the wall opposite and reminded her forcefully of the courtyard of a restaurant (JiJi's) in Delhi associated with youth and passion and blue skies deep enough to dive into, so forcefully indeed that she gave a barely audible gasp before rejoining the conversation.

"Yes," she said. "It was funny in its way. But unfortunately people got killed, even though it was an absurd place, just like the Emerald Mats factory. Too bad about that fellow Goone, though. I don't think he knew anything about it."

"He did not. He may have had commercial contacts with IRA frontmen. Indeed, he prided himself on being a canny business-man, as I understand it. But so-called canny businessmen, sorry, *people*, frequently turn out to be babes in the wood when it comes to human relations. Actually dealing with people, I mean, not just searching out their weaknesses."

"Very perceptive, Superintendent. And you're quite right, of course. I mean, look at that crazy boyfriend of his, he most certainly read him wrong, didn't he?"

"Mmm," said the super.

"Oh I can tell you the Indian press is going to just lap that one up, you know, there's an inexhaustible appetite in India for sex gossip, inex*haust*ible. I've passed most of the gory details on to my two contacts down at Haresh's Hideaway."

"Ah. The two waiter fellas?"

"Yes. Oh, they love stories like this. Especially gay dramas where one guy wears women's clothes, you know, because Bollywood dramas are so straight everybody's bored."

"Bolly . . . ?"

Rashmi took note of the super's floundering about in uncharted waters.

"The Indian movie business. Based in Bombay, or Mumbai as we say now . . . like Hollywood, you know? Bolly . . . ? Well, never mind. By the way, did you hear the lover boy has petitioned to be released from jail on the grounds of excessive solitude and mental anguish?"

"Yes, well, it's either that or . . ."

"Buggery à go go, with a life sentence. I know. But still. He *did* off the chap."

"He did. But you wouldn't believe the leniency of some of these judges. Borders on mania, if you ask me."

"Speaking of judges, what about Judge O'Mallet? What's in store for him?"

Rashmi was sitting comfortably in an easy chair with raised swivel capacity, enabling her to take the occasional, girlish spin around to catch the stodgy super off his guard. She did so now, as he grappled with a reply. When she returned to her point of departure, he had turned away and was staring at the yard, newly empty because, alarmed by the sight of a stern grown-up face grimacing through the window (the super, in his many years of bachelorhood, had developed facial tics of which he was himself quite unaware, such as a tendency to open his mouth gapingly wide whilst simultaneously uprolling his eyes and extending his tongue in the manner of a decapitated head, say that of John the Baptist as depicted by one of the old masters[2]), the small football dribbler had taken his football elsewhere. No animate movement remained. Only leaves skittered across the ground and clouds raced across the freshly wind-washed autumn sky that reminded the super of the sky over the races at Leopardstown where he'd first had a flutter, back in '72 (and had met Angela—but never you mind that).

"Judge O'Mallet, well now. He's an old friend, you know. I mean, you know how these things work."

---

[2]Good image, Jumbo lad. I'm with you here. The eyes have it, certainly. As in various canvases: Klaas Erschnitt's "Head of John the Baptist on Bed of Rice with Shallots, Button Mushrooms and a Cucumber Salad" (1649) comes to mind, along with one of my personal nonfavourites, "Removing the Head of an Oppressive White Homophobic Racist European Male Hegemonic Colonial Overlord and Thereby Symbolically Decapitating the Fascist Past" (1987) by the radical barn artist Giles Sarasate-Carmen. By the by, he's quite the *hombre*, is Giles. I met him once at a disco in Marrakesh in the early seventies, in the company of his then-mistress, Henrietta Hissler. "Oooooh," squealed Henrietta, when she clapped eyes on me, and ran away in an alluring knock-kneed fashion. I bade fair to follow, only his nibs stepped in front of me and blocked my view. "*Ola!* Are you boring?" he enquired of me. I pled guilty, upon which Giles spun on his heel and announced, *avec superbe,* "Then go away. I am an artist. Boring people bore me." Last I saw of him, he had his paint-smeared hands all over someone else's canvas (Rembrandt, I believe) and was transforming it into his own work, estimated bidding price fifty thousand dollars at Sotheby's. As for Henrietta, we met later, at Rigolo's on the Via Montenapoleone, but it wasn't the same.

"Oh I do, Superintendent, I do. Believe me, things at RAW aren't always on the up and up; quite the opposite at times."

"Well, he's been through enough, hasn't he. I expect he'll step down, just. No point harrying the man to cover when he's lost his son."

"Quite. I leave that one up to you." Charms tinkled on Rashmi's wrists as she made the expansive gesture of concession. "Completely your choice, you know. It's all your ball game, eh? Just be sure to be nice in your fax to Nahveed."

"Actually, I have my DS working on it right now. No, no, it wouldn't do to alienate your lot, Major. Youse have been a great help, and we'll be owing youse a real old debt of gratitude for uncovering all that Soldiers of Brian O'Nolan business, and we'll do what we can with the Tamil and Kashmir connection. Just thought I'd tell you."

"Good enough, Superintendent. And please also let Nahveed know I'll be back in Delhi in a week or so but that first I'm off to France or Spain or wherever those johnnies have got to by now. It's that Harry Batasuna chap I'm after. Most wanted man in at least five countries including India and Sri Lanka. Kashmiri-Tamil connections, you see."

Those johnnies. Sometimes she sounded like a character in an old Terry-Thomas or Peter Sellers flick, thought the super. *Brown of the F.O.* or one of those, with a dash of Rider Haggard. Made her all the more unusual, somehow. (Read: attractive, to certain aging superintendents of the Gardai Siochana.)

"You're a brave woman, Major . . . ah . . ." He was determined to get it right. "Vash-na-*pu*-ram." Given the super's training and background, and the stern sterility of organizational life, in which individual emotion was as ruthlessly expunged as in Stalin's Russia, it was the nearest he could come to a full-fledged pass; although, as an Irishman, and an unmarried one at that (albeit the father of a son out of wedlock, now the TD for Offaly

East[3]), he could still suggest, without being thought too forward, the two of them going for a pint; so he did so.

"Would you, um . . . ? Down the street? A drink? Just, you know, five minutes? Or the hotel? The ale festival? They're holding the pint-pulling today, I believe, postponed it for obvious reasons . . ."

Major Vashnapuram's answering laughter out-tinkled the charms on her bracelets.

"I say, Superintendent, you aren't making an advance, are you?" She leveled a gaze at him that the super was beginning to realize was very likely her specialty as an interrogator, an unblinking and somewhat taunting stare that could be interpreted variously as the penultimate stage on the road to seduction or the cool appraisal of a woman who's just about to let you have it in the goolies. So luminous and many-chambered were her kohl-lined eyes that the average Joe could easily get lost there. And Superintendent Talbott was nothing if not the average Joe.

"Well, Superintendent?"

The super turned as brick-red as the bricks of the wall opposite and fell to fidgeting with an elastic band.

---

[3]Him? You don't say. I always knew he was a bastard, being Fine Gael, but not, you know . . . well, well. But now that you mention it, there *is* something policemanlike about the set of his jaw, not to mention his shoes and trousers and that bike he rides to and from work, and the dear knows he *does* take the gardai's position on everything from salmon fisheries to driving licences, doesn't he? Odd that he married that loony schoolteacher from Oban, but. She's a Redgrave Maoist, Trotskyite wing, as I understand it. What's her name? Jocasta? Theodora? Maria Theresia? No: Noreen, that's it. Boys o boys, what a number. The Queen of Sheba of the Inner Hebrides, they call her over there. You'd reckon she'd be a dead weight on any politician's career, but word has it she's been seen helping some of his male constituents out to the privy more than once, if you take my meaning. And her hot buttered scones are nothing to sneeze at, either, according to first-hand reports. Nothing new under the sun, is there, no matter how hard you look.

"Not at all," he said, retreating behind stolidity, the policeman's friend. "Just concluding our business in the traditional Irish way, that's all."

"Well, I'd be delighted, in the traditional Indian way."

Yes, in the world there are forces at work upon men greater than the sexual charisma of women, and some of these forces are mighty indeed, ambition being one, greed and cupidity being others, and the urge to do good being the most powerful of all; but all are allied strands of the web of survival and reproduction, and none has the eviscerating immediacy of lust, or desire, or passion, call it what you will. And Superintendent Patrick Talbott's was a stern old façade that was beginning to show cracks. And before long it would be too late for repairs.

And anyway, he'd never seen a pair of knockers like that. Certainly not on a colleague.

26

Judge Gerald O'Mallet's eyes were pouched and pink-rimmed. No xenon stare left; not even a halogen stare to greet the day. Only the dim tungsten glow of a fifteen-watt, fifty-seven-year-old burnt-out case, an ashen, broken, shuffling husk, an embodiment of expired hubris, of madness aborning, of sin un-redeemed: a hollow man, an ex-Prometheus. He hated himself. God, did he ever.

"God, I hate myself, you bastard," he bawled, solo.

He hated everyone else, too, and dismissed his hated house-keeper, Mrs. Delaney, in a storm of shouting and West Cork idi-oms (although he was a Killoyler born and bred and Mrs. Delaney hailed from north Donegal) and implicit accusations of collusion with the enemy, if not the devil.

"Feck off outta here now, ya owld gutty. Ye were always spy-ing on us, werencha, ya owld sow."

"Ah get along wichya judge, sure to God me hand to me heart and before me own saviour Jesus Christ himseluf I never!"

"Balls to ya. Workin' for that bastard McArdle, ya were. Ya spilled the beans, plain and simple."

"Sure as God is my witness I never saw the man. 'Twas Mrs. McArdle I was and still am workin' for, judge. And a better employer ya would not find in the thirty-two counties of holy Ireland."

"Ya liar. And some feckin' cook ye were, sure the divil himself would turn up his nose at yer groodles. Gwan get out of it. Ye're sacked, ya owld bitch. Starting now. Go on, on yer bike. Pay? Stick it up yer arse. Pay? Don't make me laugh. Tell ya what: Take me to court, aha ha ha ha."

It was not a mirthful laugh; *au contraire.* The judge's neck muscles stood out like short lengths of stout rope; his eyes bulged, gently but obstinately, like Ping-Pong balls; the veins throbbed in his temples like earthworms; the hem of his yellow nightshirt rose and fell in sympathy with his urgent breathing and the currents of the ambient draught. Mrs. Delaney bustled hither and yon, muttering curses under her breath, and soon she was gone, spilling undergarments from her overnight bag, blathering at some length in a tongue that resembled Friesian, or English as spoken by Dutchmen.

"That's right, feck off now," bawled the judge as he watched her dumpy figure hobble down the boxtree-lined drive of Squarestairs. He made sure to signal the fig when she turned at the gate for a final look back, shaking her head at the sight of him. It was true that with his unkempt hair and yellow nightshirt he presented an eccentric spectacle to all who might be watching— not that he cared. *Let 'em watch!* In fact, he'd not changed out of his nightshirt since Tom was killed, not even to go to the funeral. There, nocturnally caparisoned, he explained he was better equipped "to head straight back to my bed and stay there until perdition throws open its gates."

But as will happen in life, perdition, when beckoned, held off. Yes, every day the judge awoke to yet another passage of misery and wanton self-contempt, his body perversely cooperating with divine punishment to delete all hints of malady or chronic ailments; in short, physically he felt great, whereas mentally he was about as fit as that mole squashed by Sylvia and Adrienne's van on the Crumstown Road at the end of Chapter 20—that is, not at all good. He was having visions, unless the Napoleonic-era hussars dancing grave quadrilles at the bottom of his garden were real. And the skittering androgens appearing and reappearing beneath the yew tree. And the furry owl he saw perched on a tree branch giving him the hairy (or furry) eyeball . . . was it an excess of vice? Hardly. Well, yes, he was letting himself go a bit, but why not, if he felt so sodding great. What was the difference between, say, ten cigarillos a day and fifteen, nay twenty in extremis? Bar the morality of it, for which he didn't give a fart in his flannels—nightshirt, rather. And it was surely a moot point if he rang in cocktail hour at half-five or five, or even a touch earlier, say four-forty-five on cloudy days. With no one to share it with, and the ever-booming television in the background, it scarcely mattered what time he tilted the old bottle, or what day it was, or who he was, or wasn't . . . and anyway, in "televisionland" they had an inexplicably insatiable (yet somehow, obscurely, reassuring) appetite for going over and over the same old shite and behaving every time as if it were the first time ever and the Almighty's own divine revelation to boot!

And dear God, how he missed sweet Tom, his own darlin' boy.

Sinatra's greatest hits, and some of his not-so-great ones (The Sands '71; Madison Square Garden '78; London Palladium '82), filled the house with a doux throbbing until, brandishing one of his old gavels, the judge fell upon his stereo in a transport of passion and reduced it to a tangled mass of wires overlaid with shards of plastic.

He regretted it the instant it was all over.

"It's all over, " he muttered, and spent the rest of the afternoon sweeping up the mess.

Then, on a morning dull and overcast, with scarcely a breath of breeze, Anil Swain came calling. Having parked his wheezing old Escort down the lane, he paused at the gate of Squarestairs to pull on his cigarette and fondle his chin, upon which a goatee was forming. Smoking, he looked the place over: red brick; Queen Anne-era or slightly after (not that Anil could have placed the era and style of construction with any degree of accuracy: "Pretty old but not as old as the bloody Taj," or words to that effect, would undoubtedly have been his verdict); square, as its name implied, with a broad flight of stairs leading up to the Palladian front door; handsomely topped off with four towering white chimneys that stuck up on the roof like an excess of donkey ears. Boxwood trees neatly lined the gravel-strewn drive, conferring a hint of the lunatic order of a surrealist painting. A hedge, untrimmed, guarded the property to the east, and on the other end stood the remains of a once-impressive brick wall against which, in the corner, autumnal sweepings were piled.

"Cool place," declared Anil, firing off his fag end. He then crunched swaggeringly up the drive and marched up the front steps, whistling—with an aggressiveness that should have been a warning to the curious—an old tune ("Maria" from *West Side Story*, which he'd caught, briefly, last night on RTE7's "MaxiMovie Mogul Madness," and yes, it wasn't too bad here and there, certainly the girl, at least—what was her name, Millie? Molly? Something American . . . no, Maria, that was it—was nice to look at, but the whole thing grew quite tedious whenever those silly staring buggers started staring at each other in that silly way as well as snapping their fingers over and over again and sort of backing up with their legs bent), and deliberately rang the doorbell, thrice. Disgruntled shouts resonated within for a few seconds, then the door opened, revealing Judge Gerald O'Mallet. It was nine, or shortly after, and the judge had heaved his large palpitating body from bed only ten minutes earlier. His hair, uncombed, formed broad protuberances on either side of his head like the fins of a manta ray. His nightshirt was scored heavily across the midriff where he'd lain all night prone and semisleepless with his blackthorn stick tucked under him in case any of those Napoleonic gentlemen came calling—and as for them androgens . . .

"Yes?"

"Good morning, judge. Can we talk?"

"Who are you, Wally? Some old tinker, eh? Nothing for you here, son."

"Oh, just let me in; my goodness, this has gone far enough."

"What has? Who the blazes are you, anyway? Some kind of Arab tinker you are, arencha, lad? Or should I say, traveller?"

"You know me quite well, I'm thinking. After all, by gosh, you arranged me to get out of prison so you could send me off with those murdering morons . . ."

"Ah, Christ. It's the wee Indian shoneen. Abdul, is it?"

"Anil. Please? May I?"

"Oh, come in, come in, who cares, make yourself at home, take over the place if you want, send for your relatives, let's turn the bloody place into a customs and immigration shed, why not, eh? Or a fucking Indian restaurant, yes let's burn it down if you like, fat lot of good it does me anymore—armed, are you? Well, shoot us both if you please, I don't care, or go and make yourself some curried rat or biryani ox or whatever it is youse lot fancy. Coffee's in there, tea's over there, and lots of it, believe me. But you can make it yourself. A drink? Not bloody likely, mate. What do you think I am, a sodding headwaiter?" Nightshirt flowing behind him, the judge swam through the air with the greatest of ease, like a dog shedding fleas . . . then he paused and looked around, as if caught by surprise.

"Who are you?"

"Anil Swain, if it please the court." (Oh, by golly, Anil was quite proud of that particular comeback, oh yes indeed, not for nothing he'd once been known as the "TV lawyer," you know, back when *Queen's Counsel* was all the rage along Marine Drive and environs and he never but never missed an episode and even went so far as to hang a pinup of Julie Barnett, that hot court secretary, oh by golly yes, on the wall of the tiny bedsit he'd shared with his cousins Musadhi, Jawa, and Sharma—Rashmi's brothers, come to think of it. . . .)

"And what is't you want, exactly?"

"I want what's fair." Anil stood stock-still, and presented the spectacle of a man standing stock-still in urgent need of fairness.

"Fair?" bellowed the judge. "Fair?"

"Yes," said Anil. "Or like I said on the phone, you will have a big credibility problem. Big," he repeated, extending his hands a yard apart to indicate the potential bigness of the judge's problem. "I'm quite willing to become a proper nuisance about all this, you know. Willing and able, as you know, judge."

Judge Jerry O'Mallet had actually been readying himself to reclimb the stairs, toddle down the hall to his bedroom, close the bedroom door behind him, lie down on the bed, take out his .22 out of the bedside table, stick aforesaid .22 into his gob and blow his fecking brains out. However, it was only a .22, and they were damn dodgy at best.[1] And Anil's even tone and steady gaze intrigued, even unnerved him; so he made other plans for the immediate future.

"All right. Come this way."

He led the way into the parlour. The flamboyant hand gestures to the left and right that he made en route—through the magazine-filled foyer, the hallway stacked high with old videos, the pantry with wall-to-wall metal tins containing an entire library of world teas from Andaman Orang-Oolong to Zanzibar Damask (one of the judge's old hobbies now fallen off the old shovel; I mean, not even an Irishman could give a flying frig about tea under the circumstances) were quite meaningless to Anil, who had no way of knowing that snacks, whiskey, cigars and cigarillos,

---

[1]True on ya. Remember Cousin Monk? He tried five times with a .22 one particularly depressing morning (the old cough troubling him again, no doubt, as well, as his prolonged uncertainty about precisely what to do with his life) and missed the first four times only to clip himself on the roof of the mouth the fifth, creating an instant cleft palate and entitling him (it was determined after prolonged and exhaustive investigation by the Ministry of Disabilities) to disability payments—which, being Monk, he eschewed.

et cetera, were concealed in the various closets and sideboards toward which His Lordship was gesticulating, mind clouded over with the pale cast of . . .

"*Thought* so."

Judge Jerry seized from atop a chaise longue a slim black monolith that Anil, even at that distance, had no trouble identifying as a TV remote control, but the judge then turned and stared in Anil's direction with such rabid intensity that he, Anil, was on the verge of saying, "I say, judge," when he realized that the judge's gaze was not in fact directed at him but at something slightly behind and to the left of his, Anil's, right shoulder. Turning, Anil beheld a carriage clock in the late-eighteenth-century Geneva style.[2] As they stared at it, the clock uttered soft chimes, indicating the half hour. The judge gaped.

"My goodness gracious, what was I thinking of? It's time for *Bonzo's Babes*," he expostulated. Majestically, he turned again and flourished the remote control in the direction of a large, hitherto discreetly concealed television, which promptly responded to the electronic stimuli by awakening into the full volume and garish lights of . . .

"Bo-o-o-nzo's Ba-a-a-a-a-bes."

A raucous television voice boomed. Strobes probed the dark. Zany titles composed of letters of rainbow colours danced across the screen. All of a sudden the lights were up and lissom lovelies dressed in clinging white leather leisure suits sashayed across a stage, pursued by an absurdly ponced-up chap in a sky-blue smoking jacket with ruffles at the cuffs. . . .

---

[2] Ah, I know the style. Nice to look at, but a quid gets you ten bob that this one was manufactured hastily in the late twentieth century by Han's Western Goods, employing current and former political prisoners in a small warehouse in Industrial Zone Number Five on the outskirts of Hangzhou (the Kinsay of Marco Polo).

"Oh, I say, isn't that Don Bonzo? By golly it is, isn't it," murmured Anil, as if beholding the god Vishnu in person. "I've heard an awful lot about him and his show, but I'm ashamed to say that I don't think I've ever actually seen it. I say, Judge, would you mind terribly if I . . . ?"

"But of course not," boomed the judge with maximum geniality. He settled himself into an armchair and tucked the fringes of his nightshirt into the pockets formed between his seated bulk and the arms of the chair. "My dear fellow. Have a seat. Let's watch some telly. A splendid notion."

The business at hand, whatever it was, receded as the two men, now on the best of terms, sat back in the warm congenial cosiness induced by the knowledge that they were wasting time in a manner pleasurable to both; thus ensconced, they enjoyed not only *Bonzo's Babes* but several of the commercials that interrupted the show (especially the one with the Mercedes and the dog with one blue eye and one brown, oh did they ever have a good chuckle at that one) and of course *The Bricklayer,* the universally respected Yorkshire TV action drama about an undercover house builder, itself succeeded by a repeat of the entirely admirable American detective series "Pete Martel, P. I." and, of course, leading into the lunchtime hour, the widely esteemed *An Nuacht,* featuring news of the Co. Killoyle Gaeltacht (population 342), an award-winning programme of which Anil, having no Irish, understand not a word; but, showing due consideration for a fellow telephile and guest under his roof (albeit uninvited, but we won't quibble) the judge translated, wearily, in a monotonous undertone.[3]

---

[3]Well, if you care: Last night at 1830 at the Anglers' Hall the An Cumann Gaelach held their annual board meeting and came up five quid short, with suspicion resting on Nuala, who'd just returned from a "business" trip to Brittany. Last Saturday night (the fifth) the Connemara traditionalists Slan Abhaile performed a programme of sixteen ancient Connacht airs and dances as well

It was well into the early afternoon by the time Anil leaned back, looked around, stretched, and came to his senses. Another American drama was on, this one, *Auden & Hitch,* featuring as prominently as the nose on a Bengali what Anil called a "carparkwallah," one of those johnnies in Yank films who like to hang about in parking garages. In this instance the blighter was wearing a white trenchcoat and staring at the camera for no apparent reason while a blond woman in a miniskirt tried to start one of those big old American Chevy Mustangs or something somewhere on a rooftop overlooking a flat boring place with a couple of tall buildings (was that what California really looked like?). . . .

"Now that's too silly," said Anil. "Eh, judge?" He looked over at his host, who was asleep, listing to starboard like an old fishing trawler run aground. Like surf pounding the reefs, the sound of a steady tidal ebb and flow energed from the judge's open mouth.

---

as their number-one hit "Slan go Foill" at Ballykilloran Orange Lodge, the Youth Centre being closed for repairs. On Sunday news came of the passing of longtime Gaeilge and local legend Seamas O Suilleabhain, who died at age eighty-six at Derrydingle Nursing Home in Crumstown after a long and distinguished illness. This account is from the *Crumstown Harpister:*

"Born in Killoyle, the nineteenth of nineteen or possibly twenty children ("I'm going for a record," his father Pedro was overheard to say one night at Mulligans' Bar, although he may have been referring to the number of rounds drunk but unpaid for by him), Seamas attended the North Killoyle Monastery Christian Brothers school on a Murphys' scholarship. There he soon showed his talent as an orator and beer drinker and became an adept midfield hurler, eventually playing for Killoyle County. While finishing school with the aid of another scholarship, this one from Guinness, he had several ardent love affairs with girls from the Loreto School across the park who were certainly old enough to know better. Seamas's first job, in 1936, was as a two-pound-a-week temporary Gaelic interpreter in the Ballydungarvan District Milk Board, which included the South Killoyle Gaeltacht, whose inhabitants, although fluent to a man, refused to speak English to milkmen. Seamas soon put a stop to that, then, inflamed by righteousness, set his sights on the law.

His nightshirt sprawled in a crumpled mass down his heaving bulk. Unexpectedly spindly legs tapered into hairy feet, sock-and-slipper-shod.

"Watch out!" bellowed the television. Anil yawned.

"I say, judge," he said. An aggressive snort-like snore was the only reply. Anil leaned over and touched the judge gently on the shoulder, then, remembering that this dozing old man, who so resembled, in slumber, Anil's long-dead *babau*—right down to that yellow nightshirt and those argyll socks, now that he thought about it— was the very same ruthless old bastard who'd betrayed him quite as much as Rama had betrayed Sita in the *Ramayana* and had then sent him off to his destiny with that fearful Spanish bugger—well, Basque was more like it, according to him; but the arrogance, the swaggering, the eyeballing, the thin lips: all those were what Anil, in his ignorance, liked to think of as typically Spanish. And the

---

He joined the Killoyle County Registrar's office, and the registrar, who was deaf, left all the court appearances to Seamas. He launched thereby his legal career, speaking only Irish, uncomprehended by all. He slipped away to lectures at University College Cork, where he took a degree in Botany Bay in 1938. Unemployed, he loafed round until 1946, when the possibilities of becoming a Gaelic bard suddenly struck him. The disadvantages promptly struck him even more forcibly, so he joined the government. His first job, from 1951 to 1954, was as a junior minister for the Western Bards, under de Valera. 'Dev would drive you mad,' he recalled. 'He'd keep on blinking at you and making silly sounds with his lips. In the end, I gave him up as a bad job.' After Seamas was called to Mulligan's Bar, he decided to leave the civil service 'on the toss of a coin,' and stood as a Fianna Fail candidate from Armagh, then as now under Loyalist occupation. Failing in that, he rushed into the mountain stronghold of the O Suilleabhains and declared his last stand, ignored by one and all—except for an experimental television crew, later known as RTE. When Seamas's impassioned features bobbed into view across the Free State's dozen or twenty television screens, a legend was born. The rest, including the Safari Park and the night he hosted the Oscars, is history. He spent his mature years hunting and riding in point-to-points. A lifelong groper, he never married."

fellow had slapped him about quite considerably, you know, not to mention clocking him on the noggin with that iron bar. One's first reaction had, of course (descendant of the Moghuls, after all, by golly) been to slug the bugger back, but that had turned out to be a bad idea, what with knuckledusters, coshes, flick-knives, fifth-belt Black Dan karate, and all that rubbish—and a genuine appetite for using these, a regular zest for sadism. That was the worst part; I mean, Anil Swain had probably met a few hundred people in his life, and in the course of walking up and down many a street and boulevard (Mumbai, Chennai, Delhi, Wolverhampton) had no doubt seen, or brushed against, or fleetingly desired, about half a million more, among whom, of course, there might well have been nasties like that Harry bloke, but it was all right if you never actually knew them, and he'd never *met* a sadist before. It was that fact that rankled, the actual certainty that such a one existed outside of Nazi movies and those Steve Kong best-sellers about chaps with green eyes and so on . . . no, it wasn't just the slapping about and the odd spot of torture the sod had so plainly enjoyed ("Now Gandhiji, a little electricity, just what so many of you don't have in India, well here's enough for a couple dozen of your quaint villages in Assam"). No, no, rather it was the certain knowledge (where before one had been able to forget about it, or pretend it was all Bollywood rubbish, or make-believe) that there was, out there, a man who enjoyed inflicting pain as others enjoyed a cup of tea, or a quick cuddle—well, it was nearly unbearable.

"Bloody hell," muttered Anil.

And there lay the man responsible, firing salvoes of sinusian vehemence.

"Wake up, you old horror," shouted Anil, stamping his feet. "Wake up, I say! Enough of this telly-watching and sleeping nonsense. We have business to discuss." With that, he boldly snatched up the remote and banished into oblivion a parking-garage scene from *Auden & Hitch* (not without fleeting reluctance, because the chap with the staring eyes seemed to be on the move at last, pretty understandable with that old Dodge Cadillac or whatever it was with that really rather nice-looking if a bit naff American bird in the miniskirt at the wheel bearing down on him at about 165 miles per—)

The judge awoke in the precise, sequential stages of the aging male of the species whose turf is challenged: eyelids suddenly wide open; full-body turn; malignant glare; upward body heave. But instead of launching an assault on Anil, as that party momentarily expected him to do, the judge stood swaying for a moment, then turned and charged out of the room, emitting noises not unlike those of a bull elephant in the fullness of *musth*. Anil watched him disappear into the voluminous chambers beyond the vestibule, from which echoes of his passage—loud slovenly footfalls, rattling crockery, wordless yammering interspersed with groans of agony and/or self- (and world-) loathing—slowly diminished into an uneasy silence. The house was still; then came the quarter-hour chimes of the Geneva carriage clock, so small and quiet that they seemed to be chiming inside Anil's head. They gently but firmly informed him that the first quarter hour after two post meridian had just expired and was now as extinct as the first quarter hour after two on, say, December 19, 1966, birthday of Anil Swain in the Sandrapore General Hospital (his parents being quite middle class enough for a hospital bed, thank you very much, even one with a beggar in the corner of the maternity ward—Dr. Abdussalam's brother-in-law Najiz the insurance salesman, it was rumoured, touching the expectant mothers for baksheesh)—or, for that matter, the same date (by an unexpected and unknown coincidence) in 1756, on which historic day the cornerstone of Squarestairs was laid, or the first or last quarter hour after six in the evening on the fifteenth of February 1758, the day of the manse's completion (delayed a month or two because of the absence of Sir Giles Wallop, the house's Anglo-English landlord, in the Low Countries fighting those damn froggies [or were they jerries?] again), or indeed as irrevocably,

irredeemably gone as the fresh dew-strung dawn of the first day
of the Moghul Empire, whenever that was . . .[4]

Anil was trembling violently, like an addict deprived of drugs.
Something inside him was half expecting the shot, but not the
deafening loudness of it that sent ripples through the subsequent
silence and left behind a watching and waiting zone of tense anticipation, as if another one were inevitable. None came, but in
the garden there came as in mimicry the soft explosion of a cloud
of small green birds ascending en masse from the top of an
unleaved autumn tree.

"Oh, son of Kunti," gasped Swain. "Oh, God. This is bad. Bad-
bad." He broke into a trot, then a full-tilt sprint, arms pumping
pistonically, hips swiveling balletically, eyelids blinking mechani-

---

[4]Well, I'm glad you asked. By an odd coincidence, the man beside me on
the upper deck of the 12A riding in to town this morning happened to be a
lecturer in history of the Indo-Dravidian Civilisations at Neo-Carthusian
Papal College in Ringsend (known for its B League hurling team) and, hard
upon consumption of the matutinal b-and-e and black tea, he said, adjusting
the long strand of grey hair that overlay his otherwise bald pate, he felt
strangely moved at the sight of me and therefore incapable of resisting the
temptation to recount to me the history of what he called "them dear owld
Moghuls, God bless 'em. Do you know that if it hadn't been for them we'd
never have mango chutney? Game ball." I shifted uneasily in my seat, attempting to banish him by dint of heavy outpourings of Capstan Full Strength
smoke, but it availed me nought but a gagging cough. He only snuggled closer,
with glittering eyes, and got properly started. "How areya? Arrah, God bless
the two eyes in yer head and the sights they behold. Mind if I smoke? Thanks,
I'll have one of yours. Oh, is that *your* pocket? Sorry. Ah, now that's better.
Now, as for them owld Moghuls, well as you already probably know the owld
dynasty was founded by a Chagatai Turkic article named Babar the Non-
Elephant (reigned 1526–1530), who was descended from that owld hoor
Tamerlane on his father's side and from Chagatai, second son of Genghis
Khan—you know that wan, they called him 'the roight bastard' all the way
from Peking to Constanti-bloody-nople—on his mother's side. Well, thrown
out of his ancestral playground over in Central Asia, like, by a ragtag bunch

cally. He dodged the expensive obstacles in his path—a humidor of Limoges porcelain, a flimsy escritoire of imitation mahogany, a mock-antique rocking chair—as deftly as if he were Cooper Lansky powering the puck toward the enemy goal line, and took the stairs three at a time. He slid backwards momentarily on the next-to-last step, which bore evidence of the recent too-hasty passage of a bulky body: stair-rail askew, loose carpet. The judge's argyll socks were for some reason discarded on the floor, one neatly lying directly behind the other, both pointing to the bedroom, like clues planted there to help investigators— and if so, they were redundant clues, for there lay the late master of the house, sprawled on his left side, a nasty bloody wound in his right temple, eyes as wide open as a dead fish's, and he was

---

of out-of-work Chinese archers—oh ya don't want to mess with them fellas, oh no, the hard men they are and no bloody mistake—Babar was in the rare old bit of a temper, you can believe it, stompin' about and swearin' like nobody's business and always at the wife to either make more chutney or drop her knickers. 'Aw shaddup,' said the missus, well you know how women are, doncha sir? Very female, most of 'em are, is what I've observed, and I've eyes in the front of me head, let me tell ya. Anyhow, owld Babar, right cheesed off at home, turned to India to satisfy his appetites and before you can say Mary Robinson there he was, in control of the Punjab, and in 1526 or thereabouts give or take he pissed all over the forces of the Delhi sultan Ibrahim Lodi at the First Battle of Panipat and would you credit it the following year he positively fucked up the arse, begging your pardon, the owld Rajput confederacy under Rana Sanga of Mewar, and as if that weren't enough in 1529 he defeated the Afghans of eastern Uttar bloody Pradesh, not to mention Bihar—and I'd rather not. Anyhow, by the time he snuffed it in 1530 there he was in charge of all bloomin' northern India from the Indus River on the west to Bihar on the east and from the Himalayas south to Gwalior, and your guess is as good as mine as to where the frig *that* is. By the by—you wouldn't have a spare bob or two, wouldya? Wouldn't you know I'd go and leave me cash at home on the dresser, you're welcome to look. Oh, is that *your* pocket again?" "My goodness!" I exclaimed in mock horror, "there's my stop!" Of course the moment he met Kathy the pleasure was all his.

just as dead as any fish Anil had ever seen, even the ones in Mangalore market (than which they get no deader).

Anil clapped a hand (left) to his mouth, repressing the gorge's urge to rise.

"Haila!"

Then, driven by an impulse to do exactly the opposite of what he should do, the silly wretch snatched the .22 out of the judge's dead hand, which had not yet stiffened into rigor mortis—it having been only about four minutes since the hand's proprietor had expired, after all—and waved it about like some idiot actor in a movie, entertaining his reflection in the dressing mirror opposite . . . then, of course, reality collapsed on top of him all at once, reminding him of his own recent scrapes and how it would look if he, Anil Swain, immigrant underemployed waiter from Sandrapore, India—already under deep suspicion (1) for the Emerald Mats caper, (2) for the Soldiers of Brian O'Nolan affair, and (3) on general principles—were discovered toting a gun in the house of a dead judge whom he had recently been threatening telephonically (they had recordings, oh, he was sure of that, oh, everything had been tapped, there were probably bugs everywhere, even now).

He tossed away the weapon (but not before wiping it hastily and distastefully on the counterpane, which overlay the judge's bare legs in ghoulish mimicry of a coy pinup pose), then pure panic impelled him out of the room, down the stairs, and out of the house. He paused on the top of the steps outside the front door, as if expecting (as indeed he was, quite consciously) a committee of witnesses and accusers: Nobody. Not a sausage. Not even a bird. He glanced about again and ran briskly down the drive and into the street and plunged into his car, a reluctant starter at the best of times; now, of course, when it was most needed, it simply cleared its throat a few times, shuddered, coughed discreetly, and fell silent with the faintest ghost of a moan.

"Haila!" screamed Anil. "Ayla! *Fucker!"*

Through the ill-kempt hedge of Squarestairs a metallic gleam caught his eye: the judge's motor, a pearl-gray 1997 Jocelyn Crannog GTX, a nice-looking car right enough, low and swoopy— although Anil, not himself an actual car guy, had no way of knowing that the Jocelyn was Irish-made and that it boasted not only aluminium heads and sixteen valves but a brake repair history as troubled as the history of the island of its manufacture. No, to our Indian protagonist, it was enough that it looked a dashed sight nicer than his old Escort, or the rubbishy Hindustans and Marutis he'd grown up with.

In any event, time was a-wasting.

"Bloody time to get out of here," muttered Anil, dismounting from his untrustworthy (and possibly, like the judge, expired) steed. Dimly suspecting celestial cameras to be filming his every move for the future amusement of the gods, he half-trotted, half-walked briskly (not wishing to do a flat-out sprint and thereby attract the eye of any member of the Gardai Siochana, or the military or legal professions, or indeed the general public, who might be passing) back to Squarestairs and crossed the drive with a maddeningly loud crunch-crunch of footsteps—and why, since he knew the judge was dead and the house was otherwise empty, did he have an almost overwhelming feeling (he didn't look, not daring) of being watched from one of the upstairs windows? He hadn't felt that way when he'd first walked up the drive—when the judge was still among the living and therefore eminently capable of standing at a window and looking out . . . ?

Well, he peeked. And there was nothing there, except the smooth reflection of scudding clouds. But still.

And why did he feel so guilty, as if he'd bumped off the old sod himself? He had to slow down momentarily and remind himself with schoomasterly sternness—"Now listen here, Swainji"— that he'd had nothing to do with the judge's extinction.

"So get that out of your foolish head right now, you *Sulemani Keeda!*"

He arrived at the car. Lucky for him, the silly old (*dead*) judge had left his keys in the ignition. The pistons in their six cylinders, being of German origin,[5] fired smoothly and willingly, and the rig was an automatic, which obviated fussing about (always liked the idea, mused Anil in the space of one or two split seconds, much more convenient than grinding the clutch and my teeth at the same time), so they were down the drive and out the front gate in no bloody time at all, flat.

Then it was, in his state of quivering panic with a fine sheen of brow-sweat (despite the chill in the air) that Anil discovered the intrinsic risk of never going on exploratory Sunday drives just to suss out the environs. So narrow was his normal daily routine— flat to restaurant, restaurant to flat, once a year drive to Dublin for dinner with the Roybals—that almost all of central Killoyle between Brendan Behan Avenue and King Idris Drive remained terra incognita. Where was he going? Again, blind faith in the sons and daughters of Vishnu guided him—and memories of Rashmi, the living avatar of Lakshmi (or was it Parvati? No, that was Rubina). Unexpected roundabouts slowed his progress, as did a traffic light or two, and damn and blast, it was the middle of the bloody afternoon and half the town was out and about—except down by the docks, now there was a dicey area he'd never really checked out—hard left at the Strand, then a quick sprint (needle hovering between fifty and sixty; lucky there weren't any strollers on this rather subpar day) along the promenade, then another red light and an impulsive right turn, then left, and presto he was fly-

---

[5]Hang on a sec, I just looked this up . . . here we are. Made by Rowohlt G.m.b.H. of Hochgroßvaterstadt, Bavaria, tuned by master engineer Herr Memminger of Memmingen to produce the galloping potential of an impressive 161 horses, as per the Deutsche Industrie Normen (DIN), with a cubic engine capacity of some three litres. The engine's fine, in other words; it's just the bodywork that tends to give out, being made on the island of saints and sculleries and all.

ing down Bedstead Lane with its array of quaint groggeries and pill shops (And I say, was that a prossie? Well if she wasn't, she damned well looked like it with those fishnet stockings and bum half hanging out of her miniskirt), but whoops, there didn't appear to be any way out, and there he went again across the promenade, near missing a bus, and then straight down a long sloping road between two walls that turned out not to be a road at all, actually, but a bloody boat ramp don't you know, and what happened to the brakes nothing's happening nothing at all. *I've no bloody brakes* oh Vishnu oh Jesus oh God oh whoever or whatever too late too late the brakes are fucked and so am I and *wham* . . .

He hit the water.

Before thought processes could rouse themselves to collate this overabundance of external stimuli, there he was, instinct taking over, struggling to free himself from the damned seat belt, struggling with unfamiliar window controls to open the window and/ or door . . .

"*Chaayla*!!! Help!!!!"

The car rocked and rolled. A fishing boat of some kind was bobbing up and down a little way off. Burly amusement was evident in the stance and gestures of the crew. One waved. Others turned away, shoulders heaving.

"Granted, I must look quite ridiculous," self-exclaimed Anil, "but the least the bastards could do is call someone on their mobiles. Ah," he amended, as that was precisely what appeared to be happening: prawn fishermen with mobile phones, a brave new world indeed. Not that they seemed in any great hurry; quite the opposite, in fact. It was astonishing how many crew members the little fishing boat seemed to have—five, six, seven, eight, ten at least, or more—twelve, thirteen, fourteen? As he counted the different sets of heads and shoulders on the fishing boat's deck, Anil slowly realized that he was making these protracted and unhurried observations because the car had settled down to a gentle listing from side to side—and, more surprisingly, there was

sufficient ambient dryness inside the car to afford him the leisure of his thoughts. Indeed, the car was quite dry inside and no
water was coming in anywhere. In other words, it was floating
across the calm waters of Killoyle Harbour as buoyantly as a
fellucah, or water buoy (or waterboy).

"Fuck me," said Anil, with uncharacteristic vehemence. "Well,
you know," addressing himself again, "I'd much rather this than
swim." (No swimmer he, apart from the odd lesson at the
Sandrapore Baths.) "Oh, most definitely. By gosh, yes."

So he folded his arms and sat back comfortably and awaited
developments as the car floated gently about. One advantage of
this latest absurdity was that he had quite forgotten about the
judge, Rubina, and (corollary to this last) Rashmi; and even the
dear old Koh-I-Noor was almost entirely absent from his
thoughts, except as the vague backdrop to a scenario wherein
his life would have dignity and purpose.

27

"Five hundred grand and not a penny more."

"Bugger that, you flaming ballocks you bugger you *ahack ahack ahack* himmmssadagadad *ahack*. Is that your final offer, you ballocks?"

Eileen was adamant, and her weapons were three:

1. Money;
2. Mascara;
3. Monologues.

1. MONEY

Actually Jimmie's, of course—or, to be precise, the parent company's, Big Jimmie's PLC—but it was hers to all intents and purposes; after all, she was the official CFO. Jimmie, the nominal CEO, "couldnae be bothered" and had signed over finanicial authority to her.

"Aye, I quite like the brass, hen," as he said, "but see them office hours? They're murder, so they are."

So he was back in the Orkneys, fishing on wild high seas with his mates Jock and Hamish from Kirkcaldy. Oh, how she wished she were with him, them, the man, the men! But, despite the ever-present danger of the heaving into view of her ex-husband Mick's puffy mug, containing as it did those pale baleful eyes, Eileen had stayed on in Killoyle because there were opportunities there, she knew which rocks to turn over, and under one of them she found the many-legged "investors" from the North, who in view of recent developments had decided to pull out without shooting anyone, or breaking anyone's knees ("nice of youse," commented Eileen, boldly, receiving an icy wink in reply) and, indeed, sold up their meagre interest without a murmur; and under another, smaller rock she came upon one Victor Hasdrubal-Scott, who (illicitly, during working hours, tut-tut) had created an amazing old newspapers web site, where somehow he'd managed not only to have consecutive issues of the same paper running for, say, thirty years (the *Dependent*, for instance, from the Emergency and Dev's dramas straight through to the attorney general belowstairs-buggery scandal of the Haughey years, not missing a single crisis on the suburban bus lines or day at the races) but also side-by-side issues of different journals covering the same topic; for example, the 1991 photo finish at Leopardstown as seen by the *Pink 'Un*, the *Hurling Addict, Own Goal*, the *Punter's Press*, and various others, in which Spanish Corvette's victory-by-a-nose was called vociferously into question and ultimately overturned in favour of Katie's Vineyard, the two-year-old filly from Kildare; also the Berlin Airlift from Stalin's perspective (he was deeply hurt, poor man), Cyprus as seen by Grivas (the British already have too many islands, they don't need another—hear, hear to that), Desert Storm (half mounted and part-executed by nonsmoking, teetotaling, churchgoing Yanks in direct opposition to the hard-smoking heavy-drinking rougher and readier Rough Riders of generations past), and so on. When Eileen, in her room at the Spurdorgan Vacation Inn (queen-sized bedroom and dining area en suite, view of the spire of Laddi's Disco), skimming along the unruffled surface of Victor's web page (he'd invited her over to his place, assuring her—spluttering unwholesomely against a background, whether real or recorded she couldn't say, of soft reports and strange cries, as of someone being gently slapped—that his wife would be there; but the hairs on Eileen's neck were gathering themselves up, so she thought better of it), came upon her own divorce notice in the Sunday *Clarion* ("Divroced [*sic*]: Eileen and Michael Greek [*sic*]"), she decided, after a short consultation with Mr. Panatella, her broker in Leeds, to lay out the nicker.

"After all, if I can find myself there, millions of others will be able to do the same," she shrilled over the phone to Mr. Panatella who, sensibly, was gently replacing his receiver on its cradle (see 3. below). In any event, with Victor, who'd had about enough of NaughtyBoy Graphics, the process was miraculously simple, once Eileen wrote out the sum: € 500,000. . . .

"Not sterling? Ahemsadad. Bugger off, ya ballocks."

"Take it or leave it."

"Well. That many zeroes, really?" sniffed the old sage. "Lemme see, one, two, three, four, five . . . ah, I reckon it'll do."

An explosive, welkin-ringing fit of coughing sealed the deal.

2. MASCARA

This worked, too, although it could be a bit of a hit-and-miss proposition, especially if applied with an excessively heavy hand, and depending on the target male's sexual tendencies, maturity, man-of-the-worldliness and inclination to respond positively to being fawned over and/or pawed by a sexually depraved middle-aged woman; actually, many were the unexpected ones who were so inclined, Victor Hasdrubal-Scott among them (although *his* inclinations were obvious from the start, what with his clumsy allusions to "spiked heels" and "riding crops, hee hee hee" and of course "stockings," every two minutes or so). Heavily applied, with purplish-rainbow hues, the mascara (Suetonius Nights by Baroness Machiavelli) made Eileen look a bit like (she fancied) a fortyish version of Fanny Steptoe, the seventeen-year-old pop phenomenon ("Juice for the Jackals," "Hip Hop Hooley," "Bigger

Breasts 'n' Mine") and could therefore ease the way through difficult negotiations—with the invaluable assistance of a bit of ju-
dicious eyelash-batting, lip-puckering, and bottom-squirming, of
course. Oddly, it actually worked from time to time, never more
so than with Jimmie, who (that first day in Edinburgh's Robert
Adam Chambers on Chambers Street) had been scrambling for
her bod with a blank canine expression in his eyes even before
she'd launched upon what was the vital and frequently conclusive part of her three-sided approach to business deals:

3. THE MONOLOGUE

Unlike many bores, who suffer others only as handy chamber pots
into which to direct the urgent stream of their own verbal piss,
Eileen was keenly aware of the extent to which she caused ennui
in her fellow man and woman and adjusted the intensity of her
blathering accordingly. It had worked a charm with Mick, for
instance, and one or two other unlikely lads whom she'd had no
luck in seeing off by more conventional means—slamming doors,
making faces, leaving monosyllabic messages on Post-its—but
who'd scarpered double quick when the honeyed drone of her
voice had entered, say, its thirtieth uninterrupted minute. More
importantly, this trick, cunningly applied, had won over, or in-
timidated, not a few businessmen, especially combined, paradoxically, with **2.** (see above).

  "They want a shag but they don't want to sit through an entire
peroration on the subject of Eileen McCreek's opinions of modern Irish economic policies or Greek holiday destinations, you
see," as she confided to her friend Libbie McBlair, staff psychia-
trist of the Dungarvan Ballet Company. "So they give me what I
want and I might give them a little of whatever they want, however unseemly."

  "Yuck," said Libbie, left pinkie erect as she imbibed Earl Grey
and mentally sketched brief longing thoughts of Vsevoyod, the

unshaven, mercurial, unshacked-up gypsy dancer from Kazan (or was it Kazakhstan?) . . .

In the end, then, Victor sold up, and out, and joyfully went in to Denny's office one gay grey morning, cheque in hand.

"You see this?" He waved the cheque under Denny's nose. "It's my ticket out of here"—here he paused at some length to describe in wordless barking sounds the extent to which congestion had risen in his bronchia during the previous night (Denny meanwhile caressed his mobile and stared inquiringly)—"you ahagsadagsadags ahack."

"Hey, well, I hope for your sake it clears, Vic," said Denny. "Because I'd say you just burned your bridges."

"Of course it'll clear, you hack ahack ballocks ahack ahem."

Victor was about to shout more abuse and taunt the man with the elaborate deception of the oldnewspapers.com web site, now a hundred pages strong, that he'd painstakingly built over several nights of "overtime" and that was now worth a cool half mil to somebody—but he remembered Mick McCreek's little crisis, and for once in his life . . .

He shut the frig up.

But not for long. With five hundred large in the bank, the first thing he saw was his way out of marriage. Accordingly, he made the appropriate legal phone calls, dreading Sheila's persistent clinging all the while; but, fortunately for him, Sheila's affair with that Mr. Thomson, long on the back burner, had resumed pride of place on the front end of the range and was simmering merrily away under everybody's noses once again, affording Victor the ideal reason for requesting separation, sequestration of mutual holdings, and divorce. Sheila protested mildly, nostalgically revisiting the Victor-loving days of yore; but Victor at his best (which wasn't very good, let's be honest) had never spun her round on her tiptoes, or taken her for a fast drive down the Corniche at Juan-les-Pins, or taught her how to dance the tango; and Mr. Thomson had done all these things, and what was more—

unlike Victor, who never went anywhere—he made regular business trips to New York and Buenos Aires, and guess who was going with him on his next one? *Yesss!* Wasn't she the lucky girl!

So Sheila complied and was stashed comfortably away with her Mr. T. in the cupboard of life's memories, good and bad. Victor's parting words to his wife—"Good-bye Victor," tearfully bade she, clinging to impassive Mr. Thomson, who waved curtly with a snappy "Bye sport"—were indicative of the extent and depth of his sentimentality.

"Good feckin' riddance to the pair of yiz ballocks."

Victor then called on his cousin Shoots, who had barely recovered from that rainy night when the Indian and the other foreigner came calling. In fact, he was still in his dressing gown, and had hardly dared venture outdoors since that dreadful night—well, maybe once, a quick dash over to the just-closed Orinoco and up to Vin's Video Van: *Long Legs, Short Words,* with Bobby Lee Irwin and that upcoming sexpot Arnette Nichon—oh, and *El Kid,* with Sonia Lloret—but Shoots was always too sensitive to be exposed to the full force of life's aberrations, poor fella. Vic confidently took charge, any lingering doubts as to his ability to do so dispelled promptly by the thought of half a million quid in the bank.

"Arrah, yer a sad old case, arencha, Shoots? Hangsadang. An old ballocks and no mistake. What are we going to do with you?"

Answering his own question, Victor, doing (as he thought) the right thing for once, invited his cousin to apply for the post of his, Victor's valet, chef, driver, handyman, and general factotum.

"Your valet?" Shoots was thunderstruck, in a very persuasive red-faced fashion, especially when combined with him drawing himself up to his full height (five-foot eleven). "Help you on with your moth-eaten old pullovers and corduroys? You're joking. You'll be asking me to wipe your arse next."

"No, I can manage that. Just keep the old motor in good running nick and fix up the house."

More expostulations followed, interlaced with vivid slurs on Victor's character—after all, Shoots did have a residual modicum of masculine pride; but in the end money abolished all scruples, as it will, and the deal was struck. Victor moved out of his, or rather Sheila's, old house into Shoots's house in Crumstown with loud instructions to have the first floor renovated "as per that telly program, you know, the one with the Yank colleen . . ."

"You mean, *At Home with Marcia Lewis?*"

"Aye. That ballocks. And see that you get in plenty of newspapers, as well, only the best, mind. The *Argus, Saturday Silence,* the *Tipperary Consitution, Le Monde.* Computers, too. We'll need lots of memory for the new Wittgenstein IV, I don't know if you've heard about it, next best thing to being there in person during the Wittgenstein-Popper debate—ahack. But that's not the only reason I want the state-of-the-art; don't imagine for a sec I'll be letting that ballocky streel of a woman get away with me old newspapers for good, like. Oh, no. I'm going to build a bigger and better web site and drive her out of the business, the fuckin' wee ballocks of a woman she is, ahack ahack ahansadagadad."

Such was the essence of Victor's endless unseen scheming when Eileen (and poor Jimmie, did he but know) took over as owner and director of Victorhasdrubalscottsoldnewspapers.com, freshly rechristened BigJimmiesUniversalNews.com, "the web's biggest worldwide newspaper resource from then till now and beyond." Eileen promptly set about enlisting sponsors and advertisers, deploying the combined elements of her standard tactics (the three *m*s) plus intimidation and working the phones day and night. Of course, until hirelings were hired, cowed, and duly underpaid prior to a lifetime's exploitation, she had also to collect, file, and collate news items; after all, the news, as many a banal-minded newsman (or woman) has pointed out, never sleeps.

Actually, one of the first items to come over the wires after Eileen took over was the bit of an eye-opener from France,

picked up by various of the select group of provincial Irish or-
gans Victor had favoured (and which Eileen was determined to
phase out in favour of greater cookery coverage from London
and Los Angeles). The second-page header in the *Offaly and
Laois Yeoman* was fairly typical: "Belfastman Found Dead on
Bizarritz Beach."

There followed a short article in which the news content was
as sparse as the general knowledge of the average Erse reading
public or its journalistic informants as to the precise location of
Bizarritz, which the article (taken from the All-Irish Union Press
Syndicate) hesitantly identified as "one of the premier resorts of
the French Bisque [*sic*] Country." Then, if the reader persevered,
resisting the lure of the sports or entertainment pages,[1] reading
keenly between the lines he or she would glean the following facts,
in no particular order: that a body had washed onto the sandy
strand of the resort city one fine late October morning (we can

---

[1]So hard to do, eh? Why, once I was all set to read a most informative, indeed crucial, article on the state of the average Irishman's investments in
overseas oil-drilling ventures—that would include me, half my manager's
pension went into those Brunei shares—but my eye was caught at the last
moment by an interview in the ShowBiz section with the Bonze of the Stars,
one Slambang Sihanouk, Buddhist monk, and confidant (and, some say, more)
to the likes of Jill-Jolie Richards, Jessica Gomez, Millie McKeown, and Judd
Carstairs, to name but a few. "Smile," was the sage's advice. "Even when I am
asleep I make sure I am smiling. And make regular movements with the bowels.
But always smile." Oddly, in the accompanying photgraph he was scowling,
possibly because he was shown leaving a disco in West Hollywood with one
arm around the ample hips of Jessica Gomez . . . anyway, thanks to that rubbish I missed out completely on the financial news and the one article that
would have told me to sell up and get out *now* because the Brunei bubble was
about to burst—as it did, the next week, which is why I'm stuck here, with
these lousy moth-eaten bedsheets and the eternal smell of chips in grease a-
frying. Still, there's always Penny, and another day . . . and you're probably
stuck in the midst of an identical haimes, convinced that you're different from
the rest of them punters. Well, good luck, pardner.

supply the telling detail: the mingled scents of French breakfast—
grand crème, tartine beurrée, croissants au chocolat—and diesel fumes,
the melancholy crimson of sunrise on the sea, the mewing cries
of breakfast-seeking gulls aloft); that small children working on
their sand castles had been startled, even appalled, at the sight of
the recumbent bulk (again, we can add the odd but significant
trifle: covered in strands of seaweed across which tiny crustaceans
skittered, the corpse not fully human-looking at first, or indeed
second, glance, its bloatedness and clayey-green hue lending it
the horrible air of some poorly manufactured effigy, one arm
mechanically flopping back and forth in sympathy with the alternating inwardness and outwardness of the tide); that the
Gendarmerie had provisionally identified the body as that of an
Irlandais du Nord, provenant de Belfast, possibly associated with
"armies of the terrorist Republicans," this conjecture based on
"police instinct" and the label on the defunct's jacket from
Clarkeson & Lowes of 485 Antrim Road, Belfast, Clothiers
(gentlemen's retail); that the British Consul in Bordeaux had been
informed; that the body bore, barely visible on its left shoulder, a
tattoo depicting a flower; that the local gendarmerie was acting
on the direct orders of the newly appointed prime minister,
Jacques Neckar, who swore at his first press conference "to strike
at terrorists wherever they rear their ugly heads" and who cited
approvingly the instant support he had received from the newly
confirmed British ambassador, Sir Carl Marcks; and that, finally,
the investigation was ongoing, with the objective of positively
identifying the dead man before the week was out. . . .

This news item, picked up in Killoyle by the _Clarion,_ had at
least two readers locally who had no need of awaiting the
Gendarmerie's verdict.

"Fuck me, it's McArdle," said Superintendent Talbott, reaching for his reading glasses over the luxuriantly prone body of
Major Rashmi Vishnapuram. She groaned in her clove-scented
semiwaking dreams (Elephanta, the Gateway of India, the Mumbai

Palace where she'd met Salman, the dark woods of Kashmir) as Talbott unfolded the newspaper with a businesslike clatter.

"Clarkeson and Lowes, eh? Notorious Rah outfitters, them boys. And aha! This does it. Have a listen to this, acushla. 'The body bore the tattoo of a small flower on the left shoulder.' Well, that's conclusive, isn't it?"

Major Vishnapuram wished he would be quiet and leave her to her dreams of India, but then she remembered that she would be on a plane to India within the week and would therefore be able to revisit in person all those dreamy places; so she sat up, alluringly tousled, and reached yawningly for wakefulness.

"I'm not with you, Super dear," she said. "Conclusive of what?"

Superintendent Talbott looked down at her through his half-moon reading glasses. On his face was an expression composed in equal parts of desire, affection, and awkwardness, each one of which she read as clearly as if they'd been inscribed in stencilled letters three feet high. It made her smile; how easy chaps were.

"Well," said the super, "when your standard-issue spotty gun-toting hooligan from the Falls or Andersonstown joins up, he's subjected to a quite rigourous series of loyalty tests, you see, along with the basic training and so on; that is, you know, detonation science, carrying weights about, wiring baby carriages, transporting plastique, and whatnot (not to mention 101 fun and easy uses for liquid fertilizer). And once he's reckoned to be a likely lad he gets a tattoo of the Easter Lily on his left shoulder if he's right-handed and vice-versa if he's a southpaw. With me?"

"So the dead man was in the Belfast Brigade."

"So the dead man's McArdle, not that fearful chancer Finn, is what I'm saying. Finn was never a real Rah man, just a malevolent toy soldier. Odd thing is, it looks very much as if he was the one who won the duel. Looks like you can call off the search for one of our fugitives, anyhow."

"Unless a third party killed them both and they just haven't found Finn's body yet."

The super looked momentarily aghast, then slowly nodded. "Right y'are, darlin.' Could be that way. It could indeed."

He brooded momentarily; then lust took over.

Meanwhile, down the street Pats Bewley was in his kitchen vigorously stirring juvenile quantities of sugar into a mug of tea with one hand and browsing the news with the other, until—you guessed it.

"Oh, shite," he said. "It's Big Martin."

So that's what Finn's crazed phone message had been about.

He put the mug down and gazed thoughtfully through the lace curtains that covered the lower pane of the kitchen window at the empty breeze-blown clothesline in his back garden. Gazing back from the first floor of the house next door was the pallid face of Irmgard, slightly retarded daughter of Herr Beuler, German commercial traveler and honorary consul of the Bundesrepublik on the Southeast coast. Herr B. was a decent, God-fearing man, so he was, albeit a Prod, as well as a Jerry, of course; and Pats had long since reconciled himself to the daily nuisance of having Irmgard's blank visage watch him, especially in the kitchen, into which, from her vantage point, she had an uninterrupted view of Pats's daily infusions of lard-spattered saucepan scrapings and heapings of frozen chips straight from the packet.

He'd considered, briefly, having her exorcised, and to that end had indeed gone so far as to consult the late Father Doyle of the former St. Oinsias Church, but both had reluctantly concluded that she probably was actually a retard.

He waved. She continued to stare, motionless.

But never mind Irmgard. This was dramatic news. Bad news, too. Quite bad.

Or was it?

"McArdle's snuffed it, eh," he muttered to himself. "Ouch."

A Basque hit, for sure. That Harry article. Subcomandante whatever it was. His signature was all over it, or rather his outfit, the Euskal Herria; oh, they loved dumping the old carcass in the briny, so they did. Easier to hide things and it made for good news copy, bodies washing up on the beach and whatnot. And not having a bullet hole—them fellas always preferred a touch of the garotte, or a carpenter's awl in the left temple.

Ouch. Even if McArdle was a right bastard. *Ouch.*

As for Finn, the old fool, Pats's heart went out to him (well, almost), because unless his corpse was scheduled by the tides to wash ashore as well this meant that he was still alive but eternally in debt to the ETA, and if Pats had the choice between these two particular fates he wasn't entirely sure he wouldn't take McArdle's. . . .

So the big fella was dead.

"Well well well well well well well well well."

Not that McArdle wouldn't be missed, mused Pats—and not only by Mrs. McArdle and the bairns. No, he'd had a few loyal fans here and there. Still, there wouldn't be any real ructions, reckoned Bewley. Something of a barney would be going on just now, anyway, what with the recent arrests and the Soldiers shutting down ops; but it wasn't as if Pats hadn't other connections elsewhere up North, not as if his life and well-being had depended on bloody Martin McArdle, for God's sake, only the big fella's exiting stage left at this juncture made things a touch more difficult, there was no getting around that—unless Pats staged a comeback and took charge himself. . . .

"There's an idea, lad," he murmured to himself.

Yes, he'd have to take steps personally. It might indeed be time to come out of hiding completely and revive the old outfit, the old name, the old accounts. He'd have to track down the "Gang of Five"—Paddy "Underfed" Colley, Seamus "Steps" Flanagan, Eddie "Two-Teeth" Hanrahan, Turlow "The Mechanic" Crowe, and Malachi "Griddle" McKing, all in Dublin, save "Steps" who was in Bradford working as a sound-stage technician at Yorkshire TV, last he'd heard. Then, assuming those boys were still alive, or *compos mentis,* or willing—or out of chokey—it would be a matter, and not a simple one, Pats reminded himself, of reclaiming what was rightfully still his, viz. the old command up in Dundalk, the cache of AK-47s and Katyushas he'd never told a living soul about (under the statue of St. Patrick on the high hill of Tara no less, a brilliant stroke if he said so himself), and the hard evidence (letters, photographs, painstakingly drawn maps) linking the lads to that Indian plane explosion over the Atlantic (pity the Indian intelligence agent they'd been after, whoever he was, had taken an earlier flight, but you can't have an omelette). Aye, it was time to wind up this phase. Pats Bewley was ready.

"I'm ready, so."

He only hoped the others were, too. He was in reasonably good nick for his age, after all. He never smoked or drank, and as for sex, well he'd not completely sussed that end of things out, after all he was Irish, wasn't he, of a certain generation . . . ? He had a nature walk every Saturday, he bowled a bit, and played golf. But what were those other fellas like, after all these years (since the bombing: three and a bit)? Paunchy? Punchy, like Turlow? Alcoholic (Steps and Griddle had certainly been heading that way)? Ill? Dead?

And they'd be needing a new name, new cover. No more of that "Soldiers of Brian O'Nolan" or "Immaculate IRA" shite. And definitely no more bloodthirsty librarians as front men. No, now it was time for the real business.

He folded the paper. There was one way to find out how the lads were doing. He went into the hallway and picked up the phone, which he then addressed in rapid, strident, fluent Irish[2]

---

[2]Fluent? Hang on a sec, isn't he the one who . . . ? Right enough, I'm with you, Francis me man. *Mutatis mutandis,* as they say.

for a few minutes. Then he withdrew upstairs and returned twenty minutes later carrying a duffel bag and wearing a shirt with cross-hatch pattern, a Trinity College necktie, and a blue down anorak, all civilian camouflage purloined from that eejit Finn just after the raid. He'd look like a Yank tourist, he reckoned.

"Cheerio, Irmgard." Pats waved as he stepped out of his front door. The girl had moved to the bay window in front and was still staring at him. "Cheerio. I'm off." Suddenly Irmgard's face collapsed and through the window Pats could hear roars of distress.

"Bloody hell, girl," he muttered, getting into his car, a silver Jocelyn Asphodel (yes, the very same jeep Mick McCreek had banged up, and a fine wee motor it was, but too bloomin' conspicuous, Pats thought; he'd have to lose it somewhere between here and the greater Dundalk area). "No need to carry on like that."

But still Irmgard roared, and the last glimpse Pats Bewley had in his car's wing mirrors as he drove off was of her pale moon of a face creased in anguish, tears (as he imagined) streaking down her face like snail trails on your driveway after the rain.

28

Well, here I am again, said Anil to himself as he was led into the jail. *Same old posters, same old stink.* Cries as of baboons in heat arose from the cells. *Same old morons.*

"Hoy!"

"A nigger!"

"Nah, dat's no nigger boy, dat's a curry-atin' Pakistani Injun die-rect from Calcutta."

"Waiter! Where's my tikka wrap?"

"Bugger that, Dermot, mine's a pint of Murphy's."

And the like.

Anil's acquaintance from his previous visit, the young guard with the Pakistani ex-fiancée, had, according to his older and less sympathetic successor, ended up marrying his "Paki gell, one o' yours, yeah" after all, so there was nothing in the place now for Anil Swain except stagnation, worry, and gloom. One or two of the inmates were leftovers from before, but many were relatively recent arrivals, and most of that lot were your common or garden wasters, regular customers at the Employment Exchange as well as jolly johnnies from the just-concluded Pint-Pulling Olympiad—an exegesis of squalor par excellence, as it turned out, having closed with champions named and prize pub[1]

---

[1] I was in on that, in the first of my dual capacities. First, using the old blindfold-and-index-finger technique, they (that is, the Awards Committee, con-

and trophies awarded but, much to the chagrin of Spudorgan Vacation Inn management, a cool fifty grand in property damage, excluding that caused by the rocket attack. Many of those responsible for the overturned brewing vats and smashed acreage of pint glasses and frosted bar mirrors were Anil's neighbours and cellmates.

"What're you in for, Abdul? Snake charmin' without a licence?"

"Eh! Where's yer turban?"

Anil maintained a rigorous silence. Nabbed for car theft and endangering others' welfare ("I mean, he's Indian, isn't he, well, they're terrible men for nicking things and setting people on fire,

---

sisting of: (1) the Rev. Granville Perker, D. Phil., spiritual adviser to Sir Phineas Finnegan, owner of Strong Liquors and Fortified Wines Worldwide, PLC; (2) Tony MacNamara, host of *Good Boy! Fetch! Sit! Want Your Walkies? Where's Your Lead, Then?* on RTE11; (3) Claudine Futtock, the model; and (4) Murphy, no less—yes, he was back, but believe you me I gave him the old cold shoulder, right enough), found Meagher's Bar in Westmeath in the phone directory under "Real Estate," so we tried to give it away before Barrabas X. Meagher, the publican, got wind of the whole affair, but old Meagher, not having after all been apprised telephonically, epistolarily, or via any other means of communication, objected in no uncertain terms (having logged in just in time to Awardsworld.com to discover his own wee pub being handed off by strangers) and went so far as to tell them to "stuff it" in a nasal baritone hoarsened by years of snuff-taking. Then, with the help of the phone directory, the committee (sans Claudine, who had an engagement in Livorno) found a pair of little-known establishments out Crumstown way, one of which, the Spittoon, was, as it turned out, nothing more than a single standing wall, consequent to a misfired practice missile from nearby overzealous patriots (is there any other kind?); but the other place (known locally as "De Udder Place (hic),"), the dear old Orinoco, had coincidentally just come onto the market after rather sudden closure by agents of the Special Forces. Upshot: One James Hynes, a deep thinker and divine from Ballybigrapids, county Laois, was awarded the place, where he now lives, alone, above the remains of the bar, with a pair of old cats. Some say he's contemplating suicide; others aver that he's on the verge of a major (or minor) breakthrough. Stay tuned.

aren't they, surely to God they're at it morning, noon, and night," in the words of learned counsel for the prosecution) but not implicated in the judge's death, as several suicide Post-it notes, written in legal sequence, signed, dated, and notarised, had been discovered adhering to various writing desks, wardrobes, and cupboards throughout Squarestairs, each note containing a countdown to the final moment: "Wednesday the 15th, only two days to go"; "Thursday the 16th, self-execution eve"; "Friday the 17th, well this is it, after about 1430 hours the world won't have old Jerry O'Mallet to kick around anymore";—he had been sentenced to a year and a day without the option, but following the advice of his legal representative Mary Rose Ryan, heiress absolute to the portfolios and prestige of O'Mallet and O'Mallet, Solicitors-at-Law, he was hoping against hope for deliverance from an unexpected quarter: Veronica and Ricky Goone-Lake, sister and brother-in-law of the late Fergus Goone. They had jointly filed a wrongful inheritance lawsuit against Emerald Mats PLC and their new owners Big Jimmie's Worldwide and had listed Anil as a possible codefendant.

"Just leave it to me," said Ms. Ryan, coolly contemplating her fingernails. "You won't be in there longer than five days, I promise."

I bloody well hope not, mused Anil, then ten days later gave up. By that time Rubina had dropped by. Relations between once-adoring husband and wife were somewhat frosty.

"I don't know, Uncle. I don't know. Here you are in the clink again. Oh, you're a silly old *gangaram*, aren't you."

"You can say that twice, Auntie."

Rubina was working at Emerald Mats.

"Don't let them cheat you, now."

"They're not cheating me. I quite enjoy it. And they're very nice, not like those bints in Wolverhampton. I'm going out with a couple of them tonight to play bridge."

"As long as it's not some good-looking *chikna*-chap or racing-car bloke or whatever." Anil rubbed his nose vigorously, prepa-

ratory to awkwardly inquiring (speaking of good looks and all)
whether Rashmi . . . ?

"She's gone back to India," said Rubina curtly. "And there she
can stay."

"Well she did save my skin, Auntie. You might bear that in
mind."

"And all you saw after that in your mind was her skin. And she's
your cousin, for goodness' sake. Anyway, what was the point of
her saving your life if all you can do is get yourself thrown into
jail again? Oh, *haila.*"

She left Anil with his thoughts and desolation.

Heels cooling well, over the next day or so he lay on his bunk
and stared at the ceiling. Occasionally, when the man's impor-
tuning became intolerable, he reluctantly engaged in desultory
discourse with Flames Nolan, his cellmate, on the subject of
motorbikes, the theft of one of which (a Moto Guzzi) had landed
Flames a three- to six-month stretch—"Jist like you, dey said you
nicked dat owld judge's wheels, yeah?"

"Not really, but it looked that way."

"Ah gwan wichya, get out of it boy, pull de udder wan. Say,
didja ever ride one of dem Gayr-man jobs, da Bee Em Double
U's, sure dey're magic dey are ah Chroist Oy remember one New
Year's Day Oy'd had a few," et cetera.

Then Mary Rose brought word that on the urging of their
attorney Veronica and Rick had dropped A. Swain, Esq. as
coplaintiff.

"Fucking jig-monkeys."

"Well, yes."

Mary Rose sat on Anil's cot and read in a dry mechanical voice
from documents: "In view of subject's erratic behaviour and previous convictions and—given his alien origins—lack of familiarity
with the Irish and British legal systems—"

"No no," Anil expostulated, waving arms. "What alien origins?
What am I, a bloody moonman? Good God, no one in this bloody

place knows more about the legal system than I do by now. And please tell me this, Mrs. Ryan, what's the Indian legal system based on, for goodness' sake?"

"Dear me, I don't know what it's based on," said Mary Rose Ryan, tugging at the hem of her skirt to block Flames's sudden fiery scrutiny, he having just awakened from a nap to find a real flesh-and-blood bit of crumpet in his cell. "Sanskrit?"

"Sanskrit! Oh, God. By golly, you lot don't know much, do you. Oh, Vishnu." His shoulders slumped, Anil bowed his head in misery. Mary Rose took out her compact and scrutinized herself, catching Flames's eye. He winked. She tossed her head girlishly.

"Don't worry, Mr. Singh," she said. "I'm doing my best."

"Arrah sure yarr darlin' and wouldn't I take half as good if I could get it from ya," purred Flames.

"Well, I never. The sauce," et cetera. Well, anyway, we can imagine how much credence poor not-Singh put in the woman's assurances. Despair, no less, folded its black wings above his head, and the velvet shades of eternal night seemed to be falling over what remained of his life; even Flames, after a long peroration on Mary Rose's likely attractions from the perspective, admittedly biased, of a red-blooded Oyrish man, fell silent, as if overwhelmed by adjacent angst. The hours turned to days, days to more days. Anil mechanically went about the poor business of a prisoner and sought relief on memory lane. Lying on his bunk, he recalled India. He delved deep and came up with his own childhood. He swaggered defiantly down Sandrapore's hot dusty summer streets that became sloshy mud-rivers in the autumn. He remembered the shopkeepers and girls, Vohraji and his plum pies and Anuprya's nimble fingers behind a hedge. He heard again the plock plack of the cricket ball during test season. He longed for the windy undulating scrubby uplands of Sandra Pradesh under hot blue cloud-streaked skies, a barren high place except for the riverlands and the old groves of jamun trees—one of which, a monster about eight thousand years old, he'd thought when he was a kid was the real Manorathadayaka, or "tree of the world," inhabited by monkey ghosts and great spidery things by night (one Dinali he'd seen them, he swore it). During a long hot summer in early adolescence he'd sold the jamun fruit to passersby. On one day he made 120 rupees. A fortune. He'd spent it all on sweets and smokes. Two days in bed and a whaling from *baba*.

And beyond Sandrapore on the main road west, the small towns all whitewashed and scrubbed as clean as the white *lungis* the people wore hitched up over their knees as they pedaled slowly along on their bikes, weaving in and out of the carts and cars and potholes and burping old lorries.

But the whitewash of the houses had a blue tint in it. Anil had never decided why.

"Like the sky," he mumbled.

He started feeling hot, then cold, then hotter. The heat he felt, he decided, emanated from the Indian sky, from his past. Oh, he'd been a hot young chap, all right. Just ask Anuprya and any of the others . . . so he raved. The chill was strictly Irish. Delirum set in and he was carried off on a stretcher to Mater Misericordiae Hospital.

"A shockin' shame, so 'tis," declared Flames to his next cellmate, Tiger McIlhenny, in for the third time for having at his old woman. "Poor wee bastard. An Ayrab, wasn't he, sure God bless yiz . . ."

"Nah. Paki or I'm Owen feckin' Parsley."

News of Anil's plight—sick, and sinking fast ("some kind of tropical bug, I reckon" in the words of Dr. Eddie Fast, FRICS) reached Rubina in the middle of the third rubber at Mary Malone's bungalow on the Strand.

"Blast his eyes," she said. "Always angling for centre stage."

But she was there, at his bedside, under the steady eye of Sister Theodore, watching wretched Anil pluck feebly at the coverlet ("you silly wretch," had been her only greeting, and Sister's intervention alone had spared the delirious Swain a slap across his finely chiselled Dravidian features) and obnoxiously issue delirium summonses to absent cousin Rashmi and others, even Rubina, once. Eyes bright, he meanderingly invoked Kalki, the white horse of Vishnu; the wind god Vayu, bearer of perfume, god of all the Northwest of India; Belinda Barnsley, hostess of the hit game show *SuperNaff*; the old *babu*, a neighbour in Sandrapore who fixed old lawnmowers (Mr. Krishnamurti); then came a chant: "Goone, Goone, I hardly knew ye . . ."

At that moment Mary Rose Ryan arrived, flushed and breathless.

"It's all right, he's out," she said. "You must be Mrs. Singh?"

"No," said Rubina.

"Oh, well, someone has to tell his wife . . ."

"But I am his wife."

"Oh. Well. Pleased to meet you, I'm sure. Anyhow, he's out, he's free, he's released on his own recognizance, at least, costs paid in full by Jocelyn Motors Limited as long as he signs this." Mary Rose extended a cool white hand in which a cool white document crackled crisply. "It's a contract. Part of the actors' union requirements, you see."

"Anil Swain is becoming a movie actor?" inquired Rubina, less incredulously than she would have done six months earlier, when the world had seemed to be run along steady, predictable lines.

"Well, not exactly. But he's likely to become quite famous on the telly."

Jocelyns, said Ms. Ryan, had flown in Claude Quiller, Q.C., superstar barrister from Belfast, Cork, and London. Quiller, in a series of lazily mesmerizing and seemingly off-the-cuff arguments he called "Quiller memoranda," had quite dazzled the judge, a thirty-four-year-old novice named Fiona Blacke-Whyte,[2] and

---

[2]Not Fiona Blacke-Whyte? Sod me, she's Gar Looney's top current squeeze, best-known for taking over the donwtown eatery Le Phacochère last year and introducing braised warthog casserole with olives on a bed of sliced

had succeeded in having charges dropped on the grounds of temporary insanity, racial discrimination, and unreliable witnesses, prawn fishermen being notorious drunks and liars.

Furthermore, the company had offered to pay all legal costs.

"What a nice company," said Rubina. "Just like that? No strings attached?"

Well, not exactly. In exchange, Mary Rose explained, for Anil's agreeing to star—turbaned, bearded—in a series of TV commercials on the theme of the fakir's waterproof magic carpet, in which he would drive a Jocelyn Crannog GTX into various harbours and waterfronts around the world—Hong Kong, New York, Trincomalee, and of course Benares—as part of a campaign to revive Jocelyn's flagging fortunes under the slogan "Jocelyn: The Car You Can Drive Anywhere!"

"Apparently they were rather impressed by the fact that the car didn't sink. And they thought he was a rally-class driver. So you see, it's a brilliant stroke."

"Good, good. I'm delighted as well. But he might die first, you know. Uncle! Did you hear that, uncle?"

Anil droned half-remembered scraps of this or that pop song or ballad.

"The pipes, the pipes are ca-a-a-lling. Michelle, my belle. *Mere sapno ki rani kab?* Oh see the moon's silvery barque. Hey hey. No milk today ..."

---

lettuce as the main dish. Man oh man was it ever a sensation. They were running up and down the street for hours afterward, and not a few had to be stomach-pumped on the spot. Well, when the restaurant was finally closed down as a public health hazard she had to find something else to do, so she and Gar cooked up this legal caper and somehow or other she got herself made a judge. Nice legs, though, don't get me wrong. I never faulted Gar Looney's taste in women—except for his missus, but he tried to put that right as soon as he could, I'll give him that much.

Dr. Fast loomed in the doorway like a voyeur.

"Oy, piss off, you lot," he said. "Come back tomorrow. We'll know by then what his chances are."

Anil passed an unsettled night, but haunting echoes of that bedside conversation seeped slowly into his throbbing brain.

"Acting contract? Telly?" he mumbled.

Of course, the minute a chink opened in the armour of Anil Swain's fever and the glorious contamination of the real world swarmed in, the disease beat a hasty retreat, fever dreams giving way to the more basic, and very familiar, ones of material well-being, restaurants, new houses, et cetera, all of it outshone by the glory of being on television; but he didn't believe it until they came back the next day and Dr. Fast pronounced him "A-OK, if he doesn't snuff it in the next forty-eight hours."

"Where do I sign?" croaked Anil, majestically gathering his hospital bumfreezer about him. Beaming Jocelyns toadies were on hand to finalize the deal. Rings flashed as they jockeyed briefly but bitterly with one another to point to the dotted line.

"Here."

"No, here."

"Here, ya git."

"I'll sign everywhere," said Anil jovially, venturing a smile that soon turned to the leering rictus of a dead man as he spasmodically heaved and shook with a monstrous coughing fit. The Jocelyns men retreated, like dogs scenting danger. Dr. Fast made a fist, and that fist pounded the ill humours out of poor Swain, who was once again able to affix his signature.

"Crikey," said Mary Rose. "I thought you were a goner."

"Certainly he wasn't," sussurated a toadie. "We knew that, ya gobshite."

"Right, that does it. You watch yer back, ya berk," hissed his stablemate.

"By the way, the car's rubbish, you know," said Anil, sinking back into his pillow. "The brakes failed."

"Well, let's just keep that between you and me, eh? No need to spread that around."

Anyway, incredible but true: Anil recovered. He and Rubina made love again, almost to their former level of proficiency, bar the actual climax (but she couldn't help wondering: Was he? Of *her*? *Not* herself?). The first Jocelyns commercial was shot in Hong Kong harbour two months later, using a heavily disguised Land Rover, as the designated Jocelyn kept on sinking in pre-trial tests. A dodgy ruse, but it worked: nobody noticed, and sales skyrocketed. They did the second commercial in New York soon thereafter, using (just to be on the safe side) an old Pontiac minivan, shot from a distance, with a substitute stuntman for the now-famous, hence valuable, Anil Swain (nicknamed Bibi on the Delhi-Mumbai-Chennai talk-show circuit); and so successful was it that Jocelyns opened showrooms in Los Angeles, Amman, Delhi, and (yes) Sandrapore.

The trade journals were, frankly, nonplussed.

"Once a byword for automotive feces, the Jocelyn Crannog has suddenly turned its image around and taken the world by storm," wrote Mick McCreek, widely respected automotive correspondent for *Glam* magazine, based in Milan. "The remarkable, if somewhat dubious, film footage of the Indian stuntman Anil 'Bibi' Swain driving his Crannog four-by-four into all of the world's great harbours, with neither driver nor vehicle seemingly the worse for wear, has—while arousing suspicions in this reviewer's jaded mind—galvanized the world's car lovers as no commercials have since the great days of Nissan's Mr. K and his Jack Russell terrier. . . ."

Then Robin Brashford, star of BTV's *Yellow Jackets* and the hit adventure flick *Mickey Munga's Revenge*, bought a customized Asphodel and Jocelyn's future was assured, for a while.

29

So Rubina quit her job at Emerald Mats, PLC and they moved into a house on End Street overlooking the Strand, and Anil shaved his beard and bought a new car (not a Jocelyn) and quite a wardrobe of Spantucci suits and Di Mangano shoes, mostly Oxfords, polished to a high gloss; then, at about the same time that the true quality of Jocelyn automobiles was becoming apparent worldwide, with concomitant lawsuits, he realized that he and Rubina were actually almost skint, but as will occasionally happen in life, luck intervened and he received, hand-delivered from the Garda Siochana along with a handwritten note of apology from Chief Superintendent Pat Talbott on behalf of the Special Services ("circumstances were unclear . . . absurd and insulting accusations . . . racism . . . deep regrets . . . dinner anytime, or drinks anyway"), the catering license to the Koh-I-Noor Restaurant.

Which was timely, because Anil's stardom went into the sewers of history, Jocelyns went into receivership again, and Rubina went into labour. Yes, the Swains finally had a baby, one of the girl type, named . . .

"No. *Not* Rashmi."

"But, Auntie . . ."

"Absolutely not. I want to name her after my grandmother. Indira."

"Indira? But half the prossies in Sandrapore are named Indira."

"Now how would you know that, I'm wondering?"

So Indira it was. And when she was born Anil returned to the fray, nervous at first in his executive capacity (with options on the franchises of other Koh-I-Noors haunting his ever-acquisitive brain); but once he'd hired Wallfish as his headwaiter and returned Thackeray and Pedro to the kitchen, overconfidence filled his veins like a hit of cocaine.

"We're home free, Auntie. Money money money! You bet. And earned honestly. Of course, it'll mean work. Real work."

"Of course."

"Know what I mean?"

"Of course I know what you mean. Work's work."

"No, no, the TV show. Look. It's just coming on."

"Accchh. *Haila.*"

Rubina made as if to brain her husband with a hippo of mock Venetian glass purchased some time ago in the duty-free at Dubai Airport during a layover en route to Ireland from home, but he was too absorbed in the magic of the gogglebox to notice her, the hippo, or his gurgling child.

"Anilji, you're hopeless."

And as if that weren't bad enough, *she* turned up again soon after, this time in the guise of a health inspector from the World Health Organization.

30

After the Pint-Pulling Olympiad fiasco, Milo Rogers—suddenly not at all desirous of being saddled with any of the blame, not to mention the debts—quit his job as managing director of the Spudorgan Vacation Inn. The reason he gave was simple: "I'm a poet, not a clapped-out feckin' arse-kissin' dogsbody."[1]

He then spent a poetic week or two brooding silently in his bungalow and writing earnest entreaties for money and drinking home-brewed ale and watching television beamed across St. George's Channel from Wales and, it is alleged (with some justification, as per what follows), penning verse. Then he started going out, first to the pubs, where he met the usual punters, then to the library, where he met Penny Burke, library director.

"Hi. Milo Rogers. Nice to meet ya. Oh. Poet, by the way. Believe it or not."

"Hi. Penny Burke. Library director."

Pen was by then, of course, having quite a while since dumped gormless Derek, once again a single woman at large—but not for long, not after the foregoing brief but meaning-pregnant ex-

---

[1]Or words to that effect. Parsimonious with the verbalizing, I am, the better to hone my other skills.

change. Yes, Milo and Penny hit it off as only fellow poets can when one's a poet and the other isn't, if you take my meaning.[2] All importantly, Alf liked Milo's mingled old-corduroys-well-sat-in and tobacco-overlaid-with-a-thousand-pints scent, and this instant friendship between man and dog ("Down, sir"; "Alf!" "Good boy!"; "Alf! Alf!") removed all doubts Penny might have had—well, *did* have—who can blame her, after two dodgy specimens like Mick and Derek hard on each other's heels.

"Bed?" she inquired, one night after a superb Tikka Masala at the Koh-I-Noor. ("Thank you, thank you, thank you," blurted the obsequious Mr. Swain, flashing hands heavily beringed.)

"Arrah."

Vigorous he was in that arena for a paunchy geezer on the aging side of life, if slightly quirky and thigh-oriented and, towards the end, heavily asthmatic—but a quick fag soon took care of that.

"Well, now, wasn't that grand, eh?"

"Arr."

So tightly did the new lovers bond, in fact, that Penny's own feelings of literary inadequacy ebbed (not disappearing completely, but) and she entered upon the golden age of her tenure as library supremo (*suprema?*) by organizing a poetry-reading evening around Milo's latest outburst of doggerel, which recounted the momentous events of the previous year from the point of view of the unhappy, and now extinct, O'Mallet clan, Killoyle branch.

Many attended the reading, including (accompanied by her obviously smitten warden, Mr. Deck) Cornelia Regan, hostess of the hit show *An Ex-Sexton Talks Sex* (Jailhouse Rock Radio

---

[2]Oh you're the sly sod, aren't you. I take your meaning, right enough. But I can tell you this much: If Penny paid half as much attention to her versifying as to her precious unemployed hooligans and hangabout louts, she'd be another Elizabeth Barrett bloody Browning, and no mistake.

360 FM/1860 AM, weeknights at 10:30); newly invested Regional Assistant Commissioner Pat Talbott, looking uncommonly serene and well disposed, as many remarked who had suffered his wrath in the past; Sean "El Maxi-Macho" McSpackle, owner of McSpackle's Spanish Cantina, sporting sunglasses and a *bolo* tie; Kathy and Mick McCreek, just in from Milan; Jumbo Wyde, best-selling author of *Zemlinsky's Chin,* munching heaping handsful of roasted Brazil nuts out of a Tesco carrier bag and conversing indifferently with this old lady, that scuttling sycophant, those nodding dozers; the suspense novelist Sinead O'Hall, known to her many fans as "the Irish P. D. James";[3] Fred Hasdrubal-Thomson and his wife Sheila, herself recently (former hard feelings gone all soft and squishy) elected to the Inner Circle of Friends of the Library, that exclusive cocktail-and-reading club restricted to donors of over £25,000 per annum (handsome PVC carrying case included at no charge except VAT, shipping, and handling); a bevy of even more minor luminaries including Stan and Terpsichore, whoever they were; Headwaiter Wallfish emitting the sated air of one who has just dined well; that Yank fellow Denny, in black T and inappropriate Armani jacket; Ramona, Den's squeeze; Inspector Sherlock Neame, who was there because the super—sorry, the A. C.—was; Maher, the developer, sporting a fine new ash-blond toupee with natural-looking curls and page-boy bangs; and not a few utter wasters.

In short: *le tout* Killoyle, together again.

In his prefatory remarks before the reading, the poet Rogers described his latest effort as "Bring the family to Tesco's Killoyle South for a Free Prize Drawing and Potluck Giveaway, Saturday April 1." . . . Oh no, that's the wrong side. I've got it now. Here we go:

---

[3]Ouch. Low blow there, pal. (Actually, the one I'm worried about is the one known as "the English Sinead O'Hall," if you follow my drift.)

"Hiya. How're ya doin'. Nice to be here, I suppose. Aren't youse in luck, the lotta youse. In for a real treat, so youse are. A right old poetry stew, as it were. A spicy blend of Dallán Forgaill, the *Vision of MacConglinne,* and Philip Larkin.[4] *Bon appétit.* And keep the noise down, in the back."

So the reading began of the verses that follow.

"Ahem." (Or should that be Amen?)

---

[4]You left out the most important part: "And seasoned with a pinch of William MacGonagall."

THE STORY OF O'MALLET BAWN
A Nonepic

Long after the brehons' great age
And soon before this night's *ard fheis*
There lived a famous Judge of Killoyle, now expired.
O'Mallet Bawn was his name (well, Jerry, actually.
I added the Bawn for poetic *élan*.)
Once I asked him this question.
"O'Mallet son of O'Mallet," I said,
"What were your habits when you were a judge?"
"Not hard to tell," said O'Mallet Bawn.

> I was a devourer of kippers
> I was a smoker of pipes
> I was a fixture in taverns
> I was infrequently in churches
> I was a listener to liars
> I was a liar to my listeners
> I was kind to some
> I was proud to most
> I was strong among weaklings
> I was fair dealing with rogues
> I was a sinner deluxe
> I was a man entire, from brow to bunions.

The judge had a lawyer son. In the courts of the kingdom
The son defended the fat half of the rabble of Eire.
(The thin could go hang.)
The son's name was Tomas,
and half Ireland was half-full of his fame.
Hangers-on came from Belfast and beyond asking for him.
Some, it is said, came eager to see the rising and setting sun's gold-
    red orb
that shone—according to legends self-created—out of his arse.

And arrived there also messengers from afar.
They came from Iberia and crazy Hindoostan,
Where young men wear old ladies' gear
And wax their beards into daggers' points
And eat fruit trees, roots and all.
There came too those from a-near,
The grease-lipped and long-shanked,
The callow and treacherous,
The lean and mischievous
From Erin's green heart to seek O'Mallet's advice.
All were made welcome in the judge's court,
Where deeply they quaffed the black hop-ale—
All save the Mahometans, who'd as lief lodge their blades
'Twixt the breastbones of an Irish knight
As touch the vile liquor they named Pipi-Tar.

"Peace upon ye, ye stupid gits," were the words of the judge,
And they fell silent at the sound of his voice, for it rolled like the
Roar of the rutting ram of Cavan.
And he spoke further.
"Eat and drink, ye shites," were his words
And the voice they were delivered in rocked the very sill of heaven
And tolled like thunderstorms over the lowering cliffs of Inishmaan.

It belled like the stag in Siodhmhuine's steep glen.
It boomed like the white waves of Magilligan Strand.
It burrowed deep into each man's soul like the memory of sin.
It sang like the harmonies of Phelim the shepherd after the act
    of night.
It whistled like the tempests of spring over the unclad slopes of
    Slieve Gallion.
It tootled like the wild swan's call in the pools of Lough Coole.
It growled like the wolf-hound of Glin on a night of high
    winds.

Truly, the judge was a stately man full five leagues in height.
Brachycephalic his noggin, as round as a loaf of wheaten bread
And his brow was high as the front side of Ben Bulben
And from his brow shone forth the light of wisdom.
Full five chariots wide was his chest from shoulder to spine
Deeper than the tarns of the great Bog of Allen his eyes
And his backside was broad as the wall of high Tara, hill of tribes.
Truly, the judge was a man to reckon with.
And true it is that we shall not look upon his like again.

Now the messengers had bewailed their folly
And like the swooping tern-flocks of harsh Inishbofin
Or the scavenger gulls of blustery Bundoran
They fell to their food and drink, of which there was an abundance
As befit the house and kitchens of O'Mallet the Bawn.

There were flitches of bacon
And sweet milk from cows' beestings
And bloaters
And bummalo
And a brace of biffings.
Filberts were there also,
And smokies from Sligo,

And Navan chaps and collops,
And Newbridge brawn,
And a pine-smoked Manx suckling pig entire
And chips on the side, with salt and vinegar
And prawns from Lough Corrib.
Beakers of ale were there beyond the counting,
And horns of honey mead,
and when the hunger of the messengers was sated and their thirst
    full quenched
and their fingers could thrum music on the taut skins of their
    paunches
        as the winter wind plays on the water reeds of Lough Erne
        as the *file* sings his verse in the chill peace of the day
        as the cockerel pipes his pride at the gates of dawn
they were brought to the judge in his place
that he might grant them their desire and learn their strange ways.

As one delivered they their message, some in squeaks, some in brays:
"We have come from afar, from places called Bilbao and Kashmir
and parts even more foreign indeed, with accents galore,
to aid the Sachsun-beleaguered soldiers of Eire,"
said the messengers of Hindoostania and Spain.

And spoke they more.
"And with our aid to our friends comes our request for aid from
    them
for from them shall be taken rocket launchers three score,
        and a gallon drum of Easi-Fert fertiliser,
        and Heckler and Koch SPG and Robar SR90 sniper rifles
        and AK-47 magazines
        and ammonium nitrate
        and sugar
        and diesel fuel, premium grade
        and Semtex

and a stalwart motorvan, Ford-tough-built,
and their equivalent gifts,"—

"Stay," said the judge, moved to the innermost of his bodhran-big
heart,
"surely your request will be in recompense for my travails and
those of my son,
for my son has within him the heart of a chief
and the bowels of a king
and the sinews of a boar from the tablelands of Gougane Barra
and the eyes of the falcon of Carrick-a-Rede
and upon him flows the golden hair of a prince
and beside him rides the shade of his grandfather the O'Mallet
of Keane
and before him blazes the silver light of kingdoms to come
and surely such a one must merit reward—and esteem."

"State your terms, O judge," yelled the envoys,
"only make it quick because our plane's leaving soon."
Hurriedly they glanced round, having quite spoiled the mood.
Of a sudden 'twas revenge they feared most
As if past their thirsting ears
The swift wind had whispered
Of the trick of the Ga Bolga
And the stout stave of Cu Chulainn.
"If you don't mind, that is," muttered a man from Spain.

And so spoke the judge in languid tones of easy command.
Now his voice was silken, but in it glinted dull iron
Like the sullen blade of Erinwatch the King-Killer.
"At the end of a year, on top of this piddling sum
In a vault, place silver and gold in the amount of a million per
Sans interest, sans taxes, sans repayment of any kind
And do this through the armies of eager in-dwellers

And overlords of wealth in the changing-places
Strewn like chaff across the six nations of Gaul
And the mountainous fastness of the Helvetii
And the rustling forests of Herman the German.
And in understanding of this I and my lawyer-son
    Who rides the waves like the god of the storm
    Who pisses high as the waterfall of Barrenglass
    Who springs from peak to peak at a single bound
    Who bestrides the four green fields of Erin the fair
    Who beats his breast and calls all to combat
Like the mighty Dinertach of the HyFidgenti
Before he fell on Aidne's sad ground (alas).
We do hereby pledge our troth, full excellent men that we are
To undertake your mission: To blow people up."

The messengers left, and sped they home
And word spread on the tongues of gossips and whores
And reached the eager ear of McArdle, high lord of the Falls.
"Shite," said he, and then he said "fock," and "fock" said he more.
And it was to Killoyle he came
From far Lagan water, the better to suss things out
In the way of the wise men of Clonmacnoise
And the shanachees of Ennis and Kilkee.
"Judge, I've also come 'coz I need
Yer fockin' help," said McArdle of Red Ulster's kingdom green.
The judge considered him and considered him well.
McArdle was a big man and a proud
And only the great tree of the world stood taller
Than did he with his head in the swirling clouds
Like the summits of the Reeks lost in summertime's squalls
And the great purple crags of the Knockmealdowns
Across which gambol the cloud-white sheep
Specks beneath the matching flocks of the sky.
"McArdle's value as a friend is no less,"

said the judge, and his voice was as the rushing stream
At Shannonford, and the fast-flowing currents
Off the Head of Kinsale.

"More," said McArdle, in the voice of a giant.
"And to give you treasure and arms
and the same amount shall be given you
at the end of a year, and close friendship will result."
"I'll think on it," boomed the judge. "Man of the North,
return then thence and await a message from me."
But the McArdle was given to loud speaking,
and expressed he then his ire, in tones of doom
That reminded the judge of the Causeway of Kings
And the stern travails of brave Finn McCool.

At length, when McArdle was gone
And behind him whirled the air in little bits
Like the flaxen strands of braided wheat
In the barns of plenty in the gold of autumn
Judge Jerry lapsed into a total funk
and in this way he was a day without drink,
without food, without sleep, tossing from side to side.
Then came to him the spirit of Shirley, his ex-girlfriend,
as was her wont, just before bed, the way she'd nagged him in life
In the low shadowy hallways of the long-ago.
And floating above him she said: "O'Mallet Bawn, you are making
a long fast. There is food beside you but you do not eat. What ails you?"
He gave the shade no answer, so the phantom said:
"Sleeplessness fell upon O'Mallet at his home.
There was something upon which he was brooding
without speaking to anyone. He turns to the wall,
the warrior of the Fían of fierce valour; it causes
concern to us that O'Mallet Bawn is
sleepless and wan."

The judge: "*I'm* wan? Look at you!"
"Jest not, O'Mallet Bawn, with the shades of the gone."
So spoke the shade, in a voice of sharp iron.
So the judge turned to his son, Tomas the brave,
And spoke to him low so the ghost could not hear.
"Son," said he, "remember what Crimthann Nia Nair said:
'Do not tell your secret to women or children.'
The secret of a child is not well kept.
And as for a woman, a treasure is not entrusted to her."
Then spoke Tomas, and his voice was as the moorhen's song at dusk
Over the barren slopes of Slieve Donard
Or the calving call of the Glas Gaibhneach
Or the hymn of the queen of Connacht, and she but a month
    enthroned
Above the long-legged landsmen of the seven tribes.

Tomas the Fair said: "Father brave, even to a woman you should
    speak
if nothing should be lost thereby. A thing which your
own mind cannot penetrate the mind of another will.
And I am your son, and to me you can talk."
"Listen to him, you eejit," hissed the spirit, and her ghostly voice
Was as the sound of an angry waterbird stalked by a fox
Or the rained-upon embers of a long-smouldering fire.
So the judge obeyed. Wearily he rose
And his gait as he walked was the sad stroll of a king
Bereft of his rule, bowed down by greed,
A prey to the yellow-eyed demons of fear.

"It is an evil thing we do for a just cause," he said, and his voice held
    within it
The cadences of long nights without love and days without light.
"Foul was it when they asked for the Semtex. Many tall and
fair-haired men will fall on account of the rocket launchers. The strife

about that fertiliser will be more than we can reckon."
"Aye," averred the son. "And unless it is given to me
it will certainly be a churl's act. The hosts of McArdle will not leave
   behind them
anything more of use than of land. He will hew down a heap
of corpses across the country. McArdle will
carry us off, he will crush us into bare ashes."
O woe is us, they wailed, like toyless brats.

"Look over the sea, then, to great Gaul," said the judge,
"where when you were a mere broth of a boy
you frolicked in the Rhenish inns and whorehouses
and took to heart the tongue of the Gauls
and the tits and bums of Gallic colleens."
"Fie on this," hissed Shirley's shade, swirling in rage,
"Like father like son"—and she was away
    Like a whirlwind in March
    Like a wisp of woodsmoke
    Like the Morrigan-bird whose call is half-heard
    Half real, half dream, on the borderlands of sleep
    Where phantoms reign and oak trees dance
    And stone turns to water
    And trickles away in the pooka's hands.
"Begone, *aisling* ghost," declaimed the judge,
"Fuck off, ye *boccanach*, ye *bannanach*. All shades, away!"
Erect then stood he, with much sternness of visage
And assemblage of extremities in oak-mimicking pose
Towering above kith and kin, the gnarled king
Of tree or mankind, sublime and powerfully malodorous
In the way of a lord of the bold Fianna Finn.

And the judge and his son did they then resolve
To take unto themselves the ill-gotten gains.
But like an axe in the brain was the judge's pain

(*There was ice on the axe*
When it hacked the king's head)
Like a spear hurled by Norsemen of old
Like the Badb's pain-warp of great Cu Chulainn
Like a blow to the noggin God-dealt to a knave.
Nonsense, said the judge, 'twas for Erin's cause
That the deed would be done. Wars were men's game
And such games playing was the birthright of Gaels
And far better 'twas, to fight in the bright
Fields 'neath treetops, beside splashing falls
Than bare-knuckled and flewtered in the Norseman's meadhall.
"And forget not our needs," warned he his son,
"Nor the viciousness of the foreign emissaries
who stack up their victims one by one
      Like the old dry bones of chattel long-dead
      Like the cordwood of a fire unlighted
      Like the mossy kindling of a hearth untended
      Like the dry mountain heather after a long summer's drought.
They're foreigners, for fuck's sake," roared the judge,
and his voice bounced off the walls of his house
      Like the echo of a storm in rain-gorged Poyntzpass
      Like the tumble of boulders in mud-drenched Glen Glum
      Like the opposing love thoughts of a lovelorn fool
      Like the swift flight of mating sparrows in spring
      Like the moods of your sweetheart, taken to bed.
And said he then this.
"Inform your friends that we have need of bank accounts
And a back-up plan—oh, and a fast solid motor
(not a Jocelyn, thanks very much),
For rapid escape, should the plan
Turn bad."

The judge stood firm.
      He was a flood: below the hill

He was a ram: master of flocks
He was a stream: beside the mill
He was an elm: among leafless oaks
He was a sword: out of its sheath
He was a cave: where spawns the fox
He was a sod: hewn from peat
He was an eel: under the rocks
He was a milestone: on a crooked street
He was the gold: in a goblet of hock
He was the breeze: cooling the sea
He was the tide: that deposits flotsam
He was the gull: that on flotsam feeds.

Then did Tomas the son his bidding,
Swift as an arrow from the bow of Brian Boru,
Fast as the ferret, keen as the hound, higher than the hawk,
With eyes sharper aglow than all the jewels of Queen Madb,
And all the treasures of fabled Foreign Parts,
And the seafoam sparkling in the winter sunbeams
Off Inishmagoole.

So secured he this one:
    A loathsome churl,
    A recalcitrant swine,
    An insolent serf,
    A bawdy kulcheen,
    A spalpeen bawn,
    An insolent rogue,
    A loud-prating fool,
    A tiresome Swain (Anil by name),
    A staggering, slavering, mewling, knuckle-dragging, low-
        browed, brown-hued, animal-cunning purveyor of meat and
        drink,
    A Hindu too, and a wayward soul, and

A naughty knave up for a lark.
'Twas in prison Tom snared him, with promises firm
and the manly air of a man born to serve,
of he who commands born to the part
with the deep-ringing voice of a leader of men.
Half-seduced was this Swain, then; yet
So maddened he was with longing for wealth,
and chests full of gold, and castles aloft
And—most especially—the lordship of Goone's,
That feasthall of khans, that unordinary dinery
Of Hindu finery
That temple of Asian sweetmeats and spice.
That he pledged Tom his troth, and with it his life—but hold, ask
    ye now:
What is this Goone?
Or who?
Or which . . . ?

Well, a merchant was Goone, and canny—one of a kind
And a tradesman sharper in wit
Than the myriad rocks of Loch Diolar's black inlets
        and the clattering hooves of MacMahon's lowing kine
        and the snapping teeth of brash Brendan the Biter
        and the snatching claws of the hawks of Howth Head
        and the flashing blades of the hall of the prince
        and the wild-wielded sword of the prince's first knight
and it was not for nothing that they called him tha' bloody wee ponce.
From Ulster's heart, then, came he, a man from Finn's hinterland.
Of plain Coleraine was Goone—'tis no mean town that place,
Of East (London)Derry the jewel, and Ulster the crown
Where Bann unfurls to the uncoiling main.

"Tell me, Goone grandson of Goone," to him once I said,
"Tell me three things that give you pleasure."

"That's easy to tell," said Goone.
"A profit in hand
The gurgling of Bann
A lad's bare glans."

(For truly was Goone a lover of lads.
No womaniser he, no
No fancier of fillies, no
No caresser of swan breast, no
No climber of Mount Venus, no
No idolator of girls, no
No seeker of she.
No.
A he-er was he, a boy-er our Goone,
A joint-staff-stiffener
A bronze-eye-baller
A gossoon-gooser
A mounter of men.)

A church charman's company
Was the seat of his pleasure
Till his churchman's mood turned and he swiveled
about; and he filled Goone with lead
Stone bloody dead.

So Goone was no more; yet, in life, he'd been more.
A maker, a dreamer, a driver, a doer,
A hunter, a fighter, a fancier of fellows
No fop, no she-man, no piteog 'twas.
And was Swain his foil? Well, this twain did meet,
And clove nearly apart
When Swain, rajah would-be
Of Chappati and Pomfret and Nan
Made sport of Goone and was promptly unsaddled

Only to be rescued by Tom, and given a van:
"Such a van as this Erin the gold has never yet seen," said Tomas
    hero maker.
        And his eyes flashed like the fire beacon on Mount Mweelrea
        And the stilt-stalking sunlight on the iron-grey sea
        And the donkey's new bridle in the square of Roscrea
        And the bronze buckled shield of Cormac, *ard ri*
        And the ring on the hand of Emer the sweet
        And the quicksilver rocks of Inishkilleen.

"'Tis a monument, this van, welded and smelted
And hammered into a stronghold on wheels,
A wagon worth seven bond maids, fit for the High King of Gaels
Like the mighty war chariots of the lords of the Celts
Worth the breadth of thy face in silver and gold
The heft of thy wife's tits in gems and bronze
The length of thy spine in raiments and ale horns
And the girth of thy fat tum in rubies and swords.
And inside the van will be chattels
And apples
And magpies and myrtles
And fine iron implements for wanderer's tents
And good goods like pillows and lanterns and stout lengths of hemp
All for the pleasure of campers and picnickers and their aunties and
    uncles,
grand people all. Rest assured, good Swain, it's all perfectly fine
And I give you the easy surety of this covenant:
when thou'st served us, we'll speak no more of thy crime
And God knows—the judge, if fairly addressed (and pleaded with well)
May relieve sad Goone of his curry concession
And make thee Hindu food lord from Killoyle to hell.

        The full of thine arm in a gold coin harvest,
        Share of field and farm,

Lordship of curry ovens
Freedom of thy person and thy wife's
    From this day to the crack of doom.
Swain Junior, son of Swain Senior,
More than that for which thou couldst hope,
Why shouldst—how couldst—thou refuse me,
    Who wishes you nought but the bloody best?

Go thou then, stout Swain, Anil of Bombay, and do what I bid thee
God speed thee then thence, and may the breezes of Rath
  Murbhuilg
kiss thy burly knees."[1]

And in such comradely tones! And so confidingly said!
Like the secrets of love in verses quite blank
(Of Ethne and Ele and their doting lovesong
Son of Fathna Fathach son of Turbech Angus),
That life-desperate Swain jumped at it—and living or dead
He vowed he'd carry through and deliver the tents
And paraffin burners and guy ropes and climbing gear
Or whatever it was. (Anil didn't care.)
"By golly, I'm yours!" and "I'm coming aboard!"
Poor fool. Not the first time Tom chose to royally mislead
And inflict his most unbrehonlike legal deceit
On a halfwit—a simpleton—a ruse-swallowing twit.

Then came McCreek.
Mick called him they, and his face—why, 'twas whey

---

[1]At this point in the original there was introduced a short episode in which the hapless protagonist is suddenly struck rhythmically about the ears by a bog hag called Lucy. For purposes of delicacy and suaveness of delivery, as well as brevity, the poet has made this episode optional, much like electric windows in a sports roadster or the American plan in a *pensione*.

Like a Sachsun's warpaint
As if fashioned of white clay
The old black-Irish way.
Hail to thee, then, Mick McCreek,
Bright banner of Killoyle, good friend always!
Mick, "Whelp of Sean" is no nickname for thee
Erin's women and rally drivers
     Her publicans and strongmen
     Her dog walkers and librarians
     Her journalists and immigrants
     Her touts and bureaucrats
     Her guards and lady editors
All contend for thee in rivalry.
'Tis a tun of man, a quite excellent lad.
Only—like George Best, or the lord Ailill mac Matach—he's fey
And he's one day here, or there, and the next—away.
Heed and beware, ladies fair.
But here's to him: Slaunch, shabby Mick!
And here follows his tale:

Well gourd-ringingly pissed was Mick one cloud-strewn day
Having lost (not misplaced) his only employ
As yeoman of cars to Jocelyn's, a maker—in this crested town,
     This silver-strand-girt citadel,
     This many-spired borough,
     This crenellated keep,
     This doughty fortress,
     This sceptr'd Killoyle—
Of same.
Then: Crash! O buggershite! O lament! O balls!
And, writhingly, a man was down
Like the sad warrior-king Ruadhri O Baoigheallain
At the bridge of Ballykilloran
Or mighty Ferdia son of Daman son of Daire

Whom Cu Chulainn, at the Feat of the Ford—
    As a mill grinds malt
    As a drill bores wood
    As a hawk swoops down
    As a vine binds trees
    As a river washes stones
    As an ax cleaves the branch
    As a bull gores the wolf
Dispatched, dismissed, discarded, disgorged
At the meeting of the kingdom's four streams
By the chalk-road and the windy banshee's rath
The very place of Dolb and Indolb's final rest—
But I digress.

No Ferdia lay stretched beneath Mick's wheels
No Cu Chulainn, neither, nor no son of Mil.
No, a mere disburser of ale,
    a stupid
    slovenly
    slatternly
    sod
Whose praises none sang, whose merits were nil
Bar setting in motion the great wheel of fate
That launched bold Mick onto high roads and low
Into the arms of more than one flax-blond lass
And the threats of—yes, you guessed it—Tomas,
Of the O'Mallet clan of the sept of Killoyle.
School chums they'd been, wary acquaintances yet they were,
Both hardened by sex and ale and the burden of hopes gone stale
And sensing Mick's travails, Tomas the Fair (fair no more: now as
    false as
    The Ga Bolga in battle
    The hound on the plain of Ailbe
    The dawn before the dawn

The rock feigning gold
The cuckoo usurping the nest
The graip in a townsman's hand
The love of a courtesan
The promises of Fergus mac Roig)
Led him a right old jig.

Yet Mick, unlike Swain, as a Milesian born
Paused here for a fondle, there for a jar,
And never let ambition take him too far—indeed
He had a job more absurd than some, quite as much as most:
Gazing at glass screens and clicking a "mouse."
Said mouse spawned a rat, that rat rebirthed a mouse,
That my fell lord of dotcom claimed for his own
And banished—the traitorous worm—poor Mick from his realm.
I place my *àer* on him
And on his kind.
        Like Bricriu Poison-tongue
        He spoke ill of a good man to others.
        Like Loegaire the Triumphant
        He despised the sight of a good man front and back.
        Like Forgall Manach
        He erased a good man's name from the rolls and his face from
            his mind.
        Like Medb of Cruachan Ai
        He in a huff flounced laterally away.
And the long and short of it saw McCreek once again
Jobless, prospectless, friendless, on the streets
Of wind-whipped tatterdemalion
Newspapers and the dirge music of empty tins
And a bottle that once in happier days
Held Lucozade.
But Mick—he was happy withal, as McCreek can be.
(Whereas you and I would mewl and whinge

And, in our tea, weep
Like mad Sweeney
In his tree.)
Yet again—this too sets him apart from the common run of men—
Unpityingly, without gobbing, or blather,
Stout Mick McCreek quaffed a quick draught and took a chance
  again
Casting round the full heart of a woman of ageless beauty aglow
That silken cord of longing that the brave man throws
At a good woman's love, and takes her troth, and turns the glow in
  her eye
To love's steady beam.

A lady of substance, with beauty fresh-blooming in place of the
  youth just gone.
The cleavage of her breasts deep enough for a warrior's hand
The cleavage of her buttocks deep enough for a warrior's shaft
Eyes clearer and more blue than the deep end of Lough Derg
And upon her head a red-gold hair-crown—

Tell us, poet, what style of beauty has she?

Well, might you ask. And I know her well. A mantle she has,
velveteen purple in hue, a soft silver-grey cloak, and in the mantle
silver piping threaded, and upon the breast of the cloak a com-
puter-shaped brooch of fairest gold. A kirtle wears she, too, long
and hooded and smooth, of emerald-green silk like the four fields
of Erin, with embroidery of red-gold that is like her crown of
auburn hair. Marvellous clasps of gold and silver in the kirtle on
her shelf-broad breasts and her milkmaid's broad shoulders and
spaulds on the sleeves. The sun always shines upon her, so that
the glistening of the gold against the sun from the green silk is
manifest to men. The hue of that silk seems to men like the flower

of the iris in summer, or like red gold after the burnishing thereof, or a car new-wax'd in the beams of sunrise. Truly she is a woman descended from the pastures of paradise. And it is true that we shall not look on her kind again.

> As Ailill loved Medb
> As Cu Chulainn loved Emer
> As Dinertach loved Creide
> As Cormac loved Roisin
> As Owen loved Nuala
> As Noisi loved Deirdre
> As Fergus loved Cornelius
> As Finn loved himself

So Mick loves Kathy.
Mealltar bean le beagán téad.
And truly Mick McCreek is a man to reckon with.
And true it is that we shall not look upon his like again.
(At least, I hope not.)
Thank you, O poet, for that metre of praise.

Sure, you're welcome.
In the way of the *fili*, I am stargazer, seer, priest,
Bard I am, and hermit, and no man's friend.
The world was made for my kind, not thine.
Word work sits with me
Word wit salts my fare
Word wizardry walks by my side
And Word wonder lights my way

> Like the glimmer of dusk at a stormy day's end
> Like the lantern of Phelim to summon his flocks
> Like the torch of the blacksmith, aglow in the forge
> Like the flames of Samhain on a braw autumn night
> Like the spark of the embers in a snug Midland hearth

> Like the shine of the shield of King Cormac mac Airt. . . .[2]

So—What of poor Swain?

Ah, poor Swain indeed, that blockhead, that jester, that Hindupe,
    that clown
That unethical ethnic, that favour-currying third-wordling
That undrinking bowsie, that televisual pimp with the spidery
    charm,
Like a madman whose intentions are fine—like Turlough, say,
    grand lout of Louth
Who, drunk but well-meaning, did an early-morning dance
For Phelim's sheep, who, being sheep, responded as such
And threw themselves blindly over the fence en masse
And of course there, when Phelim arose, they lay—
Brains (such as they were) knocked out
Of their heads.
Quite dead
Were they,
Market value:
Sweet f.-a.

In like vein did Swain undertake
A half or baker's dozen mad scrapes
And very nearly perished for his pains, first at Goone's hands
Then at those of a man from Spain feared for his name
Harry, the Butchering Basque—no genial serf from Pyrenean
    scarps,

---

[2]Here follows a conventional ode of self-praise, in highly embroidered rhetoric, of the poet's greatness and fine appearance. This, as well as the account of his ancestry stretching back to the dawn of Milesian time, is omitted. The narrative, such as it is, resumes with the chorus questioning the poet.

No boule-playing, beret-wearing, anisette-drinking *cabron*—oh no,
Before Batasuna's gaze even McArdle, fell lord of the Falls, might
    quail
And did
And choose for his health's sake valour's better part.
(Too late now—see below.)
Aye: Harry's bad.

>   In appearance a melancholy man, uncomely and dour.
>   A tunic of black, inlaid with iron, round him wound
>   Embroidered blood-red with blazing gold
>   And a long-sleeved cloak with dark hood surmounts
>   The sight of a face olive-drab and gaunt.
>   In each of his eyes glimmer fire and brimstone
>   His breath breathes sparks, like the forge of the elf mounds,
>   And on his broad thighs rests a great two-edged sword.
>   And on the night Swain met him he swore he was done for.

O Batasuna, terrible bear! O death to cowherds! O mad-angry beast,
    thou hast
Met thy match in the clash of vainglorious battle, through the shout
    of doom
When of a sudden there she is, through the swirling clouds of wrath
Killing here three men, there twice three, making nine
Three nines she slew and made a cairn with their bones
O bold Rashmi, thou Diana, Anil's wee cuz, demigoddess divine
Heroine of my telling, for thy cousin's life didst thou save (alas).

>   Her breasts round as apples
>   Her thighs firm as marrows
>   Her eyes ruby fire
>   Her shape luminescent
>   Her hair like a hawk's wing
>   Her strength that of nine times nine
>   Her voice like a trumpet
>   Her sinews like tree roots

Thus did she unmask the true villain, a moping, malicious,
   duplicitous
Mockery of a man, bent of spine, clenched of shank
A mild-mannered dissembling ox fucker of Newcastle West,
A guardian of books, once, and knowledge, and purveyor of fine things,
Twice then the depth of his villainy was dyed,
'Twas murderer, and traitor to all men: This Finn,
To spite the Judge, or Tomas, or even the Lord of the Falls
Gathered together an army of men—gamblers and reivers and
   bestialists all—
To subvert Erin's peace while cocoon'd in the mantle mirage
Of the Soldiers of Gael. Innocents who died in the rain of their
   fire—
Erin-brought by love of ale,
Bohemian-born by mishap or grace,
Killoyle-killed by false Fenian men—
Died useless as Phelim's sheep, or MacCarty's cock
(Which, when once aroused, ceased not hen-mounting
Till the last dawn he crew—for he'd mounted a fox
Itself happy to set right what Sir Cock misconstrued....)
But then McArdle, stalking revenge

     Like the wolf in the woods
     Like the rook in the field
     Like the bear at the cave
     Like the swan on the lake
     Like the stallion in heat
     Like the fox in the burrow
     Like the shrew in the stubble
     Like the owl in the gloaming
     Like the badger in the hole
     Like the bull in the pasture
     Like the trout in the pool
     Like the bachlach, the clurichaun, the sower of fear

Strike did he hard, yet missed he his man—at *Tomas* he did aim,
Not Finn. And Tomas fell hard, like Hector of old, like Ferdia the
    fair
And weep—O fell fate!—did his friends, and cacophonically wail
Bettina, his girlfriend.
And the old judge, too, mourned in his beer
All the long sad night long
His son, his likely lad, his misfortunate heir.
While Finn the Bookman, Finn the louse, Finn the false cavalier,
The cause of these ills, at dawn's first breath left he his house
To test whether the wind set fair for France.
He's there yet, and he did for the man from the Falls,
But where'er he looks Batasuna's his shadow
Finn's lease is nigh up, that much he knows
And knows he, too, that all roads lead to his barrow.

My ode's over. The rest's pure chance: How Mrs. Delaney
    o'erheard
And caused poor Tom's death, when o'erheard in her turn
Was she by McArdle, ear-eager, in his room;
How the judge, felled by loss, felled himself;
How Mick took Penny and Penny took another, and how Kathy
(The she-falcon
The she-wolf
The she-otter
The she-seal
The she-woman)
Took him.
How old fools abound
And how young ones suffer 'em.

Thus far then, the tale of O'Mallet the judge and Tomas his seed,
Dead the father, dead the son.

The gloom of Judge Jerry, hag-ridden by greed
And the happiness of youse others, whom Fortune spares—*once.*
God's will, then, be done: I am, sure.
And so, quare yoke and all
All's as it once was: *Enough.*[3]

THE END[4]

---

[3]Well, there you have it. A poor thing, but mine own. Mind you, it wasn't universally hissed. "The poem," said the *Clarion* critic, Oxster O'Callaghan, "is (or was) a remarkable contribution to the cultural and social history of modern Killhole [*sic*] and more than capable of standing on its own three or more legs as a poem." Nice, eh? Not that the *Clarion* knows poetry from a plate of cold turnips, admittedly. And 'tis true that, when the reading was done, one member of the audience bellowed "total shite," but he was promptly shouted down by the majority, and in any case was discovered to have been secretly taking nips from a bottle of Molloy's Very Special Old Pale Poteen—and furthermore, as if that weren't enough already, beneath his rambling beard and street scabs he turned out to be the former Lord Mayor, Ben Ovary, now a divorced, disguised, and disgraced life dissident and nocturnal wanderer of midnight alleyways. *Sic transit gloria* and all that, eh? Don't laugh; it could be your turn next, or mine.

[4]*Ite, missa est.*

3⁵⁰ Gen 09/614 TO